Call the Shots

About the author

Sam Tobin was born in Recife, Brazil and ended up in Manchester, England. He's been a BAFTA nominated producer, worked in kebab shops and studied law. He's lived in Moss Side, Brixton and Hollywood. *Call the Shots* is his first novel.

CALL
THE
SHOTS
SAM TOBIN

HODDER &
STOUGHTON

First published in Great Britain in 2022 by Hodder & Stoughton
An Hachette UK company

This paperback edition published in 2022

1

A CIP catalogue record for this title is available from the British Library

Paperback ISBN 978 1 399 70170 9
eBook ISBN 978 1 399 70171 6

Typeset in Monotype Plantin by Manipal Technologies Limited

Printed and bound in Great Britain by Clays Ltd, Elcograf S.p.A.

Hodder & Stoughton policy is to use papers that are natural, renewable
and recyclable products and made from wood grown in sustainable forests.
The logging and manufacturing processes are expected to conform
to the environmental regulations of the country of origin.

Hodder & Stoughton Ltd
Carmelite House
50 Victoria Embankment
London EC4Y 0DZ

www.hodder.co.uk

To Fenchurch

Prologue

Sometimes Dutch courage isn't enough. Sometimes you just need some good old-fashioned drugs. Drugs like the ones that had been promised to the man who was currently lurking across the street, keeping watch over a large Victorian mansion. It was two in the morning and parked up between street lights, under the shadow of a giant tree, he was as good as invisible.

He didn't need to be able to see to handle the shotgun cradled in his lap. He held it tightly with a finger curved around the trigger, his other hand supporting the sawn-off barrels. It had been loaded in front of him before being handed over, along with explicit instructions as to what he was to do with it. On the seat beside him was a piece of paper. Written on it in large letters and underlined twice was the address of the house across the street.

The man knew who lived there. That was why he was finding it so hard to work up the courage to get out of the car and follow the orders he'd been given.

It was hard to imagine he could be scared of anyone. The gunman was a giant. Well over six feet tall, his body folded awkwardly into the driver's seat, forcing him to stoop over the steering wheel to avoid bumping his head on the ceiling. At one time his enormous frame had been packed with dense muscle, but now his skin hung loose and sallow. It meant the tattoos that littered his body were all but indecipherable. Strange, creased-up markings that belonged to the man he once was.

Only the tattoo across his neck was still legible. In large, ornate letters it simply said 'VICIOUS'.

If someone had been sat in the car with him they would have been struck by his stale smell. A deeply unclean stench of sweat, urine and neglect. But he was alone and over the past decade of his addiction, he'd long stopped worrying about trivial things like personal hygiene or the opinion of others.

He licked his lips. They were dry. He could feel the greasy sweat starting to run down his back. He remembered the bag he'd been shown before he left on his errand. A small plastic bag, plump with an off-white powder. Ten years of drug use told him that this wasn't any old heroin. This was the good stuff. The stuff that you took when you were starting out. When you cared what was in it. Long before you found yourself cooking your drugs up with filthy canal water and shooting up in a bush beside the towpath.

The thought of that plump bag got him out of the car and on his feet. He pulled his hoodie up over his head, all the while imagining the gently sour smell of well-processed heroin. As he crossed the road and walked towards the driveway he could almost taste it.

For just a moment he stepped from the shadows and into the light. The sodium glare his own personal spotlight. He froze and took in his target. A grand double-fronted house with two large bay windows either side of an immaculately painted, sage green door. A well-kept front garden framed the building on either side with climbing plants and neatly tended shrubs. Money and taste. But most of all money.

Every house on this street was easily over a million. The casual wealth of Manchester's upper middle class – all four-car driveways, immaculate pointing and a depth of privilege totally alien to the man stood in the street holding a loaded shotgun.

He could hear himself breathing. It was a low, hollow sound. As if the mere act of walking the two dozen steps to the front door would be the end of him. Whatever strength he had once possessed was long gone.

His coarse, echoing breaths became louder as he approached the house. His world narrowed to the handful of paces left between him and his target.

Raising the shotgun, he briefly thought how small and light it felt in his huge hands, before he aimed it at the front door and pulled the trigger.

1

Craig Malton hadn't got much sleep in the last forty-eight hours. Not since someone had emptied a shotgun into his front door a couple of nights ago.

Malton had immediately recognised the sound. The distinctively dense ring of a shotgun blast. If he'd been alone in the house he'd have been downstairs, out the door and running towards the sound of gunfire. But he wasn't alone.

Instead of giving chase he had forced himself to hang back. To reassure the woman whom he shared the house with that this was nothing out of the ordinary. He had kept his head as he stopped her from calling the police before he went outside to inspect the damage.

You wouldn't know to look at it but Malton's front door was made from three-inch-thick, reinforced steel plate. It could withstand a police battering ram, small arms fire and even a grenade. But thanks to the considerable sum of money Malton had spent getting it custom-made, it didn't look at all out of place on the Victorian mansion sat on the rather nice street in Didsbury, South Manchester, which he called home.

Malton was a lot like that front door. Growing up in Moss Side, he had known the police to raid his house in the early hours. He'd ducked behind parked cars as rival gang members loosed off wild shots. Once he'd even had a grenade thrown through the window of his foster home. In all that time he'd never backed down. And now thanks to a decade of hard work and several hundred thousand pounds in the

bank, he very nearly belonged somewhere as affluently gen-
teel as Didsbury.

But all it took was one shotgun blast to blow away that
expensively won façade, revealing to the world the ugly, brutal steel beneath.

Stood on his driveway that night he had fielded questions
from terrified neighbours. Malton knew that people wanted to
feel safe; they needed to be reassured. And so when he told
them it was an attempted break-in they chose to believe him.
When he said the damage to his front door must have been
from a sledgehammer or some other blunt object they decided
to go along with it. Malton's answers were far more palatable
than the truth – someone from Malton's past had returned with
a message delivered from the twin barrels of a shotgun.

Malton didn't need his neighbours to believe him. He just
needed them to *want* to believe.

The CCTV on his home had captured a tall, masked man
firing at his front door. It wasn't much but it was a start.
For the past two nights Malton had been making enquiries.
Knocking on doors and bashing heads. So far he was none
the wiser as to the masked man's identity, but until he got
his answers there was still a business to run. His business:
Malton Security.

From doormen to debt collection, Malton Security were
experts in walking the fine line between lawful thuggery and
illegal brutality. If you had a problem that could only be
solved with the legally sanctioned threat of violence, Malton
Security were more than happy to help.

Right now it was debt collection that saw him stood in
the cluttered front room of a two-up, two-down in Hulme,
Moss Side's fractionally more respectable neighbour. There
was no need for Malton to be doing a scruffy little job like
this. A simple repo. But having drawn a blank hunting down
the gunman, Malton felt the need to get back to basics. The

day-to-day concerns of Malton Security. Concerns like the man stood in front of him holding a knife to the throat of his terrified girlfriend.

From the job paperwork, Malton knew the woman with the knife at her throat was Susannah Harper. He also knew she lived with her two sons. One sixteen years old, the other twelve. Looking at his watch, he saw it was 3.15. Home time. Malton didn't have long. He didn't really care who the man with the knife was. Malton was here to do a job and when Malton set his mind to something it got done.

'You're not taking my stuff!' shouted the man with the knife, spit flying from his mouth.

Malton was standing close enough to smell the stale weed on his breath. He raised a giant hand for calm. He knew the effect his appearance had on people. Especially white people. Malton was mixed race. Short but heavyset. His head was shaved bald and he had a deep scar running from his right eye down his cheek. While the black community had their own opinion on whether or not Malton was one of their own, as far as white people were concerned he was as black as they come. There was no disguising it. Not even with the expensive wax jacket he wore beneath the hi-vis vest bearing the logo 'Malton Security'. Not even with the custom dental work that had fixed the decades' worth of violence. Not even with enough money to buy a detached house in Didsbury. Malton saw how his white neighbours looked at him. Even more so since two nights ago when the disturbance at two in the morning confirmed all their worst fears about the black man living next door.

'He's got a knife,' said the other man in the room who was also wearing a company hi-vis vest, Dean Carter. Malton had almost forgotten he was there. Dean was a brand-new hire. Eighteen years old and fresh out of school. He was the exact opposite of Malton – pale white and visibly shaking.

Standing at least half a foot taller than Malton, Dean had one of those unfortunate faces that refuses to grow into adulthood. Malton doubted he'd even started shaving.

This was Dean's first day working for Malton Security. Malton liked to try new recruits out in a variety of positions. Getting a feel for what area of expertise would best suit them. Whether it be door work or security patrols, repo jobs or even some of the heavier, less reputable activities that Malton Security was often called on to provide.

From what Malton had seen so far, whatever Dean's area of expertise was, it didn't lie within Malton Security.

Malton took charge. 'Your missus here owes over a grand. That means as a licensed bailiff I can collect any property I find on the premises. Unless of course you can prove it's yours? Sorry, pal, I didn't get your name?' His voice was deep and oddly neutral but shot through with the unmistakable nasal peaks and glottal stops of a born-and-bred Mancunian.

'You're not getting anything. This is my stuff,' shouted the man, pressing the blade harder against Susannah's flesh.

Malton saw Susannah's eyes flash up at the clock on the wall over the fireplace: 3.20. He could tell she was thinking the exact same thing he was.

'I'm calling the police,' said Dean, getting out his phone.

Malton snatched the phone out of Dean's hand. 'No one's calling the police,' he said. He turned and glared at the younger man. He was not making a great first impression.

'I'll cut her throat,' hissed the man holding the knife.

'Go on then,' said Malton.

'Kyle, please!' cried Susannah.

'Kyle?' said Malton, giving the slightest hint of a smile. 'Now we're getting somewhere. You got a second name Kyle? One that I could check against receipts. You got receipts right?'

Malton could see the man slowly begin to realise that the situation was slipping away from him. But before either of them could make their next move they both heard the sound of someone coming in the front door. Malton saw Susannah's eyes move from the clock on the wall to the living room door. A child's voice came from the hallway, 'What's for tea, Mum?'

Susannah looked to Malton. Pleading. 'Please don't,' she begged, as if it was Malton with a knife to her throat.

A young boy in a grubby school uniform walked into the room and froze. Malton guessed he must be the younger child. He was mixed race, same as Malton. Kyle was white. He wasn't the boy's father. Malton could use that.

The sight of his mother with a knife to her throat seemed not to faze the boy. He looked older than his twelve years. Getting to an age where he knew exactly what kind of man Kyle was but still too young to do anything about it. Malton turned to him.

'What's your name, son?'

The boy looked Malton up and down with an expression that Malton instantly recognised. A hardness. 'Yaya,' he said.

Malton turned to Dean. 'Take Yaya into the kitchen and make his tea while I have a word with his mum and his . . . dad.'

'He's not my dad,' said Yaya, glaring at the man.

Exactly the reaction Malton had hoped for. Yaya's casual indifference to Kyle's fate was far more effective than any threat Malton could make.

Dean took a last look at the scene before putting his arm around Yaya and hastily leading him out of the room. Malton closed the door behind them. Now that Dean had gone he could finally get on with the real work.

'Don't think cos the kid's here I won't do it,' said Kyle. But now there was something different in his voice. A touch of fear creeping in.

Malton took in the front room. A large, new television. A couple of shabby sofas. A games console and a tablet. Garbage and old clothes thrown around. It was a mess. On the far wall a bookcase overflowed with everything except books. He decided on a course of action. Malton crossed to the bookcase and grabbed it with both hands.

'What are you doing?' asked Kyle.

With seemingly no effort at all, Malton pulled the bookcase down, showering its contents all over the floor with a loud crash. The bookcase landed on one of the sofas and lay blocking the door to the hallway. No way in. No way out.

Kyle took the knife away from Susannah's throat and pointed it at Malton. Malton had been in more than enough fights to recognise a bully. The kind of man who was used to picking on someone smaller and weaker than himself. The kind of man who in those rare situations when he had no choice but to fight a bigger man would always put his trust in a weapon. Kyle was making Malton's job easy.

Malton reached into his waxed jacket and pulled out a polished steel hatchet. The hatchet was a little smaller than a hammer and had a viciously sharp edge that glinted under the room lights. It looked deadly. Malton took a step towards Kyle.

'I'm here to collect one thousand, one hundred and eighteen pounds.' He looked around the room. 'I estimate the value of everything in this room to be approximately two thousand pounds.'

'I'll kill her,' Kyle repeated. Malton kept his eyes on Kyle as he raised the hatchet above his head.

Susannah got ready to die. If she wasn't accidentally hit by the hatchet, Kyle would surely slit her throat as his final, malicious act. She closed her eyes and waited. Three . . . two . . . one . . . SMASH!

She opened her eyes to see Malton hacking the television to pieces. She and Kyle watched in horror and confusion as Malton rained down blow after devastating blow until the television was nothing but broken plastic and shattered electronics.

Malton straightened himself up. '*Now* I estimate the value of everything in this room to be one thousand two hundred pounds.' He took another step forward.

Susannah felt a sudden warmth down the back of her legs. Kyle had pissed himself.

★★★

Twenty minutes later Malton sat on the pavement outside the house watching while Dean loaded the van. It was the lad's first day on the job and from what Malton had seen it could well be his last. Yaya sat next to Malton on the kerb, fiddling with his laces, head down.

As far as Malton knew, he didn't have kids. He intended to keep it that way. Kids made you weak. A weakness he'd not been above exploiting on occasion.

But sat on the kerb with Yaya, Malton felt something approaching a sense of duty towards the boy. He'd recognised that look in Yaya's eyes. It was the look of a kid getting ready to do what he had to do to survive. A look Malton knew far too well.

He tried to think of something comforting to say to the boy. But the words eluded him. He was built for threats and innuendo. Coercion and manipulation. In his line of work there was rarely the call for sympathy.

'You know back there, that was just grown-ups talking,' said Malton, finally breaking the silence.

Yaya looked up at him and said nothing.

'Where's your dad?'

'Dunno,' said Yaya, doing his best to look like that didn't bother him.

'Does Kyle hurt your mum?'

'What do you care? You're not my dad.'

'No. I'm not,' said Malton. For just a moment he wondered what it would feel like if he was. The thought scared him.

'When I'm bigger I'm going to protect her,' said Yaya.

Malton was suddenly very aware of the weight of the hatchet, resting in the pocket of his waxed jacket.

'You don't need to do that,' said Malton and, reaching into his jacket, he pulled out a business card and handed it to Yaya. 'You got a phone?'

'Of course I got a phone,' he replied indignantly, taking the card.

'Good lad. Kyle ever touches you or your mum, give that number a ring.'

'And what?'

They both knew what. But the boy wanted Malton to say it and he felt it was the least he could do in the circumstances.

'And I come round, break both his legs and put some fucking horrible dogs on him until what's left can't hurt anyone.'

Yaya smiled. 'Is this your job?' he said.

'One of them.'

2

Claire Minshall squeezed her husband Marcus's hand as tight as she dared. Not so tight that Marcus would know Claire was frightened. But tight enough to give her the strength to keep putting one foot in front of the other as they walked away from the hospital.

It had been twenty minutes since the specialist had given her the diagnosis. Twenty minutes of the world no longer making sense. The sounds of cars passing on the road seemed like distant thunder. The smell of rain-wet pavement came to her, impossibly strong. She could feel the muscles in her throat tight and tense, holding back the tears.

Marcus could feel Claire gripping his hand tight and he was glad of it. He was the husband. He was the healthy one. He was the one who would talk at her funeral. Receive the condolences. Go on to raise their daughter and walk her down the aisle. He was the one who would live through this.

His wife was dying and yet all he dared to think about was the time when she would be gone. To even attempt to imagine what lay before that was too horrific. Months, maybe a year if they were 'lucky'. Watching Claire slowly slip further and further away. Marcus wished it was him dying. To have the permission to give in to the awfulness of it all. But Marcus was the husband. He was the survivor. His job now was to be strong for their daughter.

They'd both dressed up for the appointment. An unspoken ceremony. Claire in a smart grey dress and the black heels she'd bought for a winter wedding the year before.

Marcus in the suit he wore for going out. The one he'd paid a tailor to line with a Manchester United team shirt.

Claire wanted to let the doctors know that they were good people. People worth saving.

There were another couple of hours before their sixteen-year-old daughter Jessica would be back from school. Two hours before they had to break the news to her and end everything.

Marcus felt the silence. He felt Claire's hand. He stopped and turned to face his wife, his expression like hers – hardly containing the grief. Seeing his pain mirrored back at him he heard himself laugh. This was ludicrous. The drama of it. This was television. A film. Other people's lives. Not theirs. Claire was laughing now too, relieved to see Marcus felt the same fearful confusion. Marcus threw his arms around his wife and held her. They both knew that once they let go it was real. Within the year Claire would be dead from the tumour growing in her brain.

Claire could hear Marcus start to cry. They clutched each other in the middle of the pavement. All dressed up with nowhere to go.

'I'm sorry . . . I'm so, so sorry,' Marcus muttered. Claire could hear the terror in his voice. There and then she made her decision. She would die. That was out of her control. But she would die with her head held high. She would make it easy on her loved ones. Give them their grief but not force them to carry hers. She would do the only thing she could do now – endure.

Marcus felt Claire's hand on his back. He hated himself. He had one job: to be strong. And here he was weeping like a child. He broke away from Claire and wiped his face on the back of his sleeve.

'I'm sorry,' he said, half smiling.

In the distance someone was frantically hammering a car horn.

'We'll get through this together,' promised Claire. 'It'll be OK. Jessica has her dad.' The words opened her up. The tears she didn't want to shed started to come. Marcus was every bit as handsome as when Claire met him all those years ago at university. Back when the future seemed like an endless open road. The square jaw, the little cleft in his chin. He looked almost comically macho. A cartoon tough guy she had thought at first, before she got to know the sweet, thoughtful man underneath.

As the emotion overwhelmed her, she didn't hear someone screaming down the road.

'I love you,' were the last words out of Marcus's mouth before he was launched from the pavement, flying up into the air. 'Like a football' is how Claire would describe it later to the police. Her dark purple overcoat billowed in the slipstream as a filthy, black car sped past her on the pavement, missing her by inches. She spun around in time to see the car slam back onto the road and keep on driving.

She turned back, her brain still trying to put the pieces together. Marcus wasn't there. She felt rain on her face. She put her fingers up to touch it and they came back red. It was blood. All over her hands and her dress. Then she saw Marcus. Lying 20 metres down the road. Folded up under himself, one leg facing the wrong way, his arms splayed like a limp puppet. An ugly red smear leading up to where he finally came to rest.

Then Claire stopped enduring. She started to scream and didn't stop.

3

The silence on the drive back to Malton Security had made Malton's displeasure with Dean plain. Back at the office in Cheetham Hill, just north of the city centre, Malton left Dean to log Susannah Harper's meagre possessions into storage while he headed home for the night.

Malton drove the long way back to South Manchester. Heading north from Malton Security before peeling off to the west and making his way slowly anticlockwise around the edge of Manchester as he headed for home.

He avoided the ring road, preferring to weave his way through backstreets. From the nostalgic grandeur of Bury with its sprawling market, through the suburbs of Prestwich full of parks and synagogues and on to the overgrown terraced streets of Salford, whose population had somehow managed to avoid the last one hundred years of British history and remain a near-all-white monoculture.

Ten years of running Malton Security had seen Malton intricately map the underbelly of Manchester. Nowhere was clean. Nowhere was too rich or too respectable or too religious that they didn't, from time to time, have need of someone like him. Someone who knew the city like a guilty accomplice. Someone who was trusted and feared and indulged.

Officially Malton Security could provide you all the muscle you needed. But if you needed more than muscle to solve your problem, and you were willing to pay – Craig Malton was your man.

There was nowhere in the city that was off limits to Malton. A combination of money and charm and reputation had seen to that. And he'd used that access to do things that no one else could.

Especially not the Greater Manchester Police.

Malton had tracked down a missing half tonne of cocaine for a sprawling family of hauliers in Beswick. He'd located the motorbike gang who'd smashed up an exclusive club in Hale, convinced them to pay for the damage and never set foot in the city again. When the body of the daughter of the biggest slumlord in Manchester turned up face-down and naked in the Manchester Ship Canal the police had closed the investigation after a year with no leads. Within a week, Malton had tracked down the young plasterer who'd met her on a night out and then on a whim, raped her, murdered her and dumped her body in the canal. Malton had walked onto the building site where he was working, led him away and left him tied up in the basement of a skyscraper that was being built by the man whose daughter he'd killed.

This past decade Malton had done all those things and hundreds more. He'd been whoever he needed to be to get the job done. And in all that time he'd been sure to keep each job separate. Every nasty, dirty thing he did for money he filed away neatly. Careful to make sure that nothing could ever come back to him. Until it now finally had.

The one clue he had, the CCTV of the gunman, had yielded next to nothing. His face was covered but one thing that was unmistakable was his height. The man was at least a foot taller than Malton if not more. It wasn't much to go on but right now it was all he had.

As he drove, his mind retraced his steps over those last ten years, starting with the people who had most to gain by coming after him and then working his way down the list.

Gratitude, fear and a desire to keep Malton onside had made getting answers relatively easy for him in the past. But none of the answers he'd got thus far had been the one answer he was after – who had emptied a shotgun into his front door?

He pulled into the driveway of his house in Didsbury. The bespoke, armoured front door had already been replaced at great cost. The CCTV upgraded in the vain hope that the gunman might return. But it wasn't enough.

Malton knew, the longer this attack went unanswered the weaker he looked. He dealt with thugs and gangsters. Killers and hardmen. He moved in a world of extreme violence where predators could smell out weakness. A place where vulnerability got you killed. Or worse.

The Manchester underworld had thrown down a challenge and unless Malton answered it and found the gunman, he knew that next time it wouldn't just be his front door in the firing line.

The clock was ticking.

4

Keisha Bistacchi scrolled through the flood of images appearing on her WhatsApp group. She'd met the women at the exclusive city centre gym she'd joined a little over six months ago. The girls were on a night out in town. From the photos Keisha could see they were having cocktails. She should have been there with them, swapping stories of dermal fillers and shopping trips. Instead she was in a deserted car park on the edge of the Peak District, bored and shivering in her car as she watched her husband Paul beating the shit out of his younger brother Johnny.

Paul Bistacchi looked exactly like what he was: an East Manchester nightmare. Hands large enough to crush a man's windpipe. A face like a clenched fist and a bald head that, day or night, hot or cold, was permanently covered in a thin sheen of sweat.

The beams from Keisha's headlights illuminated a narrow strip of the darkness in which she could clearly see Paul kicking Johnny round the small car park like a bloody football. Johnny's whimpers of pain tailed off into the night air and Keisha could see steam rising off Paul's bald head and merging with his frozen breath.

Unlike Paul, Johnny was gorgeous. Model gorgeous. He stumbled through life getting by on a combination of his good looks and the fear the Bistacchi name invoked. But neither of those were a defence when it came to his older brother Paul.

From where she sat watching, Keisha could see Johnny desperately covering his face while Paul's blows hammered down on him. Vanity overriding every other survival instinct. Keisha liked Johnny. He was every bit as much of a scumbag as Paul but unlike Paul he had a sweetness with it. A sweetness that he did his best to cover up with swagger and bravado.

Keisha wasn't the only one watching. Standing nearby was the boy they'd picked up on their way out to the middle of nowhere. One of Johnny's friends. He looked terrified. Next to him was the black car Johnny had stolen.

Keisha turned off her phone and drummed her long, diamanté-studded nails on the steering wheel. She glanced at her reflection in the rear-view mirror: the sunglasses she wore – even at night – covering the top half of her face, the rest taken up with an elegant, wide nose and a mouth permanently on the verge of breaking into a dazzling smile. Thanks to her flawless brown skin she easily looked ten years younger than she was. Younger still with a full face of make-up. Not all that different to how she looked thirty years ago.

Three decades was a long time. Keisha had almost missed the anniversary when it had rolled round a couple of months ago. It was a date that only she knew. Something just for her. A date that meant nothing to the rest of the world but to Keisha marked the moment that something inside her had hardened, forever changed.

The next thirty years had made her the woman she was today. It saw her spread her wings and become an integral part of the Manchester underworld. A friend, a fixer, a confidante. Keisha made sure that there was nowhere she wasn't welcome. No one who wouldn't bring her into their confidence. Eventually she'd found her way to Paul Bistacchi and slowly worked her magic behind the scenes to transform a small, brutal East Manchester family of drug dealers into a vast criminal conspiracy. The Bistacchis would not be where they are now without her – not that they would ever admit that.

Now she had money and she had power. Enough to help her almost forget what happened thirty years ago. But still, it *had* happened. And when, a few months ago, she realised it was thirty years to the day, she began to make plans to commemorate it, to make sure that the date didn't pass without notice.

But before all that she would have to stop the Bistacchis self-destructing.

Keisha had been all dressed up and ready to leave for her girls' night out when Johnny had burst through the door of the Bistacchi home, out of his mind with fear. Paul had been out and so it was Keisha who sat her brother-in-law down and with great patience and kindness coaxed the full story from him. After she'd heard everything Johnny had to say, Keisha knew her night out would have to wait. There was no point in building a future for the Bistacchi family if they were about to destroy what they already had.

She had called her husband Paul and given him the edited highlights. Johnny had stolen a car. There was nothing new about that. Ever since Johnny had learned about cloned keys he'd been on a spree. Stealing four or five high-end cars a week before funnelling them to a garage up in Bradford who dismantled them and sold the parts to the Middle East.

It was what happened after Johnny stole the car that mattered. Both Bistacchi men enjoyed a bit of cocaine now and then. A regular supply was just one of the side benefits of being involved in the wholesale importation of the drug. But Johnny took things that bit further. With a constant access to the white powder, he had developed a crippling addiction. When he wasn't twitching and grimacing with withdrawal he was grinning and sniffing his way through an increasingly diminished series of highs.

Johnny had been helping himself to the last of a five-gram bag when he lost control of the stolen car and mounted the pavement outside the cancer hospital in town. Not wanting to waste the cocaine, he'd taken a moment to snort up as much as he could from his fingertips. In that brief split second he had run into the well-dressed couple out walking. Smashing into the man and sending him flying. As the drug mixed with fear, Johnny had accelerated away in terror.

Keisha was only half-surprised hearing this story. Thanks to her, the Bistacchi family might have been a big name in East Manchester but they were constantly on the verge of imploding. Whether it was Paul's relentless criminal greed or Johnny's volatile combination of naivety and amorality, the family was a powder keg. It was what drew Keisha to them in the first place.

Paul had stopped beating Johnny and now opened the boot of the stolen black car. Keisha watched as he grabbed at Johnny's friend and attempted to stuff him into it. The boy was much smaller than Paul but he knew what would happen if he got in that boot and he fought like his life depended on it. Which it did.

The boy's name was Logan and he'd had the misfortune to be the first person Johnny had gone to for help. When Logan had point-blank refused to help Johnny cover up what sounded to him like a fatal car accident, Johnny had fled back home, where he'd found Keisha.

Keisha's plan had been quite simple. Johnny had run over a random stranger. The only thing to connect him to the Bistacchis was the car and unfortunately for Logan, Logan. Paul had been summoned and when he'd finally calmed down, Keisha had told him exactly what needed to be done.

They'd driven in convoy – Paul in the stolen car with Johnny, and Keisha in her silver Mercedes with Logan.

She'd used the ride to put Logan at ease. *We're all friends here. You know what Johnny's like.* She'd convinced him that just because he was being driven into the night by a family of violent criminals, nothing bad was going to happen to him.

After winding east through unlit country roads, they'd arrived at a car park up on the moors and Keisha had let the boys get on with it. But now it seemed Logan was having second thoughts. Keisha took a quick look at her phone. The girls were flirting with a handsome young waiter. Wealthy Cheshire housewives enjoying misbehaving on a night out. Keisha wondered what they'd say if they knew the kind of misbehaviour she was getting up to.

Keisha had always been good at fitting in. Back in the day in Moss Side she'd been one of the few girls with white friends *and* black friends. As far as she was concerned being mixed race meant having the best of both worlds. Everyone wanted to be Keisha's friend. It was her gift.

Now that she had Paul's money, she could be a bit pickier about who those friends were. She could join expensive gyms, drink in fancy bars and spend thousands on her wardrobe. But every so often she would be reminded where all that money came from. Drugs and the cascade of misery and violence that came with them. Once in a while she would have to tear herself away from the Cheshire set and deal with something a little more brutal.

Keisha got out of the car. The night air felt cold on her skin. She didn't have time to change and so was still wearing the sequined bodycon dress she'd picked to go out in. She'd paired it with black Adidas trainers. Keisha didn't do heels. Thirty years mixing with Manchester's criminal element had taught her the importance of comfortable footwear. Of always being ready to run. On the way out the door she'd grabbed an ankle-length Canada Goose parka. Now she pulled the long coat around her as she stepped over the gravel towards the three men.

Logan was still struggling as she approached.

'Whoa! Stop, stop, stop!' Keisha put a smile in her voice, like she'd just come across three naughty boys about to do something unwittingly foolish.

Paul and Logan broke off from their struggle and stood to attention. Johnny slowly uncurled from his foetal position on the floor.

'There's no need for any of this, is there?' purred Keisha, addressing all three of them.

'I'm not getting in the boot,' said Logan, so weakly that even he didn't believe it. He stood shivering in the night air. His arms folded across his chest, his head down. Keisha could see nearly all the fight had gone out of him.

He just needed that last, gentle push.

'I know this is tough. Christ, I mean look at me.' Keisha flashed open her parka to show the glittering evening wear beneath. She gave a little wiggle. She knew you could never underestimate the power of a bit of flesh on the male mind. 'You think I was planning to be here?'

Logan looked uncertain. Keisha continued in her light, bouncy tone.

'Thing is, Johnny here's fucked up. And that's OK, because he's family. And what are family for if not to fuck up?' Keisha gave a little laugh.

Logan almost smiled.

'He needs to get in the fucking boot,' grumbled Paul.

'And he will,' said Keisha. 'Won't you?'

Logan looked unsure.

'Come on. No one wants to be here. Johnny's had his beating. Now it's your turn.'

24

'I don't want to,' sniffed Logan. He hugged himself tighter and shuffled his feet. Keisha could see he knew how this ended.

'Why not?' she asked as gently and kindly as a mother talking to a scared child.

Logan looked from the terrifying glare of Paul Bistacchi to the beaming face of his wife. Suddenly he couldn't tell them apart.

'Please don't,' he begged.

Keisha could tell he knew it was over.

'Johnny's your friend right?' she asked.

Logan nodded weakly.

'And Johnny's in trouble. He needs your help.' Keisha measured her words.

'I just want to go home,' said Logan pitifully. He wiped his tears across the back of his sleeve.

Keisha ignored him and continued. 'Your friend needs you to get in the boot for him. That's all. You can do that can't you? For your friend?'

She made it sound like the most reasonable thing in the world.

Logan looked down to where Johnny was lying on the ground. Johnny couldn't meet his eye. Paul's wife was wearing sunglasses but he could still feel her eyes pinning him down. Logan gently shook off Paul's grip and walked towards the boot. He kept looking from Keisha to Paul, as if he couldn't quite believe what was happening.

'See how easy that was?' said Keisha as Logan climbed into the boot.

Once Logan was nearly all the way in, Paul's patience gave out. He gave the boy a quick push before slamming the boot down on him.

'The petrol's in the back of my car,' said Keisha before turning and walking back to the warmth of her Mercedes.

She returned to checking her WhatsApp group as Paul retrieved the plastic billy can of petrol. The girls had moved on to Panacea, Manchester's cocktail bar of choice for anyone able and willing to foot a five-figure bar tab. Keisha recognised a couple of footballers in the background. Glancing up, she saw that Paul had finished dousing the stolen car in petrol.

She watched as he and Johnny stripped down to their underwear before taking even that off. Their bodies were both riddled with cheap tattoos, their flesh painfully white against the dark, moorland night. Paul stuffed the clothes in the front seat of the fuel-soaked car before tossing a match in after them.

The two naked men got into Keisha's Mercedes and began to dress in the spare clothes she had told them to bring with them.

The stolen car was ablaze now. A loud thumping was coming from the boot. The car rocked from side to side but the boot remained firmly shut. Keisha started the ignition and the stereo burst into life, drowning out any sound from the night outside.

As Keisha reversed out of the car park and headed home, she marvelled at how far she'd come in the last thirty years.

The distant glow of the burning car vanished behind a hill in Keisha's rear-view mirror and she thought how lucky she was to be in Manchester, where no matter what you did, you could always burn it down and start again. Though she was still annoyed at missing her night out, that thought kept her smiling all the way back home.

5

In the three weeks since he started working at Malton Security, Dean had thought about nothing else other than how he could make up for his disastrous first day on the job. He was sure that if he had just five minutes alone with Malton he could explain how perfectly OK he was with not getting the law involved.

He could tell him about the time a boy from school beat him up and how Dean waited a couple of weeks before jumping him coming out of a nightclub. He could explain to Malton how, when the bike he'd saved up half a year to buy was stolen, he tracked it down himself on Gumtree, went round posing as a buyer and broke the thief's nose, before stealing his bike back. He could argue that the only reason he was going to call the police was that he was so desperate to keep this job that he'd wanted to do things by the book. Now that he knew the book was a considerably more racy read, he was happy to fall into line. All he needed was a second chance.

Unfortunately for Dean, he'd barely even seen Malton since that job, much less had the chance for a heart-to-heart.

***

For the past three weeks Malton had been a man on the move. Threats, favours and even the occasional spot of violence hadn't got him any answers as to who had shot up his front door. It'd been long enough that whoever did it must be starting to think they got away with it. Which means they'd be starting to think about what or indeed who they were going to aim a shotgun at next. In amongst all this, Dean's disastrous first day had quietly slipped out of Malton's thoughts.

But Dean didn't know any of this. As far as he was concerned he'd messed up on his first day out and now Malton was deliberately avoiding him. He'd begun to suspect that getting the job was one big mistake. His mum had warned him when he spotted the advert in the *Manchester Evening News* that he wasn't built for security work. Why couldn't he go back to college? Re-sit his A-Levels. He was a clever boy – he just needed to apply himself.

It's true there was a certain look to the fifty or so staff that made up Malton Security. The look that makes people cross the road to avoid it. Big, rough brick shithouses. Dean was unsure how he'd slipped through the net but it was clear that he'd been found out. He wasn't Malton Security material.

Malton Security didn't just collect debts. They ran doors for several upmarket restaurants and bars in Manchester, provided security for everything from building sites to private parties and, as far as Dean could make out, occasionally could be called on to 'have a word' when clients needed to deliver a message that only a couple of thuggish men in bomber jackets could adequately convey. All activities he'd have loved to have got involved in. But Dean did none of these things. Instead he had spent the last two weeks hosing down Malton Security's fleet of vans under the watchful eye of Alfie the office manager, who Dean had very quickly learned was a complete bastard.

Alfie was a massively fat Scouser who radiated vindictive misery. He waddled from place to place, his legs threatening to buckle under the effort of moving his 22 stone body. Heavy grey bags ringed his eyes – a result of his chronic sleep-apnoea. He ran the Malton Security office – a large, industrial unit on a nondescript estate in North Manchester. His title was office manager, which in reality meant he hoovered the carpets and made sure there was milk in the fridge and the Sky Sports subscription got paid every month. He was very much the lowest man on the totem pole. That is, until he was given Dean to watch over.

Always aware of the office gossip, by the time Dean had got back from that awful first job, Alfie knew that Dean had broken the cardinal rule of Malton Security: he'd tried to call the police. He lost no time in letting Dean know he knew this.

Dean quickly learned that as a result of his slip-up the only job Alfie was prepared to give him was cleaning vans, it being the only job that demanded being outside, getting soaking wet in the perpetual gloom of the Manchester winter. Day after day he turned up to work hoping against hope that today would be different. And day after day he left in the evening soaked to the bone and so cold he couldn't feel his hands.

Dean doubted that if he showed willing Alfie would come to respect and appreciate his contribution. He did however suspect that it was only a matter of time before Alfie would get an itch to find something more demeaning and tedious for him to do. And he was right.

On week three Dean turned up for work braced for another nine hours of freezing cold water and filthy sponges, only to find Alfie waiting for him in the office.

'Special job today.' Alfie beamed, hardly able to contain his excitement.

'Not washing the vans?' asked Dean, trying to hide the joy in his voice.

'Not today, lad,' said Alfie, with an enthusiasm that instantly put Dean on high alert.

Dean followed as Alfie led him through the front office, pausing only for Alfie to wrestle a two-foot stack of paperwork out of an ancient filing cabinet before leading Dean out the back of the building to the staff car park at the rear. They walked past the dark green Volvo Estate, which Dean knew Malton drove to work every day, past several smaller, locked sheds and over to a large, single-storey storage unit.

'Take these,' hissed Alfie, wheezing from the mild exertion of crossing the car park. Alfie dumped a mound of paperwork into Dean's arms and fumbled in his pocket for a key. Dean watched as Alfie undid the large padlock on the sliding door to the unit, hauling it back to reveal a giant room lined with metal shelves, all of them stacked to bursting point with televisions, iPads, laptops, computers, deep-fat fryers, hair straighteners, mobile phones, PlayStations and DVD players. In short, anything of value from the homes of anyone unfortunate enough to find their debt being collected by Malton Security. Items that would eventually be auctioned off for a fraction of their worth.

Alfie took the paperwork back off Dean and headed into the storage unit where he dumped it down on a small desk at the entrance.

'This,' said Alfie pointing to the stack of paperwork, 'is a record of everything we've repossessed in the last two months.' Dean took it in. He recognised the standard form as the one he'd used to log everything they'd taken from Susannah Harper's flat on his first day. 'And this,' Alfie said, gesturing to the shelves and shelves of valuables, 'is everything we've repossessed. You need to match them up. Inventory everything we've got. Good luck.'

Weeks of washing the vans and imagining that it couldn't get any worse and now this. Sure, Dean had screwed up on his first day but why keep him hanging around? Why not just put him out of his misery?

Dean broke. 'Come on,' he said. 'Mr Malton didn't hire me to do paperwork.'

Alfie looked delighted. This was exactly the reaction he was hoping for.

'Mr Malton?' he said with a smirk. 'Listen to you, soft lad. You know what *Mr Malton* thinks? Let me tell you, you don't know the first thing about the boss. There are things about the boss that would make your hair curl.'

Alfie puffed himself up. He was enjoying his tiny handful of power. Dean let him keep talking.

'And if the boss wasn't so tied up working out who it was shot up his place, you'd be gone by now.'

Dean froze. 'Someone shot up Mr Malton's house?'

Immediately Alfie's indiscretion dawned on him. The swaggering know-it-all from a moment ago turned into a cornered animal. A moment of panic crossed his face before he went straight on the attack.

'That's none of your business,' said Alfie, doing his best to loom over Dean. 'And if I were you I wouldn't go round spreading that sort of rumour. Or any kind of rumours about the boss.'

'Like you just did?' said Dean, pulling himself up to his full, scrawny height.

Alfie's brain fell out of gear. His mouth hung open as he tried and failed to find a comeback. Dean watched as Alfie ran out of road. It was uncomfortable to see. Alfie was a petty bully but Dean couldn't help feeling a little sorry for him.

'I'll get on with this then, shall I?' said Dean, throwing Alfie a lifeline.

'Yeah, you better,' said Alfie, doing his best to sound like he was still in the driving seat. Without anything else to add, he turned and waddled off.

Dean watched as Alfie headed back to the office. Alfie had said something he shouldn't and from the nervous way he hurried across the car park it was obvious he knew it. Dean didn't care about getting Alfie in trouble. He was more interested in how this revelation could help him get back in Malton's good books.

Dean was about to head into the warehouse when the office door opened and Malton walked into the car park.

Malton saw Dean stood in the open storage unit, watching him. He glanced past Dean to the contents of the unit, working out the job he'd been given by Alfie. Malton cracked a smile.

'Good luck,' he called out, then got in his Volvo and drove away.

Alone in the storage unit, Dean couldn't stop grinning. If what Alfie said was true then he had a second chance to prove that he was Malton Security material. All he had to do was find out who it was that had shot up Malton's front door.

Luckily for Dean he already had one hell of a lead to go on.

6

As Keisha drove through the rain she sang along to the car stereo, her voice making up in volume what it lacked in pitch. She was on her way to a funeral and she couldn't be happier.

Keisha used to be this happy all the time. As a child running in and out of the flats of Hulme Crescents estate, she thought she was in heaven. Thanks to a fiercely protective Irish mother and a community who stuck with each other through thick and thin, Keisha grew up never knowing that in reality she was dirt poor and living in an asbestos-riddled, concrete slum. But then the cold, cruel world came calling.

That was over thirty years ago. A lot had changed since then.

Sometimes she did wonder whether all the sadness and grief was still there inside her somewhere, rotting away in the dark. But as far as Keisha was concerned, it's what was on the outside that counted. And right now Keisha looked fabulous. She was wearing an ankle-length black dress tastefully slashed to the hip and matched with a black fur stole, black fascinator and her ever-present sunglasses and trainers. That was another reason why Keisha loved funerals. She looked great in black.

It'd been nearly a month since Johnny had run the man over and she'd had to miss her night out with the girls to help Paul clean up his brother's mess. Since then it had been back to business as usual; Keisha managing Bistacchi affairs while Paul and Johnny returned to doing what they did so well – smashing heads and selling drugs.

Keisha's plans to mark the thirty-year anniversary of her lowest point were proceeding nicely and she hadn't given a second thought to the hit-and-run until she'd seen the article in the *Manchester Evening News*.

Marcus Minshall was his name. He was some kind of lawyer, had a young daughter and even more tragically a wife who was dying of cancer. Keisha couldn't help but laugh. How unlucky could one person be? She didn't show it to Paul. Not out of secrecy, but because she knew Paul wouldn't give a shit (and besides reading wasn't one of his strong points). Paul didn't do regrets. It never occurred to him that anything bad would ever happen to him. He was the bad thing that happened to other people. That lack of imagination was what made Paul what he was today – a well-known, well-feared member of Manchester's criminal community. That lack of imagination was also the reason why Keisha was bored out of her mind.

Paul had enough money to live wherever he wanted but it never occurred to him that anyone would ever want to live anywhere other than Hattersley – a rundown, East Manchester suburb where the warmth of the people was only matched by the neglect of the council who owned most of the housing. Paul could do anything he wanted but all he wanted to do was take coke and get pissed in his local. He was a very big fish in a very small pond.

But Keisha had known that when she married him. She wasn't complaining. She made her own fun.

She pulled up in the cemetery car park and turned off the engine. It was already filling up. She saw the respectable white faces, the unmistakable softness of the educated middle class. People who had no idea how much darkness there was in the world. People who had never seen a grown man beaten until he was crying like a child. People who had never heard the sound of bones being broken with a claw hammer.

People who in their worst nightmares would never dream that someone like Keisha Bistacchi even existed.

Keisha wondered what she'd say if anyone asked who she was and how she knew the deceased. She smiled at the thought of simply telling the truth – my brother-in-law ran him over and I helped him to destroy the evidence. But today wasn't about burning anything down. Today was just about having fun. Proving to the world that despite everything she'd been through she was still the one in control.

Keisha glanced in the rear-view mirror and arranged her face into an approximation of sympathy and grief. She stepped out of her car into the rain and, bowing her head, joined the other mourners as they filtered into the chapel.

7

Malton followed the trail of bright green bin bags that dotted the canal towpath. Each one was stuffed to bursting with beer cans, soiled clothing, crisp packets and all the other detritus that clogged up Manchester's canal system. A couple of hundred years ago these canals were the expressways that let Manchester dominate the world. These days they were the domain of dog walkers and fly tippers.

Up ahead, Malton could see the group of community volunteers with their hi-vis vests on over their normal clothes. They were an assortment of bored retirees, well-meaning students and people with nothing better to do in the middle of the day than to pick up someone else's litter.

Stood watching them was a middle-aged woman in police uniform. She made no effort to help the volunteers. Instead she gazed into the middle distance, her arms folded, her mind far, far away.

'Greater Manchester Police really know how to hold a grudge against one of their own.'

The policewoman spun round to see Malton stood behind her. He held up a large, brushed aluminium flask. A peace offering.

'There better be booze in that flask,' she warned with a grin.

'Best I can do is coffee.' Malton shrugged.

'Fuck it,' said the woman. She took the flask off him and started pouring. 'How the hell did you know I'd be here?'

Malton took out his mobile phone, tapped the screen and held up a photo of the policewoman on the canal side surrounded by volunteers. She looked ready to kill someone. The caption said, 'Tameside Community Volunteer Litter Pick! #localpride #GMPgivingback'.

'If we spent half the time catching criminals that we did fucking about on social media you'd be out of a job,' she said before turning her attention back to the coffee. 'No, scratch that, you'd be in prison.'

Malton watched her drink. He had known Benton ever since they were both starting out in their respective fields. Her in the police, him as someone who was doing his best to avoid the police. Up until eighteen months ago, she'd had the kind of career that gets people spreading rumours of going all the way to the top. That was before she'd made the mistake of asking a few too many questions about the after-hours activities of some of her fellow officers.

'So who's going to blink first?' asked Malton. 'You or Greater Manchester's finest?'

'If they want rid of me they're going to have to man up and find a reason for sacking me that's better than me asking why a senior detective is palling about with a known drug dealer,' said Benton. For just a moment the defiance slipped and a bitterness came into her voice.

She turned and looked at the half a dozen volunteers. A young girl was using her litter picker to pluck bags of dog shit down from a tree, where considerate dog owners had hung them like foul Christmas ornaments. Next to her an elderly man was stuffing damp, disintegrating catalogues into a bin liner.

Malton had known Benton long enough to see that under the bluster and front, having her own colleagues turn on her had hurt Benton more than she cared to let on. He also knew that she wasn't a quitter.

'Hold on in there – you're a good cop. They can't punish you forever,' he offered.

'I think they'll give it a good go,' said Benton, laughing at the sheer absurdity of it all.

Malton couldn't help laughing along. He rarely laughed but Benton knew how to get it out of him. He had no great hatred of the police but to see the Greater Manchester Police do this to one of their own made his blood boil.

'Not heard from you in a while,' said Benton.

'Been busy,' said Malton.

'With your nice new girlfriend?' asked Benton with a grin.

Malton was never sure how closely Benton was keeping tabs on him. She was a natural detective who knew everything that went on in Manchester, above and below ground. It was always safest to assume Benton was one step ahead.

'You'd like her,' said Malton.

'Not your usual type. Didn't know you were into that sort of thing,' said Benton.

She let the silence hang, waiting to see if Malton would fill it. But when he did, it was to change the subject.

'I had a visitor a few weeks ago,' he said.

'I heard,' said Benton, not giving anything away.

'So maybe you heard a name?' said Malton hopefully.

Benton looked surprised. 'Are you humouring me or are you really that desperate?'

'I'm not humouring you. I've got nothing. No one's talking. Not even to me.'

That wasn't entirely true. People had talked to Malton. They'd begged and they'd pleaded. But nothing they'd said had proved any help in getting closer to finding the identity of the gunman.

'CCTV?' said Benton. 'I know you told the police the camera was off but that's clearly a lie.'

'CCTV's a dead end. He parked across the street in the shadows and covered his face. He's tall. That's all I got to go on. And so here I am,' said Malton.

Benton was already off in her head. Something Malton said had clearly rung a bell. She took a last sip of coffee before tipping the dregs out onto the canal towpath and replacing the lid.

She turned to him. 'After I've made sure no one breaks their neck picking up used condoms and McDonald's wrappers, I'm due at a primary school fete. Top-level police business. You sure you want my help?'

'You? The best detective Greater Manchester Police ever screwed over?'

They both knew he was blowing smoke up her arse. They also both knew it was true.

Benton started to thaw. Malton wondered if she wasn't playing with him? Maybe everything Greater Manchester Police had put Benton through really had started to get to her.

'I heard about it, looked into it out of sheer curiosity,' Benton finally offered. 'Nothing. Like you said, no one has a clue. Which is odd. As you know, there's not that many shotguns floating about, never mind people who'd have any idea where a sketchy bastard like you keeps himself.'

'Thoughts? Just now, it seemed like something I said struck a chord?' he said, trying not to sound too desperate. He knew it was a long shot but he'd really hoped that Benton would have something. A lead, no matter how small. If she said she had nothing, Malton knew her well enough to trust that there really was nothing out there.

'If they could go to that much trouble, they could have killed you no problem. They wanted to send a message,' said Benton.

39

It was pretty much the same conclusion Malton had come to himself. But it made it no less worrying to hear it come from Benton.

But she hadn't finished.

She took a quick look round. Likely more out of habit than any real worry they were being eavesdropped. Malton sensed she was debating saying something.

'I know I said I found nothing,' she said. 'And that's true. But what you just said about the CCTV got me thinking. You want my hunch?' She looked at Malton, almost apologetically.

He shrugged. 'Right now I'll take a hunch.'

'I could give you a name. But you won't like it,' warned Benton.

'I'll like it more than knowing whoever shot my front door is still out there,' said Malton.

Benton took a deep breath and looked Malton in the eye. 'Leon Walker,' she said.

Leon Walker. It had been years since he had heard that name. Once upon a time Leon Walker had been someone. A brutal bully who could subdue half a dozen men with his bare hands. A feared giant. But that was before he crossed paths with Malton.

Yet with the gunman's obvious height from the CCTV . . . it *could* be Leon Walker.

Benton sensed Malton's disappointment. 'I told you you wouldn't like it. Not my finest piece of deduction but be fair, I've got fuck all to go on. Walker's tall. He hates you. Case closed,' she said with a shrug.

'He's also a helpless junkie who can barely remember his own name. There's no way he could be behind this. For all I know he's dead,' said Malton.

And that was the problem. Malton didn't know. He had reach but a man like Leon Walker existed in the netherworld of addicts, a parallel existence populated by liars, thieves and the worst sort of abusers. Malton got information by leveraging people with something to lose – their livelihoods, their reputations, their continued good health. Addicts had none of those things. Penetrating their world was a filthy, thankless job, one which Malton had hoped he wouldn't have to undertake.

With nothing else to add, Benton turned back to the volunteers. One had stopped and looked like they might even be trying to listen in. Benton's steely glare quickly got them back to work.

She turned her attention back to Malton, looking suddenly serious. 'Whoever it is, just be careful. Every nasty piece of shit in this city knows who you are. If they want to provoke you it means one of two things: either they're insane or they mean business.'

Malton thought for a moment. 'Or both.'

8

In a strange way the three weeks before the funeral had been some of the happiest weeks of Claire's life. Jessica had taken leave from school and the two of them occupied their days doing whatever came to mind. They spent lavishly on shopping trips. They joined a health spa and took a weekend break in London where they watched a show. It wasn't that they forgot about Marcus, more an unspoken agreement to hold the grief at bay. To quietly push it back down when it reared its head. Not to give it the power to spoil what little time they had left together.

But as time went on Claire could no longer ignore the awful truth: Marcus was dead and the police still had nothing. No leads. No names. No idea who killed her husband. A lifetime of following the rules, driving at the speed limit and believing that if you broke the law terrible things would follow, meant that Claire couldn't quite process it when her family liaison officer told her to prepare for the possibility that she might die before her husband's killer was brought to justice. It didn't help that this news was delivered on the morning of Marcus's funeral.

The service took place in the cemetery chapel at Agecroft – an elegantly Gothic cemetery whose grounds boasted hundreds of war graves along with an impressively derelict Victorian clock tower. Marcus was a Salford boy and so it seemed fitting to bury him there. Jessica and Claire had planned what they both agreed was a funeral Marcus would like. The mourners came in to 'The Queen is Dead' and a vicar Claire had gone to school with delivered a short speech about who Marcus was. How he'd met Claire at university and decided to switch to study law to spend more time with her. How devoted he was to her, taking time away from his own work as a solicitor to look after their daughter while Claire, having fallen out of love with the law, went from a trainee teacher to a deputy head and finally on to running her own school. He talked about what a gentle man he was. How he cried at a good movie and despite being a fan of boxing never once raised his fists in anger. Marcus was the kind of man whose mere presence made you feel bad about your own failings. He was never angry, never impatient. Always kind, always understanding.

As the vicar spoke, Claire's mind began to wander. The chapel was full. Marcus's family, friends and colleagues all bore the same look of incredulous sorrow. *How could this happen to Marcus?* It was the smallest amount of comfort to know that so many people cared. Then Claire spotted a face she didn't recognise. A face that stood out in the sea of white faces. An elegant black woman wearing a dainty fascinator and what looked like a fur throw around her shoulders. Who-ever she was, she looked like her heart was breaking, her eyes hidden behind a pair of large sunglasses. Whoever she was, it looked like Marcus must have meant something very special to her.

With the service over, mourners streamed out of the church and into the rain to the strains of 'I Am the Resurrec-tion'. Claire was barely keeping it together.

Out of the corner of her eye she saw her family liaison officer making a beeline for her car, which was parked at the furthest edge of the car park. DC Moor had insisted Claire call her Rachel, something Claire found increasingly hard to do as the weeks went on and all she seemed able to offer were vague platitudes and pleas for patience. It appeared DC

43

Moor was more interested in defending Greater Manchester Police's inability to find Marcus's killer than in offering any real comfort. When DC Moor had dropped the bombshell that morning about Marcus's killer never being found, Claire hadn't been in the right frame of mind to ask what had changed. Why had the non-committal reassurances hardened into outright resignation?

DC Moor was getting into her car when Claire came rushing across the car park, dodging puddles to reach her.

'You're not going, are you?' said Claire.

The family liaison officer looked uncomfortable. 'I'm sorry, I've got to get back to the office.'

Claire grabbed the car door, holding it open.

'I really need to get back,' said DC Moor, avoiding Claire's gaze.

'I need to know. Why don't you think you'll catch Marcus's killer?'

The other woman looked down into her lap. She was clearly thinking something over.

'I have cancer,' said Claire. 'My husband is dead. Now I've got to go to a hotel and eat buffet food while having everyone in the room remind me of those two facts. So the least you can do is give me five minutes to explain why the hell you are so certain that you're not going to catch the man who killed Marcus.'

'OK,' said DC Moor, looking up. 'Get in.'

Jessica and the crowd of mourners outside the church watched as Claire stepped into DC Moor's car and closed the door behind her.

The windscreen was already misting up as Claire looked around. Paperwork, CDs, stray make-up. It was nearly as messy as Claire's own car. She could see the bottleneck of mourners hovering outside the chapel, unsure whether to move on to the reception or wait for Claire to emerge and receive their condolences.

The black woman was talking to Marcus's parents, offering them a hankie. Claire couldn't help but notice she was wearing trainers.

DC Moor spoke. 'We know the name of the man who killed Marcus.'

Claire snapped to attention. She suddenly became aware of every drop of rain running down the glass. The smell of the upholstery. Her own breathing as it became short and shallow.

'Who is he?'

'I could tell you his name but what good would that do you?'

'At least I'd know.'

'Trust me,' said DC Moor, 'you don't want to know.'

Claire almost felt bad for the family liaison officer. She was clearly a decent woman and it was obvious she'd already said far too much. But Claire didn't have time to be nice. She was dying and she'd just been told the police knew the name of her husband's killer but weren't going to do anything about it.

'Try me,' she said.

Before her eyes DC Moor began to change. The rigid, official kindness of a liaison officer began to melt away. She shifted uncomfortably under Claire's gaze, eventually turning away and looking out the window, towards the church.

Jessica was talking to the mourners. Receiving their condolences, directing them to cars, being the adult that her situation had forced her to become.

Finally DC Moor spoke. 'OK. How about I tell you a bit about him, the driver? When he was fourteen he got into a fight over a girl. By that point he'd been permanently excluded from school.'

'Why did he get excluded?' asked Claire, almost afraid to ask. She knew full well how extreme an incident would have to be to merit an expulsion.

'He asked a teacher out. When she turned him down he smashed up her car.'

Claire heard herself laughing. Not in amusement but in shock. She knew full well how far gone a child must be to act out like that.

But DC Moor wasn't done. 'Anyway, having been excluded, he turned up at the school. He'd brought a scaffolding pole with him. Somehow he found this boy and beat him so hard that he's now in a wheelchair. Doesn't talk all that well. Can't remember faces, names, when to go to the toilet.'

Claire swallowed hard. This pushed up at the very edges of her experience. She thought that she could handle whatever DC Moor had to tell her. This went well beyond what she was expecting. She felt sick. Her body numbly throbbed as it processed the horrific details.

'You know all this and he's just walking the streets?' Her voice was flat with disbelief.

'He went into juvenile detention for four years. Parole for a couple more. By the time he got out he'd learned enough to make sure if he was going to do something like that again, to do it somewhere private. Finish the job.'

The numbness had begun to settle in Claire's gut. It was hardening into something more useful. Something like anger.

'You sound impressed,' she said, hearing herself slipping into the head teacher's register she reserved for disciplining students.

Just like a disobedient student DC Moor smiled nervously. She picked a cigarette carton out of the car door and began to absentmindedly shred it in her hand.

'You've got to understand,' she said, 'his background. Drug dealing, car theft, domestic abuse, drunk and disorderly – his family are notorious. A problem family. Problem being they've been doing it for so long they know the game. Know how to get away with it.'

She bundled the shredded cigarette packet up in her fist and stuffed the scraps into a pocket.

'You think he was the one driving the car?' asked Claire.

'Even if we did – and I'm not saying we do – there's not enough evidence. The CPS wouldn't take it.'

Claire's brief spurt of anger faded away to nothing in the face of the sheer hopelessness of the situation. Marcus was dead. No one would do a thing about it. Finally the grief that had been held at bay these past few weeks began to swell up.

She heard her own voice, faltering with tears as she asked, 'Can you at least tell me his name?'

DC Moor glanced down into her lap. Her hands played with the hem of her blouse. She had the air of someone talking themselves into something they really didn't want to do.

Claire could see her last chance slipping away. She had to be strong, one step ahead of the grief. She reasserted herself. For one last time she wasn't a grieving widow; she was a head teacher. Someone in control. Someone who people listened to.

'Or do I have to take it up with your superiors?' Claire demanded, with all the authority left in her body.

She let the threat hang for a moment as DC Moor took a deep breath and then very reluctantly and against her better judgement gave up the name of the man who had killed Claire's husband.

9

'Five iPhone nines, two with broken screens. Twelve iPhone tens, one with a broken screen, one with a broken charger. Seventeen iPads, three with broken screens . . .'

When Alfie had knocked on Malton's office door and asked for five minutes, Malton assumed Alfie wanted to tell him the stocktake had been completed and leave it at that. That was half an hour ago. Since then it seemed Alfie was determined to go through every item in storage. Proudly reading each line out loud like a child in a school play. The only reason Malton had let him go on this long was because of Dean, who was sat next to Alfie on the large, beaten-up sofa in Malton's office.

Since Dean's awful first day Malton was dimly aware that Alfie had set the lad to washing the vans. When last week Malton had asked Alfie to do a stocktake, he was unsurprised to see Alfie delegate the task to Dean. The boy did his best but as far as Malton could see he just wasn't cut out for the work. Before Dean and Alfie had come into his office that morning he had been ready to let him go. But now something about how Dean sat, hunched over, looking at his shoes, had intrigued Malton.

The boy was thinking something and Malton was curious to find out what it was.

'. . . a child's battery-operated Ferrari. Three mountain bikes, one Nutribullet . . .'

Malton himself sat at his desk. It wasn't fancy, just a small wooden table covered in stacks of paper. He didn't have a

48

computer. Didn't trust them. Didn't use them. He didn't like the idea of putting secrets into a machine. If he wanted to know what someone wasn't telling him, five minutes alone and they would tell him everything. That trick didn't fly with computers. Though Malton was well aware how inconvenient it was, it was his company and if he didn't want to join the twenty-first century just yet then no one was going to convince him otherwise.

'. . . two dozen GHD hair straighteners. Four genuine, twenty fake . . .'

Alfie's shrill, Scouse drone continued to fill the office.

Apart from the sofa and the desk, the rest of Malton's office was given over to an expensive-looking home gym. After a lifetime of training in draughty, dirty gyms, listening to bad chart music over cheap sound systems, as soon as Malton had the cash he'd bought all his own kit. Working out alone on clean, expensive equipment was just about the only thing he did that didn't leave him with some residual sense of guilt over his success. Lifting weights sat perfectly between reward and punishment.

'. . . a bench saw, a circular saw, a jigsaw, a chop saw. All Makita . . . a DeWalt drill set, missing the driver . . .'

Malton didn't have time for this. Talking to Benton that morning had given him a lead: Leon Walker. But finding a bottom feeder like Leon would be nigh on impossible. He was a homeless junkie. A floating piece of human waste drifting through the sewers of the Manchester underworld. He could be absolutely anywhere. Malton could track him down but it would take time. It'd already been three weeks. He had no idea how much longer he had on the clock. If the attack on his home was just the start, what was coming next?

'. . . a 36-inch Samsung Smart TV, a 42-inch Samsung Smart TV . . .'

Alfie was showing no signs of winding up so Malton rose to his feet and decided to move things along. 'I'll go over the rest myself. Is that all?' Malton looked to Dean. If he did have something to say, now was the time.

'Over seven hundred thousand pounds of inventory,' said Alfie, proudly rising up off the sofa and crossing the office to hand over the paperwork.

'Seven hundred and thirty-two thousand pounds of *documented* inventory,' said Dean with just enough confidence to pique Malton's attention.

'Oh?' Malton looked interested for the first time in the last half hour.

'That's what I said,' snapped Alfie. 'Let's go.'

Dean didn't move. 'There's another thirty-five thousand pounds of missing inventory.'

Malton leaned forward. That was what he was waiting for.

'I gave you the inventory receipts. If there's no receipt it's not in there,' said Alfie sharply. 'Sorry, Boss, he's a right idiot this one.'

Still Dean didn't move. Malton stayed silent, curious to see if Dean would stand his ground.

'It took me two days to match up all the inventory in the shed with the receipts. It was all there. But there were things that didn't make sense,' said Dean. His tone was calm and he kept his eyes firmly on Malton as he spoke.

'Bollocks. I checked those receipts myself,' said Alfie, defensively.

'What sort of things?' asked Malton, his interjection silencing Alfie.

'Well you'd have receipts for jobs that were obviously domestic. You'd have the usual stuff – phones, games consoles and that. But then no telly. Or it'd be a tradesman's van and we'd get all the stuff you'd expect but then no drills.

Anyone who works in the trades knows you don't borrow drills. Bring your own or go home.'

'I'm sorry, Boss,' said Alfie, his voice puffed out with insincerity. He crossed the office to Dean and took him by the arm, yanking him to his feet. 'We've taken up enough time.'

Dean shook himself free and took a step back. Ignoring Alfie, he continued speaking directly to Malton. 'I started to wonder if there was stock missing. You know, stuff that hadn't made it onto the receipts. So I had a look what was on the computer . . .'

'And it matched the printouts! What did you expect?' cried Alfie, throwing up his hands in mock exasperation.

Malton didn't take his eyes off Dean.

'When we take stuff away,' said Dean, 'we give them a copy of the receipt. It's handwritten at the time and then we put our copy of it into the system and then we usually chuck the original paper copy. So I got the number of a couple of clients and gave them a ring.'

'I didn't tell him to do any of that,' pleaded Alfie. He sounded like a little kid, caught in the act.

'Sit down, Alfie,' said Malton. Alfie did as he was told. 'Carry on.' Malton gestured to Dean.

'I gave them a ring and obviously they weren't mad keen to talk to the people who'd repossessed their stuff. But I persevered and found a client who had kept their copy of the receipt. I went round with our printout and compared the two. I was right. Things were missing. Things that had been written down at the job and not put on the system.'

Malton silently willed Dean on, not letting his face betray his mounting excitement at Dean's detective work.

'So where could all this stuff have gone? It definitely wasn't in the storage unit. I'd checked. So I took the most recent receipt with discrepancies and went looking for the missing items – eBay, Facebook, Gumtree. Keeping it local. And I found some of the missing stuff for sale online. I looked at the seller's history and it was all there. Every receipt that didn't add up, you could match the dates and find what wasn't listed.'

Alfie was furiously running a tiny, fat hand through what was left of his hair, looking down at his feet as Dean spoke. His face had gone bright red.

'Did you find out who the seller was?' asked Malton, leaning forward expectantly while Alfie shrank back into the sofa. There was one more hurdle. One final piece of the puzzle. But it would be up to Dean. How he answered that next question would determine whether or not he had a future at Malton Security.

'Couldn't find anything out about him,' said Dean. He felt Malton examining him. Scrutinising him for a tell. Any little sign that he might be lying.

Looking Malton straight in the eye, he continued, 'He was selling through PayPal and working out of a PO box. We'll never know who it was. But I think from now on we should keep the paper copy of the customer's receipt. Make sure it doesn't happen again.'

Alfie leapt to his feet, looking like a man who'd just received a last-minute reprieve from the hangman's noose. 'I'll get on it right away!' he trilled. Malton didn't react. 'And well done, lad.' Alfie put a chubby arm around Dean's shoulder. Dean could feel Alfie shaking.

'You do that,' said Malton. 'I'd like to speak to Dean alone for a minute.'

Alfie hesitated for a second. Unsure if he'd just dodged a bullet or walked straight into the firing line.

'He'll be out in a minute,' said Malton definitively, rising from his chair.

With great reluctance Alfie left the room, keeping his eyes on Dean until the last possible second, backing out, squeezing his swollen frame through the door, which Malton shut behind him.

Malton turned to Dean. 'There's only one thing worse than a thief.'

Dean braced himself.

'And that's a grass,' said Malton with a smile.

10

Claire sat in her car thinking about how little it takes to drastically alter the course of your life. Just yesterday she was burying her husband and preparing to die from cancer. But now she suddenly had purpose. She felt more alive than she had in years. All it had taken was one name, dragged with extreme reluctance from her family liaison officer.

Claire hugged her hands around the giant thermal mug filled with the coffee she'd prepared for herself before leaving Jessica with Marcus's parents and heading out for what she told them was a last-minute staff meeting.

The piping-hot liquid filled the car with the smell of home. Of her semi-detached house in Heaton Moor. The brand-new kitchen with the fancy espresso maker Marcus had bought himself for Christmas. Sitting now, parked up in her car, in a cul-de-sac on the edge of a council estate in Hattersley, it all felt a very long way away.

It was February. Without the engine on, Claire's car was freezing. She wore a woolly hat and scarf for all the good it did her. The light went around four. For the last three hours Claire had been sat watching the estate get progressively darker. The street lights didn't come on. When looking for costs to cut, the council had decided the residents could do without street lighting. It wasn't like there was anything worth looking at. A couple of hundred low-rise flats and maisonettes thronged around patches of wasteland where one by one, over time, local amenities had been closed up and knocked down, never to be replaced.

The name Johnny Bistacchi meant nothing to Claire beyond the lurid description DC Moor had given of his teen-age exploits. She'd told Claire to forget about him. Let it lie. Johnny Bistacchi would eventually end up in prison for something or other. It might not be for running over and killing her husband but she could take comfort in knowing eventually he'd screw up and be put away. That was what happened to people like Johnny Bistacchi. They blazed a trail of destruction and then slunk away to rot slowly at Her Majesty's pleasure.

That's what DC Moor had said, but Claire couldn't wait that long. As soon as she got back from the funeral tea, she had retreated to her office and, armed with a name, had dug into online newspapers. She went from burning rage to cold fear. There were a few mentions of Johnny but mostly the articles were about his older brother Paul: his arrests for assault, drug dealing, theft, stalking, sexual assault and even murder. He'd killed a student in a bar fight a few years back, yet somehow got away with it. It was like the Bistacchis were untouchable.

Unable to stop digging, Claire began trawling social media. Within a few clicks she had everything. Johnny lived online. Between Instagram and Facebook Claire found hundreds of photos and videos. Holidays, nights out. An endless stream of different girls, all of them sporting the same dermally filled, heavily manicured, duck-pouting look. Johnny Bistacchi was gorgeous. Even Claire had to admit it. And from the looks of it he was living his best life, flaunting expensive jewellery and brand-new cars. It made her sick to see it.

But there among all the photographs was what she was looking for – the Bistacchis' home.

It started with a photograph of Johnny, shirtless and showing off his six-pack while holding two open bottles of Cristal. The effect was somewhat lessened by the fact that he was standing in a small back garden in Hattersley. But there in the background was something Claire recognised – Werneth Low, a local hill popular with walkers. She put it into Google Maps and using Street View spun around until she was sure she must be facing in the approximate direction of wherever Johnny had taken that photo.

Tracing back from Werneth Low, Claire spent the next hour slowly trailing the streets of the estate, from the safety of her laptop.

It took another few hours but she finally found the Bistacchi house. The house she instantly recognised from the hundreds of photographs taken by Johnny Bistacchi.

Finally Claire knew where they lived: 14 Burns Avenue. The home that she was now parked down the road from.

The house sat at the bottom of the cul-de-sac. A double-fronted property, it was one of the few houses on the estate that looked like money was still being spent on it. The driveway had been relaid recently and large, electronic gates installed, keeping safe the three cars parked in front of the house. A shiny new Mini, a silver Mercedes and a Jeep 4x4. The house windows were all brand new. Fashionable, grey uPVC double glazing. An ornate, metal grille covered the front door. Anyone hoping to gain entry to the house would have a job on their hands.

But it was when the Bistacchis had arrived home a few hours ago that Claire realised just what kind of trouble she was in.

She recognised Paul easily from the many newspaper articles she'd read. His bald head and squat frame were unmistakable. Johnny too was an easy spot. He was even more beautiful in the flesh. Claire couldn't believe someone who looked like that had run over and killed Marcus.

But when the final person got out of the car, Claire forgot about both of them. It was the woman from Marcus's funeral.

She was even still wearing the same sunglasses. Claire felt sick. The Bistacchis hadn't just killed Marcus. They'd been to his funeral. Why? To gloat? A warning? Was Marcus – her gentle, thoughtful husband – somehow involved with people like the Bistacchis?

Claire slid down in her seat, making herself as small as possible until all three had gone inside and she heard the sound of the heavy, metal gate sliding back across the driveway.

That's where she stayed for the next few hours. Waiting. Unsure of her next move. She wished that she had the courage to march right up and knock on the door, tell them exactly who she was and demand they hand themselves in. She imagined how shocked they'd be, finding out she'd tracked them down.

But as Claire sat watching she could feel her courage slipping away. If they were at the funeral what else did they know? Did they know where she lived? About Jessica? Was Marcus's death more than a case of being in the wrong place at the wrong time?

It was fully dark now and the inside of the car was freezing, her back stiff, the windows opaque with condensation. The smell of warm coffee had begun to curdle into the lingering odour of stale caffeine.

Claire was about to start the engine and head home when the sound of empty glass bottles tumbling into a wheelie bin snapped her to attention.

Shivering, she wiped the frosted windscreen and peered down to the bottom of Burns Avenue. She saw Paul Bistacchi on the driveway, clad only in pyjama bottoms and T-shirt with sliders on his feet. He was putting rubbish into a row of colour-coded wheelie bins lined up against the house. Since she last looked out, someone had opened the heavy metal gate that lay across the driveway.

Then, hiding in the shadows, she saw the second man.

A sturdy fence hemmed in the driveway on both sides. To the left of the house ran a cut-through, a small alley, only wide enough for a single person to pass. Houses enclosed the alley: on one side 14 Burns Avenue, on the other side number 12. The man was standing hidden in darkness, just inside the entrance to the alley, a few feet from Paul Bistacchi.

Paul hadn't seen him. The man was dressed head to toe in black, a balaclava covering his face. Claire held her breath and watched Paul sort his rubbish while a few feet away, on the other side of the fence, the man in black drew a shiny metal pole from a holster on his leg and let it slide through his hand until he had a firm grip on the end of it. The metal pole was a couple of feet long and if Claire had to guess she would have said it looked a lot like a cattle prod.

One of the bags Paul had with him wasn't going in. It was stuffed too full to fit into the top of the wheelie bin. As Paul pushed it in with a meaty forearm the bag tore and Claire saw wet rubbish spill out over the ground and all over Paul. Paul started to swear loudly. Even in her car at the other end of the street Claire could hear his choice words.

He made a cursory attempt to sweep the stray rubbish together with his foot before bending down and scooping up what he could in his huge hands. As he turned to dump the rubbish into the bin the Man in Black neatly stepped out of the alley, took another step onto the driveway of number 14 and as Paul Bistacchi dimly registered a presence, the Man in Black stuck the long, metal pole into Paul's guts.

There was a faint sound like electricity discharging and Paul fell to the ground and started fitting. The Man in Black watched for a moment before leaning in and pressing the metal pole into Paul's neck. After that Paul was still.

Claire watched as the Man in Black sheathed the cattle prod and, grabbing Paul under the armpits, dragged him off the driveway and into the road towards a waiting car. The scruffy, red Škoda Yeti had been parked there when Claire had arrived. The Man in Black must have been waiting hours for his moment.

It took him a few tries to haul Paul into the boot before jumping into the driver's seat himself and racing off, past Claire and away into the night. As he passed her, Claire risked sneaking a look. The man was alone in the car, his balaclava still firmly over his face.

Claire sat stunned for a moment. Then it struck her – if Paul didn't come back inside then eventually someone would come out looking. Maybe Johnny, maybe the woman with sunglasses from the funeral. The woman who would immediately recognise her.

Fumbling with frozen fingers, Claire started up her car, drove herself home and lay awake in bed until the early hours trying to understand what she'd just seen.

11

'You could be at university right now,' said Malton across the dirty Formica table. 'Uni girls love a bit of rough.'

Dean swallowed the mouthful of curry he was eating and smiled. 'Costs nine grand to go to uni. Accommodation on top of that. Even your shitty wages are better than that.'

Malton frowned. Dean had been growing in confidence over the last half hour. Back at the office Malton had thanked him for his work on the stocktake, going so far as to take a roll of notes as thick as Dean's calf out of his jacket, peel five hundred pounds off the roll and tell Dean to go and get himself a proper suit. He'd then taken Dean out for tea.

After seeing the few thousand pounds in petty cash that Malton had on him, Dean had been expecting something fancy. Not Café Marhaba. Café Marhaba was one of the last 'rice and three' places in the city centre. Tiny, family-owned cafés that did a spoonful of rice and three spoonfuls of curry for a fiver. The café was only a few minutes from the very centre of the city but hidden down a scruffy backstreet it may as well have been invisible.

Dean's dismay at the café's tatty façade quickly gave way to his delight at the plate of food set before him. Soft, plump rice covered in three generous spoonfuls of curry steeped in rich, spicy flavour.

The small café sat only a half a dozen diners. With its windows steamed up with condensation and the air filled with the sweet smell of several freshly cooked curries, it felt as cosy as it did welcoming.

Dean couldn't help notice how Malton had instinctively sat in the far corner, his back to the wall, facing the door. How with just a wave of his hand to the man behind the counter they had been brought two plates of food.

Dean had promised himself he wouldn't let the food distract him. As soon as they were alone he would reveal to Malton that he knew all about the attack on his house and, better than that, he had a suspect. But he was hungry and the food tasted so good.

And now Malton sat scowling at the dig over his wages. Dean tried not to look as panicked as he felt. 'Not that I'm complaining. Right now, any job's a job,' he said, trying to force a little laughter into his voice.

'You feel that enthusiastic about working for me?' said Malton, looking up from his food.

Dean froze, a forkful of curry halfway to his mouth. Malton stared at him across the small table – waiting for an answer. Dean felt all the goodwill he'd earned from the stocktake slipping away.

He lowered his fork, let out a long breath and said, 'We both know I got a bit cocky just then. Maybe overstepped the mark. I want to work for you. I want to help you do what you do.'

Malton raised an eyebrow and went back to eating. Dean knew a power play when he saw it. That knowledge didn't make it feel any less agonising as he waited for Malton to reply.

Malton swallowed his mouthful of curry and rice and set his fork down. A playful look came across his face. 'What do I do?' he asked.

It seemed to Dean like he was daring him to give the wrong answer.

'You solve problems,' said Dean diplomatically.

The smile returned to Malton's face. 'Neatly put,' he said. 'And what problem do you think you could help me solve?'

'I saved you over thirty thousand pounds.'

'Yes, but what have you done for me lately?' asked Malton.

The delicious smells coming up from his half-eaten curry, the heavy, warm embrace of the tiny café, Malton's expectation. Dean struggled to focus.

This was his moment. His second chance. It had been sheer good luck that while doing the stocktake he'd discovered Alfie had been fiddling the receipts. Dean's real trump card was a name.

Ever since Alfie had let slip about the shooting at Malton's house, Dean had been chasing a hunch. Last night that hunch had paid off.

Dean swallowed the food in his mouth and went for it. 'Do you have any idea who emptied a shotgun into your front door?' he said.

Malton leaned across the table, suddenly very serious. 'How do you know about that?'

Dean's mind raced. No one likes a grass. But it was Alfie who told him. And if he didn't finger Alfie then how could he explain away what he knew?

'Let's just say, I overheard some office gossip,' said Dean.

'Alfie,' muttered Malton, once again impressed at Dean's level of discretion.

'*However* I found out, the thing is, I think I saw the guy who did it casing your place a few weeks ago.'

Dean was expecting a little more of a reaction than the raised eyebrow he got back from Malton.

'How do you know where I live?' Malton asked dryly.

Dean's mind raced. Should he give the real reason? Without the time to think of a suitable lie he had no other option.

'Before I applied for the job I tried googling you. Absolutely nothing. That's a red flag. No one has nothing out

62

there about them. Especially not someone who owns a big company like yours. So . . .'

'You stalked me?'

'I did a bit more digging and . . .' Dean gave up and just came clean. 'A couple of weeks before the shooting I followed you back from work, just to see where you lived. I figured if you lived anywhere I knew about I could maybe drop it into the interview. Oh, you're from Openshaw, that's where I first got arrested! Crumpsall? I used to know a girl from there. Got shot. That sort of thing.'

'You know a girl who got shot?'

'It wasn't anything to do with me. I swear,' said Dean, throwing his hands up in a comic gesture he instantly regretted.

'You followed me home?' said Malton, returning to the point.

Dean sensed it was the time for full disclosure.

'You live across the city centre and drive. On a bike it's easy to keep pace with you. I just went a bit faster, waited at the lights for you to catch up. I lost you out towards Fallowfield but with a bit of searching I spotted your car and yeah . . . Then it was in the papers about the shooting. No name though. Did you get them to keep your name out?'

'I suggested they might,' said Malton darkly.

Malton sat back and sized up Dean. If he was impressed he wasn't showing it.

'You live in Didsbury?' said Dean conversationally. 'I used to hang out with a guy from Didsbury. His parents were old hippies, had a huge house. We used to take acid. Until he had a mental breakdown.'

From the look on Malton's face Dean could tell he was rambling. He quickly got back on track.

'I went for a look round. See if any of the old pubs were still there. Had a few pints. Then on my way back I thought

I'd take one more look. It was late. Nearly midnight. Anyway, I was cycling past your place and I saw him. A big guy, just stood there in the street, staring. It was only the two of us there. I went right past him, got a good look.'

Malton almost smiled. Dean was doing it. He was making a good impression.

'You saw the man who shot up my house? After you'd had a drink. Or two?' Malton said.

Dean suddenly felt a lot less certain. Sure he'd done the digging; he'd put it together. But under the bright, strip lights of Café Marhaba and pinned to his moulded plastic chair by Malton's unflinching gaze, he began to have doubts.

'I saw someone. And it was only three pints,' said Dean.

Malton went quiet. He furrowed his brow and took a mouthful of curry. For what seemed like an eternity he slowly chewed the food before swallowing, putting his fork down and wiping his mouth on a paper napkin.

Dean braced himself.

'I don't suppose you could give me a description?' said Malton.

Dean swallowed hard. This was it. The big pay-off. The thing he'd been up all night looking into. Malton was watching him, evaluating his every movement, weighing up his every syllable.

'I can do better than that,' said Dean. 'I got his name.'

12

The 1st Harpurhey Scout Hut sat between two large patches of scrubland. Twenty years ago they were terraced squares. Hundreds of two-up, two-down houses with back entries and roads and families. All that was optimistically knocked down in the hope of something better. Harpurhey was still waiting. Now the best the council could do was to ring the empty space with concrete bollards to deter families of travellers from setting up home amongst the weeds.

But the 1st Harpurhey remained. As did the Scout troop that used it. Every Thursday at 6pm the Scouts arrived, practised for their badges, watched documentaries and received talks from interesting local characters. At half seven they headed home. Then at eight o'clock volunteers arrived, laid out chairs and set up the Scout hut for the weekly Narcotics Anonymous meeting. Shortly after eight a steady stream of broken humanity trickled in, took a seat and began the weekly ritual of accounting for the addictions that had ruined their lives.

Malton was parked up in a disused car park opposite the Scout hut. There was no lighting so he sat in the late evening gloom watching the entrance of the hut, its windows illuminated by the meeting going on within.

He'd got there just in time to see the last few latecomers arriving, watching them climb the steps and disappear inside. Then he'd sat and waited for nearly two hours while the meeting inside unfolded.

Whoever had shot up his front door was still out there. But now he had a name. The name that Benton had thrown out. The name his fresh-faced new hire Dean had meticulously tracked down after his chance sighting: Leon Walker.

It was far too much of a coincidence not to take seriously.

It had been years since Malton had last seen Leon Walker. Their final meeting was the time Malton had broken Walker's spine. Leon Walker had been on a spree of senseless violence. What started as taxing bars soon escalated into a brazen show of force. Walker was tearing through Manchester, daring someone to stop him. Thanks to his enormous size and psychotic temperament, anyone with any sense was keeping well clear. Anyone who didn't, ended up regretting it.

It had fallen to Malton to put a stop to it. Not because he was a hero or because he felt the need to make a name for himself. It had been purely business. Walker robbed somewhere Malton was paid to protect – a backroom card game in Chinatown. Malton had a choice: bring Walker to heel or lose the one thing his business relied on – his reputation.

Last he heard Walker had come out of hospital a shadow of his former self, his bulk wasted away from months in traction. There was a long line of people waiting to even the score. After several, well-deserved beatings Walker swapped prescription pain medication for heroin. The rest was as pathetic as it was predictable.

Leon Walker definitely had a motive. Thanks to Malton he'd lost his livelihood, his dignity and most importantly his hard-won reputation as a man not to be messed with.

But even in his prime Walker was simply a thug. A blunt object. There was no way he could have tracked Malton down, much less had the temperament to not simply unload the shotgun into Malton himself at the first possible opportunity.

Malton might have had a name but all it did was raise more questions. He needed answers. Fast.

His chain of thought was interrupted as the door to the Scout hut opened, sending a narrow shaft of light out into the darkness. He watched as a parade of the usual degenerates shuffled out, melting into the night. Some faces he recognised; others he didn't. None of them held his attention until finally the last two people emerged from the Scout hut.

Now Malton was paying attention.

One was young. A boy in his twenties, clutching a filthy sleeping bag under his arm, his shoes missing their laces, his trousers loose around his skinny waist. From the light of the Scout hut, Malton could see his face – unshaven, scabbed and red. He felt his fingers gripping the steering wheel a little tighter in revulsion.

The woman with the boy couldn't be more different. Her skin was pale and clear; her long, black hair shimmering a little in the light from the Scout hut. She was dressed in the uniform of the Manchester hipster scene. High-waisted, wide-legged jeans, a striped top under a heavy, cotton chore shirt. Her androgynous wardrobe not quite managing to cover up her feminine curves.

The woman turned off the lights and locked the door. Now the two of them were stood in near-darkness. Only the street lights across the road illuminated them against the inky black of the empty scrubland surrounding the Scout hut.

Malton could tell from the woman's body language that she was trying to shake the boy off. He wasn't getting the message. Or maybe he just didn't care. It made no difference to Malton. He was already out of the car and striding across the car park.

'I just need ten quid and then I can get a bed for the night,' pleaded the boy, an edge of threat in his voice.

'You know I can't give you money. That's not how it works,' said the woman. Her voice was soft and even.

'What's ten quid to you, with your posh accent? I know Daddy can spare ten quid,' the boy snarled back.

He didn't quite go to grab the woman but even if that was his intention he never got the chance. Malton's thick hand wrapped itself around his scrawny wrist, yanking him back. The boy turned to see who had grabbed him but before he could clock Malton he felt a sharp blow to his kidney.

'No!' shouted the woman as the boy fell to the ground.

'He was about to attack you,' said Malton not taking his eyes off the boy.

'He needed help,' she said, sounding distraught.

Malton sighed. This conversation again. Every week he'd beg Emily to move to a nicer Narcotics Anonymous meeting. Somewhere a bit more middle-class. With schoolteachers and housewives. Not the feral bottom feeders of North Manchester. And every week Emily would smile sweetly and tell him that those people didn't need her help. The addicts in the 1st Harpurhey Scout Hut did.

If anyone else had told him that, Malton would have put it down to white, middle-class guilt. But Emily was different. She was maybe the purest person he had ever met. She saw the good in everyone, even in him. Good that he hadn't believed was there. Despite how they'd first met, she'd still wanted to see him. To understand him. When she said she loved him, sometimes he even believed her.

So when Emily bent down to tend to the snivelling runt, squirming away in pain on the ground, he stepped back and let her. He could tell the boy was playing up to her. Milking sympathy like only a junkie can.

Malton didn't like seeing someone use Emily like that.

'You can't help them,' said Malton coldly.

Emily looked up at Malton. '*You* helped *me*,' she said.

Malton knew she'd bring that up. 'You were different.' This wasn't a conversation he wanted to be having. Not in front of a specimen like the one mewling and writhing on the ground in front of him.

'How? Why help me and not him?'

Malton was done talking. He reached into his jacket for his roll of notes. He threw sixty pounds onto the ground next to where the boy was still squirming in pain.

'No!' said Emily.

The boy wasn't listening. The sight of money had a miraculous effect on his injuries. He hungrily scraped the notes off the pavement and started to back away like an animal that had just been brave enough to eat out of a strange human's hand. As he reached the safety of the street light, he gave Emily one last look and smirked before he turned and fled into the night.

'That's not what I meant,' said Emily.

'I gave him what he wanted. I told you, you should run a meeting nearer home. There are far nicer drug addicts in Didsbury.'

'The kind of people who'd fire a shotgun at your front door?'

Emily wasn't stupid. As much as Malton tried to shield her from what he did, occasionally one of the very many bad things in his world crossed over and threatened one of the very few good things. Things like Emily.

'That was my fault. Ex-employee.'

'You didn't tell that to the police.'

Despite his best efforts with his neighbours, someone had decided to call the police. Rather than fight it, he'd played his part: given a meaningless statement and lied about the CCTV. Malton knew how overwhelmed Greater Manchester Police were. Burglary, rape, serious assault – these days you're lucky to get a police car out, never mind an actual investigation. So he let his neighbours indulge in their polite, middle-class fantasy that the police were hard at work tracking down the bad guys.

Meanwhile Malton got on with actually finding out who was behind the shooting. He sighed. 'I work security. It's my job to solve things without the police. You know that.'

'This is why you don't want a family,' she said. Malton could hear the recrimination in her voice. Emily would never outright tell him how much his refusal to have children hurt her. But every time this conversation came up he knew full well how she felt.

Malton's heart sank. This wasn't the first time they'd had this discussion and he knew it wouldn't be the last. The question was: which one of them would be worn down first.

'You spend all your time seeing the absolute worst of humanity,' said Emily sadly. 'All the cynicism and cruelty. You simply can't see that the world isn't all like that.'

Malton kept his opinion on that point to himself. 'In my line of work, if I had a family . . . it's a weakness,' he said.

'Caring is a weakness? Being loved is a weakness? I know you don't believe that. I know you've got so much love to give and I know you're scared to open up. But it's me. It would be our baby. A little bit of both of us. We'd be a family.'

Malton wished he could tell Emily about the last person he'd loved as much as her. How they'd ended up getting tortured until they were begging to be put out of their misery. Finally dying after a week of unimaginable agony. And all because of him.

Deep down he knew the truth. He had resisted Emily not because he wasn't tempted but because he couldn't bear the thought of losing someone like that again.

But looking into her pale blue eyes as they shone under the street light, Malton knew that the longer he resisted the more he risked losing her anyway. If he couldn't give her the thing she wanted most in the world, what would there be to stop her finding someone who could?

'I'm not saying no,' said Malton.

'But you're not saying yes. And time is running out. I'm thirty-four. The older I get the less likely the IVF is to work,' said Emily.

Back when Emily had first raised the subject of a family Malton had gone along with it. Waiting for the right time to bail out. But as it had turned out, he didn't need to. Emily couldn't have children. At least not without help. Her past had caught up with her.

'Let me think about it,' said Malton.

Emily went silent. Malton wished he could tell her how it took all of his ingenuity and courage to keep her safe. How many people would hurt her if they thought they could get away with it. The sort of people who'd come to his house and fire a shotgun at his front door.

Protecting Emily was one thing, but a child too? Malton thought back to how he'd found his former lover when the killers had finished their grisly work. What little was left to bury. He looked at Emily and the thought made him sick.

But the thought of losing her was worse.

Emily looked down at her feet. Malton could tell she was doing her best not to cry.

'I can see you've already made up your mind,' she said, turned and headed for the car.

Malton watched her walk away from of the halo of light outside the Scout hut and into the darkness of the Manchester night.

As much as the idea of a family scared him, losing Emily was not an option.

13

Dean sat as still as he could, trying to remember an off-hand piece of advice he was sure he'd once heard about what to do if a dog attacked you. A few feet away, the Staffordshire bull terrier glared at him, every muscle in its thick, squat body tense – ready to close the gap and sink its jaws into Dean's soft, defenceless body.

It had never occurred to Dean that there was any risk involved in tracking down Leon Walker. Up until now there hadn't been. He had set off with two clues, firstly the large tattoo that read 'VICIOUS' on the neck of the man he'd seen lurking outside Malton's house and secondly, and far more importantly, his smell.

Even just cycling past, Dean had smelt it. It was the unmistakable, ground-in stench of a street junkie. Dean recognised it instantly from his short-lived Saturday job in a local supermarket, where every afternoon, regular as clock-work, the local smackhead would wander in, help himself to a bottle of cider and walk back out. It had been Dean's job to try and stop him. The smackhead always got away and Dean always needed five showers to get the smell out.

It hadn't been quick and it hadn't been pleasant but it had been surprisingly simple. Dean spent a few days cycling round Manchester with a backpack full of cans of special brew, interrogating the most fucked-up, desperate people he could find. Ever since council cuts had shut down almost all the homeless shelters in the city, there were more than enough rough sleepers to choose from. The spice addicts

72

in Piccadilly gardens, bellowing at each other, oblivious to the crowds of shoppers. The encampment of tents that had sprung up just outside Ancoats in the shadow of the relentless regeneration. Or simply going from one cashpoint to the next, each one complete with its own panhandling derelict. Dean had covered dozens of miles and given away enough special brew to ruin anyone's evening. But it had worked. The tattoo was too distinctive. He got a name. And then he got that name again and again. Leon Walker.

In fact Dean had got more than a name. But he hadn't told Malton that.

After Malton heard the name Leon Walker back at Café Marhaba, he'd gone very quiet. Dean couldn't tell if he was weighing up what he had just said or if he was looking at Dean, wondering how on earth this scrawny eighteen-year-old had come up with it in the first place. Eventually and without a word, Malton had got up from his seat, dropped a twenty-pound note on the table (easily twice what the food cost) and left.

Dean wondered if this was tough love. Was Malton simply withholding his approval, pushing Dean to go even further to prove himself? He didn't like the idea that he was being played by his boss. But he liked the idea of being wrong even less.

He hadn't told Malton everything. He kept back one final piece of information. An address: Leon Walker's flat in the tower block that loomed over Salford precinct. If Malton had jumped out of his chair and congratulated Dean on his excellent detective work then Dean would have given him that information. A final bow on the neatly tied package.

But that hadn't happened and so now Dean found himself in Leon Walker's flat, sat opposite his daughter. It was late evening when he'd rung the bell but the girl had answered almost immediately. Like she'd been up waiting for someone.

73

He hadn't counted on the dog.

'Did you know my dad before he went into hospital?' asked the girl, hopefully.

Dean felt impossibly guilty for the lies that had got him invited in.

The teenage girl sat on the floor looking up at him was clearly her father's daughter. She was tall. Nearly six foot with long, muscular legs and unusually broad shoulders. Her filthy school uniform was a couple of sizes too small, with dark grey rings around her collar and cuffs and unbranded trainers on her feet. The smell coming off her cut through the general stink of domestic neglect. It was another thing she shared with her dad.

Despite her size she looked small.

The flat was in disarray and the man who Dean suspected had unloaded a shotgun at Malton's front door was nowhere to be seen. Dean sat on a sofa without cushions, his feet on a carpet covered in scorch marks and brown stains. Everything in the place was broken and through the thin walls at least two different stereos competed to ensure that there was never a moment's silence.

The girl looked up at Dean, waiting for an answer.

'Yeah, I knew your dad. Used to go drinking with him. Good guy.' Dean hoped he sounded more convincing than he felt.

He clung tightly to the cup of tea she'd made him. It still had the teabag in, alongside a splash of milk that had long since gone off. Curdled white droplets floated to the surface.

The cross-legged girl kept staring at Dean.

'He mentioned he had a daughter,' Dean lied.

'Really?' The girl's face lit up and Dean felt awful.

As soon as Dean had walked in, the dog had come rushing out of a back room, barking wildly at him. The girl had held it back. Now it sat beside her, eyeballing him. Dean felt sure that it knew he was lying and was simply biding his time before having another go.

'You been here long?' said Dean, trying to avoid betraying his disgust at the squalid flat.

'Ever since I left the supported accommodation. I got too old for them to even pretend to care anymore.' The girl's face screwed up at the memory.

'So now you live with your dad?'

The girl looked sad. She reached out to the Staffie and dragged its giant, tooth-filled head into her lap. It let itself be manhandled, lying there as she fondled its ears with her grubby fingers, its eyes scrunching up with delight.

The girl seemed to be thinking. 'You're a mate of his, right?' she asked yet again.

Dean wished Malton was here. With his thick roll of notes and way of telling a lie that sounded better than the truth ever could. He made it look easy. Tracking down Leon Walker had been simple. Getting the teenage girl who answered the door to let him into the flat had been nothing. But once he was in there and it became clear that she was alone, suddenly everything became much harder. He wanted to just ask straight out – where's your dad? But the more he lied about Leon, the more the girl asked. Not to catch him out but to hear him speak about the man who had abandoned her in this filthy flat. She devoured Dean's lies and that just made it all the worse.

'Do you know when your dad will be back?' asked Dean, trying to sound as business-like as possible.

The girl bit her lip and looked away. 'I don't need him,' she said petulantly. 'I'm sixteen now.'

Dean was shocked. There were barely two years between them and yet despite her size she looked so young and so lost.

'Do you have anyone else to stay with?' He heard the concern starting to creep into his voice.

The girl suddenly looked up, her eyes filled with a pitiful optimism. 'I could stay with you? You're one of Dad's mates,' she said.

Dean felt the mug of hot tea burning his fingers. He set it down on the carpet. The movement attracted the attention of the Staffie, which opened its eyes and got back to its feet – watching Dean. The girl put one hand on its collar, holding it back.

Dean finally remembered what he'd been told about how to defend yourself from an attacking dog. If you can get behind a Staffie and grab its collar it can't bite you. Something to do with the shortness of its neck.

Dean wondered how on earth he'd get behind a savage dog while it was trying to rip his throat out.

'I'd love to but I don't have space. Just the one room,' said Dean.

'We could share?' She was looking straight at Dean. Making eyes.

What would Malton do now? What would he say that would make this feel less like exploitation and more like charity? That way he had of making exactly what *he* wanted seem like a win for *everyone*.

Dean couldn't think. The girl and the flat and the dog. It was too much. He just wanted this to be over. To find out where Leon Walker was hiding out and get out of there.

'Do you know where your dad went?'

The girl deflated a little. She had offered herself to him and he was still asking her about her dad.

'I don't give a shit,' she said, sounding all of her sixteen years.

'Is there anything you can tell me?' Dean reached into his pocket. His fingers brushed the five hundred pounds Malton had just given him.

The thought that the girl would rob him crossed his mind and Dean hated himself even more for thinking that of her. He reminded himself that his boss had given him that money for a suit. If he was going to buy information he'd have to buy it on his own coin.

Reaching into his other pocket he struggled to pull out his wallet. Upon opening it he discovered he had a five-pound note and some change. He took out the note. The girl's eyes were instantly drawn to it. Dean wondered if Malton felt this wretched when he produced that thick wad of notes from his jacket.

The girl seemed to be thinking before she unfolded her giant frame off the floor and headed into a bedroom, leaving Dean alone with the Staffie.

The dog stood glaring at Dean. For a moment he wondered if it was about to attack. Then with a dumb, wet grin on its face it lolloped over to him, hopped onto the sofa and flopped down on his lap, exposing its tummy expectantly.

The girl came back out of the bedroom to find Dean enthusiastically rubbing the dog's belly. She frowned. 'Fury!'

The dog slowly coiled itself off Dean's lap and returned to her side, looking guilty.

Dean leaned over and without making any sudden movements he handed the fiver to the girl. She snatched it off him, tucking it down the side of her bra before grabbing his hand and pulling it towards her. She was every bit as strong as she looked. She held Dean's wrist while she produced an eyeliner pencil and scrawled a number on the back of his hand.

'What's this?'

'Dad's last dealer.'

Dean looked down at his hand. It was enough digits to be a mobile number.

'Does he have a name?' said Dean.

'Do you have any more money?'

'I don't but if there's anything I can do for you?'

'You can fuck off.'

The girl was trying to sound menacing, but she sounded tired. It was clear she'd seen through Dean. Whether or not she believed he really knew her dad, he was no different from every man she'd ever known. He would lie to her to get what he wanted and then he would leave.

Dean felt like shit.

'If you ever need anything.' He reached into his pocket and produced one of the business cards Malton had given him. It had the office number on. Dean quickly scribbled his own number beside it.

He offered it to the girl. She didn't take it, so he gently laid it down on the filthy carpet.

'I'm Dean by the way,' he said.

The girl stared warily at him for a moment. 'You can call me Vikki,' she said.

As Dean left the flat, he promised himself that he'd phone someone about the girl. Have something done about it. But in the time it took for him to cycle home he became so caught up in planning the next step in his pursuit of Leon Walker, he'd forgotten all about her.

14

Last night Claire had seen a man knocked to the ground with a cattle prod and kidnapped in front of his own home. That much she was sure of. What to do next? That was where she hit a brick wall. This was definitely not her world. But then neither was cancer, or burying her husband, yet both of those things had happened. It was still early as she crossed the playground. She saw groups of children being dropped off for the breakfast club and the dinner ladies huddled outside the school gates – smoking away, happy in the knowledge that Claire's jurisdiction as head teacher ended at the eight-foot, chain-link fence that surrounded St Ambrose's.

One of the smoking dinner ladies gave a belligerently cheery wave. Claire pretended not to have seen and carried on inside.

She still couldn't shake the low, queasy feeling in her stomach that there was something more to all of this. That woman turning up at Marcus's funeral, the woman who she was now convinced was in with the Bistacchis. Had Marcus done something to bring these people into their lives? Was the accident that cost him his life not an accident at all? Claire felt horribly out of her depth.

The one thing keeping her going was what she had seen the night before on the driveway. Now she knew something that no one else did. If the police wouldn't move on the Bistacchis then maybe this might change their mind? But if Marcus was involved with them, what would they find?

There was already a small queue outside her office. A year seven boy and a teaching assistant. The teaching assistant nodded in recognition as Claire passed. The year seven boy kept his head down. The teaching assistant rose with something in his hand but before he could get Claire's attention, she had passed him and closed the office door behind her.

Claire dumped her bags on the floor beside her desk, sat down and turned her computer on. Desperately trying to lose herself in a routine she'd gone through a thousand times before.

But the events of the previous night wouldn't let go.

What exactly had she seen? Paul Bistacchi getting the business end of a cattle prod. As thrilling as it had been to watch the drama unfold Claire had to admit to herself that really, beyond that, she knew nothing.

Then there was the Man in Black. Who was he? How long had he been lying in wait? Claire had been there at least a couple of hours. Had he been there that whole time and if so, had he seen her?

Before last night Claire had simply been angry. Now for the first time she felt afraid. Too late she realised, it wasn't to protect her own career that DC Moor hadn't wanted to give her Johnny Bistacchi's name. It was to protect Claire.

Claire set up her desk with registers and reports and marking. All the busywork and bureaucracy it took to run a secondary school.

Spending all her time with Jessica had gone from escapist indulgence to morbid clock watching. Without work, school or Marcus, suddenly all that was left in their lives was waiting for the end. Unable to bear it any longer Claire had returned to her job and when she'd been offered compassionate leave after the funeral had turned it down.

More than ever she needed the distraction. Something to take her mind off the terrifying scenarios she had been unable to stop imagining ever since the night before.

80

She tried to focus on work. Running the school was more than enough to keep her busy. She'd been brought to St Ambrose's after Ofsted put the school into special measures. With council budgets at breaking point, what money they did have they used to poach Claire. Now every day she left her beautiful semi in fashionable Heaton Moor, got in her eighteen-month-old BMW and drove across town to teach children in inner-city Moss Side.

The school's intake was a broad mixture. First-generation immigrants – mainly Somalians. A handful of the white, working-class Irish who had once filled Moss Side and neighbouring Hulme, as well as an increasingly large number of Romani children whose parents turned up en masse to drop off their children.

Beneath the deprivation and poverty they were good kids and Claire knew how to get the best out of them. Under her watch, discipline had been bumped up the agenda. Parents were persuaded into working with the school and a sense of academic pride was beginning to break out.

Her days always started the same: checking the register for those absent. Going down the lists, the names of the usual suspects jumped out. Cody Harper missing. Again. Cody's dad had been murdered when Cody was seven and his mum's terrible taste in men meant that he was always going to be on the lookout for a substitute family. To Claire's dismay she had recently learned he'd found it with a local gang.

Next on the agenda were children who'd managed to get into trouble before the day had even started. She had seen Yaya waiting outside with his classroom assistant. Yaya was Cody's younger brother but he was nothing like Cody. He was one of the few kids with the smarts to see that St Ambrose's wasn't the entire world. That he would leave there and have to make something of himself. He knew five wasted years at St Ambrose's would mean a wasted life. Claire liked Yaya.

Kids like him made her feel as if maybe she was making a difference.

Two boys, both with exactly the same upbringing. One of them let it defeat him; the other had chosen to rise above it. Was it nature, was it nurture or was it just dumb luck?

As Claire called Yaya in, she took a deep breath, sat up a little straighter and arranged her face into a look of stern disappointment.

Yaya and the classroom assistant, a bearded young man named Ben, who was also doing his best to convey the extreme gravity of the situation, came in. Yaya sat down and Ben handed Claire a crumpled business card before taking a seat himself.

'What's this about, Yaya?' asked Claire, looking at the card in her hands. It said 'Malton Security' on it alongside a mobile phone number.

Yaya looked away.

'He was telling other boys that if they didn't let him play football he'd call that number and a man would come and break their legs,' Ben offered.

Yaya blushed.

'We don't ever make threats in this school, do we?' said Claire.

Yaya muttered something inaudible while Claire turned the card round in her hands. She held it up for all of them to see.

'What is this?' said Claire.

Yaya shrunk into his seat. 'Nothing,' he said quietly.

'So what happens if I call this number?'

'No!' Yaya looked up, terrified.

Claire shared a look of concern with Ben. This wasn't a normal playground fight.

Her voice became stern. 'Has this man threatened you?'

'Tell Mrs Minshall what you told the boy in your class,' prompted Ben, slipping into good cop to Claire's bad cop.

Yaya weighed up his options.

Claire knew most of the children at St Ambrose's had internalised their parents' instinctive distrust of authority. The daily regime of sullen silences and petty defiance was just one of the reasons she asked for and got such an inflated salary. She also knew that Yaya was better than that. Smarter than most.

Claire took a chance. Like all teachers she had the 'voice'. The voice she used to talk to children. To praise them or scold them. It was the voice an adult uses to talk to a child.

Claire dropped the 'voice' and spoke to Yaya as an equal. 'Whatever you tell me won't leave this room,' she said. 'But you have to tell me.'

Yaya looked up. He may have been young but he'd fitted more into his twelve short years than most people managed in a lifetime.

'He didn't threaten me. He said he'd help me,' said Yaya.

Claire's child protection training instantly started throwing up red flags.

Struggling to stay calm she said, 'Help you? How?'

Yaya took the plunge. 'He said if I ever had trouble with my stepdad I should ring his number and he'd sort him out.'

Claire looked at the card in her hands.

'Why would he do that?' she asked.

'He helps people. People who . . .' Yaya felt the words, heavy in his mouth. 'People who can't go to the police. He fixes problems for them.'

Claire's heart started to beat faster. She looked down at the card and then away, worried that Ben might somehow know the terrible thought that had just crossed her mind. Composing herself, she put the card into her jacket pocket and gave Yaya the standard telling-off she gave to the few kids she thought had the good sense to take a hint and steer clear of trouble in the future.

By the time Ben had ushered Yaya out and closed the door behind him, Claire was already dialling the number.

15

Dean was up early and waiting outside Reiss for when it opened at 9am. He'd found the suit he wanted online. It cost four hundred and fifty pounds – that gave him enough to buy a tie to go with it. He already had the white shirt he'd worn for school. If a four-hundred-and-fifty-pound suit couldn't make that look good then what was the point?

It was a skinny-fit suit in a dark herringbone. Not the sort of thing he'd normally wear but the model on the website had something of Malton about him, which Dean had taken to be a good sign.

As much as he wanted to tell Malton about last night's detective work, Dean was unsure that he'd really found out anything more than he'd already shared with his boss. He had seen the look on Malton's face when he'd exposed Alfie and he wanted more – he wanted to see just how impressed he'd be when he gave him Leon Walker on a plate. But right now all he had was the number Vikki had scrawled on the back of his hand. His moment of triumph would have to wait.

Malton was late getting in the office and so Dean kept himself busy on paperwork and avoiding Alfie who had become unsettlingly polite since yesterday's stocktaking revelations. There was a steady stream of Malton Security guys, coming and going in their trademark black combat trousers and black puffer jackets but no sign of Malton.

Dean was starting to feel slightly overdressed for office admin when, a little before ten, the buzzer on the front door went and Alfie showed in a strikingly beautiful, mixed-race woman. She wore enormous sunglasses covering most of her face, which she didn't remove. Instead she took a seat in the waiting area as casually as if she was settling down in her own front room.

'Is Craig in?' she said. Her voice light but with just a hint of firmness.

Dean had never heard anyone call Malton anything other than Malton or 'Boss'. But the way this woman smiled as she said his name made him think she just might get away with calling him Craig.

Alfie apologetically told her that Malton was running late but that she was welcome to wait and he'd be more than happy to make her a coffee. She declined the coffee and settled in to wait.

As Dean tried to carry on with his work he got the sense that she was examining him, her eyes hidden behind those giant sunglasses, her face framed by dark, curly hair tumbling down to her shoulders. Despite the February chill she was wearing a light cotton dress in a bright, geometric print with a Levi's stonewashed-denim, trucker jacket over the top. On her feet she wore a pair of dazzling white Adidas basketball trainers.

Dean did his best to busy himself in a pile of invoices and not to notice the way her dress parted, revealing almost all the way to the top of her thigh.

The woman took out her phone and Dean waited until she appeared distracted before allowing himself to look at her properly. She was in her late thirties he supposed. Maybe younger, not older. She had the appearance of a woman who would look this good until she died. Her fingernails were long talons in metallic purple with little diamanté crystals glued onto the tips. She'd been in the office long enough now that Dean could smell her perfume. It was thick and sweet and so distracting that Dean completely forgot that under her sunglasses he had no idea where her eyes were looking.

'You're a bit young for me.' She giggled.

Dean looked away, embarrassed.

Her laugh was fruity and rich. A powerful mixture of Mancunian Irish and a touch of West Africa. It was friendly and dirty and dangerous all at once.

The sound of Malton finally arriving for work saved Dean from this agonising back and forth. He wandered casually into the office clutching a carrier bag filled with cans of energy drink and a newspaper.

Before Dean even had a chance to open his mouth the woman dived on Malton, all hugs and air kisses which he gamely endured. She stood back and pushed her sunglasses up onto the top of her head where they rested among mounds of thick, brown curls. Her eyes shone as brightly as her smile.

'Craig! How long's it been?' She sounded breathless with excitement. No one had ever been this pleased to see Dean. Not even his mum.

As Malton weighed up his response he noticed Dean hovering in the background – unsure whether or not to interrupt. His nerves earned a well-meaning smile of amusement from Malton.

'Dean, this is Keisha,' he said and then added: 'She's an old friend.'

Hearing this Keisha beamed. 'We've already met,' she said, in a tone that made Dean blush.

Dean watched as they both disappeared into Malton's office. Before Malton closed the door behind them he paused for a moment and looked Dean up and down before giving him an approving nod.

'Nice suit.'

16

Malton sat at his desk listening to Keisha talk and did his best not to betray any trace of emotion. She went straight for the sofa, kicking off her trainers and tucking her feet up under her bum, just like she used to when they'd stay up talking all night. That was a lifetime ago but the way she looked at him, the way she called him 'Craig' – she was doing her best to carry on as if it were just yesterday.

Of course, they'd bumped into each other since then. Manchester talked a big game but there was only so much Manchester to go round. They moved in similar circles and neither of them were willing to stay away from Moss Side, where they had first met. But on the handful of occasions when their paths had crossed, they had stuck strictly to pleasantries.

Yet here Keisha was chatting away in his office as if the last thirty years had never happened. Malton wondered what had changed.

Keisha dove straight into small talk, asking him about his business, what he'd been doing. Questions he felt sure she already knew the answers to. He answered as briefly as he could, staying upbeat and gently steering the conversation away from the secret things in his life that even Keisha would have had a hard time discovering.

The whole time she kept up that winning smile. Malton thought how much he missed seeing her smile. It was what had kept them together for so many years – never wanting to see that smile go away.

87

'How's Emily? It's Emily, right?' said Keisha, her voice so light and chatty that Malton could almost believe she didn't already know everything there was to know about him and Emily.

He played along. 'She's very good. Nothing to do with any of this.'

Keisha smiled. 'You've gone up in the world. A nice Jewish girlfriend from Hale? Didn't think that was your type. I bet her old man loves you.'

Emily's father Lawrence went drinking with Malton. He had retired early on a small fortune and was living his life without any of the studied wariness that Malton depended on. He seemed happy. Malton envied him. But he knew what Keisha wanted to think – and he let her.

As fun as all this was, eventually Malton addressed the elephant in the room. 'You've managed to steer clear for the last thirty years. What's changed?' he said.

'If I could have gone to anyone else I would,' said Keisha. She sounded almost apologetic. As if she was imposing on an old friend.

'So I'm the last resort?' said Malton, one corner of his mouth turning up with the faintest suggestion of an in-joke between friends.

'You know, no one else can do what you can,' said Keisha taking the bait and playing along.

As much as part of Malton wanted to enjoy this trip down memory lane, a larger part of him still remembered just how dangerous Keisha could be when she set her mind to it. It was time to let her know she wasn't the only one who'd been keeping tabs on an ex.

'Not even the Bistacchis?' he said.

Malton held back mentioning Keisha's new husband. When he heard Paul Bistacchi was marrying his ex, he felt sure that something bad was coming down the pipe. But that was three years ago. Since then the unexpected union of a hard-as-nails girl from Hulme and a roid-addled, mid-level drug dealer from Hattersley had moved to the periphery of his radar.

'You heard?' said Keisha, sprawling, uninhibitedly on the sofa in a way that Malton was sure Paul Bistacchi would not appreciate.

'I nearly sent flowers,' said Malton. 'Must be . . . interesting. Married to the Bistacchis.'

'No worse than what you used to get up to. No worse than what you still get up to,' she said with a teasing familiarity.

'I don't get hammered and run people over outside the Christie', said Malton. It was time to close this down.

Keisha looked impressed. 'I wasn't sure you'd have heard about that.'

'The Bistacchis aren't known for their discretion.'

'But they don't get caught.'

'Yet. So what problem is so difficult that even the combined IQ of the Bistacchi clan can't solve it?'

Keisha slipped her feet out from under her bum and leaned forward. Malton caught her perfume – *Obsession*. It was the first perfume he'd ever encountered. His dad reeked of Guinness and his mum had left when he was still a baby, so growing up he never knew the wonderful, magical fragrance of a woman. When he'd first smelled Keisha it was all he could think about. To this day when he walked past a woman in the street wearing *Obsession* he felt his heart leap. Just for a moment he would get a memory of how it felt to be in love for the first time with a gobby girl from down the road in Hulme called Keisha McColl.

'Paul's gone,' Keisha said, shaking Malton back to the present.

'Left you?'

'No. Taken. Kidnapped.' The lightness was gone from her voice. This was all business.

Kidnapped? You'd be safer kidnapping a rabid dog than Paul Bistacchi. Malton tried, unsuccessfully, to think of anyone from the Manchester criminal fraternity who would even dream of doing something so dangerous.

'By who?' he said, making sure to keep the curiosity out of his voice.

'You tell me,' said Keisha, throwing down the gauntlet.

This wasn't what Malton expected and if he was honest with himself he was intrigued. But unless she asked him outright, he wasn't going to offer.

'I run a security firm. Work doors, guard stuff. You need the police,' said Malton, rising from his desk.

'Are you going to make me spell it out?' said Keisha.

Malton kept quiet. Yes, he was.

'You're the police for people who can't go to the police. Villains. You're the man who can find people, return property, make amends. When Gary Werner's daughter got in with those lads up in Rotherham, ended up on the brown, you went up there, found her, brought her back. Along with the ones that got her hooked on it in the first place. Remind me, what did Gary do to them?'

'Not my business. He paid me for his daughter and the men who got her hooked on heroin.'

'I heard he had them raped by a couple of guys, made them confess everything on tape. Sent the video to their parents.'

'You don't want to get mixed up in heroin,' said Malton as an end to the matter. A few things about the Gary Werner case never had sat right with him. He made a policy of never getting involved once a job was over but privately he thought sending the tape to the lads' parents crossed a line.

'Mixed up like Emily?' said Keisha with a smile that said she knew exactly what buttons she was pressing.

Malton hardened. 'I'm not interested.' He walked over to the door and held it open.

In the office beyond Dean tried to look like he wasn't eavesdropping.

Keisha stayed sitting. 'Sorry, that wasn't fair. I'm upset. I'm not thinking. Paul's my husband. I love him. I'm scared for him. I need you.'

There was the smell of *Obsession* again. It was overpowering. Keisha's big brown eyes, her lids lowered just a little, started to work their way through the defences Malton had spent decades building.

'Not interested,' he repeated, firmer this time.

Keisha shrugged. She reached over to her discarded trainers and started to slowly put them on.

'Shame. I thought we meant something. That I could come to you.' The lilt was gone from her voice. It was now all Moss Side aggro.

'No.'

'Shame too, all those clubs you run. Hard enough keeping a door. What if every night a pack of idiots with weapons came down, started making trouble, beating up bouncers, beating up punters. You remember the old days, right?' Keisha had finished putting on her shoes and was standing. 'The Bistacchi name means something out in Hattersley. I give the word and East Manchester comes to you. Filthy, brutal, fucking horrible East Manchester. Not Moss Side rough. White rough. Every night. Every club you run.'

Malton weighed up the threat. And just for a moment, how much he enjoyed being threatened by Keisha.

He shut the door and walked back to his desk. 'I charge two grand a day.'

'Doesn't your ex get a discount?' asked Keisha sweetly. Then she let out a laugh. 'I'm fucking with you. You should see your face.' Keisha always knew how to lead Malton on.

She reached in her handbag and pulled out a bundle of some of the filthiest-looking banknotes he'd ever seen. Street money. 'Here you go, that's you for the next two weeks. Any longer and I'll sort you out.' Keisha dumped the money on his desk and it spilled onto the floor.

She leaned in over the desk, giving Malton a prime view of cleavage. He kept his eyes firmly on her face. She held his gaze, daring him to look down.

Finally Keisha broke first. 'And if you need any more, just ask,' she said.

On the wall next to Malton's desk a small light started flashing. Keisha had her back to it but Malton saw it clear as day. This had been fun but now he was needed elsewhere. He got up and held the door open.

'I'll be in touch. Don't worry – I'll find him,' he said.

Malton held Keisha's gaze, holding her in place with his eyes so she wouldn't turn around, see the red light flashing behind her and realise that it wasn't confidence speaking, it was urgency. He needed her gone and if telling her he'd find her husband was what got her out of his office, then that was what he was going to tell her.

'Don't you want to ask me anything?' said Keisha as Malton steered her through the door.

'I prefer to find things out for myself. That way I can trust what I hear.'

'You don't trust me?' she said with a mischievous smile, the lilt back in her voice.

'I'll be in touch.'

Keisha thought for a moment, stepped to Malton and before he could stop her, gave him a peck on the cheek. She was slightly taller than he was. She had to stoop a little. 'I know you will,' she said and left the office.

Dean, who was still sat waiting, watched her go. Malton caught Dean staring past him to the red light flashing on the wall.

There was no time to explain.

'We got a job,' said Malton.

Dean snapped to attention. 'What is it?'

Malton threw a last glance to the flashing red light as he pulled on his Barbour jacket. 'Manageable. If we get there before the police,' he said.

17

Lorraine's used to be a match-day café. A Moss Side institution. When Maine Road was still standing, hundreds of thousands of football fans would flood the streets of Moss Side on match days and the café would make as much in one day as they'd make the whole rest of the week. Packed full of warm, noisy bodies; the smell of sweet, hot bacon and strong cups of tea. Then during the week players would drop in for breakfast after training. Their faded photos still hung on the walls – arms draped around the owner Lorraine, like she was a second mum.

She wasn't just a second mum to Malton. She was as near to a mum as he ever got. Back when he was a scruffy Moss Side kid, breaking into cars and nicking from corner shops, Lorraine had caught him trying to set fire to her bin and instead of calling the police she did something Malton had never forgotten – she had invited him in and fed him.

She had sat him down with a full English and talked while he ate. She hadn't asked him why he was setting fire to her bin. She hadn't asked why his clothes were so dirty or his hair half combed out. She'd just talked and smiled and laughed. Malton had wondered if this was what mums did. He wouldn't know. His dad had said his mum had left because of him. That she didn't want a son. As an adult Malton knew he was only saying that to hurt him. It didn't mean that on some level he didn't still believe every word.

There was none of that at Lorraine's. Malton would drop in and she would feed him. She would introduce him to the players who came in from training for their breakfast. He thought of her as the mum he deserved.

That was over thirty years ago. In that time Malton had left Manchester and Maine Road had been knocked down. Manchester City had moved to the Etihad and with it the fans, the match-day crowds and the money. Lorraine's had limped along getting ever closer to bankruptcy until three years ago, on the brink of closing, Malton had finally returned.

Before then he'd deliberately avoided Lorraine's. He'd told himself he was busy, which he was, but deep down he knew the real reason – he was scared Lorraine would have forgotten him. That like his real mum, she never really wanted a kid like him in her life.

The moment he'd stepped in the door all his fears vanished. The place was deserted. Just him and Lorraine, like old times. He'd ordered a full English and as he'd sat eating it, they'd talked as if he'd never been away.

Lorraine was just like he remembered her, laughing, heaping food on his plate, talking non-stop. The smell of the fat cooking, the scalding hotness of the builder's tea, the low hum of the refrigerator behind the counter. Malton had felt like he'd come home.

As he was licking the last of the grease from his fingers he'd come right out and asked how business was doing. Lorraine didn't have it in her to lie. She'd cried a little as she told him she was on the verge of closing. After the years of work she had put in she was going to lose it all. Malton knew this already. This was exactly how he'd planned it. He told himself that what he was about to do was helping Lorraine, repaying her kindness. Which in a way it was.

Malton had made Lorraine an offer. He would save her café and all he would expect in return was a little favour.

Now, as Malton's car sped through Manchester traffic towards Lorraine's he checked his watch. He'd promised

Lorraine a lot of things as part of their agreement. But the most important of those was that within five minutes of her pressing the silent alarm he'd had installed, he'd be there at the café. It had already been three minutes.

After Lorraine accepted Malton's offer of help he'd overseen a few changes: a sturdier back door as well as a hidden safe in the kitchen. In return Malton promised Lorraine she would get a steady stream of customers. All she would have to do was keep on doing what she had always done: cook her food, mother them and make Lorraine's feel like your second home. And from time to time these new customers would give Lorraine a package. A package that she was to put in the safe. Not open, not interfere with, not store anywhere except the safe. Then at the end of the week someone would come and empty the safe.

Malton jumped a red light and pulled onto Princess Parkway. Out of the corner of his eye he could see Dean getting thrown about in the passenger seat. They were a couple of minutes away at most. The speedometer was pushing seventy as Malton hurtled down the dual carriageway that skirted the edge of Moss Side.

Whenever possible Malton made sure it was him who did the weekly pickup. He'd arrive and Lorraine would shriek with delight. She'd sit him down and fill him with hot, greasy food, washing it down with strong, dark tea. She'd then join him, asking him about his life. His job, his girlfriend, his favourite football team. Malton never said a word. He just let her talk while he ate. Lorraine didn't need a second person to hold a conversation.

Malton had never felt like he belonged. Ever since he was young he had taken that feeling and made it work for him. He had made himself useful. A fighter, a negotiator, a peace maker. Whatever would make him needed, make it harder for him to be cast out. But for half an hour a week at

Lorraine's he wasn't trying to be anything. He was just eating his fried breakfast and it never once crossed his mind that he could do or say anything that would ever make him unwelcome in that little café.

It had been six minutes since the alarm went off. As Malton pulled up outside Lorraine's he heard the first gunshot.

18

Malton was already out of the car, racing across the pavement and into the café before Dean had even had time to get his seat belt undone. But Malton wasn't waiting for him. He crashed through the door, reaching into his jacket for his hatchet as Dean followed hot on his heels.

Malton didn't break stride as he took in the scene. Lorraine was slumped behind the counter – a carving knife clasped in her hand and her clothes drenched in blood. From the way she lay Malton knew she was already gone.

The knowledge that she went down fighting was the smallest possible comfort to Malton as he made up the distance between the front door and the counter where a youth in a balaclava was standing, the warm gun still in his hand.

Malton kept pace as the boy wildly swung the gun round to face him. He lowered his left shoulder, ducking under the gun barrel and as he did so, swung upwards with the razor-edged hatchet in his right hand.

'Duck!' screamed Malton, without bothering to look behind him to check whether or not Dean was even there. He was there and he did duck as the gun went off a second time, the bullet lodging in the ceiling before the hatchet connected with the boy's hand, cutting clean through his wrist, severing the hand, gun and all.

The hand flew high in an arc across the café, bounced off a table and landed on the floor. Malton kept moving, vaulting the counter and rushing to the side of the woman slumped behind it.

The boy started to scream, holding the bloody stump up in sheer disbelief at what had just taken place. Dean kicked the hand with the gun into a corner, tore off his brand-new jacket and threw it over the boy's stump. Clasping it tightly, he looked over the boy's shoulder and saw Malton knelt over the woman's limp body.

Malton bent down to cradle Lorraine. She felt impossibly light in his huge hands. The bullet had smashed into her cheek and passed out the back of her head, taking a good amount of skull with it. The last look on her face – defiance.

Malton could smell the chip fat on her hair. It mixed with the salty, metallic stink of blood. Rage and grief boiled up inside him. His teeth clenched as his breath became short and fierce.

'Boss?'

The sound of Dean's voice pulled Malton back from the brink. He wasn't here to grieve or to get bloody revenge. He was here on business. Lorraine was dead, her killer was screaming on the floor of the café, minus a hand. It was time to take control.

Malton laid Lorraine gently on the floor before standing up and grabbing a roll of cling film from the counter, which he threw at Dean who just about caught it. 'Get him in the car. Now!' Malton ordered, pointing to the gunman.

Dean opened his mouth to ask what he was meant to do with the cling film but before he could get an answer Malton was already heading into the back.

The safe had been installed beneath the deep-fat fryer. It was an ingenious design. The fryer itself rested on top of the safe and was held in place by a hidden catch. Once you unlocked the catch you could lift the entire fryer upward, revealing a top-loading safe. Unless you knew it was there you'd never find it. And if you knew it was there then you knew who owned what was in it. And if you knew who owned what was in it you knew just how suicidal it would be to try and take it from him.

The only thing that made sense to Malton was that somehow whoever had told the kid about the safe had neglected to give him the full story. They had put a gun in his hand, sent him into Lorraine's and as good as signed his death warrant.

Malton punched the combination into the safe and quickly stuffed everything he found inside into a carrier bag. With the safe empty, he turned to go. It was then that he saw it. On the wall in the kitchen, away from the paying customers. It was a photo of him and Lorraine. He remembered the day she took it. He was only four-teen. He'd come in wearing the first real clothes he'd ever bought for himself: a Fred Perry polo and Levi's jeans. Sure, he'd bought them with stolen money but it was his stolen money. Lorraine had made such a fuss over him. She'd insisted on taking a photo there and then. It was a lifetime ago. But here it was. Printed out and framed. Just like the photos of the footballers in the front.

Malton took the picture off the wall, smashed the frame to get it out, folded the photo up and stuffed it in his jacket.

By the time he was back outside, Dean was helping the gunman into the car. He'd lost the balaclava and Malton saw with dismay just how young Lorraine's killer was.

'Get in the back with him,' Malton said to Dean as he walked round to the driver's side door.

Dean nudged the boy over and got in beside him. He reached across and buckled the boy in before doing his own seat belt. Malton got in the driver's side and dumped his bag on the passenger seat.

He calmly wove his way into the traffic on Princess Park-way before hitting a number on his phone and putting in a call to the man who three years ago had paid him to turn Lorraine's café into a drop house.

The man who right now had the power of life and death over all three of them.

19

Carnforth Road wasn't posh but it definitely wasn't the kind of road where someone would buy a £500,000 detached house and then leave it to rot like they had done to number 36. Number 36 had been the main topic of residents' meetings, angry letters to the council and repeated attempts to track down whoever it was behind Destiny Property Management – the only identifying name on the title deeds.

Malton knew exactly who owned Destiny Property Management. What's more, he'd come to 36 Carnforth Road with Dean and the boy who shot Lorraine to meet the elusive owner.

Every window of number 36 was unsentimentally covered with steel shutters, screwed deep into the brickwork. The front door with its carved wood details and stained glass windows had been replaced with a unsentimental metal door held firmly shut with a giant padlock. The general consensus was that the house was empty, but the late-night sounds of raised voices from inside – some even said screaming – kept the fear of squatters alive in the minds of the residents' association.

The apparent lack of occupation meant that number 36 had become something of a favourite spot for the casual fly tipper. Its front garden was strewn with black bin liners, broken bed frames and discarded suitcases.

Malton, Dean and the boy picked their way through this assortment of trash and headed for the back of the house. It was less than ten minutes since Malton made the call and there was already the tell-tale Man-City-blue Range Rover parked across the road waiting for them.

Malton could feel his phone buzzing in his pocket. Someone wanted something but they could wait. Right now there was nothing more urgent in the world than being here at number 36 Carnforth Road.

They would have been there sooner, but Malton had been forced to pull over on the way to treat the wounded kid. In the panic Dean had taken the cling film with him but failed to do anything with it. Instead he'd wrapped his new jacket around the stump to stop the bleeding. There was so much blood it had saturated the jacket and was pooling on Malton's upholstery.

With the boy barely clinging on to consciousness, Malton took over from Dean. Slapping the boy to something like awake, he had wrapped his bloody stump in cling film before raiding the highly specialised first aid kit he kept in the car for occasions just like this.

First Malton forced a handful of antibiotic tablets down the boy's throat before the final touch: a small bag of what Malton assured him was medical-grade cocaine. The boy took a small bump, shuddered and sat up, suddenly alert.

Malton had Dean mop up the worst of the blood with what was left of his jacket and they continued on their way.

The back garden of 36 Carnforth Road was worse than the front. What once was a decent-sized lawn had grown to head height with weeds and stray plants. Only the well-trodden path round the side of the house to the back door gave any indication that anyone had been anywhere near the back garden in decades.

The back door itself had been replaced like the front door but instead of a padlock there was a numerical keypad.

While Dean kept a firm grip on the boy, Malton pressed in a keycode: 1.1.1.2. There was a buzzing noise and the door clicked open. All three of them headed inside to meet the CEO of Destiny Property Management. The very same man who owned the drop house at Lorraine's.

A man whose name was a byword in the Manchester underworld for violence, cruelty and fear.

A man called Danny Mitchum.

20

It was 1999 and Paul Bistacchi had just kissed a complete stranger full on the lips. He was drunk. The good drunk where everyone loved you and you felt pretty much the same way. United had just won the treble and every pub in the city centre was disgorging bodies as the whole of Manchester made their way to Albert Square, drawn by an unspoken certainty that they were in the midst of history.

Sounds of joyful shouting filled the air. This was the old Manchester. No skyscrapers, no building sites, just the reassuring canyons of the warehouses and the dozens of pubs offering nothing more novel than a pint of Guinness Cold. Paul Bistacchi had never felt a happiness like this. Every face was smiling. Everyone equal. The joy of watching Manchester United not just secure the treble but do it in extra time against Bayern Munich.

A young man grabbed Paul and bellowed in his face, 'WE BEAT THE FUCKING GERMANS!' Paul didn't raise his fists, he just bellowed back a wordless acknowledgement. Two complete strangers shouting noise into each other's faces in a gesture so full of love that they would both remember it for the rest of their days.

The crowds were getting thicker now. There were already thousands in Albert Square. The statues were covered with bodies who'd scrambled up and over the stolid elders of the city. Someone had shimmied up a lamppost and was hanging from it while those below egged him on. The few policemen that were there seemed oblivious to their duties – too swept up in the emotion of the moment to care.

It didn't matter. There was nothing here but love. Defiant, beautiful love. As Paul Bistacchi entered Albert Square his heart was swollen to burst. There were no camera phones, no one recording anything. This was a moment exclusively for those who were there. To remember it exactly how they chose to remember it.

It started to rain. Paul stopped dead. This wasn't right. It was a hot, Mancunian summer evening. The sort of weather that saw lily-white torsos lining the tables of pub beer gardens. It didn't rain.

Paul looked up in the confusion. The rain was warm. Too warm. It was getting in his eyes. In his mouth. He fell to his knees on the cobbles of Albert Square. It felt like drowning.

Paul Bistacchi woke up to find himself bound by his ankles and wrists to a solid, metal chair with someone pissing in his face.

Shaking from his reverie, he spat out a mouthful of piss only to have it fill right back up. He made the mistake of going to shout and only succeeded in swallowing a good amount of the urine. Choking and spluttering, he turned his head to the side as the hot stream gradually lost pressure and stopped, leaving him soaked and stinking of piss.

'I'm going to fucking kill you!'

The man standing over him said nothing in response. The room was dark and he was wearing the same balaclava he'd been wearing the night before. The cattle prod at his side.

'You know who I am? My family?' Paul squinted in the half-light. The man didn't look big. A few inches taller than Paul maybe, but slight. Nothing compared to Paul's steroid-filled frame. 'You're fucking dead, mate, fucking dead.'

The man didn't say a word. He turned away and walked to the far end of the room. Paul glanced round. The air smelled damp. There was a single, tiny window. Too filthy to let in any light. The walls were old, red brick except for the far wall, which looked to have been newly constructed from breeze blocks. The space was empty but he could see faded marks on the concrete floor. Until very recently someone had been storing something in here. But now the room was empty save for him and his captor.

'I'm Paul Bistacchi. I do what I want, mate. Do what I fucking want!' Paul flexed against the bonds holding him to the chair. Nothing.

The man was coming back. In his hand he had a power drill.

'You fucking dare,' said Paul. 'YOU FUCKING DARE!' He started to rock back and forth, bellowing at the top of his lungs. At the back of his mind was something that felt horribly like fear.

The man watched as Paul managed to upend the chair and topple sideways, still firmly attached. Paul landed with all his weight on his left arm. He let out a cry of pain.

'Youfuckingfuckyoufuckingfuckyoufuckingfuck!' Somewhere between breathless threat and violent mantra, Paul was hyperventilating. His muscles strained ineffectually against his bonds. His head rocked back and forth, his mouth a pinched orifice of profanity spewing an unpunctuated stream of menace and spittle.

The man was behind him. Struggling to lift the chair upright, he finally righted it before retreating a little, bent double with the exertion.

'Who the fuck do you think you are?' bellowed Paul.

Without saying a word, the man bent down and picked up the power drill before getting down to the messy business of drilling holes into Paul Bistacchi's legs.

21

Malton knew only one person who drove a Range Rover painted the sky blue of Manchester City. The one person in Manchester who scared Malton. A man who was an unreadable blend of cruelty and outright insanity. A man who had been hideously disfigured in an attempt on his life and who had not only survived but when it emerged that Greater Manchester Police knew about the threat and hadn't passed it on, had sued the police for a multi-million-pound settlement. And won. Disfigured psychopath Danny Mitchum.

To Malton's eternal relief it wasn't Danny Mitchum who was waiting for them inside 36 Carnforth Road, but Danny's dad Stevie Mitchum. Six foot four and shaven-headed, Stevie had the money to dress well, he just didn't have the taste. Malton had a lot of reasons to despise Stevie Mitchum but near the top of the list was how cheap Stevie made the soft Italian suits he always wore look. Several grand of tailoring ended up looking like a twenty-quid suit from Asda on Stevie's gym-bloated frame, his illiterate tattoos peeking out from the collar and cuffs of his shirt.

Malton was used to dealing with men like Stevie. That toxic mixture of ego, insecurity and horrible upbringing was Malton's home turf. After Danny had taken his settlement and used the police's money to start a drug empire, he'd appointed his dad Stevie as his right-hand man. Father and son, a family business. Stevie may have been the older man but it was Danny calling the shots.

Malton and Danny knew who each other were. They moved in the same worlds and traded in the same currency of respect and fear. Two alpha predators who purposefully steered clear of each other.

That was until Danny had approached Malton to set up a drop house. As wary as Malton was of working for Danny, he was even more wary of saying no to him. Especially when Danny revealed where it was he wanted the site to be.

Malton was under no illusions. Danny could have set up a drop house anywhere in the city. He had asked Malton to set one up at Lorraine's in order to fuck with him. It was Danny Mitchum letting Malton know that if he wanted something then he'd get it.

Malton had talked himself into it. He couldn't go up against Danny even if he wanted to. If he didn't do it then Danny would go to Lorraine directly, his way of punishing Malton. He hated himself for not reaching out to Lorraine sooner. Letting his fear of her rejection keep him from helping her on his own terms. Once Danny Mitchum was involved the best help he could offer was to put himself between Danny and Lorraine. Make sure she didn't get hurt.

It hadn't worked out like that.

They found themselves in what was formerly a large, well-lit front room. Thanks to the metal shutters, the only light that came in was through cracks in the walls and a large hole in the floor above that opened directly up to a roof destroyed by rain and neglect.

Malton couldn't help but notice that Stevie was alone. A man like Stevie didn't turn up without backup. That is, unless he was in a hurry. Malton thought back to the phone call he'd made on the way here only a few minutes ago. How it was Stevie who'd answered and set up this meeting. He'd sounded rushed. Like he was putting a plan together in his head on the spot. Malton wasn't handing over anyone without hearing it from Danny himself.

'This the idiot that tried robbing us?' said Stevie, nodding towards the boy.

'This is the idiot,' said Malton. He didn't move a muscle. Stayed exactly where he was and made no move to hand the boy over.

Stevie crossed the faded green carpet to where Dean stood, half restraining, half supporting Lorraine's killer. Malton stepped forward, subtly putting his body between them.

'He had a gun. He shot Lorraine. She's dead,' said Malton.

Stevie smirked. Malton kept a straight face while mentally adding Stevie Mitchum to his very long list of people who would, one day, get theirs.

'Did you get the money?' asked Stevie.

Malton held up a bag.

Stevie snatched it and looked inside. 'Is it all there?' he demanded.

Malton knew Stevie didn't have a head for figures. Unlike his son he was just as stupid as he looked. This was all for show.

'It's all there.'

'I got some questions for you, pal,' Stevie said to the boy. 'What's the little shit's name?' he asked Malton.

'I'm working on that,' said Malton.

'You don't even got his name? People talk about you like you're Sherlock fucking Holmes. You're just a fucking Moss Side bouncer, thinks he's smart. Give him here – I'll get him talking.'

'No.' Malton was done humouring Stevie Mitchum. It was time to call his bluff.

Stevie looked confused. 'You remember who you work for?'

'I work for your son,' said Malton truthfully.

Stevie planted his feet and puffed out his chest. He jabbed a chubby finger in Malton's direction. 'And that means you work for me,' he spat.

Before he had entered the building Malton was undecided what he was going to do with the boy. If Danny Mitchum had been there then there would have been no question. Whether he wanted to or not, there was nothing in this world worth crossing Danny Mitchum over. Right now, the lad would be in the back of that Man-City-blue Range Rover with Danny Mitchum sticking sharp things into him, laughing his head off while he did it. But Danny wasn't here.

'Does Danny know you're here?' asked Malton.

For just a moment Stevie hesitated. 'What the fuck that matter?'

'So he doesn't know you're here?' chanced Malton.

'You wanna be fucking careful, Craig,' said Stevie. The thick muscles of his neck bulged and flexed beneath his suit jacket. His feet shifted into a boxing stance, his whole body gearing up for action.

Stevie was, Malton reflected, stupid enough not to be scared of him. And that made him a lot easier to handle.

'I'm paid to run a drop house for your son. And that means when someone tries to rob him I'm paid to find out who and why. I work for you.'

'So fucking give him here,' hissed Stevie. He was on the balls of his feet, shuffling side to side. He wasn't listening anymore. He was getting ready to solve the situation the only way he knew how – violence.

'Suppose I give you him? And you go to work on him? We all know what you're like.' Malton said this last sentence halfway between a compliment and an insult, knowing full well that a man like Stevie would always see it as the former.

Stevie smiled proudly. 'Yeah you know what I'm like,' he said, making psycho eyes at the boy who kept his gaze firmly on the floor.

'Suppose you get carried away. Lad's already lost a lot of blood. He's not ready for a session with Stevie Mitchum. Let me look after him. Get him strong again, find out exactly what he knows. And once I know who he's working for then I can deal with it. Let me do the leg work. Earn my money.'

Stevie stopped shuffling his feet and fell out of a boxing stance. He shook out his arms, cracked his neck and exhaled. For a moment he was perfectly still. Then without warning he reached into his coat and pulled out a foot-long machete.

'Why don't we just find out here and now,' he said, pointing the long blade towards the boy.

Malton was pleased to notice that Dean barely reacted. He was learning.

'No!' The boy spoke for the first time. His voice low and slurred.

Stevie advanced. 'See? You're soft, Craig. That's your problem. Think you can talk everything out. Sometimes you just need a bit of fucking steel.'

Malton threw his hands up and turned to Dean. 'Hand him over.'

Dean looked shocked. He hesitated.

'I said hand him over,' ordered Malton.

The boy turned as if about to flee. Stevie grabbed him by the arm and tore him away from Dean.

'Now we'll find out what you know,' he said raising the machete.

'We'll be off then,' said Malton. 'I'll give Danny a ring to let him know that the drop house was robbed, Lorraine was shot dead and that you're handling everything.'

Malton was halfway out the door by the time Stevie called after him. More than anything Malton hated how predictable men like Stevie were. Whatever else you could say about Danny, you had not the first fucking clue what was going on in that cracked head of his. At least it kept things interesting.

'I don't have time for this shit. I got an empire to run.' Stevie pushed the boy back towards Dean. 'I'll tell Danny myself. Whatever you find you come to me. You understand?'

'Of course,' said Malton. 'That's what you pay me for. And tell Danny I'm sorry about the drop house. Let me know if he wants me to set up a new place.'

'You think you're the only one on the payroll?' sneered Stevie, putting his machete away. He turned to the boy. 'This is your lucky fucking day.'

They watched Stevie let himself out of the house and waited until they heard his engine start up and then the squeal of tyres pulling away.

Once they were back in silence, Malton turned to the boy. The image of Lorraine's dead body flashed across his mind. The gunshot wound. The blood. Malton closed his eyes for just a second. Just long enough to push down the urge to tear the scared young lad in front of him into a million tiny pieces.

He opened his eyes and took a breath.

'You've done one really stupid thing this morning but I'm hoping it doesn't mean you're that stupid all the time. You've just been given a second chance. A second chance to tell me absolutely everything. And if you don't? Then that roided-up monster will ask you the exact same questions but he'll be holding a blowtorch on you while he does it. Not my place to tell you what to do but I know who I'd rather spill my guts to. So why don't you start with your name?'

'Cody. Cody Harper,' came the terrified reply.

22

Keisha returned home to find the front door open and several items of furniture dragged onto the driveway, where it looked like someone had been smashing them apart with an axe. From inside the house she could hear screaming and the sound of breaking glass. The Bistacchi family were clearly not doing well without Paul.

Walking into the front room it looked even worse than it sounded. The sofa had been upturned and the bottom torn out. Every cupboard and drawer had been emptied into a pile in the middle of the room. A section of the laminate flooring had been ripped up and a couple of floorboards removed. And in the middle of it all Johnny Bistacchi was still going. Still looking for hidden nooks and crannies. Still smashing the place to pieces. Presiding over the carnage was Keisha's mother-in-law Maria Bistacchi.

Maria had the exact same face as her son Paul, with her eyes constantly on the swivel for the next eruption of violence. Unlike Paul, Maria was always groomed to within an inch of her life. Long, acrylic nails and salon tan, twice-weekly hair appointments and a wardrobe that would make an Alderley Edge WAG jealous. She was never without at least a couple of grand's worth of jewellery hanging off her. Today she was dressed in her go-to, low-key outfit of wet-look leggings and fashionably sloppy knitwear paired, as always, with a defiantly high pair of stilettos.

Marrying Paul Bistacchi had always been a trade-off. Keisha liked a bit of rough and Paul had more than enough money and a certain kind of status among a certain kind of scumbag. Most importantly Paul had power. The kind of power that you earned through broken bones and bellowed death threats. Keisha was onboard with all of that.

The downside was that deep down Paul Bistacchi was just an angry bully who got lucky. That meant never moving out of Hattersley. It meant the endless parties where aspiring local hardmen would kiss Paul's drunken arse until it all ended in the inevitable fight. But worst of all, living with Paul meant living with his entire family under one roof. Not just his idiot younger brother Johnny but also his bitter, spiteful mum Maria.

For all their numerous flaws the Bistacchis stuck together. Partly out of loyalty, partly out of convenience and partly because living in a council house registered in Maria's name meant that despite having no earnings on paper, Paul and Johnny could at least explain how they still had a roof over their heads.

In her time Keisha had lived in condemned tower blocks, women's hostels and crack houses. None of that had prepared her for living with Maria.

Maria was used to getting her way. Johnny and Paul were true mummy's boys and went above and beyond to indulge her. The house was decorated to her taste: a jarring mixture of outdated design clichés and fussy, garish kitsch. Maria always insisted on cooking despite her culinary knowledge consisting of little more than the microwave and frying pan. Every move Paul made he ran it by his mum first. Nothing happened that Maria didn't agree to. In the Bistacchi house Maria's word was law.

Until Keisha had arrived.

Keisha realised that while Paul was eager to please his mum he was more keen to show off to his new wife just how well he'd done for himself. Working on Paul's ego, Keisha had very deliberately rolled back as much of Maria's influence as she could. The commemorative plates and faux driftwood picture frames were replaced with chrome and glass. The regular diet of potato waffles and sausages gave way to jerk chicken and goat curries, dishes Keisha knew Maria wouldn't touch but that Johnny and Paul wolfed down.

Bit by bit Maria was pushed back until all that was left of her domain was the gaudy pink master bedroom with its dated en suite.

While this left Maria in a state of near-constant fury, Keisha had made it a point to play nice, to antagonise the woman with kindness. With a beaming smile and eyes hidden behind dark glasses, Keisha was charm personified. It gave her a certain thrill to deny Maria the showdown she knew her mother-in-law so desperately craved.

Maria was so busy hurling invective at Johnny she didn't even notice Keisha come in.

Keisha took a breath and put on her best smile. 'Everything OK, Maria?'

Maria spun round on tottering heels. 'Where the flying fuck have you been?'

A lifetime of cigarettes, shouting matches and male company had given Maria's Hattersley accent a gorgeously deep, aggressive timbre.

Ignoring the chaos around her, as if it were just another day chez Bistacchi, Keisha said, 'I had to run an errand.'

'An errand?' spat Maria, waving a handful of long, neon-pink nails in Keisha's direction. 'A pissing errand, she says, like lady fucking muck.'

'Looking for Paul?' said Keisha innocently, motioning over to where Johnny was busy tearing up floorboards.

Maria creased her immaculately plucked brows. She knew when she was being mocked.

'Don't think I won't give you one of these, you cheeky cow.' Maria waved a small, manicured fist in Keisha's direction.

Johnny had momentarily stopped deconstructing the front room to catch his breath. Maria turned on him, a look of angry incredulity on her face.

'You fucking found them?' she said, her voice dangerously loaded with sarcasm.

Johnny mutely shook his head.

'Then keep fucking looking!' screamed Maria.

Johnny gave a tell-tale sniff, wiped his nose with the back of his hand and dived back into the demolition derby.

Keisha kept smiling sweetly. Rising above the chaos. 'What are you looking for? Maybe I can help?'

'You know! You know!' Maria was shaking with rage.

'This is bollocks.' Johnny stood up and stopped looking. 'We should be out looking for Paul. It's been over twelve hours now. What if something's happened?'

'Paul's a big boy,' said Maria. 'You get back to it.'

Maria smacked Johnny round the head. Keisha couldn't help but smirk.

She quickly wiped the smile from her face and turning to Johnny asked, 'What are you looking for?'

'The guns,' said Johnny glumly. 'Paul borrowed a load of guns off Danny Mitchum and he wants them back.'

'Danny Mitchum?' said Keisha with bland curiosity. 'Melted faced, murderous lunatic Danny Mitchum?'

'If that limp-dicked schoolboy thinks we're scared of him then he's got another think coming,' said Maria.

Keisha knew Maria well enough to be able to discern between her mother-in-law's different shades of aggression. From casual aggro to truly offended nuclear meltdown. Right now it was clear that, whatever Maria might say to the contrary, she was scared half to death.

Keisha keenly felt her role as the only responsible adult in the room. She'd only been gone a couple of hours and in her absence Maria and Johnny had managed to demolish half the house.

Since that fateful, thirty-year anniversary had rolled round a few months ago Keisha had been making all manner of plans. Plans she wasn't about to have ruined by the Bistacchis and the chaos they inevitably brought with them.

It was easy enough to avoid being pulled into the drama. The hard part would be calming things down before they escalated.

Keisha lowered her voice and attempted to inject a little bit of common sense into the situation.

'I don't know where the guns are,' she said, 'but if Danny Mitchum threatened you that's serious.'

'That's what I said!' said Johnny, his brief outburst of defiance instantly squashed with a severe look from Maria.

In managing the Bistacchis' day-to-day affairs Keisha had done her best to avoid Danny Mitchum. If you wanted to grow old it was a good rule to live by. When Danny got involved everyone tended to end up dead.

'You don't fuck with Danny Mitchum,' said Keisha to Maria. Her tone making clear that this was less advice and more a statement of fact.

Maria smiled back belligerently.

'What's so funny?' asked Keisha.

'He never told you, did he? You think you're so clever. Going round acting like you're a big deal. But Paul didn't tell you about the guns, did he? He told me. He trusted his mum,' said Maria.

Annoyingly Maria was right. Paul hadn't told Keisha about the guns. That didn't mean she didn't know about them. Nothing that happened in the Bistacchi house escaped Keisha's attention. Whether it was Maria sleeping with the teenage lad from a few streets over or Johnny gradually becoming incontinent from hitting the ketamine a little too hard. There were no secrets too shameful or buried too deep for Keisha not to ferret them out.

What Keisha didn't know was what Maria was planning to do with these guns if she ever found them. If Danny Mitchum was involved that was something she needed to find out with the utmost urgency.

'Why would he tell you and not me?' asked Keisha, doing her best to sound just a little bit wounded by Paul's omission.

Maria took the bait. Her face settling into a condescending look of pity. 'Cos he was making a move on Danny Mitchum. Using his own firepower against him,' said Maria proudly.

From the way she said it Keisha knew Maria wanted her to be shocked. She was. The plan was suicide.

Maria revelled in Keisha's reaction. 'That cocky little toad didn't have the first clue,' she said.

'You sure about that?' said Keisha.

'You what?' said Maria.

'If Danny Mitchum had no idea Paul was planning a move against him, isn't it a bit of a coincidence that Paul's gone missing?'

Maria stopped in her tracks. From the look on her face, Keisha could tell this had honestly not occurred to her. Maria could keep one thought in her head at a time. Any more than that and things got messy.

'You saying someone told Danny?' said Maria, accusingly.

Keisha shook her head. 'I'm saying until we get Paul back let's not do anything hasty,' she replied.

'That's what I said,' added Johnny, earning yet another murderous look from his mum.

'Fuck that,' said Maria turning her back on Johnny and Keisha. She grabbed her nearby handbag, pulled out a packet of cigarettes and lit up.

The silence was broken only by the click-clack of Maria's heels on the laminate as she paced up and down, lost in her own world.

Johnny gave Keisha a look. It was clear he wasn't brave enough to break into whatever train of thought Maria was riding.

This was all getting very messy. Missing guns, Danny Mitchum, revenge plots. Since marrying into the Bistacchi family Keisha was used to fighting fires but this was threatening to burn the whole thing to the ground with her still inside.

The older woman's fear could derail everything or Keisha could use it against her. It was time to stop being coy and take control.

'I'm going to find Paul,' said Keisha.

Maria rolled her eyes. 'Oh are you? Thank fuck for that. You hear her, Johnny? She's going to find Paul. Crisis over. You arrogant bitch.'

Keisha didn't rise to the provocation. 'This morning, that's what I was doing. I went to see an old friend of mine. A man who can fix this sort of thing.'

Maria's face darkened. She stormed across the living room, getting right up in Keisha's face.

'You went telling some stranger our family business?' Maria's dermally enhanced lips curled around her chemically whitened teeth in disgust.

Keisha hadn't wanted to mention going to Craig. She was pretty sure Maria had barely left the East Manchester postcode she was born in, much less ever set foot in Moss Side. The chances of her and Craig crossing paths seemed remote. Ideally Craig could get on with what he did best and Maria could remain in the dark about the whole thing.

Unfortunately that was no longer an option.

'He's good at this sort of thing,' said Keisha, doing her best not to retch at the older woman's cigarette-steeped breath.

'No. We take care of our own,' said Maria.

'He can help us.'

'He can go and fuck right off.' Maria wasn't shouting now. Her voice was low and gravelly. Her eyes fixed on Keisha. 'This is a family matter, you understand?'

'Paul's missing . . .'

'Do you understand?' Maria Bistacchi wasn't a tall woman but Keisha had been in more than enough fights to recognise someone you didn't want to get physical with. Maria came from a long line of women used to being booted down the stairs and smacked around the kitchen table. Just because she was the first generation to hit back didn't mean that she'd lost the genetic memory of taking the kind of beating that would put most men in hospital.

Keisha glanced round the room. Paul wasn't just the head of the family. He was the glue, the threats and the bribes that held everything together. In the twelve hours since Paul had been missing everything had gone to shit and now Danny Mitchum was on the horizon. There was no time for any of this.

But she would make time.

'I understand,' Keisha said. 'But I also understand that if Danny Mitchum turns up asking for his guns back and we can't deliver then there's going to be hell to pay. Never mind the fact that if his guns aren't here, then where are they? More importantly who's got them now?'

'You think I've not thought of all of that?' said Maria, gesturing to the destruction. 'It's getting sorted,' she said, daring Keisha to disagree.

Maria was cornered. But being a Bistacchi that meant that there was never a better time to come out fighting. Keisha knew nothing she said or did would change that.

It was time to pivot towards the chaos and throw petrol on the fire.

Keisha made sure to look as tiny as possible. She mirrored Johnny's body language. In Maria's presence he always reverted back to being a scared little boy.

'Danny Mitchum's not the only one in this city with guns,' said Keisha. 'We could get our own guns. For protection, if nothing else?'

'Protection? Who do you think we are?' said Maria grandly. 'I told you, we're hitting Danny Mitchum. Johnny and the boys.'

'But how can we, if we don't have guns?' asked Keisha, trying to sound disappointed to miss out on the opportunity to take on the most dangerous man in Manchester.

This was all about Maria now. Keisha had laid the trap, now all Maria had to do was walk into it.

Maria stalked round the smashed-up room sucking the last dregs out of her cigarette. Keisha couldn't tell if she was thinking or if she was simply trying to look like that was what she was doing. Finally she crushed the wet fag end into an ash tray and turned to Johnny.

'You know who you need to talk to,' said Maria.

Johnny didn't look so sure he did. But Keisha knew. She had put the seed in Maria's mind and now it had taken root.

'Should he go alone?' offered Keisha, doing her best to sound as uncertain and directionless as Maria might want her to be.

'Of course fucking alone,' said Maria.

'And you trust him?'

Maria paused. She was fiercely protective of her boys. Paul was obviously the golden child. First born. Never gave her a moment's worry. Johnny . . . well, Johnny did his best.

There was one last thing Keisha needed from Maria.

Maria turned to her daughter-in-law. 'You're going with him,' she said.

Keisha hid her delight at how simple it had been to outma-noeuvre the older woman. But it wasn't enough for Maria to think this was the best plan of action. To make it stick Keisha needed to appeal to Maria's sense of petty sadism.

These last thirty years had taught Keisha a lot of things, among them to never give in to fear. That didn't mean in those last three decades she hadn't seen more than her fair share of fear from other people.

Fighting her nature, Keisha willed her face into that look of mounting horror. She remembered the look Logan had given her as he climbed into the car boot. The sad resigna-tion of prey meeting predator. For Maria's benefit she did her best to recreate that look.

'Shouldn't I stay here in case . . .' she said, pleased at how she managed to make her voice quiver just slightly.

'I said you're going with him. Strength in numbers. Watch his back. That's it. End of discussion. The two of you are off to get us some guns.'

Maria was triumphant. Her plan, her orders and a help-ing of cruelty to wash it all down. She lit a new cigarette in triumph.

After three years of dealing with her mother-in-law it was no trouble whatsoever for Keisha to disguise her delight at how easy it had been to play her.

Maria pulled herself up to her full five foot two, a general addressing her troops. 'We're going to get our own guns and we're going to hit Danny Mitchum so hard it'll make what happened to his face seem like a birthday present.'

Keisha knew what was coming next but she played her surprise just right as Maria continued.

'First thing tomorrow,' Maria said, 'you're off to see the Squaddie in Saddleworth.'

23

After giving Malton his name, Cody hadn't said another word on the drive back to Malton Security HQ.

When they got to the office Malton was about to lead him out back when he noticed just how much blood Dean had got on himself. He stank like a butcher's shop on a hot day. Blood wasn't just on his suit but on his hands and his face too. It was even in his hair. He looked like he'd been dipped in it. He was surprised Cody was still standing the amount he'd lost.

Malton turned to Dean. 'You're done for the day,' he said.

'But I could help,' protested Dean.

'You're done. Tell Alfie to burn everything you're wearing and sort you out with some clean clothes and then you can go home.'

As disappointed as he was, Dean rightly sensed now wasn't the time to push the matter. He watched as Malton led Cody through the office and out back. Part of him wondered what was about to happen to Cody. Another part of him was glad not to know.

Cody stayed silent as Malton led him through the office to one of the smaller storage units at the back of the car park. From the outside it looked like the kind of place you'd keep garden tools or maybe a bicycle. It was only after Malton had unlocked the formidable combination padlock and opened the doors that it became clear that this storage unit was built to hold something very different.

A single bed covered half the floor space. The metal bed frame had been bolted to the floor. Beneath the bed was a plastic bucket and a roll of toilet paper. A clinging smell of piss and bleach rose up from the bucket, filling the tiny room. Beside the bed was a small table with a few well-thumbed porn mags and a mountain of snacks – the kind of thing you could get from any newsagents: chocolate bars, crisps and chewy sweets. Nothing with any nutritional value. Two pallets of bottled water sat beneath the table. And that was it.

An LED light was built into the low ceiling and when Malton turned it on, it was brighter than the sun, every nook and cranny of the storage unit remorselessly lit.

Malton steered Cody into the makeshift prison before shutting the doors behind them.

Malton sat on the bed beside Cody, who was cradling his stump, rocking slightly. Somewhere at the back of Malton's head the incandescent rage he felt at what had happened to Lorraine was still burning. However, alongside it was a dull sense that maybe if he had never come back to Manchester, Lorraine would have simply lost her café and retired broken-hearted but alive.

Danny Mitchum had singled her out to get to him. This was all his fault. He'd let himself have feelings for someone and now they were dead. It had happened again.

Long ago Malton had got over what other people might call guilt. He'd seen people with nothing commit terrible crimes and blame it on their deprived upbringing. He'd also seen people who had been given every chance in life commit even worse atrocities and plead leniency based on their priv-ilege. Either morality applied to everyone or it applied to no one. From what Malton had seen these last thirty years he knew which side he came down on.

And so he lived from moment to moment. A constant state of vigilance as he balanced the sins of one world against the good deeds of another. Cody had killed Lorraine. Malton had maimed Cody. Cody had robbed from the most dangerous man in Manchester but Malton had saved his life. As far as Malton was concerned, whatever he might feel about Lorraine's death, that meant Cody owed him something.

Sat in the tiny, locked storage unit, the one thing Malton wanted to know more than anything was how a teenager knew about the safe at Lorraine's. Who had sent him there to rob it?

Malton took the hatchet out of his jacket and laid it on top of the pile of yellowing porn mags. Cody's eyes were irresistibly drawn to the bright, polished steel smeared with drying blood. Cody's blood.

'This doesn't have to be the end. When I was your age I'd already killed two men,' said Malton, matter-of-factly.

Cody started to cry.

'Later on things got very bad, very quickly. And I left Manchester. Left everything. Started again with nothing.'

'Can I start again?' asked Cody. The hope in his voice was pitiful.

'Right now? No. Right now you have less than nothing. You owe me a drop house. You owe me the life of the woman you just killed. You owe Danny Mitchum the opportunity to torture you to death.'

Cody started bawling.

'Stop crying,' ordered Malton. 'Pull yourself together.'

The boy did his best to do as he was told, wiping his tears with his one remaining hand and holding himself as tightly as possible to avoid shaking with the fear he so obviously felt.

'You weren't very helpful back there in the car. But now you've got a second chance. Your last chance. I'm going to ask you some questions. If I like the answers I can help you. If I don't like the answers then I can't. If you don't tell me anything then I'm driving round to give you to Danny Mitchum. To make sure you know exactly what that means, I want to show you a video.'

Malton got out his phone and held it up for Cody to see.

'Last year someone was stealing from Danny Mitchum. Someone who worked for him. He hired me to find out who and I did. And this is what Danny did to him. What I'm about to show you is hard to watch, but you're going to watch it all. You understand?'

Cody nodded blankly.

Malton tapped the phone and a video started playing. Malton didn't look at the screen. He'd seen it once already and that was more than enough. He kept his focus on Cody's face and did his best to ignore what he now knew was the sound of a man having his leg cut off and then slowly having his skull beaten in with his severed limb.

The video finished and Malton put his phone away. Then the boy told him everything.

***

With Cody locked away for the night, Malton took a moment to digest the day's events. First Keisha, then Lorraine and now, if Cody was to be trusted, the name of the person who had sent him to rob the drop house. On top of that Leon Walker was still out there, the shotgun attack on Malton's home still going unanswered.

Things were threatening to get complicated.

Malton took out his phone. He had two voicemail messages waiting for him. Both from earlier that morning. Both from the same number. He'd been so preoccupied with the robbery at Lorraine's he hadn't had time to check. Malton didn't like people leaving him messages. It felt like potential evidence.

He dialled up his voicemail and listened.

'Hello, my name is Claire Minshall and I understand you can help people? If that's right, if I've got the right number, please can you phone me back? Thank you.'

Puzzled, Malton listened to the second message. It was sent forty-five minutes after the first.

'Hello, I called earlier. Claire Minshall again. Sorry. I called . . . I called because a man ran over and killed my husband and the police say they know who he is but they can't find him and I don't think they want to find him and I don't know why and I don't know what to do because I'm dying. I've got cancer and I know it's wrong but I don't want to die knowing that the man who killed my husband is still out there. And I don't want you to hurt him or anything. I just want you to find him. And that's it. And if that's what you do I can pay you.'

There followed a long pause. It sounded like the woman on the other end of the phone was crying or at least making an effort not to cry.

'I need you to find the man who killed my husband. I need you to find Johnny Bistacchi.'

Now things really were complicated.

24

Claire's day had featured three playground fights, an over-flowing toilet, a suspected allergic reaction in the canteen and one parent turning up unannounced to complain about the council hounding her for unpaid council tax. More than enough to keep her so preoccupied that as she was unlocking her car to head home, the last thing on her mind was the phone call she'd made that morning.

'Claire Minshall?'

Claire turned to see a thickset man in a Barbour jacket with a scar running down one side of his face. 'We have CCTV,' she warned, pointing up at the cameras covering the staff car park. Having established that everything was on film, she calmly asked, 'How can I help you?'

Malton looked up at the CCTV camera. It was a cheap model. One rung above a convincing fake. Whatever footage it was taking would be next to useless in identifying anyone who wasn't stood directly in front of it. His firm would never install anything like that. But he knew why the woman had mentioned it and he did his best to look harmless.

'My name's Craig Malton. You called me earlier,' he said, standing a respectful distance away from Claire.

Filtering through the events of the day, it took Claire a second to connect what she was being told by the man now standing in front of her. But when she did make that connection her blood froze. Instinctively her fingers curled around the keys in her hand.

'I shouldn't have called,' she said. 'I'm sorry. A boy I teach had your card and it was early and I was . . .'

'We're just talking. We're on CCTV. It's nothing unusual. I bet you get all kinds of people just walking into this place. I remember when I was at school round here, we had to get a security guard just to stop random people walking in.'

'Where did you go?' asked Claire, desperate to keep the conversation away from the voice messages she'd left earlier that morning.

'Birley. It's not there anymore. They knocked it down. Built flats.'

'Birley High?' said Claire, her mind racing. 'I remember that place. I did one of my first placements there.'

'And you still wanted to be a teacher?'

Claire laughed. The man didn't.

'We can talk here or we could go somewhere more private? It's up to you. Wherever you feel safe,' said Malton.

Claire knew that was coming. It didn't make it any easier to stomach. 'Talk about what?' she said, desperate to put off the inevitable.

'Talk about Johnny Bistacchi and what exactly you'd want me to do when I find him.'

Hearing the name 'Johnny Bistacchi' in the man's unmistakable, Moss Side accent finally made it real. She was no longer a spectator of this world. She was in it.

But if she was going to be involved then it would be on her terms.

Claire didn't want to talk anywhere near the school. Too much risk of being seen by parents. And she definitely didn't want this man knowing where she lived, although she suspected he could easily find that out if he wanted. So she led Malton away from both those places and they found themselves parked up in Ancoats, just beyond the inner ring road.

Ancoats was awash with building sites. Where once there had been terraced streets you wouldn't dare walk down, now luxury apartment complexes had sprung up. Building sites plastered with hoardings of the aspirational lifestyle you could expect to be living for just a ten per cent deposit.

There was no one nearby but from where they had parked they were clearly visible from the nearby tram stop. It was isolated but not so much that no one would see a woman being bundled into a Volvo. Or hear her screaming. Claire hoped it would be enough.

'We'd just got the news. About the cancer,' she said. She was wearing a coat and scarf but still felt the late afternoon chill.

They stood leaning against Claire's car. Malton's Volvo was parked up nearby. Claire kept her eyes forward – on the Manchester skyline filled with cranes and scaffolding. Not on the intimidating stranger who stood stock-still, a blank, open look on his face as she revealed her innermost secrets to him.

'It's . . . it's impossible to describe. But what can you do? We knew we had to keep going for Jessica's sake. She's my daughter. Do you have kids?'

Malton shook his head. This was exactly the sort of reason why up until now he'd avoided even the thought of it.

Remembering why she'd called this man in the first place Claire cut to the chase. 'We'd come out of the Christie. We'd just got the news. A ninety per cent chance that I'd be dead by the end of the year. We were stunned. Of course we were. And maybe that's why I didn't hear him coming. But he was speeding. He was on the pavement. Everything already felt so unreal. I just watched it happening and it was like . . . oh right. This makes sense. This is how things go now. People can die. Just like that. It's normal.'

Malton didn't react. He didn't shiver with the cold or interrupt to offer his condolences. He simply carried on taking it all in with just the occasional nod, every so often his eyes glancing to the side for a second as if correlating what Claire was saying with some internal record of his own.

After weeks of people tiptoeing around her terrified of saying the wrong thing, Claire found it surprisingly comforting to be able to just talk.

'And of course I thought, well there's cameras. They caught the number plate. It happened outside the Christie for God's sake. A hospital.'

'So what happened?' asked Malton.

'Nothing. Nothing happened. I buried my husband and nothing happened. And then the worst part. The family liaison officer. She comes to the funeral and tells me they know who did it. They've got a name: Johnny Bistacchi. And guess what?'

'They won't do anything about it?' said Malton.

'Yes! Can you believe it? The police know who did it and they say they can't do a thing.'

Claire hadn't spoken to anyone about this. And here she was unburdening to this man who half an hour ago she'd thought was about to attack her in the school car park. She had the feeling that there was nothing she could tell him that he didn't already know. This wasn't about him finding out about what happened. It was him finding out about her.

'What do you know about the Bistacchis?' Malton answered her question with one of his own.

Claire glanced at him. She saw the scar on his face and the shaved head. She saw a man who had heard her entire story and not once seemed the least bit shocked at what she had to tell him. Suddenly the absurdity of the situation crowded in on her.

'I shouldn't have called you,' she said, more to herself than to Malton.

'But you did. And that means there's part of you that wants something done. You've done the right thing. You've gone to the police and the police have let you down. What else were you meant to do?'

Malton looked Claire up and down.

'You've never broken the law, have you? Never put a foot wrong. Always thought that it was enough to be a good person. Now your husband's dead and you've been cut loose.'

'Am I meant to be impressed at your insight?' Claire's initial fear was beginning to wane. This man was playing with her. First the police leaving her in the lurch, then the Bistacchi woman at Marcus's funeral and now this. Did the entire world think she was fair game? She had been a teacher long enough to know what happens when a bully smells weakness.

'My insight is this,' said Malton. 'You were in a place where you'd do something you'd never have done before. You called me. Those feelings, they're still there. They made you make that call. I wonder what else those feelings might make you do?'

'You want to know why I called you? I was scared to go to the police. She came to Marcus's funeral. Paul Bistacchi's wife. At least I think that's who it was. Black woman, sunglasses. She knew about the funeral. She was there. They killed Marcus and they came to his funeral. I don't know if he was involved with them somehow or if it's just some kind of sick warning but what if I go to the police and find out Marcus *was* involved? That this wasn't just some tragic accident? What then?'

Claire realised she was crying angry tears. She frowned and wiped her eyes with her scarf.

133

Malton was genuinely surprised by this new detail. It definitely made things a bit more complicated. 'So you don't want me to deal with Johnny Bistacchi?'

'No.'

'You don't want him lifted off the street? Tied up somewhere? Beaten, burned and begging for mercy?'

'I don't want you to kill him!' Claire blurted out.

Malton looked hurt. 'I never said I'd *kill* anyone.' Then: 'Do you *want* me to kill him?'

'No,' said Claire too quickly. 'I want . . . justice.'

Claire wondered what she imagined justice looked like. Whether or not it looked like Johnny Bistacchi's beautiful face, mutilated beyond all recognition at the hands of this man. The thought made her sick.

'I shouldn't have called you. When I realised they were at the funeral I got scared. I'm sorry.'

Claire looked at Malton. He seemed so calm. So confident. So unlike the police she'd dealt with. With all their practised sympathy and impotent promises. But there was something more going on. Two decades of teaching had given her a sixth sense for when she was being lied to. When children thought they could game the system, work your sympathy and play everyone off against each other. Claire had seen enough kids like that to know that they would never imagine they'd get caught. And that was their weakness: the unshakeable belief that they were smarter than you.

'Thank you for meeting me. I'm sorry to have wasted your time.' Claire turned to get back in her car.

'Did you kidnap Paul Bistacchi?'

Claire froze. He knew about Paul Bistacchi. If he knew about that what else did he know? Did he know Claire had been there? If he knew, who else knew? Somehow Marcus had brought the Bistacchis into her life but now her own stupidity had brought this man with them. She turned back to him, mustering all the courage and composure she had left.

'You think I kidnapped Paul Bistacchi? I thought I never broke the law? Never put a foot wrong.'

'And yet you called me.'

Claire held Malton's gaze. He wasn't quite staring her down; it was more than that. He seemed certain. As if he already had the answers. Asking her these questions was a mere formality.

Every so often in teaching you'd meet them: the kid who lied and cheated and got away with it, the kid who *was* smarter than the adult. Claire had often wondered what they would go on to become. Now she had her answer.

She took a breath. She was in deeper than she would ever have imagined. Whether or not she trusted this man he was her only option.

But if she was going to make a deal with the devil, it would be on her terms.

'I didn't kidnap Paul Bistacchi,' she said firmly. 'But I saw who did.'

Malton couldn't help but raise an eyebrow. It was the smallest of tells but Claire caught him doing it. Finally she'd found a chink in his armour.

'The man who kidnapped him, he was dressed in black. I didn't see his face.'

'But you saw him kidnap Paul Bistacchi?'

Claire felt light-headed. Turning to face the fear suddenly made everything seem easy. The shadows disappeared and all that was left was the man before her. Craig Malton.

'If you don't believe me, I can give you his number plate.'

Claire saw Malton's eyebrow twitch a second time and she knew she had him.

'But in return I need you to find out what my husband had to do with the Bistacchis.'

25

A colourful selection of fruit was spread out across the black granite worktop before Malton. He started by taking a couple of bananas, peeling them and dropping them into the blender. Then he stopped and tried to remember what sort of smoothie it was Emily usually liked after working out.

Malton had come home to find the kitchen deserted and the sound of loud music coming from the home gym at the back of the house. Emily usually worked out first thing in the morning. She only hit the gym this late when she was angry. As a recovering addict, Emily steered clear of the usual comfort blankets. No booze, no binge eating and obviously no drugs. Emily's only vice was endorphins and so when she needed to feel good about herself she would retreat to the gym, turn the music up loud and run until her legs gave up.

Malton guessed she must still be dwelling on last night's argument. The smoothie he was attempting to construct was his idea of a peace offering. He scanned the rest of the fruit and tried to work out his next move.

Malton was never that interested in food. Like so many things in his life, food was other people's pleasure. He grew up constantly hungry. For him food was just one more good thing in life that deep down he doubted was meant for him. It was one more piece of leverage that was useless against him.

It meant his mind was clear and his thoughts were his own. Right now, those thoughts were trying to arrange the day's events into some kind of sense. Keisha was back in his life. He hadn't seen that coming. Much less that she would be asking him to track down a kidnapped Paul Bistacchi. It would be hard to find anyone who'd met Paul and didn't wish him ill. The list was endless. But then he'd had the phone call from the schoolteacher asking him to look into what linked her dead husband to the Bistacchis. In Malton's experience just because the connection was currently eluding him didn't mean that coincidence had anything to do with it.

Malton felt into his jacket and pulled out the photo he'd taken from the café. Lorraine had her arm around him, holding him tight, hugging him in the daft, loving way that Malton imagined a real mum would hug you. And he was smiling. Not just his mouth, his eyes too. He looked so young. Like he had no idea what was coming down the track. About the same age as the boy locked up back at Malton Security. The one who'd spilled his guts, giving Malton even more to think about.

Suddenly his mind went to Leon Walker. The boy in the lock-up was a callow teenager who'd turned up with a gun to rob a secret drop house. Leon Walker was a washed-up junkie who'd arrived on Malton's doorstep with a shotgun. Two gunmen, both as clueless as each other but both pointed at targets that only a handful of people in the city could possibly know even existed.

It didn't make sense. His years of wading through the random chaos of the criminal underworld told Malton that this felt different. Something more was going on. But at that moment, what that something was lay just beyond his grasp.

Malton snapped back to the task in hand. He selected a mango, a handful of blueberries and half a punnet of raspberries. In short order he sliced the mango with a knife from a block of very expensive Japanese kitchen knives. The sweet, wet smell of freshly cut fruit filled the kitchen. He then dropped the chopped pieces of mango into the blender along with the berries. For good measure he threw in a handful of nuts, a dash of soya milk, put the lid on and hit blend.

Emily wandered into the kitchen as he was pouring the gloopy, yellow liquid into a tall glass. She was glowing. The sweat from her workout left dark patterns beneath her breasts and armpits. A damp circle had formed on her chest bone and the skin on her face and arms glistened.

He could tell from the look she gave him that despite the workout she was still hung up on last night. He handed her the smoothie, guessing she was too worn out to refuse it on point of pride.

He was right. Emily took the glass and greedily drank nearly half in one go. At least he was good for something.

Malton washed the sticky residue off his hands as he watched her drink the rest of the smoothie. He wiped down the knife in the kitchen's large Belfast sink, dried it and replaced it in the block. Emily took the glass away from her lips and with one hand wiped the moustache of fruit pulp off her face.

He jumped in before she had the chance to speak.

'About last night – I've been thinking.'

'It's OK. I mean, it's not OK. But maybe that's my problem, not yours.'

Her words made Malton feel sick inside. He spent his entire life convincing people that his way was the right way. Gaslighting the world with well-chosen words and softly spoken threats. It didn't feel good to see it working on Emily.

'No. It's not OK. It's not you. It's me. And I want to change.'

It took a moment for Emily to register what she was hearing. But once she had her eyes lit up. Just as Malton hoped they might.

'What I do, my work . . . if I had a child, some of the people I work with, they might try and use that against me,' said Malton. He thought back to Claire Minshall, getting ready to die and leave her daughter utterly alone in the world.

Emily reached out and touched his arm. 'You think I don't know anything but I know. I know about what you do. I've seen how people look at you. I know about the axe you carry around. I've seen you come home with blood on your clothes. I know. But I also know that you would never, ever let anything bad happen to me.'

Emily looked Malton in the face with those huge blue eyes.

'Or our baby,' she said.

Malton was taken aback.

It suited him not to think too deeply about what Emily did and didn't know about the darker side of his life. He'd chosen to shoulder that burden alone. But here she was, not only telling him that she knew but also telling him that she didn't care. She trusted him to be her protector.

Suddenly the soft, innocent girl from Hale looked very different to him.

'You take care of people. It's your job. It's who you are. I know you'll take care of us. I trust you,' she said taking his heavy, gnarled hands in her own. Her soft white fingers felt like velvet to Malton against his own calloused brown skin.

Malton was cautious, he was careful, but he was never scared. He minimised risks, made sure he had a plan. He never backed down. So why was this any different? Why should he let his past hold back his future? The thing he feared most was losing Emily.

Malton pulled Emily towards him, his thick arm easily encircling her slender waist. She felt warm, still damp from her workout. He could smell the animal musk of her fresh perspiration.

He looked down, searching her face but he saw nothing but love.

The world shifted.

'Let's do it,' he said.

139

Emily's eyes widened; her mouth broke into a smile of pure joy. She wriggled free of Malton, took his giant, shaved head in her hands and kissed him.

Malton let himself be handled. He surrendered as her tongue explored his mouth, her soft, wet lips stealing kisses from all sides.

Emily kept her mouth pressed against his as he felt her hands, eager and quick at his belt. Her fingers fumbled with the heavy denim of his jeans and his own hands joined hers, loosening his clothing. Her fingers slipped his briefs down over his muscular thighs and neither of them could fail to notice his enthusiasm.

Leaving him half unwrapped, Emily turned to face the island unit. With a playful wiggle, she slipped her knickers and running tights down over her petite backside and leaned forward, spreading herself across the granite surface.

Her perfect, alabaster bottom offered itself to Malton.

He didn't need to be asked twice. His thick, muscular hands wrapped around her thighs, his fingers encircling her body. He pulled her towards him and she arched her back a little as he slid, unprotected, inside.

Malton held Emily in place for a moment, enjoying how warm and soft she felt against his skin. Emily pressed her body into the cold granite of the worktop. Letting herself be trapped between the hard stone on one side and Malton on the other.

Malton felt his heart beat faster as the chains that held his every waking thought together loosened just a little. Beneath him Emily's thin, slick body moved in time with his own. She felt warm and soft against Malton's thick, hard body.

All the compartmentalised fears and desires in Malton's head began to blur together. He clenched his jaw and concentrated on the feel of Emily's flesh against his own. How little of her there was but how she completely overwhelmed him.

He kept his right hand on her waist and with his left hand he leaned over Emily and entwined his fingers with hers. Their two hands splayed over the black granite as they slowly made love.

As Emily closed her eyes with pleasure, Malton found himself looking across the room to the kitchen table. He tried to imagine himself sat there – a father, a husband. Emily filled out and maternal. Bliss. All the things he'd never dared dream about.

But then the vision shifted in his mind's eye. Suddenly Emily was gone. Keisha was there. Eyes boring into him from behind those ever-present sunglasses.

Malton thrust harder into Emily. He looked down at her tiny, prone body pressed against the worktop and tried to focus.

When he looked up Keisha was gone. Sat at the table was the bloody remains of his former lover. Beautiful features reduced to wet meat. A body broken and contorted with obscene violence.

Malton pulled Emily close and focused on the gentle curve of her back. He kept his eyes down, using all his powers of concentration to keep his ugly thoughts at bay.

Emily slid her free hand from the worktop and slipped it between her legs. She began to softly moan. The sound brought Malton back with an urgent clarity.

He thrust into her and let the sensation fill him up. The sound of her pleasure, the warmth of her body, the smell of exertions still fresh on her skin.

Malton screwed his eyes shut, pulled her close and they finished together.

When he opened his eyes it was only him and Emily in the kitchen.

★★★

Twenty minutes later and Emily's smile hadn't faded. She hadn't gone to shower yet; instead she was singing to herself as she got ready to cook them a meal. It was harder than it sounded. Despite being amply appointed with a range cooker, double-sized fridge-freezer and acres of worktop space, Malton's kitchen had very little actual food in it.

Malton watched Emily search the dozens of empty cupboards, assembling a random assortment of tins and long-dead spices.

'If we're going to have kids, we're going to have to start shopping and cooking proper dinners,' said Emily, surveying the ingredients she'd found. 'Tinned tomatoes, old chives, frozen mince and rice. What do you fancy?'

She was smiling as she said it and just for a moment the kitchen felt warm and safe. The kind of place you would raise a family.

Malton's phone started to ring. A reminder that outside this beautiful dream the very real, very ugly world was waiting to pounce. Checking who the number belonged to, Malton took a few steps back, turned away from Emily and answered.

Emily watched as a few seconds later he hung up and turned back to face her with a look she immediately knew meant that their evening was over.

'Work?' said Emily. She sounded so understanding that Malton almost felt guilty.

'Yeah,' he said. 'I've got to go.'

Emily looked at him fondly. Whether it was the sex or the knowledge that she was going to get the family she always wanted, she was beaming.

'Stay safe. One way or another, you're going to be a dad!'

Malton did his best to look happy at the thought of it. He'd finally given the ground. There was no going back now.

As he pulled out of the driveway, the fact that Emily had got what she wanted and he had agreed to do the one thing in the world that terrified him the most made him feel a little less ashamed about the rush of excitement he felt for the person he was on his way to meet.

Dean had managed to fit a lot into his first proper day working alongside Malton. Death, dismemberment and the upper echelons of Manchester's criminal underworld had all made an appearance. It went a long way to cushioning the blow of his new suit being first soaked in blood and then being dumped in a burn barrel and torched by Alfie.

He still hadn't had a chance to ask Malton what it was the woman in the sunglasses had wanted from him. Dean secretly quite fancied her but judging by the way Malton acted around her he thought it would be best to keep that to himself.

Then just when things were reaching some kind of resolution with the kid from Lorraine's ready to spill his guts, Malton had sent Dean home. Dean was nowhere near ready to call it a day. He'd had a taste of the way Malton did business and he was eager for more.

That was why half an hour ago he'd called the number he'd got from Vikki Walker and was now loitering beneath a street light outside a shuttered shop in one of the warren of backstreets surrounding Strangeways prison, nervously waiting to meet the man who sold drugs to her dad Leon.

The streets around Strangeways were an oddity. While most of the rest of the city centre had succumbed to the gentrification of student housing, investment properties and artisanal bars, the area around Strangeways was as rough as it had been for the last couple of hundred years. The looming presence of the prison was clearly failing to serve as any kind of deterrent as the streets around it were filled with shambling addicts, tragic prostitutes and, most famous of all, a thriving counterfeit goods scene.

It had been dark for several hours now but the streets were still thronged with the men acting as salesmen for the counterfeit goods their bosses kept hidden in backstreet lock-ups to avoid the attention of the law.

Dean looked around trying to work out if any of the touts he saw lurking on street corners might be the man who he hoped would give him the next piece of the puzzle he needed to track down Leon Walker and get one step closer to delivering him to Malton.

An Asian man across the street caught his eye and broke into a smile. He was middle-aged but with a chubby, fresh face. He wore a shabby leather bomber jacker and beige slacks over a pair of bright white trainers. Dean wasn't convinced he looked like the kind of man who sold drugs for a living.

'All right, Boss, what you looking for?' said the man, crossing the street and making a beeline for Dean.

'It's OK. I'm waiting for someone,' said Dean. This clearly wasn't Leon Walker's dealer and whatever he was selling Dean wasn't interested.

This didn't in any way deter him. 'I got everything, Boss. All low, low prices. All designer. All proper. Half price of the shops. All genuine. Yeah?'

'It's OK.' Dean tried his best to make a show of ignoring the man who was stood right in front of him.

'I show you, Boss,' said the man with a conspiratorial smile as he stepped past Dean and started to unlock the shutter of the shop behind him. A second later he had pulled the shutter up to reveal, to Dean's astonishment, every conceivable counterfeit item your heart could desire.

There was the ubiquitous Louis Vuitton luggage, rows and rows of branded trainers. A rack of Canada Goose jackets.

A couple of shelves of boxed iPads and iPhones and, jumbled about on the floor, dozens and dozens of boxes of various designer perfumes competing for space with an assortment of Ugg boots.

The man stood back, proudly displaying his wares.

'Whatever you want, Boss.'

Dean was so taken in by this display that he nearly missed the young lad who had appeared across the road and was impatiently scanning around, just as Dean had been doing moments earlier.

Dean took a last look at the Aladdin's cave of counterfeit tat. It was his mum's birthday coming up and she'd love a new pair of Uggs.

'Give me ten minutes, mate,' said Dean, as he turned and jogged across the road to where the lad who'd just arrived had started looking at his phone.

'I got your number off Leon Walker?' Dean said to him hopefully.

The boy looked up from his phone, scowling at the mention of the name. The boy's hair was freshly cut into an immaculate fade. It stood in comical contrast to the messy fluff that passed for a moustache across his top lip. He couldn't have been more than fifteen.

'He dead then?' he asked casually.

Dean looked confused. 'No? Why? Is he?'

'One of my best customers. That smackhead robbed. Like really robbed. He was like a business. Then he stops calling. Happens.'

'So you've not heard from him?'

'What I just say? Now what do you want?'

Dean's mind raced. If his own dealer thought he'd died then wherever Leon Walker was, either he *was* dead, in which case Dean had wasted his time on a wild goose chase, or he had gone to ground somewhere. From what Dean knew about Leon Walker he didn't seem like the kind of man who would be much good at lying low.

'I said, what you want? You wasting my time?'

The boy stepped to Dean and drew back his puffer jacket. To Dean's absolute horror he saw his second gun of the day. This one tucked into the tracksuit bottoms of the boy now threatening him.

'No. Of course not. I'd like . . .' Dean stopped. He had no idea what he'd like. He didn't take drugs. And he wasn't mad keen to be caught buying them openly on the street either. Plus he only had thirty pounds on him.

Across the road the much more friendly criminal selling fake Ugg boots was waiting and smiling expectantly. Dean wondered just how cheaply he could get those Uggs for.

'What can I get for ten pounds?' he asked.

The boy screwed his already screwed-up face even further.

'Ten quid? You brought me out here for ten quid? For ten quid you can fuck off.'

'Sorry.' Dean turned to go.

'No. You can give me the ten quid and then fuck off.'

'Of course. Sorry again.'

Dean was sure that this wasn't how Malton would have handled it. But luckily for him Malton wasn't there to see him messing up quite so badly. He opened up his wallet and before he could stop him the boy reached in and snatched a twenty-pound note.

'That'll do. Fucking idiot.' He pocketed the twenty and turned to go.

Dean looked in his wallet. The final tenner had been folded in the crease and so had been missed. It was the smallest possible of victories.

Today was what he'd been dreaming of for all those weeks stuck out in the stockroom but now it appeared he was as inessential to Malton's plans as he'd ever been. Plus he'd lost four hundred and fifty pounds' worth of suit, been a willing victim of street robbery, and worse than that was no closer to redeeming himself by finding the whereabouts of Leon Walker.

He was defeated and demoralised. Dean's phone buzzed. It was a text from the number Malton had given him – his personal mobile. His heart racing, Dean opened the message. Was this Malton relegating him back to washing cars and taking orders from Alfie? Or had today actually been a resounding success?

The message was two words long. It read, 'Paul Bistacchi.' A smile broke across Dean's face. He wasn't getting canned and he wasn't getting congratulated. He was getting something better: the chance to prove himself.

Dean resolved that by the time he got into the office tomorrow he would know everything the internet had to say about a man called Paul Bistacchi.

But first Dean had a birthday present to buy. Buzzing with confidence, he crossed the street and prepared to haggle his way to a pair of ten-pound Ugg boots.

27

Malton had been doing this long enough to know when he'd been played. And he'd been played.

On the phone Keisha had said that they had to talk and that it was urgent. She'd sounded almost scared and Malton had fallen for it. Ditching Emily, he'd raced to meet her. As he drove across town he'd allowed his imagination to run riot. Casting himself as the great white knight riding to her rescue.

Sitting outside a derelict pub in Moss Side, waiting for Keisha, gave Malton time to reflect that Keisha would never need rescuing. Not really. It's the people who got involved with Keisha that ended up needing saving.

Keisha had asked to meet by the Gamecock – a classic, flat-roofed estate pub from old Moss Side. These days the Gamecock was boarded up but it was still standing, one of the last reminders of what Manchester used to be. It survived the riots, Gunchester and the IRA. But even the Gamecock couldn't survive gentrification. Student flats and privately owned houses. Money. The sort of people who didn't want to drink in a pub that screamed meat raffles and beer garden brawls.

It had been Malton and Keisha's local.

That was all in Malton's past. The Gamecock was derelict and would soon be knocked down and turned into flats. Things change. People move on. Emily was his future now. A future Malton promised himself he would do absolutely everything in his power to protect.

A knocking on the passenger side window shook him out of his thoughts and he leaned over to let Keisha in.

She got in, slamming the door behind her. Instantly the car was filled with the smell of her perfume. An intangibly delicate scent that went a long way to covering up the absolute steel of the woman wearing it. Even at this time of night she was wearing her sunglasses.

'You came,' said Keisha.

'You said it was an emergency.'

Keisha broke into a smile. 'And you came right away! You do care!'

Malton knew there was no point in getting angry with Keisha. She never got angry unless getting angry was the thing that would get her what she wanted. She measured out her emotions and never spoke without thinking five steps ahead. Everything Keisha did or said was some kind of game. Right now Malton had been suckered into playing but that was OK; now he was on to her he would be ready for it.

'I came. So what is it?'

'You *have* changed. All business.'

'You're paying me. I'm working for you. This is business.'

'And not just a little pleasure?' Keisha smiled widely enough that Malton could see the gold tooth at the back of her mouth. There was laughter in her voice. It was very hard to resist.

'You remember this place?' said Keisha, pointing to the Gamecock.

'I remember,' said Malton.

'Your first door job. Where it all began. The Craig Malton empire.'

Despite himself, Malton smiled at the memory.

'You were so proud,' said Keisha, grabbing his arm like an aunty recounting an embarrassing story. 'Remember we went to the market and got you some proper trousers and everything?'

'I remember you making me wear them,' said Malton, ruefully.

'You looked adorable. You were so skinny back then. You had hair!'

Keisha ran a hand over Malton's bald head. Malton wondered if he should stop her. But he didn't.

'And I remember you getting me fired on my first shift,' he said. He was enjoying this trip down memory lane more than he felt comfortable with.

'Oh yeah,' said Keisha feigning surprise at the recollection. 'Those three guys who wouldn't leave. They were about to beat the shit out of you.'

'They were about to try,' said Malton. 'And then you glassed one of them and the whole place kicked off.'

'Anything for my man,' said Keisha with a smile.

She looked across at Malton and both of them were right back there. The stink of cigarette smoke and sweat. The crappy jukebox. The feeling that it was them against the world.

Malton knew what she was doing. But he also knew it was working. He tried to focus on the here and now. The cold of the Moss Side night. The post-coital warmth he still felt deep in his belly from his evening with Emily. The child he'd agreed to have with her. Anything but Keisha.

'Craig,' said Keisha, her voice suddenly serious. 'I'm in trouble.'

Keisha was lining him up and he knew it. He told himself that he needed to keep her onside if he was to untangle whatever it was that held together the events of the past few weeks. It made the guilt feel a little less acute as he gladly fell into her trap.

'More than just Paul?' he said.

Keisha frowned. 'Since he's been gone certain things have come to light,' she said.

He thought about Claire. Bereaved and terrified. Was it possible her husband had crossed paths with Bistacchis? Malton put a pin in it and let Keisha continue.

'Before he went missing, Paul borrowed a load of guns off Danny Mitchum. I think he was planning to use them against him.'

There weren't many things that could take Malton by surprise but that did. Danny Mitchum seemed to keep cropping up today. Malton would have to look into why that was.

'You're paying me to find Paul, not deal with Danny Mitchum.'

'What good is finding Paul if by the time you've worked out who's got him the rest of his family are dead?'

Malton couldn't decide if Keisha was exaggerating or if she really was that scared of Danny Mitchum. It would make sense for most people to be scared of him; even Malton was. But he'd never known Keisha be scared of anyone before. He remembered the fight at the Gamecock. Watching Keisha swinging a pool cue, cracking skulls and breaking bones. Her damsel in distress act didn't quite ring true.

'Paul's mum wants us to go buy a load of guns off the Squaddie. She's going to start a war,' said Keisha, her tone inviting Malton to share her exasperation at this turn of events.

'I'm sure you'll handle it.'

'You could handle it,' suggested Keisha.

So that was it. What started with finding Paul Bistacchi had suddenly become putting Malton between Danny Mitchum and Maria Bistacchi. No man's land.

'I'm not touching that one. I took this job as a favour. To you,' said Malton.

'A favour? Craig Malton is doing me a favour? I'm flattered,' said Keisha tartly.

'I'll give you your money back and let you deal with it yourself,' said Malton.

Keisha put her hand on Malton's thigh and gave it an affectionate squeeze.

'I'm sorry,' she said, her voice low and vulnerable.

Malton tried to ignore the memories dragged up by the feeling of Keisha's hand on his leg. The gulf between the present and the past felt far, far smaller than the three decades it was.

'Marcus Minshall, were you in business with him?' he said, hoping the abrupt change of topic might catch Keisha out.

Unable to help herself, Keisha burst out laughing. Clapping her hands together with glee at the very idea.

'Marcus Minshall?' Keisha could barely breathe for the peals of laughter. So much so that despite everything Malton found it infecting him. His mouth turning up and the unusual sight of Keisha uncontrollable with mirth.

'Craig, trust me. The closest Marcus Minshall came to getting involved with the Bistacchis was when Johnny wrapped him around his bumper.'

As Keisha kept laughing Malton wondered if she had any idea that the woman who Johnny had made a widow of didn't just know who had run over her husband, she'd watched while Keisha's husband was kidnapped off his own driveway. And what was more she knew Keisha had gatecrashed her husband's funeral.

But there was no way she could know any of that and so Malton stayed quiet.

'You're a funny one, you,' said Keisha, choking down the last of her mirth.

She seemed to have forgotten she was meant to be in fear for her life.

'We used to have a laugh didn't we? Back then,' she said, her hand finding its way back onto Malton's thigh.

153

Malton thought about their time together all those years ago. It was passionate, it was violent, it was intense. He wouldn't describe it as a 'laugh'.

Keisha's face became solemn. The hand squeezed his thigh a little tighter. 'I meant to say the other day. I'm sorry about what they did to James.'

At the mention of that name Malton froze. He felt his heart start to beat uncontrollably. With only the slightest tell he let his breath slow down. Long, deep lungfuls.

Keisha carried on, seemingly oblivious to the effect the mention of that name had on Malton.

'What do you know about James?' said Malton. His voice leaving no room for any confusion as to just how serious the conversation had just become.

Keisha took her hand off Malton's thigh and crossed her arms, making her own show of being put out.

'You pissed off to Liverpool, Craig. Not the other end of the world. You think I didn't check up on my ex once in a while?' she said.

Malton hadn't. After he left Keisha, he had never looked back. In fact until she arrived in his office the other day he'd not said more than ten words to her since the day he walked out.

'My twenty-first birthday and the love of my life tells me he's gay and he's leaving? You don't think I'd be just a bit curious?' said Keisha indignantly.

'I asked, what do you know about James?' said Malton. Even saying his name out loud was painful. Malton wished he could mask his feelings but he knew his body was giving him away. His shoulders high and tense, his fists clenched into tight balls in his lap. The way he felt inside it was all he could do not to wrench the steering wheel off and smash it through the windscreen.

'I know what those bastards did to him,' said Keisha, softly.

So did Malton. He thought about it every single day. The man he loved, butchered because of him.

'Nothing compared to what James's brother did to them,' said Malton darkly. The thought gave him the barest shred of comfort.

They both sat in silence for a moment. Neither one of them quite daring to carry on down this path.

'But now you're with Emily?' said Keisha, breaking the silence.

Malton wasn't ashamed of his sexuality. It wasn't complicated. He was bisexual. Like everything in his life it made most sense to him to keep things separate. When he slept with men he was gay. When he slept with women he was straight. That worked for Malton.

Before he could put that into words, Keisha spoke.

'It's fine,' she said. 'I get it. You like a bit of both. Just a shame you couldn't have worked that out before you fucked off. Could have come to some kind of timeshare arrangement.'

Keisha burst out laughing. Malton stayed silent.

Malton remembered how conflicted he'd been the day he left. How he'd dreaded Keisha's reaction and hated himself for being the way he was. It was over thirty years ago but he definitely wasn't ready to sit here making jokes about it. Especially not with Keisha.

'You asked me to find Paul. I'm going to find him and then we're done,' he said. He meant it.

Keisha stopped smiling. Malton could tell that beneath her sunglasses her eyes had gone dead.

'You know it's never done,' said Keisha. 'What we do? It follows you right until the end. You can't live this life and then hang up your Malton Security vest, go home and pretend to be a nice, middle-class white guy. It doesn't work like that, Craig. Our world is always there. Always waiting to pounce and hurt you. It's James; it's Paul. Who's next? Emily?'

'Get out,' said Malton.

Keisha lingered just long enough to let Malton know she was leaving on her own clock, before she turned, got out of the car and walked away into the night without saying another word. Her perfume lingered in the car for several minutes after she'd left. When he felt like it had finally dissipated, he put on the vents just to make sure and headed home to Emily.

He'd still do everything in his power to find Paul Bistacchi. There weren't many things Malton believed in but he did believe that when someone asked him to do a job he'd see it through to the bloody end. Whether or not he thought it was in their best interests and regardless of whether they changed their mind along the way. Everyone knew that if you hired Malton, whatever else might happen, the job got done.

But it was now clear to him that the safe return of her husband wasn't the only thing Keisha wanted from him.

As he drove back across town he did his best to fathom what else it was she was looking for and more importantly how far she would go to get it.

28

Claire was used to not sleeping. In the months leading up to her final diagnosis she had hardly slept at all. The not knowing was awful. But this was different. Claire knew exactly what she was afraid of. She'd been awake all night turning over in her head every way that things could play out. None of them gave her any cause for reassurance.

She clutched a mug of tea and stood in her front room, peering through slanted blinds at the road beyond and the morning serenity. It was a narrow street lined with large, semi-detached houses facing onto the road. No driveways so parking was always a bone of contention. Every house had at least two cars and so there were constant arguments about who parked where. It also meant that Claire could match every car on the street to its respective household.

She went down the road, one side at a time, counting off each car, making sure she knew whose car it was. Checking for any vehicle she couldn't account for. Having done it once and with every vehicle allocated to a house on the street she didn't feel any less scared and so she started over.

She'd told Malton everything. She hadn't meant to and she definitely didn't want to drag her dead husband into things but somehow he'd got it out of her. Every last detail of what she'd seen the night before. Right down to the car number plate.

Now all she had was his word.

Part of Claire hoped that maybe she'd given him something he could use. Something that would lead to him finding out what Marcus's connection was to the Bistacchis. And if along the way he roughed up Johnny Bistacchi then maybe she could live with it. But the moment she had that thought she was struck with sickening dread.

She'd asked him not to kill Johnny Bistacchi, but nothing about the way the man conducted himself convinced her he'd taken her request to heart. As much as Claire might wish Johnny dead, she knew without a shadow of a doubt that her conscience could never live with the knowledge that she'd ordered a man's murder. That wasn't what she wanted Marcus's legacy to be.

She was going to be dead inside of the year. Already she was starting to get headaches that painkillers could barely touch. Soon the symptoms would get more physical. She should be preparing her daughter Jessica for life without either of her parents, not pursuing a murderous vendetta.

And besides the morality of it, what if it got back to the Bistacchis that it was her who had set Malton on them? If they really had deliberately targeted Marcus what would stop them coming after her? Or Jessica?

As she squinted through her blinds she wondered how easy it would be to find out where she lived? Malton had tracked her down to her school. Was it that simple?

Right now was the last of the good times. The last bit before the cancer started to really kick in. These should be the times when Claire was making the most of every moment with Jessica. Not morbidly dwelling on what the stocky man with the scar on his face was going to do to Johnny Bistacchi and what that would mean for her and her daughter. She hated that she was now worrying about the man who had killed Marcus. Wondering how she could save his life.

'I'm off, Mum!'

Jessica's voice came from the hallway. Claire snapped to attention, spilling cold tea as she did so. Putting her mug down and wiping her hands on her trousers, Claire checked the time. Half seven. She was late.

'I'll drive you,' she said, taking a last look out the window and hurrying into the hallway to join her daughter.

Jessica was already opening the door.

'I said I'll drive you!' Claire hadn't meant to shout but that was how it came out. Both of them heard the edge of fear in her voice.

Jessica shut the door. 'It's OK, Mum. I'll be fine. It's the school bus. Same as always. Yeah?'

Claire realised that whatever she did, Jessica must never know. It was knowing that had dragged Claire into this. Knowing Johnny Bistacchi's name, where he lived, Malton's phone number and the number plate of Paul Bistacchi's kidnapper. She wished she'd never leaned on DC Moor to tell her anything.

Now the only thing she had to protect Jessica was her ignorance. Claire hoped that if her daughter had no idea of the terrible events she'd set in motion that would be enough to protect her.

'Please, let me take you. For me?'

'Oh, Mum.' Jessica put her school bag down and threw her arms around her mother. Claire held her back, screwing her eyes tight to not cry.

'I'm sorry. I know it's silly. You're a big girl.'

Letting go, Claire started to wipe her eyes with her sleeve. Jessica reached into a pocket and passed her mother a tissue, which Claire gratefully accepted.

'I know it's hard – what happened to Dad,' said Jessica, her voice play-acting at a maturity beyond her years. 'It was just so random. And you getting sick. It doesn't make any sense. But you can't live your life in fear of the unknown. Dad wouldn't want that. Whatever time we've got left together, we've got to just keep going. Make it count?'

Claire wondered what she'd done to deserve such a wonderful daughter.

'You're my hero, Mum,' said Jessica.

Claire felt herself welling up again.

Suddenly it all made sense to Claire. Jessica was right. She had terminal cancer. Her husband was dead. There was nothing left to be afraid of. Especially not someone like Malton or the Bistacchis. Let them fight it out amongst themselves and if they wanted to try and drag her family into their world then they'd have to go through her first.

29

Dean hadn't slept. Enthusiasm and caffeine had seen him pull an all-nighter, cramming his head full of as much information as he could find about Paul Bistacchi. There were three Paul Bistacchis in Manchester. One was a dentist, one was a retired tailor and one was a notorious gangland criminal. Dean hoped that Malton wasn't going to be asking him about the first two.

Dean could hardly keep still as he sat waiting for Malton to arrive. Since losing his suit yesterday he was back to wearing the school trousers, school shirt and pullover combination he'd worn to his first interview at Malton Security.

When Malton finally arrived just after eight, he seemed distracted.

Dean still had no clear idea why exactly Malton had sent him the text. There was still a small part of his brain telling him that it wasn't even meant for him. So Dean decided to play it cool. Keep things light.

'What did the lad locked up out back say the other day? Did he tell you who put him up to it?' asked Dean.

Malton stopped dead. He took a quick look around to make sure there was no one else in the office and grinned. 'You're keen,' he said.

Dean had no idea if this was a good thing or not.

Malton picked up on his uncertainty. 'Let's talk about it in private,' he said, walking past Dean and into his office.

Dean followed Malton and made a point of closing the door behind him.

Malton sat at his desk. Without thinking Dean took the seat across from him.

'So did he say who put him up to it?'

'If I know who put him up to it, then whoever that is, I've got to deal with them,' said Malton knowingly. 'And right now, I'm a little bit busy.'

Dean couldn't work out if this was another test or if Malton was being deadly serious. He suddenly felt like he was back in his job interview.

'But don't you need to know? What if they come looking for the kid?'

'I don't know where he is. Do you?' said Malton.

Dean had a strong suspicion Malton was fucking with him. They'd witnessed an armed robbery turned murder, mutilated the culprit, saved him from being tortured to death and locked him in a storage unit. It felt like it deserved at least a little urgency.

Malton ignored Dean, went over to the weight bench on the other side of the room and started loading 20-kilogram plates onto the bar.

'I got your text,' said Dean, trying to get back on slightly firmer ground.

'Good,' said Malton, removing his Barbour jacket and peeling off the chunky knitted sweater underneath to reveal a white Airtex vest and arms coiled solid with muscle. 'Right now our priority is Paul Bistacchi.'

'Even more than Leon Walker?'

Dean had struck out with Walker's dealer but he was still sure given enough time there were only so many places a near seven-foot junkie could hide in this city.

'Leon Walker can wait,' said Malton.

Dean saw all his good work disappearing down the drain. He got desperate. 'But what if he's connected to Paul Bistacchi? Or Lorraine's?'

Dean couldn't parse the look Malton gave him. Whether it was disbelief or whether he'd actually stumbled upon something.

Whatever it was Malton quickly went back to loading weights onto the bar.

'You're eager,' he said. 'And that's good, but Leon Walker's not business. Right now I'm getting paid good money to track down Paul Bistacchi. So what do you know?'

While Dean's mind raced through the hours of online research he'd spent the previous night doing, Malton finished loading the plates. He lay back and wrapped his fingers around the bar. Dean counted 80 kilograms on each side. Along with the 20-kilogram bar, that was a 180-kilogram bench. He'd once lifted 40 kilograms and it'd nearly killed him.

'Spot me,' said Malton, getting ready to lift.

Dean did as he was told, taking up position behind Malton. If the older man couldn't lift the weight, Dean wasn't convinced there was much he could do to stop the bar crushing him to death. Malton braced, his arms went taut and the bar lifted up off the rest and took position above his chest.

'Paul Bistacchi?' muttered Malton, lowering the bar to his chest, his entire body tensing with the effort.

Half mesmerised by the sight of a man benching over twice his body weight, Dean took a second. Malton raised the bar with a solid grunt.

'Paul Bistacchi,' said Dean. 'He's been done for growing cannabis. Mixes with a lot of mid-level dealers. Big family, bit famous round East Manchester. One brother: Johnny.'

'I don't want his life story,' said Malton, lowering the bar again. 'Who'd want him gone?'

Dean's mind raced. The *Manchester Evening News* had articles about the Bistacchis going back years. They were constantly coming up in relation to drug importing, antisocial behaviour, sexual assaults, property damage and casual vio-lence. There were hundreds of people who would want to be at the front of the queue to see the Bistacchis get taken down a peg or two. Dean tried to remember anything concrete. Anything that would help. Then it came to him.

'He killed a guy and got away with it.'

Malton raised the bar with a smile. 'Who?'

'A student. There was a fight in a bar. And this kid got involved. He was in the wrong pub at the wrong time. Took a punch and died. They said there wasn't enough evidence. No CCTV. No one in the pub would talk. Lewis something I think . . .'

'Lewis Cornforth,' said Malton, lowering the bar once more. With every rep, more and more muscles stood to attention. His torso bulged with a strength that his stature went a long way to conceal.

'Yeah that's the one,' said Dean. 'Happened last year. It seemed like an open-and-shut case. Then the police just dropped it and suddenly everything went quiet. It was really weird. Like there was something else going on.'

Malton let out a panicked groan and suddenly the bar he was holding started to lurch to one side.

'Spot me!' he shouted.

Dean was there, his skinny, white hands around the bar. He felt the impossible weight. Like dark matter dragging the bar down. He knew there was no way on earth he could move it. Malton's arms were shaking, the bar pressing on his chest. Dean could hear his lungs start to wheeze as the enor-mous weight bore down on him.

Dean bent his knees, using all the power in his back and legs, putting everything he had into the bar. It wasn't moving. Malton was making a low gurgling noise. Still Dean didn't stop. He could hear himself making his own set of incoherent grunts as the effort of it all began to overwhelm him.

With teeth clenched together he spat out, 'Mother . . . fucker . . .' closed his eyes and waited for some Hulk-like outburst of power. Mind over body. A hidden reserve of strength that his sheer will would unleash . . .

The bar moved. Not just a little. It moved all the way up, out of Dean's hands, over Malton's head and onto the rests with a solid clunk.

Dean staggered backwards, spent. Malton sat up looking like he'd just jogged up a short flight of stairs.

'Good effort,' he said and started pulling on his jumper.

'You didn't need me at all.'

'You think I'm fucking with you,' said Malton perceptively. 'I'm not. I need to know you've got my back. And now I know that you do, I need you.'

Dean felt this still very much came under the umbrella of being fucked with but he kept quiet.

Malton stood up and put on his Barbour. 'Our one-handed friend out back isn't going anywhere, so what say we go ask the police why they decided not to prosecute Lewis Cornforth's slam-dunk murder case?'

30

Keisha gripped the metal handrail as she skipped down the stairs of the narrow alley that linked Stockport's covered market with the twisty, cobbled streets below it. Stockport had changed nearly as much as Keisha these past thirty years. It used to be that the only thing you'd smell coming down this alley was stale urine and the only people you'd meet were the kind of people who didn't mind hanging out in an alley that stank of piss.

Today all Keisha could smell was the floral aromas of the homemade candle shop that had taken up residence in the tiny premises halfway down the stairs. She glanced through the window to see a couple of white women in aprons, one of them arranging a display of candles while the other took photos with her mobile phone.

Johnny was parked up a few streets away, waiting in a transit van. Keisha had followed in her own car. It had been easy to convince him to make a quick detour on their way to source guns up in Saddleworth. Johnny was doing his best to hide it, but it was clear Paul's disappearance had him scared. The search of the house had failed to turn up the guns or any clues as to who might have taken them.

Without Paul, Maria would expect him to take the lead and become the face of the Bistacchi family. That meant as soon as they had more guns it would be Johnny taking the fight to Danny Mitchum. Even someone with Johnny's lack of smarts knew that it was a one-way ticket to the morgue.

That worked just perfectly for Keisha. Johnny needed her help and she was more than happy to give it. For a price. As long as Johnny didn't have to think for himself he was happy. And as long as Johnny did what she said and didn't go blabbing to Maria then so was Keisha.

Despite how it ended Keisha had enjoyed seeing Craig the night before. And on home turf too. It reminded her of the old days when in no time at all Craig had gone from an aimless kid from Moss Side to the upcoming prospect everyone was talking about. It was no coincidence his rise had coincided with them getting together. She'd shown him the world outside the M14 postcode. Taken him to clubs and parties.

Introduced him to the black spaces where thanks to an absent mum and a white dad, Craig had never felt he belonged. She'd built Craig Malton. He was her creation and it felt good to see just how far he'd come.

It was almost enough to make her forget how it had all ended.

Keisha emerged into the lower levels of Stockport town centre. Stockport Council's grand scheme to regenerate the town centre had turned around large swathes of the town. Where once there were decaying newsagents and empty premises, now were thriving independent businesses, cafés and bars. She caught sight of her reflection in a shop window and for just a moment she felt old. She shook it off and carried on picking her way along re-cobbled streets.

Last night hadn't gone exactly how she'd hoped. Even so, she'd called Craig and he'd come running. They still had that connection. That was something Keisha could work with.

She peered through her sunglasses into newly opened shops, counting all the usual suspects as she did so – young, white and tattooed. Beards and knitted caps. Dyed hair and enthusiasm. People who had never had to work retail and so for whom the idea of serving the public day in, day out held a quaint fascination. Having spent one long, shitty summer working in a greengrocers in Moss Side Precinct, there were few things Keisha would prefer less than going back to working in a shop.

A shop like the one she stopped in front of. 'Cakes by Emily' said the sign above the shop window. The window itself was home to an elaborate display of handmade cakes. Pride of place was a giant cake sculpted to resemble Miss Piggy from *The Muppets*. It was exquisite. A genuine piece of art.

Even Keisha was impressed.

As she entered, a bell over the door rang and a woman's voice shouted from out back, 'I'll be with you in one second!'

Keisha looked round. It wasn't a large premises. Just big enough for the kitchen out the back, the counter displaying three dozen cupcakes and four or five grand layer cakes and half a dozen chairs clustered around two tables.

Keisha perched on one of the chairs and looked over a noticeboard of community announcements. Yoga and Extinction Rebellion and a couple of flyers for local bands.

A young woman emerged from the back, wiping her hands on a tea towel and smiling. She radiated an enthusiasm that Keisha instantly picked up on.

'This place is cute!' said Keisha.

'Thanks,' replied the woman behind the counter. 'And everything's vegan.'

'Oh. I didn't know that,' said Keisha.

'But it's all delicious! Hi! I'm Emily.'

The woman with the long, black hair and pale white skin reached over the counter, offering her hand.

Keisha made no move to shake it. Smiling all the while until Emily retracted her hand and stuffed it into the pocket on the front of her apron.

'So what can I get you? The brownies are amazing, the millionaire's shortcake is also amazing. In fact it's all amazing,' said Emily with a nervous laugh.

'I wonder if you could help me then. I need a cake.'

'You've come to the right place. We've got layer cakes or if it's a special occasion we can make you something unique.'

Keisha took in the shop.

'And this is all yours?' she asked.

'Yes. I say we, it's me really. My dad sometimes helps with deliveries but mostly it's just me.'

Keisha decided that Emily was no threat whatsoever. She could afford to be a little more friendly with the girl. Draw her in.

'The occasion – it's a bit of an odd one,' she offered, sucking in her cheeks and inserting a note of apology into her voice.

'We like odd!' reassured Emily.

Keisha fixed on Emily's clear blue eyes from behind her sunglasses.

'I need a cake for an ex of mine,' she said conspiratorially.

Emily jumped on it. 'Ooooh. An ex? Are you getting back together?'

Keisha smiled and wrinkled her nose. 'Maybe. Who knows? Depends how good the cake is,' she said with a laugh.

'So is it a surprise or a birthday or what?'

'He's doing some work for me. And once he's done I'd like to thank him. Let him know I'm thinking about him.' Keisha went back to inspecting the cakes on the counter.

'And you're hoping once he finishes the job then maybe you two could have another shot?' teased Emily.

Keisha looked up. Her glare hidden by the dark lenses.

'Sorry, I'm being nosy,' blurted Emily, suddenly flustered.

'To tell you the truth,' said Keisha, 'I don't even know if I want another shot. It ended so badly. After everything we'd been through he just upped and walked out.'

'What a bastard,' said Emily.

'Next thing I hear, he's over in Liverpool shagging around with men.'

'Oh my gosh,' said Emily, putting a hand to her mouth to hide her genuine surprise.

Emily's reaction to this indiscreet gossip was exactly what Keisha had been hoping for. The fast-tracked intimacy of a stranger oversharing her most personal secrets.

'He was gay?' said Emily.

'Gay, bi, it doesn't matter to me. I just wish he felt he could have talked to me. I loved him,' said Keisha.

Emily's face was the picture of heartfelt sympathy. 'Sounds like you're the one who could do with cake,' said Emily.

'I just think it's sad that some men can't talk about their feelings. You can be so close to someone but not really ever know them. You know what I mean?'

Keisha knew full well Emily knew exactly what she meant.

Emily was nodding. 'Some men are like that. But if you love them, you've got to just keep trying.'

Suddenly the gravity of their conversation hit Emily and she laughed nervously.

'Are you seeing anyone?' asked Keisha, innocently.

A huge smile broke out over Emily's face. She lowered her eyes, self-conscious of how badly she was concealing her joy.

'Yes,' she said. 'Sorry.'

'Don't be sorry,' enthused Keisha. 'At least one of us has a functioning love life.' Keisha laughed, filling the little shop with the rich, uninhibited sound.

'Actually, it's going really well,' said Emily. She leaned over the counter, suddenly eager to share with this woman she'd only just met. 'We're trying for a baby.'

Keisha's guts turned to lead. She felt every bit of her body become dense and cold. Emily's delighted laughter sounded very far away.

For just a moment she was back thirty years ago, in a flat in a condemned tower block in Hulme. Outside something was aflame. Craig was long gone and she never even got to tell him . . .

Keisha willed herself back to the present with a huge, congratulatory smile. 'That's fantastic news,' she said and took pride in how sincere she sounded.

'Thank you,' said Emily. 'It's early days, but fingers crossed.'

Keisha watched as Emily actually crossed her fingers.

'And hopefully your ex will see what he's missing out on,' said Emily, with genuine sympathy.

Keisha squeezed all the levity out of her voice, fixed Emily through her sunglasses and with complete conviction said, 'I'm definitely going to give him something to think about.'

She could tell Emily felt the air leaving the room. Keisha savoured the other woman's brief moment of discomfort until the irrepressible smile came back to Emily's face.

'Listen to me, I'm the last person to give anyone relationship advice,' she said. 'But I do know cake and I am going to make you a cake that'll show that ex of yours just what he's missing.'

Keisha could see what Craig saw in this woman. No edge, no side, no agenda. No nothing. Just smiles and cake and a life with enough privilege to still believe the best in people. Even someone like Craig Malton.

'Could you do a message on the cake?' said Keisha.

'Of course,' said Emily, getting a notepad out of the pocket in her apron.

'I want a big cake. Really huge. As big as you can make it. Chocolate, he likes chocolate. Or at least he said he did when he was with me. And on the top I want it to say, *"ONE LAST CHANCE".'*

31

From the front seat of his car Malton dialled 999 and when asked what emergency service he required, told the operator: police. A moment later he was put through and explained to the voice on the other end of the phone that he was watching someone breaking into a house. Number 89 Gosley Street to be exact. Not the posh Gosley Street in Bramhall. Gosley Street in Blackley. When asked for his details Malton gave one of the dozen fake names he always had at the ready, hung up, took the SIM card out of his phone and dropped it out of the car window down a grid.

Across the road Dean was breaking into number 89 Gosley Street. Or at least he was trying. Dean had asked why they couldn't just call the police and tell them someone was breaking in. All that Malton had said was that it never hurt to practise. Which was why Dean was now furiously kicking at the white, uPVC door.

Dean turned back and looked to Malton, shrugging as if to suggest that maybe, now he'd had a go, he could come back and sit in the car. But Malton gave him an encouraging thumbs-up and gestured to keep going. As Dean booted away he wondered what Malton's plan was. Who it was he thought was coming and why they'd stopped at Greggs on the way to pick up half a dozen steak bakes. Any doubts he might have entertained had long since gone since the spotting incident back at the office. Malton had decided to trust him and now he was going to trust Malton.

Dean could feel beads of sweat forming beneath his work shirt, running down his back and soaking his underwear. He wiped the perspiration from his face and tried to catch his breath. He'd never kicked a door in before. It was harder than it looked. In the distance he was sure he could hear sirens. He gazed up at the row of terraces just across the road. Grimy curtains, rotting window frames and yards piled with wet cardboard boxes and litter. If anyone was watching him they weren't going to do anything about it.

Dean took a step back. The frame of the door seemed immovable but the panels inside the frame shuddered and flexed with each kick. He thought maybe if he could kick out a panel he could reach through and unlock the door.

Dean focused on the bottom right panel. He took a step back and swung. His foot connected bang centre of the panel and kept going. The rectangle of white uPVC gave way and Dean's foot went with it. Thrown off balance he found himself on his arse on the doorstep as a police car slowly pulled up outside the house.

Scrambling to his feet, Dean was met with the sight of a police officer exiting her car – one hand on her baton, the other on her radio. She was short and middle-aged but radiated the kind of terrifying intensity that reminded Dean of his mum. She didn't hurry but moved with a weary inevitability. Never once taking her eyes off Dean.

'I lost my keys,' said Dean with a confident smile.

He saw the officer looking at the missing door panel. She looked annoyed that he'd even try to bullshit her. Dean noticed how the lines on her face were fixed into a frown of unending disappointment.

'I should probably fix that,' he said, optimistically.

The officer kept her eyes on Dean and spoke into her radio. 'Control, this is Benton at Gosley Street now. Suspect still at the scene. I'm going to need backup.'

Dean began to wonder at what point Malton's plan would reveal itself. 'It's my house. I swear.'

'It's OK. He's with me.'

The officer turned to see Malton getting out of his car, holding up a greasy paper bag and smiling. She got back on her radio, 'Control, cancel that request for assistance.'

The three of them sat on the low garden wall of number 89, eating. Or rather Benton and Dean ate. Malton just watched. Dean had skipped breakfast and was too hungry to wonder if he should have joined in eating the bag of steak bakes. As hungry as he was he couldn't help but be impressed with how quickly Benton demolished her food. Giant mouthfuls and minimal chewing. Someone used to eating on the go.

'This your new chicken?' said Benton, looking at Dean.

'Something like that,' said Malton, not rising to Benton's bait.

'You want to watch this one,' Benton said to Dean. 'Known him since he was a little bastard in Moss Side, smashing windows, nicking bags of crisps.'

'I heard they got you back on patrol,' Malton interrupted. 'I told you they couldn't bear a grudge forever!'

Benton finished her steak bake, wiping greasy hands over her trousers. 'They got me sitting on a wall eating steak bakes with you two champions. It's hardly Nipper of the Yard, is it?'

'What was he like, back then?' Dean asked her, nodding to Malton.

Benton looked to Malton who almost imperceptibly shook his head.

'You want to know what this guy got up to you ask him yourself.' She turned back to Malton. 'Thanks for breakfast but I got nothing more on who shot up your front door.'

Dean's ears pricked up at the mention of the shotgun attack.

'That's not what I'm here for,' said Malton. 'I had a bit of a question. About Paul Bistacchi?'

Dean saw Benton give a slight grimace.

'Last year, Paul Bistacchi sucker-punches a student. Gets away with it. What's going on?'

Benton ignored Malton, making a show of brushing stray crumbs off her uniform. 'I gave you Leon Walker for free. Out of the goodness of my heart,' she said.

Dean desperately wanted to ask this woman what she knew about Leon Walker. To share his own, ongoing investigation. But he had the common sense to keep it to himself. For now.

He watched as Benton made the same survey of the surrounding street as he had done. She was seeing if anyone was watching.

'It costs a fuckload being a single mum. Thousands and thousands,' she said.

Malton didn't seem thrown by this at all. He sucked his teeth and shook his head sadly.

'Could it cost hundreds and hundreds?' he said.

Benton rolled her eyes theatrically. Dean began to realise that this wasn't the first time this conversation, or something like it, had taken place.

'It could cost a single, piss-taking thousand. At a fucking pinch.'

And there in Malton's hand was that thick roll of cash again. His chunky fingers peeling off fifties too fast for Dean to even count them. Notes that folded neatly into his palm as he leaned across Dean and shook Benton's hand. A hand that Benton slipped into her trouser pocket without hesitation.

Just like that she started talking.

'Paul Bistacchi isn't clever. But he's not stupid either. He's that sweet spot of just clever enough to do it and just dumb enough to not think why he shouldn't. He knows a lot of people. Does a lot of business. Hundreds of thousands. Maybe a couple of million a year.'

'And who decided to let him keep that up?' asked Malton.

'Paul Bistacchi is a worker. Every day he's grafting. Cos he hasn't got the vision not to. He's a nasty sod but he's a small-time nasty sod who knows everyone.'

'He's the weak link in the chain,' said Dean, spitting out steak bake.

'The weakest, thickest, noisiest link. And you did not hear this from me but Greater Manchester Police have been working for the last three years to finger every major player in the North West. And what do they all have in common?'

'Paul Bistacchi!' cried Dean.

Benton and Malton both glared.

'He's a keen one this lad, isn't he?' said Benton.

'He's getting there,' said Malton. 'I guess you know Paul Bistacchi's missing then?'

'We got fuck all money to do anything these days. God help you if someone breaks into your house or nicks your car. The big lads stuck it all on a spreadsheet and decided to put everything they had in the budget on this one operation. Called it Operation Euston. Fuck knows why. When two years into it Paul Bistacchi kills Lewis Cornforth, it's already cost far too much to shut it down. He's the key to it all. So he got a pass. CCTV lost, statements rewritten. But now he's done one. Or someone unpleasant has realised their good mate Paul maybe isn't the most discreet scumbag you could do business with. Let me tell you, there are a lot of people high up the food chain absolutely shitting themselves right now.' Benton started on her second steak bake, talking with her mouth full. 'Where do *you* think he's gone?' she asked.

'I've got a few ideas I'm looking into,' said Malton. 'You got any names?'

'Not for a grand I don't. But if you work it out remember your good mate Benton. Caught you with a shopping trolley full of stolen car radios and let you off with a warning. Finding Paul Bistacchi's the kind of thing that might just drag my career out the toilet.'

'It's like you don't enjoy these little get-togethers,' chided Malton.

Benton's radio crackled to life. 'Report of a Domestic Disturbance, Pointer Lane. Benton, confirm.'

Benton swallowed her mouthful and slowly rose to her feet, rubbing her hands together.

'Social media bullshit or old-fashioned domestic violence? Only one way to find out.'

'Before you go,' said Malton, 'there's a number plate I need checking.'

'I've got water coming through my kitchen ceiling and my teenage daughter's going out with a wanker. Sadly there's only so many hours in the day.'

'Tell you what,' said Malton, 'why don't you run into some car trouble? Call up, get a lift back to the station. Have a quick look on the database while you're waiting for a new car?'

Benton looked unsure, sucking her teeth as she weighed up Malton's offer. Malton raised a finger – wait – and produced a large Stanley knife from his jacket. Benton and Dean watched him walk across the road to Benton's squad car, kneel down and methodically slash his way all the way round the two front tyres. With a loud hissing sound the whole car sagged forward over the newly flat tyres.

'Car trouble,' said Malton.

'Can't argue with car trouble,' said Benton and sat back down on the wall. 'You see Paul Bistacchi on your travels, be sure to give him my love.'

Malton gestured to Dean and they returned to the car, leaving Benton to polish off the remaining steak bakes.

'Thoughts?' said Malton, once they were back on the move.

'Could Paul Bistacchi really be under police protection?' said Dean.

'Never underestimate how badly Greater Manchester Police can fuck things up,' said Malton.

Finally Dean got where all this was heading. He tried to sound less excited than he was at working it out.

'If the police weren't interested then what if someone took the law into their own hands?' he said.

Malton gave a little smile.

'You mean someone like the family of a promising young student who got murdered on a night out?' he said.

32

Terry Morefield's eighty-three-year-old mum made her slow, shaky progress across the chintzy living room carpet, a tray loaded with biscuits and cups of tea gripped firmly in her knotted, arthritic hands. With every step a little more tea sloshed onto the tray.

Keisha could see Johnny wondering if he should get up and give her a hand. She gently shook her head and Johnny sank back down into the decades-old floral sofa on which he was sitting. Meanwhile Terry hadn't moved a muscle to help his ancient mother. He stayed sitting bolt upright on the high-backed armchair he'd been in when his mum had first led Keisha and Johnny into the living room.

It was on Maria's orders that they had driven out of the city up towards Saddleworth Moor to the tiny village of Diggle where Manchester's number-one underworld gunsmith, Terry Morefield – aka the Squaddie – lived with his elderly mother. Terry was by no means the cheapest. But he was the most reliable. He could bring deactivated guns back to life. Turn starting pistols into deadly weapons. Through his contacts Terry could source whatever ordnance you wanted. But most importantly he was strictly neutral. You bought guns off Terry, no one else knew about it. Now that Danny Mitchum was on high alert, the Bistacchis couldn't risk tipping their hand by going to any of the cheaper but less discreet places they might usually go to.

Keisha had goaded Maria into sending her to accompany Johnny, and Maria had taken the bait. Now that Keisha was along for the ride she was going to make sure things happened exactly how she wanted them to.

That included the second detour they'd taken in order to visit the car park where a few weeks earlier they had burned Johnny's friend Logan to death in the boot of a car in order to cover up Johnny's mistake. Driving over to Saddleworth, Johnny had been following Keisha's silver Mercedes in his van. So when she'd led them up to the scene of the crime Johnny had followed along, oblivious.

They'd stood in the windswept car park for nearly ten minutes, staring in silence at the yellow police incident board beside the scorched patch of tarmac. Then, as Keisha had secretly hoped would happen, Johnny pulled out a spliff and angrily smoked it down to the roach before stomping back to his van. Johnny was nothing if not predictable.

Keisha knew that Johnny's constant drug use had given him a high tolerance for weed. Even for the super-strength skunk he liked to smoke to get to sleep after indulging in his favourite white powder. But today Johnny had left the house stone-cold sober. Maria had seen to that. He was smoking on an empty stomach.

As they drove the rest of the way, Keisha was gratified to detect a newfound sloppiness to Johnny's driving as she watched him following in her rear-view mirror.

Whether it was the car park or the skunk or a bit of both, by the time they'd arrived at the Squaddie's stone cottage and parked up, Johnny seemed determined to take charge. Keisha had watched from her car as Johnny got out of his van and started marching up and down, talking to himself, psyching himself up for what was about to come.

Before they'd left, Maria had handed Johnny a satchel stuffed with all the emergency cash that Paul kept stashed around the house with instructions not to let it out of his sight. Keisha knew exactly how much money Paul had hidden around the house and exactly how much of that money Maria knew about. From her estimate the satchel must have contained around ten grand, no more.

Johnny had clutched the satchel to his chest as he'd walked up to the Squaddie's front door and rung the bell. So intense was his focus that when Terry's mum had asked him to take off his shoes he'd marched straight in as if he'd not heard the request. Keisha had followed on behind, apologetically taking off her bright white, shell-toe Adidas before following Johnny into the front room.

Once Terry's mum had made sure everyone had a hot cup of tea in their hands, silence descended.

Terry was ex-army. He had the neat, upright bearing of a man who'd been in the forces. His shoes were buffed to a mirror shine. He wore the same beige, army surplus chinos and short-sleeved shirt day in, day out. Always crisply pressed. His hair always buzzed to short stubble. He blew daintily on his cup of tea, drinking it in small, polite slurps.

Terry didn't speak much but Keisha couldn't help noticing how every once in a while he'd look down at Johnny's muddy, size 10 trainers on his mother's floral carpet and shudder just a little.

Keisha looked down at her tea. Terry's mum used sterilised milk and so the tea was boiling hot with a faint whiff of something clinical about it. She could see Johnny doing his best to drink the scalding liquid.

'I'm really more of a coffee person,' she said to the room with a smile, tipped the full cup of tea into a nearby houseplant and placed the cup back on the tray on which Terry's elderly mother had brought it.

Terry did more than shudder just a little. His mother stopped smiling. The temperature in the room dropped.

Johnny glanced at Keisha. What was she playing at?

'It's good tea. Really good,' said Johnny. He went for it, guzzling back the rest of his own tea and replacing his mug on the tray. The boiling tea felt like it was stripping layers off his teeth.

'You've not come for the tea,' said Terry.

'We need guns,' said Johnny.

Terry's mum grimaced.

'Not in front of Mum,' Terry said, downing his tea and getting to his feet. He looked to Johnny. 'You, downstairs.'

Johnny jumped to his feet.

'Make sure you get some guns though,' said Keisha.

'What did I just say?' said Terry, through tightly clenched teeth.

'Sorry,' said Keisha. 'It's just we need them. Today. We're desperate. We'll take whatever.'

'Fuck's sake,' said Johnny before he could help himself.

Terry spun round and grabbed Johnny. He was nearly half a foot shorter but Johnny looked terrified.

'Don't you dare use that language in my house,' said Terry coldly.

'I'm sorry,' said Johnny.

'He's sorry. He's just nervous. Cos we need those guns. Urgently. Whatever it costs,' said Keisha.

'Follow me,' said Terry, and he headed out the back.

Johnny turned to Keisha and gave her a look of frustrated annoyance that Keisha pretended not to understand. She gave him a thumbs-up. Johnny gave up and followed after Terry.

Keisha was alone with Terry's mum. The old woman's jaw was slowly, angrily grinding away to itself. Her sunken eyes locked on Keisha.

Keisha looked around the room and then back to the old woman with a look of friendly curiosity. 'You ever think of redecorating?' she said.

33

Malton knew exactly where to find Lewis Cornforth's parents. They lived round the corner from him. The Cornforths were as much part of Didsbury as the Victorian library or the wrought-iron shopping parade. Lewis's dad Adam was an accountant and his mother Sam had been a local councillor. A *Vote Labour* sticker a permanent fixture in the front window.

They were old Didsbury – a couple who'd bought thirty years ago when Didsbury was full of draughty, unrenovated Victorian semis. Back then it was teachers and lawyers and doctors who made up the neighbourhood. They drove battered cars, walked muddy dogs and drank dirt-cheap wine from places no one had ever heard of.

When Lewis was murdered, the entire community felt it.

Malton never forgot his first time in Didsbury. A girl he met at a club in town had snuck him back home. He was less interested in shagging a posh girl than seeing how that posh girl lived. Back then he was only dimly aware of the world of the scruffy upper middle-class. It was eye-opening. The pile of *Private Eyes* in the toilet, the ramshackle collection of furniture. Heavy throws, thick with dog hair, draped over sagging sofas. He remembered everything had smelt faintly damp. The house was freezing and even fucking didn't do much to warm him up. But it left an impression. A kind of wealth he didn't know existed. The comfortable certainty of it all.

But that was then. Nowadays the teachers and doctors had retreated to the optimistic poverty of Levenshulme. The lawyers were clinging on by their fingernails and every piece of housing had been done up to within an inch of its life. Front gardens disappeared in favour of monoblock driveways on which Land Rovers parked – their noses spilling out onto the pavement. Every window was covered with bespoke wooden blinds and the brickwork no longer sprouted plant life. A lot of people were paying a lot of money to live in Didsbury. Malton was one of them.

The Cornforths were one of the last of the old guard. Their house sagged a little in a street of basement conversions and double glazing. Unlike so many of their neighbours they hadn't installed thick wooden security gates across the entrance to their driveway. In fact their driveway was hardly visible thanks to the overgrown front garden. A dilapidated garage sat at the end of the driveway, nestled against the house – its roof almost falling in under the weight of the ivy that covered it. The whole house had a crumpled, picture-book quality that made Malton's job all the easier when it came to breaking in.

He stood with Dean at the back door, well screened by garden walls and the sprawling shade of mature trees. The door itself was a flimsy wooden affair with a large, single pane of glass filling its top half.

'Break in,' said Malton.

Dean stood for a moment looking unsure. He was glad to get a second chance. This door looked an awful lot more expensive than the scruffy uPVC door back in Gosley Street.

'You want me to pick the lock?' he asked, seeking clarification.

'Break in,' said Malton.

Dean decided that if he was going to end up kicking this door in he could at least have made a token attempt to pick the lock first. He bent down and peered at the lock. He stared at the keyhole and the handle.

Malton noticed he was moving his lips as if deep in thought. Or at the very least giving the impression he was. He put a hand on Dean's shoulder. 'You know what the first thing you do is?'

'Some kind of lock-picking device?' said Dean, hopefully.

Malton reached past Dean and tried the handle. It turned and the door opened inwards. 'Try the handle.'

Malton gestured towards the open door. Despite working security for the past decade, Malton never ceased to be amazed at how many people simply didn't lock their doors.

'Go in, see what you can find,' ordered Malton.

'Are you coming?'

'I'm waiting out here. Don't want to get caught breaking and entering, do I? Not look good on my SIA renewal. Off you go.'

Hoping that he looked half as prepared as his boss apparently thought he was, Dean stepped into the kitchen.

'Hold on,' said Malton.

Dean stopped and turned to see Malton pulling a pair of blue latex gloves out of his pocket.

'Don't want to leave any prints,' he said holding out the gloves.

Dean took the gloves and, pulling them on, disappeared into the house.

Malton took out a handkerchief and wiped his own prints off the door handle. It'd been a long time since he'd had anyone working for him whom he actually trusted to go over a house like this. Longer still since he'd had anyone he liked enough to offer the gloves to.

Malton looked around the back garden. Like a lot of larger houses in Didsbury the back garden was something of a comedown. Not much bigger than a terraced yard, most of the plot was an overgrown lawn. There was a wrought-iron bench placed beneath a halo of ivy growing up the back wall.

A large, mature willow ensured enough cover to not be overlooked, so Malton took a seat and caught his breath.

It was warm for the time of year and the garden smelled of damp earth. The beds around the lawn were filled with evergreen shrubs and the bare branches of plants waiting for the spring. Creeping vines covered the side of the garage – blocking the small, rotting window set into the side of the building. It wasn't perfect but it had a kind of shambolic beauty that spoke to Malton. Anyone could neglect a garden, anyone could pay someone to level a garden and fill it with neatly clipped plants and turf. But there was a special kind of elegance to the barely maintained shabbiness of a garden like this.

Malton planted his feet in the grass and tried to feel like he belonged.

His brain gave him around ten seconds of grace before the hundreds of other thoughts that occupied his every waking moment started to crowd in on him.

On any normal week the armed robbery of a Danny Mitchum drop house would be taking up all of his time. Never mind the teenager he had stashed away back at the office, Malton would be tearing Manchester apart to get Danny Mitchum his pound of flesh. But this wasn't any normal week.

Paul Bistacchi was operating with de facto police immunity. The implications were huge. It was almost enough to make him forget that Leon Walker was still out there. Yet another dangerous loose end to tie up.

To make matters worse he'd finally caved in to Emily. Did he really want a family or was he just afraid of losing her? The events of the past few days proved beyond any doubt that there was no room in his life for family. No room for anything approaching normal.

Was that why when Keisha called he came running? Was she his way out of committing to Emily? Were the last thirty years just postponing the inevitable?

Malton pushed that thought to the back of his mind and focused on the here and now. It was clear that something *was* happening. Something big and dangerous that he needed to get out ahead of before it was too late.

Looking up, he saw Dean pass by a staircase window, heading upstairs. The boy was doing well. He'd rolled with everything Malton had thrown at him. Malton saw big things in his future. Provided he lived that long.

Malton's phone rang. It was Benton.

'You're quick,' he said.

'I don't have to be,' said Benton.

'What was the number plate?'

If Benton could give him a lead on the car that kidnapped Paul Bistacchi, all this could be over very quickly indeed.

'A car that was stolen in Liverpool two weeks ago.'

Malton groaned. A dead end. He was about to ask Benton where the car was now when he looked up and saw Dean hammering on the staircase window, shouting, desperate to get Malton's attention.

He looked like he'd just seen a ghost.

34

The last time Paul Bistacchi's heart had beaten this hard he'd just snorted an eight ball of what had turned out to be uncut cocaine. The price of the drug that drove Manchester's black economy had fallen so low that it was no longer worth the effort to cut it. The time and outlay – not to mention the increased risk of getting caught – had meant that for a time there was near one hundred per cent pure cocaine going up the noses of anyone in Manchester lucky enough to be buying.

Paul had always been able to drink and snort and swallow more than anyone. He was always the last one standing. The one still awake come morning, hunched over the wreckage of the night before, hoovering up the aftermath. But even for him an eight ball of pure cocaine was a shock to the system. From the first greedy sniff he'd sensed something was wrong but rather than appear to back down he had done the exact opposite and consumed what was meant for him and three mates. What followed was the nearest Paul had ever felt to death in his life. Until now.

He clenched the muscles in his glutes and thighs. He couldn't bring himself to look down at the half a dozen holes that had been drilled into his legs. With every clench he could feel blood oozing up out of those holes. Nerves scraping on flesh and bone. A shooting agony. He wondered if he could still walk.

The tighter he flexed the slower his heart became as the volume of blood left in his body became too low to maintain any kind of blood pressure. The slower his heart became the more his rage came into focus. He concentrated on the sound of his breathing. With each breath he tasted the air – it had a dank, moist flavour to it.

He couldn't cry out if he wanted to. He could barely keep his eyes open. The outside world sounded very far away. Every ounce of strength he had went in service to staying conscious.

He'd been pissed on and had holes drilled in him and now he was done. Paul tensed his entire body – feeling the strain as what blood he had left swelled into his enormous back and chest.

He could tell he didn't have long left. If he didn't use what little strength he had left this would only end one way.

Paul drew his arms to his sides, the zip ties that bound him to the chair cutting into his wrists. And still he kept going. The muscles in his shoulders popped; his back strained with the effort of it all. He planted his feet on the ground, pushing his strength through his legs. Ignoring the pain that came with it.

His head felt ready to explode. He felt like he could hear the blood rushing in his veins.

Every sinew of his body flared with inconsolable rage. The metal of the chair began to distend and twist under the intense force being exerted upon it. Then with a bestial roar from the bottom of his lungs, one arm of the chair finally gave way and like some blood-soaked prize fighter, Paul Bistacchi held aloft his free right hand.

Burning with the low cunning of revenge, Paul lowered his free hand back to where it had been bound to the chair and waited for his captor to return.

35

As Malton hurtled through the kitchen, his double-soled brogues slamming on cracked terracotta tiles, he saw stacks and stacks of packing boxes. Newly folded, freshly filled. Empty shelves and drawers hanging open, their contents already decanted into yet more boxes.

Hammering up the staircase, he could hear Dean shouting upstairs, calling out for Malton to hurry, that he couldn't hold on for much longer – whatever that meant.

Malton ran past the faded patches on walls where until very recently something had been hanging. Mirrors or paintings or family photographs. Whatever it was, they were no longer there. Someone was slowly emptying the house. Getting ready to leave.

Malton paused at the landing. It opened out into a large square of polished floorboards over which had been lain a threadbare Persian rug, the edges long since frayed white.

'I'm in the bedroom,' Dean shouted, his voice sounding urgent and strained.

Malton headed to the front of the house. Bursting into the bedroom he found Dean, his arms wrapped around the waist of a middle-aged man who was hanging from a thick nylon rope, which had been looped over the back of a cupboard door.

The man's face was a dark blue colour, bright white spit foaming around his lips. His eyes livid red and bloodshot.

'I can't hold him much longer,' implored Dean.

Malton was across the bed, reaching into his Barbour jacket and producing the steel hatchet. Brushing Dean aside, Malton took the weight of the hanging man with one arm while with his free arm he reached up and quickly cut through the rope holding him.

The man fell: a dead weight. Malton caught him and laid him across the bed, tugging loose the rope around his neck as he did so. He recognised him straight away – it was Adam Cornforth, Lewis's father.

'Is he dead? I saw him hanging. He was moving. I swear he was moving. I tried calling you but you didn't come and I couldn't keep holding him . . .'

Dean's words carried on in the background as Malton pushed down on Adam's chest with his giant, gnarled hands, urgently performing the compressions he hoped would bring him back to life.

Out of the corner of his eye, Malton saw Dean instinctively take out his phone before thinking the better of it and slipping it back into his trouser pocket. Malton smiled to himself – he could trust the boy.

But this wasn't looking good. Adam was lifeless. His flesh a deep shade of purple. His tongue limp in his mouth.

'What if he's dead?'

Malton didn't have an answer to that. He didn't like questions he couldn't answer. He always felt that if you were asking the question you should already have the answer. That was only good manners.

He stopped the compressions and stood up. Adam didn't move. Malton raised his right hand and without hesitation slapped him across the face with his open palm.

The force of the blow knocked the man halfway across the bed and, as his body spun like a rag doll, he let out a strangled cry before rolling off the end of the bed and landing on the floor on all fours. He started to heave in great lungfuls of air.

Dean ran over to him, bending down so he was level with his face. The man looked up into Dean's eyes and then past him to where Malton stood towering over him.

'The good news is: you're not dead,' said Malton.

36

Keisha watched Johnny toss the holdall full of guns onto the passenger seat of the van. She detected a definite spring in his step.

Johnny and Terry had been downstairs in Terry's basement workshop for nearly half an hour before they finally emerged. Meanwhile upstairs Keisha endured half an hour of increasingly hostile small talk with Terry's mother. The longer they were down in the basement the more Keisha had started to suspect something was up.

Ten minutes in she could hear animated voices coming from downstairs. Fifteen minutes in the laughter started and then it didn't stop until Terry and Johnny emerged back into the living room all smiles and with Johnny struggling to carry the bulging bag of guns that Terry had just sold him.

So great was Terry's newfound affection that he seemed to have completely forgotten about any problem he had with discussing firearms in front of his elderly mother. Going as far as to unzip the bag that Johnny was carrying and to eagerly pull out an AK47 in order to show off how he'd modified the firing pin.

Keisha was handed a second bag, which was a source of great amusement to everyone there when they discovered she could barely lift it. Johnny had not only managed to purchase a small armoury, he was also walking away with hundreds of rounds of ammunition.

It would seem being incredibly good-looking wasn't just an advantage in nightclubs and on Tinder. Even flinty, ex-army gunsmiths weren't completely immune to a pretty face. Once again Johnny Bistacchi had got away with it.

Unable to do anything else, Keisha was forced to join in the post-gun sale bonhomie that culminated in Terry's mother sending them on their way with a neatly wrapped tea loaf for the journey home.

The tea loaf was sat on the passenger seat of Keisha's car while up ahead the guns and ammunition were in Johnny's van. Johnny had driven off in the lead before Keisha had even started her car. He was returning the triumphant hero and was clearly eager to get home and boast to Maria about what a good job he'd done.

This was not what Keisha had in mind.

Nor was it what she had in mind when before her eyes a dark red van came speeding out of a side road, smashed into the side of Johnny's van, rammed it off the road, through a drystone wall and into a ditch.

Keisha slammed on her brakes, stopping 20 metres or so from the crash. Before she had a chance to even undo her seat belt two men in masks had leapt out of the red van and rushed to the driver's side of Johnny's van.

She watched in horror as the men tore open the door and a stunned Johnny tumbled out into the ditch.

The larger of the two masked men grabbed her brother-in-law and flung him in a fireman's lift over his shoulders while the second masked man dragged the holdall of guns and the smaller bag full of ammunition out of the van.

Unable to carry both the guns and ammunition together, the second man carried the guns to the red van where the larger man had slid open the back door and deposited Johnny's semi-conscious body. The larger man took the bag of guns and threw it in the back before leaving the smaller man to zip-tie Johnny's arms and legs while he went to retrieve the ammunition.

All of this happened in under a minute. They were clearly professionals.

The larger man looked up to where Keisha's car had come to a halt.

She saw him reach into the back of his waistband. She didn't need a second warning. As she pulled her car into reverse the man raised his gun and fired. The bullet went through her windscreen and lodged in the passenger head-rest.

Keisha kept her cool. Checking her rear-view mirror she saw the road behind her was empty. She put her foot down and her car reversed away at speed.

The man loosed a second shot but by then she was pulling into a full U-turn. Her car swung round one hundred and eighty degrees and the bullet sailed past. She slammed into first gear and accelerated away.

In her rear-view mirror she saw the man consider a third shot, think the better of it and jump into the back of the red van, pulling the door shut behind him.

Keisha didn't wait to see if they would follow her. She crunched through her gears and was nudging seventy as she drove over the top of the Peak District and back towards Oldham, taking care to go the most twisty, unlikely route she could think of and stopping only briefly to throw the tea loaf into a field of semi-curious sheep.

This was exactly what Keisha told Maria would happen. Danny Mitchum had made his move. But he'd made one fatal mistake. He'd gone for Johnny, not Keisha. Clearly he didn't think she was the threat. People had been making that mistake her entire life.

Most of them were dead now.

37

One of the last traces of family life in the Cornforth household was the fridge. Its entire surface was covered in photographs. Starting at the bottom with shots of a young Lewis
Cornforth at Disneyland, beaming to the camera as he posed
alongside Mickey Mouse. Here was Lewis proudly holding
up his first Scout badge. Further up the fridge and Lewis
grew older – a teenager before a dance, reluctantly photo-
graphed in front of his parents' house in a badly fitting dinner suit. And here he was in a circle of friends, surrounded
by beer cans and laughing at the camera – drunk and young
and happy. Towards the top of the fridge there was a photograph of Lewis, his parents either side of him. All three of
them at ease in each other's company. Three adults with a
lifetime of shared memories.

Lewis's father sat crying into the cup of tea Dean had
made him. It'd taken a while to locate cups and a kettle. As
Dean searched the stacks of boxes it became clear that entire
drawers had simply been emptied into the boxes, stopping
only when the box was full. Clothes mixed with crockery,
old magazines, out-of-date tablets and tins of food. An entire
lifetime of possessions jumbled beyond coherence and held
together with packing tape.

Finally he'd found a couple of mugs in the sink along with
the evidence of last night's meal. Beans on toast and two plates.

Malton looked through the wallet he'd taken from the
man's pocket. The picture of innocence he asked, 'Adam
Cornforth? You Lewis Cornforth's dad?'

'Who called the police?' asked Adam, looking up tearfully.

'No one called the police,' said Malton.

Adam looked confused. 'How did you know to come and rescue me?'

Malton smiled. 'We didn't. It was pure dumb luck.'

Adam processed this for a moment. A smile broke across his face. 'Pure dumb luck? It was pure dumb luck.' He was laughing now. His red eyes tearing up with the humour of it. He turned on Dean, shaking with laughter. 'It was pure dumb luck! I was due some of that!'

Dean started to laugh along nervously. Malton kept quiet. Adam shook his head and took another sip of his tea.

'You can never find a policeman when you need one and when you're trying to top yourself you get two dropping by unannounced.'

'Oh we're not police,' said Malton.

Adam stopped laughing. The manic joy drained from his face.

Malton crossed the kitchen and took a seat opposite Adam at the sturdy wooden table that dominated the room.

It was a big kitchen. Even with everything removed and stuffed into boxes, Malton could feel a lifetime of family steeped into the plaster and tiles. The sound of laughter and argument and the day-to-day intimacy of family life. This was the kitchen table where Lewis Cornforth had eaten his meals, done his homework, drunk with his mates. This was where he'd grown from a little boy at Disneyland to a solid, young man. Right up until one night out drinking, by the dumbest of dumb luck, he'd bumped into Paul Bistacchi.

Even packed away in boxes it was clear what kind of family had lived here. A loving mess of lives intersecting, leaving their mark on each other. Malton thought back to his own kitchen. The clean lines and empty cupboards. Then he looked at Adam Cornforth, wretched in his grief for a murdered child. He couldn't help but feel like he was staring into his own future. A cruel warning – children make you weak.

Malton put the thought to the back of his mind. He was here on business.

'I didn't say I was the police. Did you?' Malton gestured towards Dean.

'No,' said Dean, gamely playing along.

Adam pushed his chair back and got to his feet. He started to back away.

'So if we're not police, who do you think we are?' said Malton. He had the man totally in his thrall. Soon there would be nothing he wouldn't tell him.

'I don't want any trouble,' pleaded Adam.

'I would,' said Malton. 'If a piece of work like Paul Bistacchi killed my boy and the police did nothing? I'd want trouble. I'd want the worst sort of trouble. And I'd go looking for it. Is that what you did, Adam?'

Adam looked from Dean to Malton and then back to Malton. He thought for a moment, turned and fled.

Malton watched him go. He was almost impressed. Adam Cornforth still had a little fight left in him.

'He's getting away,' he said casually to Dean who took a second to cotton on, before jumping out of his seat and running after him.

Malton stayed sitting at the table. From the hallway he heard the scuffle and Adam pleading. He heard Dean telling him that they weren't going to hurt him and they just had some questions. It didn't sound like Adam wanted to answer any questions. Malton heard Dean getting more and more out of breath. And then the sound of someone getting punched and Adam Cornforth falling quiet.

Malton looked over to the fridge. They looked like such a happy family. If this wasn't work, he'd almost feel bad for

Adam. But this was work and when Dean finally dragged a bloodied Adam back into the kitchen Malton rose from his chair and got ready to do what he did best.

'Sit,' he commanded.

Dean forced Adam down into the chair.

'Everything's packed up. Where are you going?' said Malton.

'Just kill me,' sobbed Adam.

'If you want to die, why pack up first?'

Adam hung his head. 'Just leave me be,' he said quietly.

'We're not here to kill you,' said Malton.

'Then beat me up or whatever it is you're here to do.'

Once again it struck Malton – just how deep and profound the death of a child was to the parent left behind. Lewis Cornforth died a year ago at the hands of Paul Bistacchi. Adam Cornforth had been dying ever since.

Malton spread his hands out on the table and finally got round to why they had come here in the first place. 'Paul Bistacchi's gone missing. We're here because we thought you might know something about that.'

Adam went quiet. Whether he was pleased or shocked or scared, he was so broken it was impossible to tell.

Very quietly he said, 'Fuck him.' He looked up. A spark had returned to his face. 'He killed my son. He ruined my life. I couldn't move on. My wife said we had to move on. How do you move on after that? Lewis is dead.'

Malton looked at the fridge. A tall, blonde woman was in every other photo. Good-looking too. Sam Cornforth had taken care of herself. He could imagine a woman like that having a second chance. Getting restless if her husband was determined to wallow in the past.

Malton looked back to Adam Cornforth. Poor, sad, broken Adam Cornforth. Nothing left but topping himself. And he couldn't even get that right.

'Where is your wife?' he asked.

For a moment Adam looked angry. 'Gone. She left. I've not seen her for months now. Said she couldn't handle it. *I've* got to handle it. Why does she get to walk away?'

It was clear to Malton she'd made the right choice.

Dean thought back to that second plate in the sink. If Adam hadn't seen his wife in months who was he eating with the night before?

'Out of curiosity,' said Malton, 'what did the police say about Lewis?'

Adam slumped back in his chair, utterly beaten. 'They said there wasn't enough evidence. It was a full bar and no one came forward. They said the CCTV wasn't on. My son was murdered and it's like I'm the only one who knows it happened.'

Malton reached into his coat and produced a thick wad of bills. He peeled a few off and left them on the table.

A look of disgust and anger came over Adam's face. 'You're paying me off? You think that makes it better?'

Malton kept cool. 'Don't be stupid. I don't carry that sort of money. This is for information. I had some questions. You answered my questions. I'm getting paid to ask. Only fair you get paid too.'

'I don't want your money,' said Adam firmly.

'Your money now,' said Malton, pushing the pile of notes across the table towards Adam.

They left Adam Cornforth alone at his dinner table, in his empty house, his life packed away in boxes.

Back in the car Malton asked Dean what he made of it all.

'I feel sorry for him. He's lost everything,' said Dean.

'And so has nothing to lose?' said Malton.

Dean looked unconvinced. 'Back when he did a runner, I didn't even hit him hard and he just folded. Like it was the first time in his life he'd ever been punched. Someone like that kidnapping Paul Bistacchi? It doesn't make sense.'

'Then who?'

Dean wished he knew. Something about that second plate was still bothering him. He couldn't put his finger on it so he kept his mouth shut. For now.

'Paul had just got away with murder. He'd have to have been feeling pretty untouchable. If the police aren't going to do you for murder, what do you do next?' asked Malton.

'Whatever you want,' said Dean.

Dean was right. Paul Bistacchi would never have put two and two together and realised he was being set up as the key to bringing down the entire Manchester underworld. He would have imagined he was untouchable. If he could kill a civilian and walk away from it, there was only one place left to go. Turning on his own.

When he'd met Keisha the night before, Malton was sure she was trying it on. Playing the damsel in distress in a way she knew would hook him in. But what if what she was saying was true? What if Paul Bistacchi had taken his shot? What if he really was planning to bring down Danny Mitchum?

More to the point, what if Danny Mitchum had found out before Paul had the chance?

38

Claire put down the phone. It had been Cody's mother Susannah on the line. She sounded distraught. Or drunk. In all likelihood a little of both. Susannah Harper was typical of the kind of parents Claire found herself dealing with. Young girls with absent fathers and traumatised mothers, alienated from education and railroaded into becoming parents themselves by a series of feckless men who wasted no time in moving on once the children arrived.

Susannah had four kids. Two of them were already in care. She'd managed to hang on to the two youngest: Cody and his brother Yaya. Claire had helped convince a judge that Susannah had grown as a person and that Cody and Yaya would be safe living with her. It was a decision she had questioned more than once since then.

Despite his home situation, Cody's brother Yaya had got his head down and thrived. Cody had gone the other way.

Claire had tried several times to talk to child services about Cody. How he had drifted into associating with gang members. That he had patchy attendance and dozens of red flags raised by his behaviour those rare times he was in school. She knew that there was no money or will to do anything about it, but if she didn't try then who else would?

Claire had barely got into the office that morning when Susannah called. Cody hadn't come home. That started a frantic day of phoning around, trying everywhere Claire could think of. Cody might be a belligerent thug who disrupted lessons and assaulted teachers, but he was still a child at her school and that meant she had to do everything she could to protect him.

She'd been so busy she'd hardly had time to worry about whether or not Craig Malton had discovered anything linking Marcus to the Bistacchis. She was in her element, doing the job she loved. Making a difference. She'd promised Susannah Harper that they'd find Cody together and she meant it.

Claire was about to start calling round her network of youth mentors when the knock on her office door made her heart freeze.

The young detective standing in her office doorway was clean-shaven and looked nearly as young as some of Claire's pupils. He even smelled of Lynx body spray. He would introduce himself as DC David Ward and go on to tell Claire that they had recovered a severed hand from a murder scene. A fatal shooting Claire had read about in the paper that morning. DNA had matched the hand to a name already on file – Cody Harper.

Claire sat numbly listening to the tale of horror. A woman dead from a gunshot wound. Cody's severed hand clutching the murder weapon – the rest of him missing presumed spirited away for torture, murder and disposal. As a headmistress she would occasionally find herself in these situations. But something about this coming so close on the heels of her meeting with Craig Malton made the hairs on her neck stand on end.

'Sorry to dump all this on you,' said DC Ward. He was a nervous talker. Constantly moving about in his chair. It was as if being sat in the head's office was bringing back unpleasant memories. 'You're down as the point of contact for the local authority? I understand the mother has issues?'

'She's doing her best,' said Claire. She sounded like she was scolding him. Which in a way she was. DC Ward was giving off the energy of a guilty child and so she was responding in kind as a stern, disapproving headmistress.

Cody and Yaya had bounced back and forth between Susannah and several foster parents. Somewhere along the way Claire had volunteered to put her name down as a point of contact. A way to lend a friendly face to the local authority who bore ultimate responsibility for the boys. Better her than a rotating carousel of care managers and social workers. She never imagined she'd be in a situation like this.

'We've kept the hand detail out of the press for obvious reasons. But now we've got the DNA result. If you could maybe . . . ?'

Claire knew what he was fishing for. He wanted her to be the one to break the news to Susannah. After everything Claire had done today she would now have to tell Susannah Harper her son was dead.

'You said you don't have a body. What if he's still alive?'

'Our gang team, the ones who deal with this sort of stuff, know that usually when someone goes missing like this, after a robbery . . . They'll be taken somewhere safe, tortured to death and the body dumped. The odds he's still alive, well, they're negligible.'

The exact same odds the doctors gave Claire.

'That's what you want me to tell his mother?' said Claire sternly.

'I think it'd be better coming from someone she trusts.'

They both knew that DC Ward was taking the easy way out in dumping this on Claire. She thought back to that morning when she told Susannah that she'd find her son. It was no comfort but in a way she *had* kept her promise.

Susannah's entire life had been one long running dispute with the police. For it to be them who came to her door to break the news about Cody would be too cruel. This was the final kindness Claire could do for Cody.

'OK. I think I've heard enough. Unless there's anything else to add?'

DC Ward looked panicked for a moment. Like whatever thought he'd just been entertaining had vanished from his head. 'Wait! There is one thing. Bit of a long shot though. We got one vehicle on CCTV, outside the café around the time we think it all went down. I know you've had your fair share of gang activity around the school. Maybe you might recognise something?'

Claire bristled at the suggestion her school was some kind of haven of criminality. The children she taught had it hard enough already without the world assuming the worst of them.

'If there is gang activity around the school then that sounds a lot like a police matter. The sort of thing someone like you should be out dealing with. Doesn't it?'

It was petty but Claire enjoyed seeing the detective start to blush.

'I'm sorry,' he stammered, fumbling with the photos he was about to pull out of his briefcase. They slipped from his hands and fell to the floor. DC Ward dropped to his knees, scrambling to pick them up.

He babbled nervously as he gathered up the photos, 'Thing is, there's something off with the plates. Someone's deliberately masked them. You can get special plates, totally illegal of course, the colour of the numbers and the background are just near enough that on cameras it appears blank. Like these.'

He stood up and placed a couple of blurry photos printed on A4 paper, in the black ink of an office printer. They showed a car parked outside of a café. It was true, the number plates appeared blank. But the make of the car was plain to see.

The car was an old Volvo. Or to be more accurate it was the Volvo Craig Malton was driving when he met Claire outside of the school yesterday evening.

39

It had been at least five minutes since the last brick had come through the front room window. From where she was crouched behind the upturned sofa, Keisha eyed the stretch of living room that would take her to the kitchen and the handgun Paul kept hidden inside the extractor fan above the oven. The floor was covered in broken glass and house bricks.

'Get the gun!' cried Maria as she cowered behind a bookcase on the other side of the room. At the sound of her voice another brick sailed through the already broken front window and slammed into the far wall – leaving a dent in the plasterboard.

Keisha looked over to where her mother-in-law was huddled cowering in fear. It wasn't much consolation seeing her like this, but it was definitely some. They'd been arguing when the first brick came sailing through the window. Keisha had returned home and broken the news that Johnny and the guns were gone. They were on their own. She tried to explain to Maria just how bad things were but the older woman wouldn't budge an inch. When Keisha offered to ask Malton to intercede with Danny Mitchum she'd point-blank refused. Keisha suspected Maria was taking a suicidally perverse pleasure in doing the exact opposite of what she was told.

A brick flew in and made contact with the 60-inch TV. From where she was crouched, Keisha heard Maria's anguished swearing and the sound of the giant television toppling off its stand and onto the carpet.

Johnny's frantic searching for Paul's hidden guns had already torn the place apart but now the hail of bricks had broken every window and was slowly smashing what was left of the place into smaller and smaller pieces.

Keisha risked a glance over the top of the sofa. She saw the jagged remains of the double glazing, and beyond to the bottom of the driveway where she made out at least two masked men – each clutching yet another brick – waiting for signs of movement.

She recognised them immediately as the two men who'd kidnapped Johnny.

'Still think you can take on Danny Mitchum?' hissed Keisha.

'Get in that kitchen and get the one fucking gun we do have,' growled Maria.

'After you,' said Keisha, defiantly.

Maria looked out from behind the bookcase to the driveway. Nothing. She raised herself up onto her feet, arthritic knees audibly cracking as she did so. She stole a glance across to the kitchen – just a few metres away – and then back to Keisha.

'You fucking . . .' Maria didn't get to finish her insult before a brick sailed through the window and clipped her on the shoulder, sending her sprawling to the floor with a shriek.

Maria lay on the carpet in amongst the glass and debris swearing loudly. Keisha could hear laughter coming from outside. She looked from Maria to the kitchen and back.

'Go!' screamed Maria.

Keisha thought for a moment and started shuffling the other way. Back along the sofa towards the hallway.

'Where the fuck are you going?' demanded Maria.

Keisha looked around. She was just a few feet from the stairs and the chance to run up to the back bedroom, squeeze out of the window and jump onto the conservatory roof and down into the garden. Then over the back wall and out into the scrubland beyond the back of the house. If these were Danny Mitchum's goons hurling bricks at the house, Keisha wasn't keen to be around when they got bored and finally decided to storm the place. Maria was the one who wanted to antagonise the most dangerous man in the North of England. This was her fight.

'Don't you dare leave me,' cried Maria, still lying on the floor half-stunned and surrounded by glass.

Keisha started crawling with purpose towards the hallway. There was a metre or so gap between the end of the sofa and the hallway. The floor was covered in glass and broken ceramic from where a brick had smashed into the display cabinet filled with Maria's mail-order china. Keisha could see a triangular shard of Princess Diana's face lying on the soft pile carpet. At least it wasn't all bad.

With her one good arm Maria started to crawl across the front room floor, hauling herself through the broken glass. 'Get back here!'

It seemed like the bricks had stopped coming. Keisha got ready to run. She counted down in her head.

Three.

Two.

One.

There was a knock at the door.

'Now we're both fucked!' shouted Maria gleefully.

'Is anyone home?'

Keisha froze. 'Craig?'

'So you are home,' said Malton from the other side of the front door. 'Can I come in?'

'What happened to the guys with the bricks?'

'They ran off when they saw us,' said Malton.

Very, very slowly Keisha got to her feet. No bricks came hurtling towards her. Through the broken windows all she saw was Malton's Volvo and the skinny lad she'd met at his office. He was standing next to a half-full wheelbarrow of house bricks.

She opened the door to a grim-faced Malton and threw her arms around him.

'What the fuck are we paying you for?' Maria had hauled herself up and joined Keisha in the hallway. She was clutching her bloody shoulder and looking ready to kill someone.

'To find Paul,' said Malton.

'I'll do your job for you. Danny Mitchum's got him. Same as he's got Johnny,' said Maria. 'And you're going to get them back.'

40

It was Malton's decision to go to Moss Side. It was Keisha's decision to go to the Silver Spoon. The Silver Spoon was an old-school Caribbean takeaway. It reminded Malton of his days back in Moss Side. Back when, despite all its problems, it felt almost like home.

The Silver Spoon was simple and clean. It wasn't trying to appeal to anyone who didn't already know. It was a black place. A place where the occasional curious white face would be met with polite indifference and sent on their way with some of the best food they'd ever eaten. Malton didn't feel any more at home here than he did in Didsbury.

He watched as Keisha flirted with the man behind the counter and swapped gossip with the middle-aged woman manning the kitchen. He couldn't tell if Keisha knew them or this was the first time they'd ever met.

She had seemed genuinely shaken by the attack on the Bistacchi house. Rightly so. The house was wrecked. It was unthinkable a few days ago that anyone would dare drive down Paul Bistacchi's cul-de-sac and lay siege to his home. But now Paul was out of the picture it seemed anything was possible.

Malton had suggested a drive and Keisha jumped at the chance. He'd left Dean to help Maria with the clean-up.

Two trays of hot rice and chicken slid across the counter along with a single paper napkin folded round a white plastic fork. Keisha paid and they left the warm, inviting smells of the Silver Spoon to take a walk around Moss Side.

Eating as they walked, they drifted towards the missing heart of Moss Side: where Maine Road stadium had once stood. It was now a puzzling collection of new-build homes. All stuffed slightly too close together.

Keisha was managing to talk and shovel food in her mouth at the same time. Malton contented himself to simply listen and enjoy the rich, satisfying heat of his jerk chicken.

'Can you believe they knocked down Maine Road for this? Look at this place?'

Keisha waved a greasy plastic fork towards the nearest house. It was squat and covered in white render, at odds with the red-brick terraces that made up the rest of Moss Side.

'Fucking criminal is what it is.'

It seemed Keisha was already moving on from the attack on her home a few hours earlier.

'You miss this place?' she asked.

'No.' Malton didn't even have to think. There were hundreds of reasons he loved Moss Side but that didn't mean it hadn't been time to move on.

'I guess if you did you wouldn't have just walked out on everything. On me.'

Malton didn't respond.

'It was never as bad as they said it was,' said Keisha. 'Moss Side. Manchester's South Central LA? Course it was never like that. Just white people looking in and seeing a few too many black faces. And now they're tarting up terraces, building new homes and flats. Still Moss Side. Same people. Same landlords. Same everything. This place never changes.'

Malton couldn't argue with that. The more they tried to change Moss Side the more it reminded you exactly what kind of a place it was.

The sun was going down. As they walked on to Claremont Road they got a view all the way down towards Princess Parkway. The sun rested just at the line of the rooftops, painting the terraces in a radiant, golden glow. For just a moment Moss Side looked a little bit like heaven.

'You've got to have a word with Danny Mitchum,' said Keisha.

Malton knew this was coming.

'You heard what I told Maria. You hired me to find Paul. That's what I'm doing.'

'You were there – you saw what he did to the house. And what if it was Danny Mitchum who took Paul? You thought about that?'

Malton had thought about it. A lot. It annoyed him that he still didn't have a clear answer.

'I'm looking into things,' was the best he could do.

Keisha flared up. 'Really? Cos it looks like you don't have anything to suggest Danny Mitchum isn't suspect number one. He kidnapped Johnny for fuck's sake. I saw it happen. And then they attacked the house. If you hadn't showed up I'd be dead. Or worse.'

For just a moment Keisha seemed genuinely rattled. Malton wasn't used to seeing her like this.

'You don't know it was him,' he said.

'Who the fuck else?'

Without any adequate answers to give, Malton wanted to end this particular line of questioning and so he threw Keisha a bone.

'I got a witness. Someone who saw Paul getting kidnapped.'

Keisha fell silent. She stopped eating. 'Who?'

'You know I'm not going to tell you that.'

'What did they see?'

'Enough. They gave me a number plate,' said Malton.

'You didn't tell me any of this.'

Malton instantly regretted telling Keisha anything. He had wanted to give her some small crumb of reassurance. Instead he had simply provoked a dozen new questions, none of which he had answers for.

'Because I didn't need to tell you,' said Malton.

'Whose plate was it?'

Malton ignored Keisha's question and headed down a back alley away from the city centre and towards where the old bus depot used to be. Keisha trotted after him, pausing to throw what was left of her food into one of the large, communal bins that dotted the back alleys, overflowing with rubbish and attracting fly tippers.

'My contacts tell me the plate was from a car stolen a few weeks ago. It's a dead end,' he said truthfully. What he was hiding behind that truth wasn't for Keisha to know.

'So go after Danny Mitchum. What else *can* you do?' There was an edge of desperation to her voice.

There were dozens of things Malton would rather do than put himself in Danny Mitchum's sights. Not least because he had yet to hear back from him about the robbery at Lorraine's. However you cut it, the robbery was partially Malton's fault. He was being paid to run the drop house and it'd been robbed. That was on him. As long as he had Cody tucked away he had a bit of red meat to throw Danny. But Malton knew the sooner he handed Cody over the sooner Danny Mitchum would be done with Cody and move on to him.

'I can't play both sides,' said Malton.

Keisha laughed out loud. 'That's not what I heard.'

Malton shot Keisha a look. She just smiled, shrugged innocently and kept walking. It was starting to annoy him how easily she got under his skin.

They stepped out of the back alley and stopped. It was Lorraine's café. Alongside the police incident board were floral tributes. Dozens and dozens of them lining the road and blocking the pavement.

Keisha frowned. 'I heard about this. Robbery, nasty stuff. You remember this place back in the day?'

Malton walked over and began examining the flowers. There were so many. As well as notes and individual flowers there were huge floral tributes, several in the blue and white of Manchester City. Kneeling down Malton read a few of the cards and realised he recognised the names of several former City players. Players from decades ago back in the heyday of Lorraine's café. They remembered her. Malton was briefly touched before he recalled the desperate state he had found Lorraine in on his return to Manchester.

These millionaire footballers sprung a few hundred quid for flowers when she was dead. Malton was the only one who bothered to look out for her when she was alive.

But they weren't alone. There were dozens of smaller bunches. Many of them obviously handpicked from nearby Alexandra Park. And with them the notes. Scrawled on scrap paper or graffitied straight onto the shop window. An outpouring of love.

Lorraine never had any family of her own. She was drawn to lost causes. People like Malton. Lorraine's wasn't just a café. It was a lifeline.

Every Christmas Day she'd open up and feed a dozen local families. She'd invited Malton these past few years. Malton had thanked her, given her an extra grand and stayed home. Part of him wanted to imagine that he was the only waif and stray Lorraine had ever paid attention to. Knowing that she had enough love to share around made his memories of her feel somehow less special.

Malton thought about Cody, huddled in the storage unit out back of Malton Security. Whether he would turn up alive and well wasn't up to him. Danny Mitchum still needed to even the score card.

'Told you. This place never changes,' said Keisha. 'Neither do the people.'

Malton looked up to see Keisha stood beside him, examining the floral tributes as she spoke.

'You're the only person who ever made me feel safe. That's why I came to you about Paul. Why I called you the other night. You think I'm tough? I'm not tough. No one's really tough. We're all just terrified and doing our best not to show it. When you're around . . . I feel like I can drop the act. Just for a while.'

Malton had tried so hard not to let Keisha in. He'd promised Emily her family. He'd focused on the job: finding Paul Bistacchi. He'd kept on asking after Leon Walker. He'd done paperwork, lifted weights. Anything to keep his mind busy because the moment he stopped moving all he could think about was the girl he walked out on all those years back.

The moment Keisha was in his head, it was like driving in heavy fog. Everything became indistinct. Vague shapes looming up. Clarity coming far too late to avoid the danger.

'So what are you going to do about Danny Mitchum?' she said, her voice switching straight back to business as if the preceding conversation had never happened.

Malton gladly followed her lead. 'I'm not going to help Maria Bistacchi get killed fighting Danny Mitchum. But I'll talk to him.'

It had been a mistake to do this. To risk revisiting the past without a clear plan. Now Keisha had manoeuvred him into confronting Danny Mitchum. She knew once he agreed to do something that was as good as a contract. Malton always followed through. Everyone knew that.

That was why later, when Malton received a phone call, after he had dropped Keisha safely back in Hattersley, he put Danny Mitchum, Leon Walker and Paul Bistacchi on the back-burner and headed off to make good on an entirely different promise.

41

Dean bounded up the steps to Leon Walker's daughter's flat, taking them two at a time. He'd been on his way home when he got the call. After spending nearly the whole day clearing bricks and debris from Paul Bistacchi's house he was just about ready to throw in the towel.

He was sure now Malton *was* fucking with him. Giving him just enough encouragement to get his hopes up before dashing them again with some humiliating piece of grunt work.

It didn't help that he was starving. Maria Bistacchi hadn't offered him anything to eat or drink all day. As soon as she realised Malton wasn't coming back, she had spent the time barking orders at Dean and reminding him that she was paying Malton, his boss, and so he had to do exactly what she told him to.

Dean occupied himself taking in everything he could about the Bistacchi house. Looking for any clue as to who it might be that had kidnapped Paul. Malton had given him the bare details of how the snatch had happened. Paul was taken from the driveway in front of the house by an attacker hiding down the back alley.

Looking out of the shattered front window Dean had a clear view of the street. That meant that if the Bistacchis didn't shut their curtains then anyone in the street could see everything going on inside. More than that, Dean couldn't help but notice the thick, metal gates on the drive. Whoever took Paul had got lucky with those gates being open. Unless they knew they would be open.

Vikki's call had come in while he was waiting for the bus. It had been brief and panicked. The dealer who Dean had met last night was in the flat demanding money. Dean had given her his card and mobile number but why had she called him? Didn't she have anyone else?

Whatever the reason, Dean had grabbed the nearest taxi and made his way over as fast as he could persuade the driver to go.

After arriving at Vikki's tower block he'd hurtled up the several flights of stairs to her flat, barely pausing for breath. Dean was so caught up that in his rush to get there, as he finally emerged on Vikki's floor, it dawned on him he hadn't given any thought as to what he'd do when he finally arrived.

The door to the flat was ajar and he could hear the sound of raised voices and of things being broken. Given how little there was of value in the flat, it couldn't be long before whoever was inside got tired of breaking worthless furniture and turned his attentions to Vikki.

Bursting in, Dean was confronted with carnage. Vikki was stood in the doorway to the bedroom, her arms and legs spread, blocking the doorway while she screamed at the boy who was taking great pleasure in destroying what little she had. It was the lad from the night before. The one who had stolen twenty pounds from Dean.

Both of them stopped what they were doing and turned to face Dean. Before he could say a word Vikki spoke.

'You're in for it now. Fuck him up!'

Dean had no idea he had made such a strong impression the other day. Maybe he *was* Malton Security material after all. Part of him was secretly flattered that whatever it was he'd said or did had given the idea that he was someone you'd call to 'fuck someone up'. A much larger part remembered the gun in the dealer's waistband and how meekly he'd opened his wallet to him on command.

From the sneer Vikki's order elicited, it was clear the dealer remembered Dean too.

'You got any more money for me?' The young lad put his hand on the butt of the gun sticking out of his trousers.

'You need to leave,' said Dean.

'Come on! Fuck him up!' screamed Vikki, gesturing impatiently.

'I've got this,' said Dean, not taking his eyes off the dealer.

'Really? You got this? How you got this?' The dealer pulled the gun out and Dean took a step back. He noticed out the corner of his eye the firearm had no effect on Vikki. She hadn't even flinched.

'Let's all just take a moment,' Dean said. He needed a moment. Enough time to think what Malton would do in this situation. Malton with his giant frame that could bench hundreds of kilograms. Malton who carried thousands in cash and a razor-sharp axe with him at all times.

Frantically Dean scanned the room for anything that would be a half-decent weapon against a gun. His eyes fell on what was behind one arm of the sofa: lying asleep there was Fury, the Staffordshire bull terrier.

'What is it you want?' said Dean, keeping his eyes locked on the dealer and hoping that he wouldn't notice that he'd started to slowly edge towards where the dog was sleeping.

'I want my money. Her dad owes me hundreds.'

'Her dad, not her,' said Dean. He was moving more quickly now, taking tiny sideways steps across the room.

'I'm getting my money. Or something else.' Dean watched the dealer smirk and look towards Leon Walker's daughter. It was obvious to everyone in the room what he meant.

Dean was only a foot or so away now. He'd moved half-way across the room unnoticed. It was now or never.

'You're leaving. NOW!' As he shouted Dean bent down and grabbed Fury's collar from behind, dragging the dog in front of him. The sleeping animal looked up curiously and half-smiled at the sight of Dean.

Dean dug his fingernails into Fury's neck as hard as he could, all the while making sure he was behind the dog, holding its collar as tightly as possible.

Fury erupted into loud barking. Suddenly Dean was holding on for dear life as the thickly muscled dog thrashed and writhed, desperately trying to turn around and bite its antagonist.

He prayed that what he'd been told about how to avoid getting savaged by a dog was true.

'You get out or I set him on you,' cried Dean.

The dealer went pale. Momentarily he seemed to forget the gun in his hand but as Fury's barking got louder and more angry he raised the firearm, aiming it at the dog with a shaking arm.

'I'll shoot him,' he threatened.

'You better kill him,' said Dean. 'Cos if you only wound him, he's going to eat your fucking face.'

The dealer took a step back.

'You got your shot lined up?' said Dean. He could feel his muscles burning. His entire body was clenched, every part of him straining to hold on to the dog's collar and stop it turning on him. As he did so he dug his nails deeper still, driving the animal to even greater heights of primal fury.

The dealer seemed to be having second thoughts. His eyes turned to the door and then back to Vikki.

'I'll be back,' he said unconvincingly before sticking his gun into his waistband and making for the door. Slowly at first and then once he had a few feet between him and Fury, he made a dash for the exit.

Dean heard his feet hammering down the stairs and away into the night.

Now all he had to worry about was getting torn to pieces by Fury. He'd stopped jabbing his nails into the animal's neck but it was still bucking wildly, threatening at any moment to shake free and turn on him.

'Calm him down!' he shouted to Vikki.

The girl took one look at Fury and rushed out the room, leaving Dean alone with the savage dog.

'Where are you going?'

'He needs something to eat!' came the voice from the kitchen.

Dean heard the sound of cupboards being rifled. Looking round the flat he wondered just how much food Leon Walker would have left in for his daughter.

'I'm sorry, I'm sorry!' Dean shouted at the dog to no effect.

Vikki came running back out clutching a box of cereal.

'Is that it?' said Dean.

'That's all I could find.'

Dean could feel his grip loosening. His arms were shot. His muscles played out.

Vikki emptied what was left of the box of cereal all over the carpet in front of Fury just as Dean felt his fingers begin to uncurl and slip from the collar.

Fury gave a final, ferocious tug and Dean's grip broke. He fell backwards into the wall and instinctively curled up, waiting for the attack.

A second passed. Then another. Then he heard laughter. Tentatively looking up, he saw Fury greedily hoovering cereal off the carpet while Vikki knelt down beside him, rubbing his side and laughing.

An immense wave of relief flooded over Dean. All he could do was join in, laughing at the utter absurdity of what just took place.

The two of them sat on the floor of the filthy flat, all their fear melting into uncontrollable, cathartic laughter.

When they finally stopped, something had changed about Leon Walker's daughter. It was like the laughter had finally shaken off the hardness she'd been forced to wrap herself in to survive. Under all the filth and bravado was still a sixteen-year-old girl.

'I've got something for you,' she said.

'It's OK,' said Dean. 'I just wanted to make sure you were safe.'

'You don't understand,' she said and headed into the bedroom.

Dean pulled himself together and stood up. He was getting ready to politely make his excuses when the girl emerged holding something the size of a cricket bat wrapped in a filthy towel. Dean knew straight away what it was.

She gently unwrapped the towel to reveal the shotgun she was holding.

'It's my dad's. You were asking about him. He came in late one night, a few weeks ago. He wouldn't speak to me; he just went straight to his room. He was only in there five minutes or so before he left. That was the last time I saw him.'

Dean marvelled at the shotgun held out in Vikki's hands. Was this the same gun that had been used on Malton's front door?

Vikki continued, 'I went in to see if he'd stashed anything. You know, money or drugs, drugs I could swap for food. I found this.' She offered the gun to Dean.

Gently Dean took it from her. It was the first firearm he'd ever held. The weight of it surprised him. Without thinking he broke the barrel in the same way he'd seen in countless films and computer games. To his surprise both barrels were loaded.

Vikki saw his shocked expression and smiled. She leaned in and took the shotgun off him, emptying out the two cartridges into her hand in a gesture it was clear she had performed more than once before.

Finally Dean felt like he'd arrived. He'd nearly tracked down Leon Walker, he'd scared off an armed drug dealer and protected a vulnerable (well sort of vulnerable) young girl. He was Malton Security material.

He just wished Malton knew about any of this.

While Dean helped Vikki clean up the worst of the damage she told him about the woman who'd given her dad the shotgun and exactly what had been going on in Leon Walker's flat.

42

Claire took a moment before she rang Susannah Harper's doorbell to tell her that her son was most likely dead. This wasn't the first time Claire had done this. As a head teacher there had been the occasional untimely death and she had found herself accompanying police to break the terrible news. But this was the first time she'd done it solo.

She tried not to think that just the other day she'd been speaking to the man she now suspected had killed Cody. The man she had asked to investigate her dead husband's connection to the criminal family who had killed him. The man whose car was captured outside the café where Cody's severed hand was found. She focused only on her anger. It was the same anger that led her to set up a food bank at the school. The anger that had seen her testify in court against abusive partners on behalf of the children she taught and fight child services tooth and nail to see the children in her care get what they needed.

Anger had its uses.

Claire took a last look around the road of already-scruffy new-build houses and rang the bell.

Instantly there was noise from inside. Shouting. She heard Susannah's voice and another voice with her. A man's. They were arguing whether to open the door.

Claire knocked this time and shouted, 'It's Claire Minshall. Cody and Yaya's head teacher?'

The shouting stopped and then a moment later the door was opened a crack and Susannah peered out through a black eye.

'What?' snapped Susannah. She was looking past Claire as if expecting someone else.

'Can I come in?' asked Claire.

'No,' said Susannah, her eyes were wild. Her brain clearly racing.

This wasn't how Claire had wanted to deliver the news. Cody could wait.

'Are you OK?' she asked.

'Who is it?' a voice called from inside.

Susannah turned back to answer, 'It's OK. It's not him.'

'Who's there? Do you need help?' said Claire, trying to see through the crack in the door and into the house beyond.

'He just beat the shit out of Kyle,' said Susannah, starting to get angry.

'Kyle?' asked Claire, confused.

'Yeah Kyle. My boyfriend,' said Susannah amazed that Claire wasn't keeping up. 'He just came in here and started smacking him around.'

'Who is "he"?' asked Claire.

'The black bloke. One who was here the other day repossessing my stuff,' said Susannah.

Claire got a sick feeling in her stomach. 'Did he have a scar?' she asked.

'Yes! That's him,' said Susannah relaxing a little and in doing so letting go of the door. It opened just a touch wider but Claire was still none the wiser.

'Did he hit you too?' Claire gestured towards Susannah's black eye.

Susannah looked away and didn't answer. That was all Claire needed to know – that whatever else Malton had done here, he wasn't the one responsible for Susannah's face.

The front door swung fully open and a man stood in the doorway next to Susannah. He was a mess. His mouth was swollen half-open to reveal missing teeth. Both his eyes were starting to bruise and close. From how he moved it was clear he was in a lot of pain.

'You know the black bastard that did this?' he said. His voice lisped through his busted mouth.

'Sorry who are you?' said Claire.

The man turned on Susannah. 'Didn't you fucking tell her?' He turned back to Claire. 'I'm her boyfriend Kyle. Who the fuck are you?'

Claire looked from Kyle's broken face to Susannah's black eye and decided it was time to take control of the situation. Ignoring Kyle, she focused on Susannah.

On any other day, whatever had gone on here would have been Claire's top priority. Nothing took precedence over knowing that the children in her care had a safe and secure home environment. But today was different.

She needed to deliver the news about Cody before getting dragged any further down this road.

Claire squared up and ignoring Kyle addressed Susannah. 'I've got bad news. About Cody. The police have found a hand.'

Susannah looked confused. 'What do you mean? Where? Whose hand?'

Claire held firm and continued, 'It's his hand. It was severed during what they think was a robbery gone wrong.'

'So where's the rest of him?' Susannah looked confused.

'The police don't know but they're working on the assumption . . .' Claire paused. Not for dramatic effect but to master the overwhelming sense of grief that she felt saying the words out loud. 'They're working on the assumption that he's dead.'

Claire watched as the unbearable truth began to solidify in Susannah's mind. Her son was gone. Susannah looked blank. Her eyes darted about, unable to settle. For a moment she almost grinned as if unsure what her face should be doing in response to her world ending.

'Fuck him,' said Kyle. 'What about me?'

For once in her life Susannah was numb to Kyle's reflexive self-pity. A thought hit her and dragged her back from the edge. 'But they don't know he's dead? You said they were working under the assumption. They don't *know*?'

'They haven't found a body so . . .'

'So he might be alive?'

'It's possible but . . .'

Claire could see the insidious tendrils of hope starting to worm their way into Susannah's heart. The stubborn refusal to accept the intolerable pain of loss. Before her eyes Susannah was retreating to her own, tiny, internal world of grief. A world where she could still believe there was a chance that Cody was alive.

'He'll come back. Forget about him. What are you going to do about the bloke who did this?' said Kyle.

Claire stiffened. She rearranged her face from sympathetic to stern.

'Firstly, I am not the police. I am Cody's headmistress and a named person in Cody and Yaya's care plan. Secondly, in both of those roles I'm going to be forced to report to the police my suspicion about the domestic violence taking place in the home of two of my pupils. And thirdly, despite what you seem to think, the most important thing here is that a child may well have lost his life. Your partner has lost a son; Yaya has lost a brother.'

Kyle was quiet for a moment. He looked annoyed. Then a thought hit him and a sneer came across his face. 'It was that little bastard Yaya did this to me. I saw him talking to that black guy. He did this. If you care so much about her fucking kids, you talk to him before you come round here having a go at me.'

Kyle pulled Susannah back inside and slammed the door behind him, leaving Claire alone on the doorstep.

Now it was clear why Yaya had that card. Malton had given it to him and promised to take care of the man who'd been beating his mum. Yaya had done exactly the same as Claire. He'd made a phone call and asked Malton to hurt someone. Part of Claire was glad to see the damage he'd done to Kyle. The irresistible thrill of seeing a bully get his comeuppance. But a bigger part of her returned to the anger. Kyle was a bully who used his fists to get what he wanted. So how was he any different to Craig Malton, the man who had killed Cody? And what would happen when Yaya returned home? When Malton wasn't there to protect him?

Somehow this man had wormed his way into the lives of not one but two of her pupils. He had dangled the carrot of easy violence and drawn them into his world. Just like he'd done with Claire.

Claire had spent her entire career teaching children right from wrong. Telling them that the only way to go through life was to play by the rules, to treat others as they wanted to be treated, to solve their problems with words and forgiveness.

If Malton got away with this then Claire's life's work was meaningless. She'd die and it would be like she had never even existed.

Walking back to her car Claire thought about her next move. She would be dead in the next six months but before that happened she swore to herself that she would make sure Craig Malton was behind bars.

She was about to get into her car when she saw exactly what she needed to make sure Craig Malton never hurt anyone ever again.

227

43

Paul Bistacchi watched in silence as the man in the balaclava let himself into the room. Paul kept his free arm by his side, ready for the moment the man got close enough to grab. He watched as the man wheeled in a hostess trolley piled with bandages and an assortment of half-used packets of pain medication.

There was something different about him. He seemed brisker. More sure of himself. He barely seemed to notice Paul.

Paul waited. He wasn't entirely clear how long he'd been in this room but he was fairly sure it was night-time. During the day he could hear traffic and the sounds of people nearby. He'd tried shouting but when he opened his mouth all he had the strength for was a voiceless rasp, and so he decided to save his energy. Now all he could hear was the occasional passing car but nothing more. A slow, suffocating silence.

But not for much longer.

Paul's legs had gone numb a few hours ago. He felt a little dizzy from the blood loss but that was more than made up for by the adrenaline pumping through his body at the thought of finally getting his one free hand on his captor.

But the man didn't come any closer. Instead he stood examining the contents of the trolley. Wordlessly, he picked up packets and rolls of bandages, tossing them back seemingly frustrated with what he found.

'You need to bandage my legs,' said Paul.

The man stopped what he was doing and looked over to Paul.

'You drilled holes in my fucking legs. I'm going to bleed to death.'

Paul couldn't be sure but it looked like beneath the mask the man was smiling. As if the thought of Paul Bistacchi bleeding out wasn't maybe the worst thing that could happen.

'You got bandages right? For me?'

The man looked down at the trolley as if he were seeing it for the first time.

'On your little hostess trolley? For me? At least give me some water? Please?'

It pained Paul to beg but the thought of the impending violence made the deceit bearable.

The man thought for a moment and picked up a bottle of water from the hostess trolley. He paused.

'That's it. Come over here. I can't do it myself, can I? You tied me up.'

Paul tried to see through the eyeholes in the man's mask. But in the darkness of the room it was impossible to see what was going on beneath.

'I just need water.' Paul's free hand clenched tightly. He shifted himself in his seat, getting ready. When the man got close enough he could throw his entire weight behind his grab. It wouldn't matter if he toppled over on the chair. As long as he had hold of the man, the rest would be simple. He'd make him untie him. Make him tell him who he was and why he was doing this. Then he'd just hurt him for the fun of it. Beat him. Ruin him. Break him into bits.

The masked man unscrewed the cap on the bottle of water, stayed exactly where he was and started to pour it out over the floor.

'What are you doing?'

Water cascaded onto the concrete floor until the bottle was empty. Then the masked man threw the empty bottle at Paul, upended the trolley and turned to leave.

Paul dropped the act.

'DON'T YOU FUCKING DARE WALK OUT ON ME, YOU DEAD FUCKING FUCK!'

Paul was ranting. So much so that he was gesturing with his free arm. Waving it in the air before he even realised what he'd done. At the sight of Paul's free arm the masked man took a step back, stumbling with shock.

'Get back here!'

But the man was already briskly sliding open the locks on the door. Not panicking but not loitering either.

'GET BACK HERE!'

The door shut and then Paul could hear the sound of locks being fixed.

'YOU GET BACK HERE!'

For the first time in his life the thought crossed Paul Bistacchi's mind – *I might die here.*

But before he could dwell on that thought he heard the sound of raised voices coming from outside. Two voices. One was a man's voice. He sounded broken, hoarse and tearful. It was the other voice that got his attention. It was shouting back, barking orders, running the show. It was that voice he recognised.

44

Malton felt physically sick. The unshakeable sense of distraction that he'd started to feel every time he thought about Keisha was one thing. But now he had the full-blown, bilious terror of having just watched himself almost lose control completely. Keisha had not just got under his skin, she was in his head. Pulling apart the carefully constructed defences upon which Malton relied to simply exist.

He parked up on his driveway. Daylight was going and the street lights shone through the trees that lined the road. Reaching across to the passenger seat, he heaved out the large bag of Chinese takeaway he had bought on the way home. He'd tell Emily he'd bought it to apologise for getting home late but he knew full well the reason he'd so massively overspent on Chinese food: he had just nearly beaten a man to death and was terrified she'd somehow know. The food was his unspoken atonement.

Letting himself in, he found Emily sat at the kitchen table working away on cake decorations.

The deliciously savoury smell of takeaway filled the room. Emily glanced up from what she was doing and looked apologetic. 'I didn't know when you were getting back so I already ate.'

'No room for a bit of chow mein?' said Malton, stacking tinfoil boxes up on the counter. He looked around the kitchen. It was only six months old and looked as clinically immaculate as it did the day they'd installed it. His mind went back to Adam Cornforth's kitchen. The lifetime of living it had taken to imbue it with the faded sense of the familiar. Dinner parties, birthdays, Sunday roasts and the everyday life of a family. How Lewis Cornforth's death had suddenly turned all of those good things into unbearable reminders of loss.

'Good news! We've got an appointment at the IVF clinic next week,' said Emily, looking up with a smile. She returned to her work, hunched over a cutting board, painstakingly carving decorations from icing.

Malton took a seat opposite Emily, clutching a carton of special fried rice and a fork. He was already shovelling it into his mouth as he sat down. Emily had seemed so happy the night before when he'd agreed to the IVF. He hadn't expected that things would start moving so quickly. He felt desperately unready.

Malton watched Emily work, her delicate hands cutting copperplate letters out of fondant icing.

He tried to ignore the aching in his knuckles. Before he'd got home he'd stopped by the office, bathed his torn-up hands with rubbing alcohol and wrapped bandages around the worst of the damage.

The damage was still obvious but it was better than the bloody mess that had been left by the time he'd stopped beating the boy's stepdad. He hoped Emily was too into her cake decorations to notice.

'You know your work?' said Emily without looking up.

'Mmmm,' said Malton, chewing on a mouthful of rice and king prawn while giving one hand an experimental flex beneath the table as he tested for broken bones.

Malton suddenly remembered Claire Minshall. He needed to let her know that there was no connection between her husband and the Bistacchis. Tell her that his death was simply bad luck. For all the comfort that would bring her.

'You know how you run doors and clubs?' asked Emily leadingly.

Malton stopped thinking about work and relaxed. This was going to be about favours. Favours were easy. Easy and safe.

'You know the new members' club that's opening in town tomorrow? Club Brass?'

'I've heard of it,' said Malton, putting his tray down and dropping his other hand, away from sight beneath the table.

'You're not going to make this easy, are you?' said Emily with mock outrage.

'You mean I'm not going to ask you if you would like me to get a couple of tickets to the opening of Club Brass?' said Malton with a calculated grin.

'Could you?'

'If you want them?' he teased.

'And could you come with me? Take the night off? Once the IVF starts I don't how I'll respond. I thought it'd be nice to have one last night out before it all gets underway.'

Malton started to work through all the plates he had spinning in his head. Trying to guess which one would require his attention most urgently.

'You need a night off,' said Emily.

Flexing his battered knuckles beneath the table, Malton couldn't disagree.

'I'll come but I can't stay late,' he said.

'I knew you could swing it! And, there's one more thing?'

Malton felt himself relaxing. He liked making Emily happy.

'Can you get four tickets? It's Greg and Lucy's anniversary tomorrow. It'd be awesome to go together? Have a double celebration?'

Malton would rather have had Emily to himself. Lucy, an old school friend, was harmless enough and it wasn't like

233

Malton couldn't play nice for an evening. Though he'd yet to meet Greg, he could imagine the sort. The thought made him shiver.

They both knew he could never say no to Emily.

'Four it is,' he said.

Malton stood up and walked behind where Emily sat. He was about to wrap his arms around her but then remembering the state of his hands he elected to simply hover at her back, looking down as she worked.

As he tried to focus on her delicate, soft fingers, cutting out letters from the sweet, white fondant icing Keisha's words from earlier that day came into his head – people never change.

His life was bathed in violence. His bloody knuckles bore witness to that. Violence had cost James, the one man he'd ever loved, his life. It had brought Keisha back into his world with increasingly dire consequences. He'd kept Emily safe up until now but with the IVF he would be bringing yet another innocent life into the crosshairs.

If he didn't change then something would have to give.

Emily was silent as she worked. When she was really concentrating she unselfconsciously stuck her tongue out the corner of her mouth. She was doing it now. Malton found it adorable. The thought of anything happening to her was overwhelming. It crowded out everything else.

He felt himself losing his grip on events. Danny Mitchum, Leon Walker, the whole lot of them. Malton would gladly put his body between Emily and the darkness. But what would happen to her and his as yet unconceived child if he were to falter, even for a moment?

'What you thinking?' said Emily, still clutching a piece of icing in the shape of a letter N in one hand, a fine, craft knife in the other.

'Just work,' said Malton.

He looked down at what Emily was doing. Several letters were already cut out and had been laid across her board. They spelled out O.N.E.L.A.S.T.C.H.A . . .

45

The gun that Paul had stashed in the house for emergencies sat on the kitchen table. This was definitely an emergency. Paul and Johnny were gone. Since the attack that morning every window of the house was now boarded up and Keisha was sitting across the table from her mother-in-law, neither of them able to go to sleep lest Danny Mitchum come back to finish the job.

Maria had a bottle of vodka and a carton of orange juice open in front of her. The harsh smell of the cheap spirit mixed with the sweetness of the juice. Her mother-in-law was halfway through the bottle and to Keisha's eyes seemed unchanged for it. At least if Danny Mitchum did make his move it would be a lot easier to slip out unnoticed past a half-cut Maria rather than stay and go down with the ship.

The house was silent except for the sound of Maria mixing her drink. Keisha could tell Maria was doing the same as her, straining to listen for any noises coming from outside. The sound of armed assassins creeping down the cul-de-sac or killers clambering over the garden wall.

At least she'd managed to convince Craig to speak to Danny Mitchum. Keisha didn't really care whether or not he'd be able to persuade Mitchum to back off. At this point it didn't really matter. Keisha was just about done. What did matter was that it'd be clear who put him up to it. If she could put the seed into Danny Mitchum's head that Craig Malton was now working for the Bistacchis, then Craig would be forced to take sides. Her side.

Without Paul around there was nothing to stop it happening. Even if Craig did eventually find Paul, things had moved on. The Bistacchis' illusion of control had been shown to be just that – nothing more than threats and intimidation. All it had taken was for the brothers to be lifted off the streets and the whole thing had fallen apart.

Keisha tried to figure out how it had all gone wrong. Johnny had been snatched on their way home. How could Danny Mitchum have known about the visit to the Squaddie? Her plans would have to change and fast.

Maria stiffened. 'Did you hear that?'

'Hear what?' asked Keisha.

'Shut up!' hissed Maria.

They both listened.

'It's nothing,' said Keisha at the same time as the sound came again. A heavy sound coming from the path that ran up the side of the house leading to the garden.

'You heard that,' whispered Maria, reaching for the gun.

Keisha had. Events had overtaken her. Whatever Craig would have said, didn't matter now. This was it. This was when she'd have to make the decision. Fight side by side with the Bistacchis or live to fight another day.

There was the noise again. A scraping sound. Like something heavy being dragged across the concrete slabs on the path.

'They're coming in the back way,' said Maria. After grabbing the gun off the table, she rushed across the room and pulled down the kitchen blinds before turning off the lights.

Keisha squinted in the dark and wondered if now was the time to make a run for it. Down the side of the house someone had started kicking at the back gate to the garden. It was always stiff and needed a swift boot to the bottom to get it open.

They both heard the gate swing open and slam into the side of the house.

As her eyes adjusted to the gloom, Keisha saw that Maria was clearing the table.

'Give me a hand,' Maria said and started dragging the table towards the back door.

That was it. There was nothing for it. Keisha was in. She bent down and helped Maria quietly tip the table over to form a makeshift barricade before grabbing a kitchen knife and joining her behind the upturned table.

Maria aimed her gun at the door. The back door was reinforced uPVC, built to withstand a police battering ram. Keisha wondered if it would be enough.

Maria was smiling. Whether it was the booze or plain craziness, Keisha wasn't sure. But whatever else Keisha thought of her mother-in-law, she couldn't deny that if it was going to come to a fight she'd rather be fighting with Maria than against her.

Neither woman was even breathing. Keisha could feel her heart beating. The adrenaline was starting to flow, not with fear but excitement. The knowledge that the talking was done. Now was the time for the violence to start.

Someone turned the handle of the back door. It was locked.

Maria levelled her gun on the door.

A new sound. A key. They had a key.

The lock turned and the door began to open. Maria's finger curved on the trigger as Keisha realised what was happening.

'NO!' she cried out as the door swung open and Maria opened fire.

The silhouette in the open doorway went down.

Keisha grabbed Maria's gun.

'What the fuck are you doing?' Maria said.

'They've got a key.'

Maria looked blank.

'They knew about the stiff back gate. They've got a key. It's not Danny Mitchum.'

'Then who is it?'

Keisha stood up. A body was lying prone in the back garden just beyond the back door. Keisha walked around the table and turned the light on.

The kitchen light flooded into the garden, illuminating it enough for both women to see the writhing, moaning shape of Johnny Bistacchi clutching the side of his head, blood pouring through his fingers.

Maria clambered over the table and strode into the garden. She looked down at her injured son. Next to him was a holdall, which had fallen open. It was full of guns.

Maria broke into a smile. She turned back to Keisha.

'Fuck Danny Mitchum,' she said.

46

Malton was standing wrapped up against the early morning Manchester air in a replica jeep coat lined with lambswool. Beside him Dean shivered in a thin anorak.

They stood side by side next to the small, demountable office that sat in the middle of the building site where Malton had arranged to meet Danny Mitchum.

When he had called Dean late last night, Malton didn't tell him why he was needed so early today. He had just told Dean to dress warm and be ready for anything. By now he knew he didn't have to tell Dean twice. Malton felt bad leaving Dean to clean up at the Bistacchis', but he was glad to see it hadn't put a dent in the lad's enthusiasm.

The site used to be a Chinese Cash and Carry on one of the busy arterial roads connecting Manchester with the hillside villages to the east. That was before it burned down. Now all that was left was a charred metal fence that ran around the perimeter, protecting what remained of the hardstanding. A large hoarding boasted about the two dozen new homes that were to be built on the site, and a couple of bright yellow earthmovers stood by, ready to make good on that promise. But now, at six in the morning, the site was empty. Occasional buses sailed past, carrying those unfortunate enough to have to be working at this hour, but no one took any notice of the two men waiting where the Cash and Carry had once stood.

Malton had parked up a few streets away and walked. It helped him collect his thoughts, feeling his feet in contact with the wet, litter-strewn pavements. This part of Manchester was all brownfield sites and industrial units. Half a mile up the road sat the new site of Smithfield Market, built at a time when no one could imagine anyone wanting to live this far east. But that was a long time ago and development had begun to creep out of the city centre. Now everywhere you looked building sites were springing up. Malton Security guarded most of them. That was how Malton knew no one would be turning up to work on the site of the former Cash and Carry for at least the next hour.

It was only a few hours since he'd promised Keisha he'd speak to Danny Mitchum. But it was more than enough time to start putting things together. Even though he knew from Benton that the car used to kidnap Paul Bistacchi had been stolen over in Liverpool, Malton had a good idea who had stolen it.

The car was only half the picture. Paul Bistacchi was close; he could feel it. The incestuous world of Manchester criminals was a small one. The nest had been poked and soon the rats would start emerging. But before that it was time to make peace with the rat king himself: Danny Mitchum.

Keisha had been desperate for him to talk to Danny. From what Keisha said Maria couldn't have cared less. Malton wasn't surprised that a woman like Maria was planning to move on Danny Mitchum herself. The Bistacchis came from that class of people for whom violence was simply another tool in the box. Nothing out of the ordinary and untainted by anything as cumbersome as morality. Malton knew that sort of person well. He was one of them.

He'd told Keisha in no uncertain terms – if he was talking to Danny she'd need to make sure Maria didn't do anything stupid. He was relying on Keisha to pass that message on and hoping against hope Maria Bistacchi had the good sense to listen. If she didn't, things would get very bad, very quickly. That was why he'd asked to meet Danny so early – get to him before Maria could.

Malton tried to tell himself that this was all business. He was working for both Keisha and Danny. Now their paths had crossed, for the sake of business, he needed to make sure there were no misunderstandings about where his loyalties lay. Malton's neutrality had kept him alive this long; he wasn't about to give it up now.

But deep down he knew there was more. Summoning Danny Mitchum at this hour, especially when Danny would still be mad about the drop house – it was a needless risk. He could have passed Keisha's message to Danny in any number of ways. Ways that didn't risk coming face to face with Danny's unpredictably violent temperament.

Malton was here because he needed to guarantee that Danny wouldn't make a move against the Bistacchis. Against Keisha. Whether it was loyalty or guilt or something else entirely, when Keisha had asked him to speak to Danny last night he knew that he would end up here. In harm's way.

He'd chosen this semi-public location because whatever else he was, Danny Mitchum was still the most terrifying man he'd ever met. Having his face burned off with industrial brick cleaner had only seemed to encourage him.

If Danny did move on the Bistacchis, Malton would be forced to pick a side. Either way, it'd be a bloodbath.

On the drive over, Malton sensed Dean was distracted, like he had something he wanted to get off his chest but wasn't sure the best way to go about it. Malton reasoned that whatever it was he wanted to say, if it was that important he'd have already said it. Anything else could wait until they'd met Danny and survived to tell the tale.

'Look lively. He's here.' Malton nudged Dean and indicated down a side road, past a railway arch, where the Man-City-blue Range Rover was picking up speed and heading their way.

Dean straightened up a little, put some steel into his eyes.

'Don't say a word. You're only here to make killing me more trouble than it's worth.'

Dean's face dropped as he processed what Malton just said. 'What?'

'Getting two unwilling people into the boot of a car is harder than one,' said Malton as Danny's Range Rover pulled into the remains of the Cash and Carry and stopped a few metres away from where the two of them stood.

A couple of bull-necked men got out of the front of the car, both of them dressed head to toe in black, Under Armour tracksuits and trainers. One of the rear doors opened and Stevie Mitchum unfolded himself out. It was too early for him to have bothered to squeeze into a suit and so instead he was dressed like his goons, in a tracksuit, over which he'd thrown a heavy, tweed overcoat. Malton silently winced at the overall effect. In his right hand Stevie was holding a white stick and seemed far more subdued than when Malton had seen him the other day. Back when he had demanded Malton hand over the boy who'd tried to rob the drop house.

Malton nodded. Stevie didn't nod back.

'Fuck you want, Malton?' came a voice from inside the Range Rover. Unmistakable North Manchester aggression mixed with a strange nasal echo, as if the person speaking was doing so from behind their hand.

'To see your beautiful face,' said Malton, cautiously.

Both the men in Under Armour tracksuits took a step forward. Stevie Mitchum glared. From inside the Range Rover came a wet, coughing sound. Danny Mitchum was laughing.

'You're a cunt, Malton. That's why I like you,' said the voice from inside the Range Rover.

'At least let's do this face to face – as it were.' Having broken the ice Malton decided to go all out. Hide his fear behind bravado.

There was a pause and then Danny Mitchum emerged from the back of the Range Rover. Stevie handed his son the white stick.

Malton kept his gaze on Danny but out of the corner of his eye he monitored Dean's reaction to what he saw.

The man who got out of the car was young and scrawny, mid-twenties at most. He was wearing a white and gold tracksuit. The tracksuit top was open to reveal a chest covered in tattoos. But Dean wasn't looking at Danny Mitchum's chest. He was looking at what was left of his face. Both eyes were gone. In their place – two sunken, flesh-covered sockets. Danny's nose was also gone and instead there was a dark, raw-looking hole in the centre of his face. His upper lip had melted away only to be reconstructed with skin from somewhere else on his body. It hung over his mouth, a miscoloured flap barely concealing his leering teeth and gums.

Malton was quietly impressed as Dean swallowed hard and kept his cool.

Danny ignored his dad and the white stick and walked without hesitation towards where Malton and Dean stood. The hardstanding was pitted and broken but Danny seemed to know instinctively where to put his feet so as not to fall. He stopped a few yards away from them.

'Before you say a word, can I just say . . .' Danny paused for dramatic effect before bursting into a foul grin. 'You owe me the little prick who shot Lorraine.'

Malton knew this was coming. Now he had to decide just how much Cody's life meant to him.

'Three years I had that drop house,' said Danny. 'That was you that set that up. Good bit of work. Poor fucking Lorraine. No more Christmas dinners for needy kids. Real tragedy. You ever try one of her breakfast rolls?'

Malton didn't reply. He knew Danny Mitchum was simply enjoying the sound of his own voice.

'Well?' said Danny, shaking the warmth out of his voice. 'You got him for me?'

'He's helping me with my inquiries,' said Malton firmly. 'You can have him when I'm done.'

Malton had already got everything he needed from Cody but he wouldn't be handing him over to Danny Mitchum unless he absolutely had to. As long as the boy was alive he had his uses.

Danny's jaw hung open with disbelief, the only tell on what was left of his face. 'Or I could just tell you to give him to me now.'

Malton knew if Danny did demand it, then there was nothing he could do about it.

'Where's Johnny Bistacchi?' Malton said, changing the subject.

'Why'd you want to know?' asked Danny.

'I heard you snatched him up.'

'Well I heard you and Keisha had got back together,' said Danny with a rictus grin. 'Now that Paul's out the picture.'

Behind Danny, Stevie and the two goons were leering provocatively. Malton ignored them.

'You heard wrong. I'm helping her find her husband.'

'Wait, so are you looking for Paul or are you looking for Johnny? I'm fucking confused.'

'Both,' said Malton.

'She's careless with her relatives that one. Good job you got out while you could.' Danny laughed. Behind him his dad and the goons laughed along.

If Danny Mitchum had had eyes, Malton would have sworn after he'd said this he was staring right at him. Waiting for a reaction. He got nothing.

'So you don't know where they are?' asked Malton.

'Not seen a fucking thing. And that's not why you asked me here. You said you wanted to talk about guns. So let's talk about guns. Wherever the fuck they are, the Bistacchis owe me a whole lot of them. Borrowed them. Never got them back. And I want them back. Now.'

'I've not got them.'

The men in Under Armour tracksuits started to look restless.

'You haven't? Or they haven't? You said you weren't back together with that mad bitch.'

'I'm not. I'm just the messenger. The Bistacchis haven't got your guns.'

Malton had no leverage. He had no proof of where the guns were or if they had even ever existed. All he had was Keisha's word and his own nerve. With no other cards to play he put his trust in both of them, held his ground and met Danny's eyeless stare.

'That makes it easier for me.' Danny laughed again.

'You're not to touch them,' said Malton.

Danny raised his hands up and feigned terror.

'I'm not to touch them?' mocked Danny. 'So you are working for the Bistacchis?'

'I'm finding Paul Bistacchi. And they're paying me. And if you kill them all then I don't get paid.'

Danny's ragged lips curled down into something approaching a frown.

'So give me my fucking guns,' he said, soaking every word with the violent intent Malton knew full well he could easily make good on.

Malton reached into his jacket and Dean watched as he pulled out that thick roll of notes and weighed it in his hand for a moment.

'I'll cover the guns. You back off the Bistacchis.'

'You cover the guns and you waive your fee for clearing up the drop shop and I'll think about it.'

In one swift movement Malton threw the entire roll in a high arc towards Danny Mitchum. Without hesitating, Danny's hand flew up and plucked the roll out of mid-air. He held his arm aloft clutching the roll of money like a victor holding his trophy.

Dean stifled a gasp.

'And I still want those guns back,' snarled Danny, stuffing the roll of notes into his tracksuit bottoms where it created an unseemly bulge.

'I'll see what I can do,' said Malton. 'And if you happen to come across Paul or Johnny Bistacchi, do let me know.'

Malton held his breath. He was as good as accusing Danny Mitchum of kidnapping one or both of the brothers, but he'd come this far. He couldn't leave without at least seeing how Danny would react to the charge. There was a sickening moment of silence. Malton became very aware of the intense cold coming up through the concrete of the hardstanding.

Then Danny Mitchum burst out laughing.

'You're a cheeky fucker you. That's why I like you,' he said. As he laughed, spit flew from his mouth and dripped down his chin.

Malton watched unmoved as shaking with mirth Danny wiped his face on his sleeve, turned and was about to head back to his car when a thought struck him. He spun back around to face Malton. He wasn't laughing anymore. His shattered face quite still.

'You're working for them, paying for their guns and doing their fucking errand-boy shit. Looks a fuck of a lot like you and the Bistacchis are in business together,' he said holding out his arms in a theatrical shrug.

'I told you, we're not,' said Malton, not moving a muscle.

Danny tilted his head to one side and scrunched up what was left of his face. 'Better hope not. Cos if those Bistacchi pricks even think of trying to fuck me over, I'm coming for your junkie Jew missus first.'

Before he could stop himself images of James's mutilated corpse flashed across Malton's mind and then just as quickly they were replaced with yet more horror – the vision of Emily, her delicate white body torn asunder with the most unimaginable brutality.

But his face betrayed none of this.

'Remember, Malton, I'm blind. Not a cunt.'

And with that Danny Mitchum was away.

A few minutes later in the car with Dean, Malton was still doing his best to choke down his fury. He was so angry that as they drove in silence back to the office he'd completely forgotten any curiosity he had as to what it was that Dean had to tell him.

Dean for his part was far too thrown by what he'd just seen to say a word of what he'd been told by Vikki Walker the night before.

And so he didn't tell Malton that he suspected Keisha Bistacchi, the woman who he'd just put his life on the line for, had been the one who paid Leon Walker to unload a shotgun into his front door.

47

'With proton beam therapy you're looking at fifty-fifty, maybe even better.'

Dr Rosenbaum was a short, kindly woman whose long grey hair was held back off her face with an Alice band. She delivered Claire her verdict in a softly upbeat American accent.

'What do you think?' she asked her patient as she sat back in her chair smiling.

Claire was dizzy. With everything that had been happening she'd nearly forgotten that she had this appointment. Because of the nature of her cancer she'd had an automatic referral to the proton beam department of the Christie Hospital and for the past ten minutes she'd been told that everything she believed about her illness was wrong.

'I know,' said Dr Rosenbaum. 'It's a lot to take in. And I'm sorry you had to wait so long to hear this. We're still kinda new here but we're swamped – just us and the unit down in London. I know you've had it hard recently, but you're lucky as hell to get cancer in Manchester.'

Claire didn't feel lucky. Yesterday everything had finally started to make sense. She had her reason to keep going. To bring down Craig Malton and die knowing that she protected her daughter and did the right thing. She'd felt noble.

But now this woman was telling her it was fifty-fifty. Or more. Suddenly nothing made sense.

'You're saying I might live?' asked Claire, barely daring to say the words out loud.

'Yes.' Dr Rosenbaum beamed. She couldn't stop smiling. 'We start with chemo to reduce the tumour and then proton beam to blast it without harming the surrounding tissue. It's not a promise, but it's a chance.'

Claire started shaking. Dr Rosenbaum reached out and held her hand.

'It's good news,' she reassured her.

But Claire wasn't thinking about chemotherapy or radiation treatment. She was thinking about the footage she had on her mobile phone. The footage she had been planning to use to bring down Craig Malton.

Seeing the state of Kyle's face had been the final straw. The thing that had shaken her to her senses. Kyle was a violent, manipulative abuser but even then, seeing what Malton had done to him turned Claire's stomach. Underneath all of Malton's steady words and cool charm he was no better than the people he brutalised. Claire couldn't believe that she'd been taken in.

She'd been leaving Susannah Harper's house when she saw the video doorbell across the street. After some sympathetic gossip with the homeowner about poor Sue Harper and her awful boyfriend, she'd obtained a copy of that evening's recording. The footage was now on her phone. Footage that clearly showed Malton going in to Susannah's house and emerging a few minutes later looking like Satan himself. Claire didn't know if it would be enough but she figured along with Kyle's evidence and the footage of Malton's car outside the café where Cody had vanished, it had to be something.

And if it wasn't enough, it wouldn't matter because Claire would be dead within the year. Or so she thought before Dr Rosenbaum had ruined everything.

Claire looked around the consulting room. It was brand new, like the rest of the proton beam department. Clean white walls, white furniture and no traces of the usual signs of a well-used hospital. No laminated signs from HR. No posters or piles of surplus medical kit. Just Dr Rosenbaum, her warm, enthusiastic smile and hope. Fifty-fifty. Maybe even better.

In that moment everything changed.

48

Malton woke early from a restless night of nagging dreams and, without disturbing Emily, slipped out of bed and into the box room that he used as a walk-in wardrobe.

He slept in tracksuit bottoms. They were casual enough to pass for sleepwear but meant that should he ever be surprised in his own bed he was just about dressed enough for whatever he would find waiting for him.

The walk-in wardrobe had been fitted with mirror-doored cupboards. It was a remnant from the previous owners but one that Malton was happy to retain. As austere as most of Malton's life was, clothes were a secret vice of his. Emily used to tease him that he took far longer than she did to get dressed when they were going out. She was only half-wrong.

It was still dark outside as Malton slid open a large, floor-to-ceiling mirrored door and took out his running kit. Grey technical fabrics designed to wick sweat away from the body. Shutting the door, he couldn't help but stop and feel a small sense of pride in his physique.

Despite being forty-six years old Malton was in great shape. While he had neither the time nor the inclination for the kind of diet and regime that would have given him a shredded definition, his torso spoke of a deeper, more abiding strength. A bone-deep hardness that didn't need to boast of its presence.

He could see the bullet holes, the stab wound, the places where bone had broken through skin and been reset.

Everything that he'd endured to get himself to this point – yet nothing could have prepared him for the last few days.

Leaving the house, he shivered in the morning cold, his breath a thick cloud of mist. Malton glanced back at the new front door. All trace of the attack was gone. He almost looked forward to when he could pour all his energies into tracking Leon Walker down. But right now Leon would have to wait.

Running through the wet, dark morning under the fading glow of sodium street lights, Malton tried to shake off a growing sense of dread.

His night had been filled with disturbing images. James's carved-up body. The crumbling flat in the Hulme Crescents where he had walked out on Keisha. Emily, as she was that first time he saw her. Over them all hovered Danny Mitchum like a psychotic angel of death.

Even now as he pushed his legs to their limit, heaving in great lungfuls of air to propel his squat body forward, he couldn't shake the feeling that something terrible was about to happen. It stalked his thoughts. Interrupted the cool, unemotional logic that was needed to parse the Gordian knot of the past few days' events.

Malton hurtled downhill, away from Didsbury village and towards the path that ran along the River Mersey. He had passed a couple of joggers already but upon seeing the intense focus of Malton's face and the masochistic pace he was setting himself, they refrained from issuing the usual 'hello' or 'good morning'.

He ran on alone along the river. It sat deep in a valley, civilisation rising up above it on either side. In the early morning its surface was obscured by dense mist. It felt to Malton like he was running into hell.

He broke cover from the river and emerged beside a giant blue glass pyramid, an unwanted corporate landmark that competed with the neglected Victorian viaduct to be the definitive sign that one had arrived in Stockport, one of Manchester's larger suburbs.

Malton stopped and bent double, sucking in the cold morning air. Running hadn't done a thing. It had simply baked in the night's confusion and distress. The weak Manchester sun told Malton that his time was running out.

Things were about take a turn for the violent and unless Malton could get his head together then there would be no telling who would be left standing when the dust cleared.

49

Dean woke up early to give his mum her birthday present only to find that she had already cooked him breakfast and left for work.

Ever since his dad had died just before his sixteenth birthday she'd been working three different care jobs. Driving from one end of Manchester to the other, changing beds, wiping bottoms, cooking meals and far too often providing the only human contact people would have all day.

Dean missed seeing his mum but it couldn't be helped. When Dad died everything had to change. Dean had to shape up. His mum had to sell their house and downsize to a two-bedroom flat. Dean had to get a job.

His mum hadn't wanted him to apply to Malton Security. She worried he'd get hurt. But when he'd come home and boasted that he'd saved the company over thirty thousand pounds she looked so proud. Her son was finally using his brain for once. Just because he was working for a security firm didn't mean he had to be out getting into trouble.

Then he'd met Danny Mitchum. He'd seen Malton's reaction to Danny. How even though he did his best not to show it, even a man like Malton was rattled.

Dean was no angel. He'd been a tearaway in his time. But by meeting Danny Mitchum, suddenly a whole new terrifying world had revealed itself. A world that scared Dean to his core.

He opened the oven and took out the still-warm breakfast of eggs on toast his mum always left for him. The kitchen was far smaller than their old house, but it was enough for the two of them.

He promised himself that he'd master his fear. He'd stick with Malton and he'd make himself so indispensable that in no time at all he'd be earning enough money to get him and his mum out of their tiny flat and let her quit the job that took up all her time and kept them apart.

He filled the sink with water and added a squirt of washing-up liquid. The heating in the flat was off to save money and Dean enjoyed plunging his hands into the warm water.

Scrubbing his plate clean, he thought about what he'd found out from Vikki. He added it to the list of things that didn't quite make sense. The gate being open when Paul Bistacchi was kidnapped. The second plate in the sink at Adam Cornforth's. On their own they didn't mean anything but together Dean felt like there was only one thing they could mean.

He had wanted to hold back from accusing Keisha before he had concrete proof. And then they'd met Danny Mitchum and it seemed like Malton had other things on his mind.

But the longer he left it, the more it felt like he had no choice. He needed to say something.

Unable to come to a conclusion, Dean headed off for work, but not before he wrapped a bow around the pair of knock-off Uggs and left them out on the worktop for his mum to discover when she came home for her lunch.

50

'So they just let you walk out of there?' Keisha asked for the third time.

Johnny looked up from his plate of fried breakfast. His head was still swaddled in the makeshift bandage Maria had wrapped round him the night before. The bandage on the side where Maria had shot off most of Johnny's ear was wet and red.

'He escaped,' repeated Maria, returning from the stove with yet more fried bread which she heaped lovingly onto Johnny's plate.

Keisha sipped her black coffee and tried to ignore the thick smell of fried food that had filled the kitchen. It had been a long time since Maria had made one of her signature fried breakfasts. Keisha had seen to that. Now here she was, stood at the stove just like the bad old days. She even had a cigarette in her mouth, the tobacco fumes mixing with the haze of hot fat.

'Tell me again,' said Keisha, 'how did you escape?'

'He's told you once; what do you want from him? He got out of there and got us our guns,' said Maria with maternal pride.

'That's another thing I don't get. The guns – are they all there?'

Johnny looked unsure what to say. He glanced at Maria expectantly.

'He got as many guns out as he could,' said Maria, spilling grease over the edge of the pan as she carelessly tossed more slices of bread in an unhealthy amount of hot fat.

'Back at the Squaddie's place, I saw the AK he sold you. Where's that?' drilled down Keisha.

'Fuck's sake,' snapped Maria. 'Where were you when he got kidnapped? Where was your black boyfriend?' she jabbed a spatula in Keisha's direction. Small drops of fat flew all over the kitchen table.

None of this made sense. Johnny would have trouble finding his way out of a mid-sized Wetherspoons. The idea that he could somehow escape Danny Mitchum beggared belief. That he could do it with a haul of firearms was beyond credibility.

After Maria had patched him up the night before, Keisha was keen to get as much information out of Johnny as possible. Who took him? Where did they hold him? What did he tell them? Did they have Paul? But Maria had stepped in and insisted that her little boy needed his rest.

With barely a word, Johnny was ushered up to bed and knocked out with painkillers. Maria was still dosing him.

'If he did escape from Danny Mitchum . . .' said Keisha.

'If? He's here now. He escaped. My boy outsmarted Danny Mitchum,' said Maria, putting an arm around Johnny's shoulder and hugging him with a reckless disregard for the still-wet bullet wound on the side of his head.

Keisha continued. 'OK, assume he did all of that. Then right now Danny Mitchum is coming for us. And what have we got? An injured Johnny and a bag of garbage.'

'They're all the guns I could find,' said Johnny, looking up from his breakfast. His voice was too loud. He was clearly having problems adjusting to only being able to hear out of one ear.

Maria hauled the bag off the floor and dropped it on the table, scattering crockery and condiments. She ripped the bag open.

'Is this garbage?' she said, holding up an ancient-looking revolver. 'This garbage?' She plucked out what looked to Keisha like a converted starting pistol. 'And ammunition too!' Maria dug a hand clad in long, acrylic nails into the bag and pulled out a fistful of bullets. To Keisha's eyes they were all different calibres and with no way of knowing if any of them fit the guns that were in the bag.

'All I'm saying is: what if Danny Mitchum let you escape? What if he let you escape with just enough guns to think you had a chance?'

'Why the fuck would he do that?' said Maria, casually waving around a dusty-looking sawn-off shotgun.

'Because he knew what you'd do next,' said Keisha accusingly.

'What we do next is hit that bastard and hit him hard,' gloated Maria, pointing the shotgun in Keisha's direction.

'Exactly,' said Keisha, pushing the shotgun barrels away from her.

'Exactly,' agreed Maria, totally missing the point. 'I've already put out the call. Everyone we've got.'

'Can't you see it's a trap?' said Keisha.

'Can't you see no one gives a shit what you think anymore?'

Maria reached over and with immense glee stubbed her cigarette out in Keisha's coffee cup.

'Paul Bistacchi means something round here. You never got that. You waltzed in and enjoyed it all but you never really understood. How could someone like you know what family really means? What loyalty means? Your lot didn't want you and neither do we.'

Keisha had wondered when that would come out. She was amazed the old woman had lasted this long.

'Then you're on your own,' said Keisha, rising from the table.

'When Paul gets back I'm telling him you walked out on his family,' warned Maria.

'That's not going to happen,' said Keisha. 'Because if Paul ever does get back, thanks to you, his entire family are going to have been murdered by Danny Mitchum.'

'Get the fuck out of my house,' spat Maria.

Keisha couldn't have been happier to oblige.

51

Claire had been waiting in the police station reception for nearly an hour now. Before that she'd spent a fruitless forty minutes attempting to phone her family liaison officer.

When it became clear that DC Moor wasn't going to be picking up Claire had decided to handle things in person and had gone to her nearest police station, which was Greenheys, tucked behind the Heineken brewery on the edge of Moss Side. It was an ugly, dated station with the staff inside looking as worn out as the building itself.

Claire had introduced herself as the headmistress of St Ambrose's and told the officer on the desk she had vital evidence concerning an assault.

When the expected immediacy failed to materialise Claire found herself sitting in the waiting room on a hard plastic chair alongside the station's regulars – the homeless and those who were legally obliged to register at the police station. Those on probation or licence who the police considered dangerous enough to need to know their whereabouts for at least twenty minutes each day but for whom limited resources would stretch no further.

The room stank of bleach and, beneath the bleach, vomit and urine. Everything that could be bolted down was bolted down. The place looked like it was on a war footing.

Claire did her best to ignore her surroundings and focus on why she was there. The video on her phone was damning. It showed Malton parking up and barging into Susannah Harper's house and five minutes later emerging wiping blood off himself. It was frightening. The Craig Malton in the video was very different to the cool, composed man who'd met her days earlier. This, Claire was sure, was the real Malton. An out-of-control thug who flattered himself with airs and graces.

Claire was angry with herself that she'd asked him to look into Marcus's connection to the Bistacchis. That she'd given him the car number plate and taken him at his word. But now she saw clearly who Craig Malton was and she was determined to do something about it.

Harder were the mental gymnastics required to unlearn the idea that she was already dead. Proton beam therapy had given her hope and hope was far trickier to deal with than despair. Despair made going up against a violent criminal seem like nothing. Hope made Claire tremble at the thought of what might happen if the police weren't interested in what she had to offer. Or worse still, they took it and bungled the job, letting Craig Malton know that she tried to bring him to justice and that she had failed in her attempt.

Watching as one by one the regulars were seen to and left, Claire started to wonder if maybe she was the odd one out. Was she the only person who thought any of this mattered?

On the other side of the waiting room two homeless men had started arguing. In a matter of seconds, they went from raised voices to fists. Two filthy bodies went to the floor, arms flying as blows failed to connect. Both men shrieking garbled threats as they rolled around the waiting room.

Claire shrunk away as half a dozen police in shirtsleeves poured out from behind the desk and dived on the brawl. They worked as one, effortlessly separating and subduing the men. It was mesmerising to watch.

'Claire Minshall?' Claire turned at the sound of her name and found herself staring up at a solid-looking policewoman.

'Yes,' said Claire.

The policewoman looked over to what was left of the fight and shook her head wearily.

'Sorry about that. Happens all the time. One of the perks of the job. My name's DS Benton. I hear you've got a video to show me?'

52

Malton was running out of ideas. He'd never felt like this before. He felt unprepared, unable to find a fixed point from which to marshal his thoughts. It felt like he was being dragged down into the darkness of his past and there was nothing he could do about it.

His morning run had left him no clearer as to a course of action and now he sat at his desk in his office at Malton Security, staring at the well-used Ordnance Survey Maps of Greater Manchester that had been patched together on the office wall, laying out the whole of the vast conurbation, road by road.

Malton knew it all. The invisible geography of the criminal city. The gang allegiances and unresolved grudges. The territories and turf wars. Faces current and long buried. The maps on the wall were covered in thousands of unmarked pins, each one a memory.

No matter how hard he stared at the maps they refused to give up any answers.

Since meeting Danny Mitchum the other day he'd been deliberately keeping busy, taking calls from various clubs and bars, the places who paid him to supply security. Legitimate businesses who treated him like one of their own. People who'd been to university and paid taxes. People who knew all the thousands of invisible rules that meant the world treated you like you belonged. Rules that no one had ever taken the time to teach Malton.

He'd always told himself he had something they never would. The one thing that let him do what he did so well. He wasn't scared.

He had houses and cars and nice clothes, but if he had to walk out on it all he wouldn't hesitate. He'd walked out on Keisha and made a new life in Merseyside and after James's death he'd left his life in Liverpool and returned home. The world hadn't ended.

But now he wasn't so sure. He thought of losing Emily and the family they hadn't even yet begun, of letting Keisha drag him into the dark chaos she surrounded herself with, Danny Mitchum's leering face and Leon Walker out there somewhere waiting to make his next move.

Suddenly Malton felt a lot like he had everything to lose.

His thoughts wandered over what he'd learned, what he suspected and what he knew for certain. Paul and Johnny Bistacchi were still missing, both kidnapped. Keisha seemed to be losing her grip on what was left of the Bistacchi family and Danny Mitchum still wanted his guns back. And then there was the teacher who'd called him out of the blue and ended up giving him that number plate. And of course there was the boy still locked up out back, missing a hand.

It felt like there was something he wasn't seeing. Something bigger that pulled all these random events together. Gave them shape and meaning. But whenever it felt like he was nearly there, suddenly he'd be dragged back to Danny Mitchum's threats, to Keisha's warnings and, with tragic inevitability, to vivid memories of James's bloody fate.

Malton had always done everything in his power to keep each part of his life neat and separate. Now all that work was for nothing. Every part of his world had begun to blur together. He could no longer see anything clearly.

He spread his hands out on the desktop. His knuckles were still raw from two days ago. He hadn't planned for things to go like they did. Before he knew what had happened he was in the house and smashing the man to pieces. Beating him harder than he'd beat anyone for years. This wasn't the carefully rationed violence that Malton prided himself on. This was something else.

As he'd felt his fists smashing against flesh and bone, the dull sense of unease he'd been feeling over the past couple of weeks had begun to work its way to the surface. The harder he'd beat the man the nearer he'd crept to some sort of clarity. Maybe if the boy hadn't come in and seen his handiwork he would have kept going. He would have reached some kind of resolution.

But the fear in the boy's voice had brought Malton to his senses. He had deluded himself to think he and the boy were from the same place but now he saw that he was alone.

Malton had always known getting close to people was a mistake. He hadn't left Keisha because of his burgeoning sexuality. He had left her because he loved her too much. A childhood of abandonment and neglect taught him that anyone you loved would leave you in the end. He was getting his punches in first.

Before he met James he had thrown himself into the world of gay sex clubs. In amongst the writhing bodies he'd found a kind of peace. An easy, safe intimacy; free from the risk of hurt. Back then he'd been able to see things so much more clearly.

But then James had come into his life and suddenly there it was again. That fatal weakness. Loving and needing someone so much that in no time at all he found himself terrified of losing them. He had lost James. In the worst way possible.

He stared hard at the map. A thousand pins representing a thousand stories. It finally hit him. They weren't a thousand stories. They were the same story told a thousand times.

He rose from his desk. It was clear to him now. He had been seduced by complexity, drawn in by ambiguity. He'd allowed events to assume an elaborate aura of mystery that they didn't deserve. Underneath all the posturing and half-truths this was simple, criminal thuggery. Something Malton understood completely.

He stripped off his jacket and lay down on the weights bench. He had all the pieces in front of him. Now all that was needed was just the right amount of exertion to pull those pieces together.

Malton wrapped his hands around the bar and began to lift.

53

Having arrived at Malton Security before his boss, Dean had decided to keep busy and get the warehouse up to date. There was something very meditative about the paperwork. It gave him time to weigh up what he'd learned from Vikki.

It also gave him a chance to stew on his cowardice. Malton had made it crystal clear that he saw potential in Dean. And when he finally had a way to reward that faith what did he do? He bottled it. He promised himself that the next time he saw Malton he'd just come out with it. Tell him about Keisha and Leon Walker, maybe even throw in his thoughts on the open gate and the dishes in Adam Cornforth's sink. To hell with the consequences.

Dean was logging property when his phone went off with a message from Malton asking him to come to his office right away.

Halfway across the car park, Dean paused by the low, locked container where – to his knowledge – Cody was still being held. For a moment he considered knocking on the container. He had a question for Cody. Something Leon Walker's daughter had said had rung a bell. Something that if it was true made things even worse.

As much as he wanted to talk to Cody he remembered how Malton had been when he first locked him in there. He'd sent Dean away and since then hadn't mentioned the boy. For all Dean knew Malton had handed him over to Danny Mitchum.

Malton looked up as Dean let himself into his office. It looked like Malton had been lifting. His shaved head glistened with sweat and the veins on his neck stood to attention, thick and vigorous.

Before Dean could say a word Malton launched in. 'I need you to head over to the Bistacchi house and keep an eye on Keisha. If she leaves I want you to follow her. Wherever she goes. And I don't want her to know you're watching. Keisha's a funny one. If she thinks that I think she needs my help she's likely to do something stupid. Just to try and prove me wrong. Do you have a car?'

'No.'

'But you can drive? It said on your job application you had to be able to drive.'

'I passed my test. I just didn't have the money for a car. Why I wanted the job.' Dean thought about his mum in their tiny flat. 'One of the reasons.'

Malton dug in his jacket and tossed something across the room to Dean. He caught the keys to Malton's Volvo mid-air.

'Borrow my car. Be careful. It's got more poke than you'd think and spare parts are a proper nightmare to find.' Malton made for the door.

'Where are you going?' asked Dean before he realised how it sounded.

'I've got to tell you where I'm going now?' Malton sounded different. Benton said he was from Moss Side. Now he sounded like it. He sounded serious.

'No, I, I, I . . .' stammered Dean.

'I'm going for an evening out with my partner and her friend and her friend's husband. To a very expensive, very exclusive club where I expect I shall be paying for everyone's drinks while I drink tonic water and hope that you're keeping Keisha Bistacchi out of trouble. Is that OK with you?'

The Moss Side edge had retreated but still something seemed different about Malton. The way he snapped. Like something inside had come a little too close to the surface.

'Yes,' stammered Dean. Malton flashed him a smile and disappeared, leaving Dean alone in his office.

Dean looked down at the car keys in his hand. He swore quietly to himself. The shock of Malton's outburst had thrown him and now not only had Malton just left without knowing that it was Keisha Bistacchi who'd set Leon Walker on him, but he'd ordered Dean to guard the very person he had wanted to warn him about.

He was wondering if he should run after Malton when the door to the office opened.

'Look . . .' said Dean, ready to tell Malton everything. But it wasn't Malton. Alfie came in carrying a box.

Dean was sure Malton knew it was Alfie who had been stealing from the storeroom, even if Dean hadn't named names. But Malton hadn't fired Alfie. And as far as Dean could tell, Alfie was still the same disagreeable Scouse prick he'd always been. Maybe he'd got lucky and caught Malton with too much on his plate. Dean hoped when all of this was over Alfie's name was still on a list somewhere.

'Where's the boss?' Alfie asked.

'He's gone,' said Dean ruefully.

'Shame. Just had a courier drop this off for him,' said Alfie, putting the box down on Malton's desk. He opened it up. Dean looked in the box. It was a beautiful cake iced with the message: *'ONE LAST CHANCE'.*

'One last chance? What the fuck does that mean?' Alfie said.

Dean didn't know. But he had a gut feeling this was bad. Like when Leon Walker's daughter had told him about how one night the woman in sunglasses who had started hanging round her dad's flat had invited over a boy she recognised.

He didn't go to her school but he was in a gang with some of her mates. A proper gang. His name was Cody. The woman had given him a gun.

The more Dean found out the less he understood how it all fit together. He didn't have a choice anymore. No matter how scared he was – Malton had to know.

54

When Malton was a teenager he'd sometimes walk into Manchester from Moss Side. For most of the people Malton knew back then, Manchester city centre may as well have been the moon. Leaving Moss Side was unheard of for anything other than football or being taken to Strangeways. So, Malton would walk along Princess Parkway alone, past abandoned terraces and scrubland. Past the spectre of the already crumbling Hulme Crescents and on into the city centre.

Back then Piccadilly Gardens was an unlovely pit of an open space. The dead centre of the city, filled with scruffy flower beds and rotten benches. It was where all the street drinkers of Manchester eventually found themselves. Back when there was money to pay for homeless shelters, they'd wake up late and wander into town clutching cans of special brew ready to spend the day drinking, begging, shouting and fighting. Making Piccadilly Gardens an eyesore. An embarrassment.

That was then. Thirty years later little had changed. The council had filled in the hole and thrown up some concrete civic furniture but decay always finds a way.

Walking through Piccadilly Gardens, Malton clocked four different youths selling spice. He spied a machete – its handle wrapped with masking tape – badly hidden beneath a dustbin. Two dozen rough sleepers approached anyone who looked halfway respectable, for the few quid it would cost to buy the spice that would make their night out on the streets almost bearable. A group of young African men sat at the feet of the statue of Queen Victoria. Dressed immaculately in market-stall jeans and jackets, box fresh trainers and newly minted fades. The water feature was broken again. Where there should have been leaping jets instead there were a few disappointing gurgles and a handful of filthy pigeons getting no less filthy for it.

In a few hours he had to meet Emily but first he was about to do something that felt like an act of desperation. As he walked through the late afternoon air he tried to put it out of his mind.

Danny Mitchum was right about one thing: to the outside world it looked uncomfortably like he was working for the Bistacchi family. Malton had spent his entire life avoiding taking sides and he wasn't going to start now. But Danny threatening Emily had told him one thing: the thought of Malton taking sides with the Bistacchis scared Danny enough for him to openly challenge Malton like that. It didn't make the threat any easier to live with.

Malton had spent the afternoon lifting ever heavier weights, pushing his body to its absolute limits. Still his head swam with thoughts of Emily and the terrible danger she was now in. All thanks to him. Nor was he any nearer to cutting through the maze of questions he still had about Paul Bistacchi. And he didn't have a clue where Leon Walker was hiding.

Malton felt his grip slipping.

He'd tried violence, he'd tried running, he'd tried lifting until his arms burned and his lungs screamed. None of it had helped clear his head. This was his last throw of the dice.

Malton pulled his Private White VC car coat tighter around himself and shivered a little in the late February air. He'd been home and changed for the evening into a soft-tailored, bespoke suit and a pair of very expensive split-toe Oxfords. He was massively overdressed for an evening with Emily and her friends but he wasn't dressing for them. He was dressing to try and convince himself that despite what he was about to do he was still a good person.

Heading up Oldham Street, he pulled out his phone. Half a dozen missed calls from Dean. Malton couldn't fault the lad's enthusiasm. Didn't mean he was going to call him back. Alongside all the calls from Dean there was a single missed call from a very familiar number. Intrigued, Malton dialled.

The phone rang as Malton passed the huddle of semi-reformed addicts outside the homeless support centre.

'Turn your phone on,' said Benton's voice on the other end of the line.

Malton always had time for Benton. For as long as Malton had known her Benton sounded like she had somewhere better to be. Whether it was arresting him for breaking and entering back in the day or these days when he needed the kind of favour that only a disgraced police officer can do for you. He took her harried hostility as a sign of genuine affection.

'You called?' said Malton.

'We've got a mutual friend,' said Benton.

'You know I don't do friends,' Malton replied.

He heard what sounded like someone screaming abuse at Benton's end of the call.

'Sounds like you've got company,' he said, teasingly.

'Oh nothing special. Just the rewarding life of a beat officer. Mental illness, relationship counselling and the occasional macing. You know. Police business.' Benton seemed to have a near limitless capacity for swallowing all the shit Greater Manchester Police fed her. Malton found it immensely endearing.

He swerved down a back alley to get out of the flow of pedestrians and afford a little privacy for his call. He picked his way around the litter and puddles as he talked.

274

'So who's my new friend?' asked Malton with genuine curiosity.

'Claire Minshall? Name ring a bell? I mean I know it does because she came into my station and told me she asked you to find Johnny Bistacchi,' said Benton.

'Really?' Malton was impressed. He hadn't credited Claire with the guts needed to fold herself into the mix like that. 'Did she tell you she asked me to look into her dead husband's connections with the Bistacchis?'

'She told me everything,' said Benton. 'What did you find?'

'Nothing.'

Maybe he'd need to move Claire Minshall up the running order. As soon as she knew her husband was innocent she'd quickly lose interest.

'Is that all?' asked Malton, pleased to be one step ahead of Benton.

'No. She had a video.'

In the background it now sounded like someone was barking. Malton heard Benton put her hand over the phone and shout something indecipherable before returning.

'Sorry about that. Apparently smoking spice *isn't* great for your mental health.'

'A video of what?' said Malton. He racked his brains as to what on earth he'd done that anyone could have on film.

'You leaving Susannah Harper's house couple of days ago? She says you duffed up Susannah's boyfriend.'

Malton stopped dead beneath an iron fire escape. He'd messed up and he knew it.

'And what did you do with this video?' he said almost as an aside.

'Funny thing, I asked her to give it me and she refused. Said she wanted to hold on to it. Just in case.'

Malton clenched his jaw. Right now this was the last thing he needed. It was a complication and what's worse, a complication that he'd caused. If he hadn't given his card to the boy. If he hadn't followed through and gone round. If he just hadn't got so carried away. If he'd called Claire and told her that her husband was in the clear. He had so many chances to avoid this and he'd blown through them all.

'You still there?' said Benton.

'Still here.'

'Well here's something to cheer you up. That number plate you gave me? The car that was nicked in Liverpool? We found it. Someone had burned it out. Second one this month.'

Malton's heart began to beat again. He quickened his pace and headed out of the warren of backstreets, emerging at the edge of the fashionable Northern Quarter with its tap rooms and coffee shops.

'What was the first?' said Malton.

'Car that ran over Claire Minshall's husband outside the hospital. Only that one had someone in the boot. A mate of Johnny Bistacchi. Small world.'

Malton had stopped breathing. Something was coming into focus.

'I've got to go,' he said and hung up. He couldn't stop smiling. He knew who had taken Paul Bistacchi.

But first he had to do the one thing that would cut through the noise in his head. The one thing left that he hoped would blow away the dust and let him bring this all to a conclusion.

Malton turned his phone off before putting it in his pocket and stopping in front of the discreet black doorway that opened onto a flight of stairs leading down to the Locker Room: the largest gay sauna in Manchester. Out of habit, Malton checked the coast was clear before ducking through the doorway and down into the depths.

55

The blood was flowing freely from the wounds in Paul Bistacchi's legs. Every agonised step he took he felt more of it leaking out, trickling down his legs. His faltering movements about the room in which he was trapped were made clear by the trail of crimson footprints he left in his wake. Movements that were becoming more and more lethargic and less and less coherent.

What was left of the chair was still lashed to his right hand with zip ties but with his free hand he had torn the chair to pieces – allowing himself finally to stand and walk about. So intently had he gone about this activity that only when, with a triumphant bending and snapping of metal, the chair finally fell away had he realised just how much it had cost him.

With every muscle in his body turned to the task he had neglected the caution that his injuries required. Blood had seeped out of the wounds, covering the chair and making his job even harder as his grip slid and slipped over the blood-slick metal. It was only when he stood in triumph that it hit him. He fell to one knee, his head light as if it had been suddenly inflated to several times its size. He staggered, his vision blurry, his heart rate slowing. His eyes closed for just a moment – long enough for his blood-starved body to blink into blackness and back again. Long enough to have momentarily forgotten he was bleeding to death in this strange room.

Getting back to his feet, Paul Bistacchi moved with an intensity of focus. Like a drunk putting one foot in front of the next, he gritted his teeth and struggled to keep the singular purpose at the front of his thoughts: escape.

He made for the tiny window. Dragging himself across the room, he took longer than he should have taken to realise that it was far too small for him to climb through and even if it were not, someone had screwed a long-rusted mesh of firm metal across the pane.

Turning away from the diffuse shafts of light coming through the glass, Paul screwed his eyes shut and counted to ten. A childhood trick that had stuck with him his entire life. Upon opening his eyes he saw that the light in the room had reset. He saw for the first time where he was and he saw the door through which his captor had come and gone.

A thin border of light framed the tatty wooden door. Partially painted years ago before whoever was doing the job realised the futility of their task and left it half done. There were three different locks on the door – each from a totally different time period. As the world became a less safe place new locks had been added. But best of all – it opened outwards.

For years Paul's father kept a small allotment where he used to go to escape the daily hell of Paul and his brother. On that 20-foot-by-10-foot patch he'd erected a shed. Built it himself. Paul remembered as a young boy being shown around the newly constructed shed – his dad immensely proud to tell him where he'd scavenged each different piece of wood: an unattended skip, a demolished public house, the building site on which he worked during the day. He'd shown Paul rows and rows of inset shelving and the small table where he had a gas stove and kettle ready to make cups of tea.

Paul lost interest as his father explained how he had built the door of the shed to open outwards, meaning that anyone who wanted to boot the door in would find it held firmly in place by the doorframe. The shed was, he boasted, virtually impossible to break into. In later years Paul had discovered this was indeed the case and rather than admit defeat had burned his elderly father's shed to the ground.

Woozy from blood loss, fatigue, hunger and fear, Paul found himself staring at a door just like the one on his dad's shed.

But now Paul was on the inside.

With an incoherent yell of defiance, Paul Bistacchi ran the short length of the room. With every step his legs threatened to buckle beneath him until they did and he fell, smashing his body into the door. Old, rusted hinges tore from soft, rotten wood and all the locks in the world made no difference as the door flew open and 18 stone of Paul Bistacchi tumbled through the broken doorframe, falling heavily onto wet grass.

The fall knocked the wind out of him. He lay on his back looking upwards at an early evening sun as it filtered through the tangled branches of a willow tree.

Squinting against the brightness, he hauled himself to his feet, oblivious to his surroundings. He took a step. Then another. Each one feeling like he couldn't possibly manage more. He could see the road now – parked cars, people.

Paul opened his mouth but it was dry. He tried to call but what came out sounded hollow and weak. The last of his energy was leaving his body. Finally the wounds in his legs overwhelmed him and first one then both legs folded beneath him. As he hit the brickwork of the driveway the pain caught up with him. He lay where he fell, gasping, barely alive.

The smell of wet moss rose up into his nostrils. His breathing became shallow as his body unclenched and poured itself into the ground.

The last thing he remembered before he passed out was the uncovered face of a man looking down at him. The face of the man who had kidnapped him.

56

Keisha was two cars ahead of Dean as they crawled through the traffic of Manchester city centre's inner ring road. Despite his best efforts, a minicab and an aggressively driven white Audi had managed to squeeze themselves between his car and Keisha's silver Mercedes. But with everything moving at a crawl Dean had managed to keep eyes on Keisha's car. If anything, the distance made Dean relax into his role of Keisha's unseen shadow. Malton's green Volvo 960 Estate was hardly difficult to spot. So much so that he wondered if Malton had deliberately sent him out in it. Was he there to be seen by Keisha? Was Malton sending a message?

Dean had driven as carefully as possible to the Bistacchi house. He'd not gone above fifty, even on the motorway out to their estate. But then as he was turning the nose of the Volvo into the narrow cul-de-sac where Keisha lived, he had been forced to jerk the steering wheel to one side and slam on the brakes as Keisha tore past him in her silver Mercedes.

Without time to worry whether or not he'd been made, Dean had to perform the tightest three-point turn of his life. After three points had ballooned to fifteen he finally turned the long estate car around without scratching it on any of the cars that were double parked either side of the cul-de-sac.

Racing back to the main road, he was lucky with the lights and saw Keisha far in the distance, pulling onto the M67 and heading towards town. Throwing caution to the wind, Dean put his foot down and was soon on her tail.

The interior of Malton's car smelled of lovingly polished leather. Dean breathed it in. It smelled like old money. Showy but not too showy. Obviously expensive but not flashy. Dozens of CDs littered every available pocket. Mainly hip-hop and mostly from the Eighties and Nineties. Dean chose to drive in silence. Driving Malton's car made him intensely anxious. Maybe that was why Malton had sent him? To keep him on edge. Dean reflected on how paranoid he felt about Malton's every intention. He wondered if that was the point of it all? Was Malton trying to teach him something? Get him to see the world five steps ahead like he did?

Dean still hadn't told Malton about Keisha's connection to Leon Walker, the man he suspected of shooting Malton's front door. Nor had he passed on the information that it was Keisha who gave Cody the gun used in the café robbery. Now he worried the moment had passed. If he was to tell Malton now, how would he explain the long delay between him discovering the possible connection with Leon Walker, and him finally getting round to telling his boss about it? He'd tried, but Malton hadn't answered any of his calls. Eventually Dean gave up, figuring that if Malton wasn't picking up, it was because he didn't want to speak. That made Dean feel better. If Malton asked he could, at least, point to his reasonable effort to fill him in.

Keisha hit the inner ring road and led Dean around Manchester. Dean wondered if she'd made him and was trying to lose him in the complexities of Manchester's city centre traffic flow. Just as they were about to drift into Salford, Keisha turned and, after cutting through the heart of the city, headed out east on Fairfield Road.

The line of traffic crawled slowly towards Piccadilly station, passing the grand Victorian building that was formerly home to the University of Manchester Institute of Science and Technology. When Dean was growing up the building dominated the approach to the station. Now it was matched on all sides by newly constructed flats and office blocks, all built within the last five years. This newfound prosperity filled Dean with a sense of optimism. His city shared his youthful confidence. Manchester was on the up and so was he.

As soon as the lights – which took traffic past the drop-off for Piccadilly station and out towards the brownfield debris of East Manchester – turned green, the car in front of Keisha's began to indicate a right-hand turn. Dean edged forward a few feet as the entire lane of traffic halted behind the car waiting to make the turn. With no filter light it was at the mercy of the heavy oncoming traffic.

'Come on . . . come on . . .' Dean muttered to himself. Keisha's car was still behind the line. As long as the light turned red before the car in front of hers made the turn then they'd all still be together.

The driver of the white Audi slammed on his horn, setting off a wave of horns from the backed-up traffic. Startled by the noise, the car making the right-hand turn pulled forward a few feet and made a token effort to pull to the side. The road was too narrow and the oncoming traffic too relentless to fully clear the lane but the sight of the few feet of clear road set off the horns once more.

Keisha's car didn't move; it hovered there, behind the line, as finally the lights faded from green to amber. The oncoming traffic sped up as drivers attempted to beat the light. The car making the right turn was forced to stay put, unable to risk getting T-boned by the cars who were now openly gunning to jump a red.

The light went red, and then to Dean's horror Keisha's silver Mercedes hauled to the left, bumped one wheel up on the pavement and, running the light, steered around the car that had been blocking the lane of traffic. As the cross traffic began to move, Keisha's car accelerated away, past Picca-dilly station towards Depot Mayfield and the warren of roads that lay beneath the railway arches.

Dean watched the silver Mercedes vanish eastwards before turning a sharp left and heading north towards Ancoats. He watched with agonised impatience as cars spilled across the junction, blocking his way, every second that the light stayed red another second that Keisha had put more distance between them.

Barely had the amber light come on than the white Audi hammered forward, aggressively chasing a straggler out of the junction and speeding off in the same direction as Keisha. As Dean was getting ready to follow, the minicab directly in front of him hit its indicator for a right-hand turn. Dean didn't hesitate. Following Keisha's lead, he bumped Malton's Volvo up onto the pavement. With the sickening scream of metal on metal he hit the pedestrian barrier and scraped round the minicab before flooring it in Keisha's direction.

Dean had only ever driven his driving instructor's Ford Fiesta. He'd never handled anything like a Volvo. He tore past the train station pushing fifty miles an hour and found himself having to brake in order not to swerve out into oncoming traffic as he threw the car into the left-hand turn down which Keisha had disappeared a few minutes earlier.

Dean gripped the wheel and pushed himself back into the soft leather seat as the Volvo hugged the road and turned into the darkness beneath a railway arch. No sooner had he made the corner than he had to hammer on the brake and bump to a stop up on the pavement. There was the silver Mercedes. A few hundred metres up ahead, just beyond the railway arch, in the fading daylight. Dean hoped the shadows would be enough to hide his presence. Had Keisha seen him? Was she waiting for him?

Suddenly a figure appeared out from the scrubby under-growth of a disused patch of land, rushed up to Keisha's car and grabbed the door handle.

Dean stared with disbelief as he watched the man he rec-ognised from outside Malton's house all those weeks ago. A man who until now had been a ghost to him: Leon Walker.

Walker jumped into the back of Keisha's car. Dean didn't have time to feel the satisfaction of seeing the final piece of the puzzle fall into place because, with a screech of tyres, the silver Mercedes took off behind Piccadilly station and back towards the city centre.

Dean put his foot down, the Volvo roared to life and he set off in pursuit.

57

Malton watched as the two men shook off the small white towels that had been covering up their naked bodies. With both of them now completely liberated, the larger of the two pulled the smaller one towards him, one hand behind his head as he put his tongue down his throat, the other hand sliding between his legs.

None of the other sauna-goers seemed fazed by the display taking place in the middle of one of the Locker Room's communal areas. The room was dark and lit with subtle red underlighting. Fitted seats stretched the length of two of the walls, padded and deep enough to accommodate writhing bodies.

In the middle of the room, pride of place, was a large, round, padded mattress, covered in a wipe-clean, PVC sheet.

Malton split his attention between the two men who were now lowering themselves onto the round mattress, and the various other patrons who wandered in and out by the room's two exits. It was a mixture of younger, more toned men and a decent number of more out of shape, older men.

One in particular caught his attention. Sat across the room from Malton was a man who was obviously a newbie. A soft, white-bodied, middle-aged man who sat tugging at his towel as if hoping it might cover just a little bit more of his unappealing body.

It was easy to tell the first-timers from the old hands. The ones who came all the time walked around without even a towel. Whether their body was gym fit or a middle-aged disaster, they seemed utterly unconcerned. The newbies tended to hover, arms folded over bare chests, clutching on to their towels for dear life.

They needn't have worried. Places like the Locker Room thrived on mutually assured discretion. Whether you were a seasoned regular or a nervous first-timer, what happened in the Locker Room, stayed in the Locker Room.

Malton couldn't stop thinking about Emily. He'd never discussed this part of his life with her but at the same time, he never treated his bisexuality as a licence to be unfaithful. But between Keisha's warnings and Danny Mitchum's threats, he needed to do something to shock himself out of this fog.

Malton used to come to places like this all the time. He'd strip off, fuck the first guy who caught his eye and head off. All inside of half an hour. It left him feeling refreshed and with a clarity that had fuelled his meteoric rise in the world of security.

He desperately hoped that somehow retracing his steps, reminding his body who he once was would provide the jolt his mind needed.

The two men had moved on in their courtship. The larger one had broken away, leaving the smaller waiting on the circular mattress while he went to the side of the room and fished a condom out of the large bowl of them, thoughtfully left by the management for just such an occasion.

On the other side of the room the Newbie's eyes were bulging out of his head as he watched the larger man return and with the smaller man's help, made an extravagant show of putting the condom on.

James had hated places like this. Malton had taken him once and felt hugely embarrassed as James spent the entire evening fully dressed and talking about the latest developments in *Coronation Street* with the middle-aged cleaner whose job it was to sporadically freshen the club up over the course of the evening.

The message was loud and clear. If Malton wanted James he'd have to commit. So that's exactly what he'd done.

The two men were going at it full tilt now. Both of them were in good shape, their bodies shaved and clipped to best show off their muscular definition. Malton watched their taut forms slide over each other as they noisily enjoyed each other's company.

The Newbie couldn't take his eyes off them. He had uncrossed his arms and now rested his hands in his lap, ineffectually covering up his obvious arousal at what was going on in front of him.

After James died Malton never thought about being in a relationship ever again. He hadn't gone back to the saunas either. With nothing left to lose, he doubled down on his work and built up Malton Security. He wanted to become so strong, so powerful that never again could anyone ever dare do what they did to James.

When he'd met Emily that was put to the test. Once again he had a weakness. The fear was still there but Malton was a different man to the man who lost James. By now he was an untouchable figure in the Manchester underworld. He told himself he could keep Emily safe against anything.

Then Leon Walker unloaded a shotgun into his front door. And Keisha Bistacchi came calling and with her came Danny Mitchum and all the hell he brought with him.

Everything about this felt wrong. The clarity Malton had hoped to find wasn't coming to him. He needed to go all the way.

Malton stood up and made his way around the circular mattress to where the Newbie was sitting. He sat down, provocatively close to him, making sure that their legs were touching. Malton's solid brown thigh against the Newbie's thin, white chicken leg.

The man wasn't Malton's type. He was short and soft. His flabby body folded in on itself and from the way he sat it was clear he felt a good deal of shame about it. But Malton wasn't here for fun. He was here as a last, desperate attempt to regain control.

He pressed his leg against the Newbie's and waited for the electric feeling that comes the first time you touch a stranger's skin. He felt nothing.

The man turned to Malton and gave a feeble smile before looking away, pretending to be engrossed in the noisy sex going on a few feet from them.

Malton reached out and took the man's hand. He put it on his own thigh. The man didn't stop him. His fingers pressed into the solid muscle and he let himself edge just a little closer.

Something was wrong. Malton felt the man's hand as a dead weight on him. All he could think about was the smell of office-stewed sweat coming off this stranger. The messy job he'd made of shaving his jowly chin that morning. His mind flashed back to Emily and he felt sick.

'I shouldn't be doing this,' said the man suddenly. 'I'm married. It's my anniversary,' he added. Immediately he realised how odd this sounded and smiled apologetically. His hand started to move up Malton's thigh.

Malton reached out and grabbed his wrist, pulling it away from him.

The man let out a little shriek of pain. Malton didn't let go.

'I'm sorry, I thought . . .' he said.

Malton held his hand in place for a moment as he tried to marshal his thoughts. He'd hoped this would be transactional. A purely physical connection. Enough to jump-start his head back into the game.

But all he could think of was Emily. He had told himself he was doing this for Emily, to think clearly about their future together, and now he realised how delusional that sounded.

'You're hurting me,' said the man, an edge of annoyance in his voice.

Malton let go of his wrist and the Newbie pulled it back, clutching it to his chest, unsure what his next move should be. He dared to snatch a glance over at Malton.

Malton finally got it.

Everything was separate for a reason. Not just to protect each separate part but to keep all the finely balanced parts of Malton's being in alignment. His homosexuality and his heterosexuality. His criminal violence and his dreams of middle-class respectability. His blackness and his whiteness. It wasn't to protect Emily, it was to protect himself. And here he was about to sleep with a stranger for Emily's sake. It was madness.

His mistake was to try and stop thinking about Emily. He couldn't and he wouldn't. He loved her and would do anything for her. She was as much part of his world as Keisha or Danny Mitchum. But as long as he accepted that then, like everything else in his life, he could keep her where she belonged, safe and protected. Separate.

He would make room for her and their baby. He would create a ring of steel so strong and unyielding that nothing could touch them. And finally inside that sanctuary he would feel whole and safe and happy.

On the circular mattress the larger man began to noisily groan as he grabbed the hips of the smaller man who lay beneath him and pulled him upward, thrusting into him as hard as he could.

Malton stood up and gave the man beside him one last look.

'Leave your wife or leave here. You can't do both,' he said, and then turned and left.

Ten minutes later Malton was fully clothed and walking up out of the Locker Room's sunless world of anonymous, homosexual sex and into the fading sunlight of a Manchester evening. He was already running late.

Emily was right. He had definitely needed a night off. The fog had lifted. His mind felt sharp again. He had come right up to the edge of what it would feel like to lose Emily. Not to Danny Mitchum's threats but to his own stupidity.

The fear was still there but now he knew what to do with it. He knew how to proceed.

What's more, thanks to Benton's tip-off about the burned-out cars he was now certain that he knew who had Paul Bistacchi.

As long as Dean kept eyes on Keisha, everything would be downhill from here on out.

58

There could be no doubting that Dean had been spotted. Keisha's silver Mercedes lurched to the left and, travelling at speed, disappeared down a backstreet barely wide enough for a single car to pass through. Dean followed in Malton's green Volvo, swerving to avoid the communal bins that hung off the slivers of pavement making the narrow alleyway even narrower.

Central Manchester was in near gridlock as rush hour traffic fled from one end of the city to the other and out towards the suburbs. On the roads the average speed was little better than a crawl but in the tight Victorian back alleys Keisha hit forty miles per hour as she threw her car around what was left of old Manchester.

Any pretence of stealth was gone. Dean found himself smashing through piles of bin bags, hearing the nerve-shredding sound of the car's undercarriage scraping on raised paving and hammering the horn whenever a worker on a fag break threatened to end up beneath his wheels.

Every so often Dean would get within a few feet of Keisha's car. When he did, he could see Leon Walker being flung around in the back seat. Walker wasn't wearing a seat belt and when Keisha turned suddenly he would slide across the seat, slamming into the side of the car and disappearing for a moment before hauling himself back upright.

Without warning Keisha jerked her car right and accelerated up a one-way street. Dean didn't even think, he turned after her, gunning Malton's car as he did so. The road was two lanes wide, ferrying traffic out of the one-way slog around the middle of town and towards the Mancunian Way. For a couple of hundred metres until the junction, the road was clear – the lights on green.

Dean put his foot all the way down, pulled across to the empty lane and started to draw alongside Keisha. The Volvo ate up the road as Dean dragged himself level with Keisha – the two cars racing neck and neck as the lights changed to amber.

Propelled not just by the car's powerful engine but by the heady thrill of the chase, Dean turned to eyeball his quarry. He saw Keisha smile, grip the wheel and then disappear as she hit the brakes leaving Dean the split second in which he saw the red light before flying out in front of her and into the path of the now-moving stream of cross-traffic.

The sound of horns was Dean's first warning. He hammered the brake, yanking the steering wheel away from the cars heading towards his flank. The wheels locked and the entire back end of the car looped away from him in a shrieking donut, stopping only when it smashed, at speed, into a lamppost on the corner of the junction.

His car had spun a full 180 degrees to face the oncoming traffic. Dean saw Keisha complete her three-point turn and head off the wrong way down the one-way street before turning onto the overpass out of the city. The last thing he saw was Leon Walker smirking through the rear window at the sight of Malton's Volvo wrapped around a lamppost.

59

Club Brass sat on the seventh floor of a newly constructed five-star hotel. Despite tonight being invitation only, by the time Malton arrived there was already a queue. Soap actors, a smattering of reality stars and influencers, and half a dozen footballers with their heavily tanned, barely clothed dates hanging on their arms.

Malton found Emily stood on the opposite side of the road, nervously glued to her phone. She looked gorgeous. Dressed up in a way Malton rarely got to see her. She was wearing a loose black playsuit and had her hair teased into a bouncing mass of curls. She looked up, grateful to see him.

'I didn't think you were coming,' she said, relieved.

'Sorry. Work,' said Malton. 'Why aren't you in the queue?'

Emily looked embarrassed. 'I know you do a lot of this sort of stuff. And I know you said our names would be on the door. But . . .' She groped for the words. 'I'm just no one. I can't walk up and demand they let me in.'

Malton held out his arm to Emily. 'I can,' he said with utter confidence.

Emily shook her curls out and took his arm with a smile. Malton crossed the road with her and walked straight to the head of the queue. He could hear a few voices further down muttering in disapproval. Exactly as he'd intended.

As he approached he didn't have to say a word. The two giant men in dinner suits manning the door turned away from the couple at the head of the queue and held the door open as Malton led Emily through without so much as a backwards glance.

Stood in the elevator, heading upwards towards the exclusive club, Malton felt Emily push herself against him and hold him tight. Since leaving the Locker Room Malton felt a renewed gratitude for all he had. The smell of her hair, the warmth of her body, the way she trusted him completely. Everything he ever wanted was already his. It was only now that he finally saw it.

Malton wanted to tell her how he would move heaven and earth to keep her safe. How no one, not even Danny Mitchum would touch a hair on her head and the terrible price they would pay for even trying. But instead he kept quiet and held her and savoured the moment.

As the lift carried on upwards, Malton looked down at Emily and thought about the first time he saw her.

When people asked how Malton and Emily had met, Emily always jumped in with a story about a chance encounter, an instant connection and a happily ever after. Malton was happy to let her lie for the both of them. How could you tell someone the truth? That Malton had been hired by Emily's father to rescue her from the boyfriend who had decided that rather than steal to fund his habit, he'd make more money pimping Emily out on the internet?

Malton had turned up to the hotel room posing as a client and spent his allotted hour just talking to her. Explaining who he was and why he was there. At the start of that hour Emily would have done anything for the boyfriend who was feeding her drugs and selling her body to strangers. By the time the hour was up she willingly took herself to the bathroom and locked the door while Malton waited for her boyfriend to return.

Malton never asked Emily what she could hear in that bathroom. He did his best to make it quiet. He'd choked the boyfriend out as quickly as he could. Gagged him and wrapped him in a duvet before bringing him round and taking his time while he broke his body to pieces with a claw hammer.

When he was done with the boyfriend he'd knocked on the bathroom door and told her to close her eyes. He put his hands on her shoulders and led her out of the hotel and down to his car. He drove her directly to a treatment facility and left her there, his job done.

The last thing he expected was a couple of months later to get a phone call and hear Emily's voice on the other end of the line. At first he tried to shut it down but then she told him how she couldn't get him out of her head. His calm, low voice. The way his heavy hands rested on her shoulders, how safe she felt as he guided her out of that room and out of her old life. How she had pestered her father relentlessly until finally he'd broken and given her Malton's phone number.

Malton knew all too well you can't reason with an addict. Emily was an addict and she'd decided what she needed most of all in the world was Malton. But he couldn't get that hour in the hotel room out of his head. What started as a job had sparked something inside him. More out of curiosity than desire Malton had agreed to meet her again. That was over a year ago.

The elevator doors opened and they were greeted with a short staircase leading upwards. The walls had been clad in polished, riveted metal and a bright neon 'CLUB BRASS' sign let them know they had arrived.

The sounds and smells of the bar flooded in. Drunken conversation; low, warm jazz music; and the strong, boozy smell of cocktails. The bar area was, true to its name, decked out in brass fittings, brightly polished and perfectly designed to show off the hundreds of different bottles of spirits on offer. The wood-panelled walls went down into chocolate-coloured leather seating that mixed with brushed metal and industrial lighting to give the feel of expensive exclusivity.

Malton looked round, taking it all in. Every table was packed full of people – women in figure-hugging dresses and strappy heels, men in skin-tight suits with fashionable tattoos on their necks and hands. Everyone split between their own enjoyment and the awareness that they were the chosen few – Manchester's beautiful people. Hardly anyone was without a phone in their hand. Every few seconds a group of people would bunch together and an arm would shoot out to take a selfie and immortalise their privileged position at the top of the social food chain.

Wealth and talent and luck had brought these people here. Not Malton. He'd snatched his place here through sheer force of will.

Club Brass had three outside terraces. Small seating areas where you could look down on the city as you drank among its elite. Two of the terraces were packed with revellers. But the final terrace lay empty, a velvet rope sealing it for who-ever was yet to come and claim it.

Without waiting to be asked, Malton led Emily through the throng towards the empty terrace. Heads turned as he lifted the velvet rope and ushered Emily to her seat. For the first time in the last couple of weeks he felt fully in control. With Emily by his side he had something worth fighting for. A life he wouldn't walk away from. A reason to overcome it all.

Malton felt eyes on him – wondering who he was and why he was afforded the honour of this prime piece of real estate. Impervious to their gazes, he called over the waiter and ordered two Diet Cokes. One for him, one for Emily.

While they waited for their drinks to arrive they looked out over Manchester. They were high up, but not so high up that the surrounding buildings didn't close in around them.

A forest of glass and steel and light. Way beneath them at street level Manchester seemed like a deep ocean of shadows. Teeming with light and life. High up in Club Brass it felt like another world.

The drinks arrived and Emily made a toast. 'Here's to our family,' she said, her voice rising nervously as she suddenly realised what she was saying. Doubt stole over her face.

'Here's to our family,' said Malton, raising his own glass. He had wasted too much time already. Now he had made the decision. He would let himself be happy and he wouldn't let the fear of losing that happiness ever have a hold over him again.

It felt like the start of something wonderful.

The sound of Emily's name being screamed across the bar shook Malton out of his reverie.

Emily looked up to see her best friend in the whole world, Lucy, stood at the velvet rope – eyes wide open with delighted disbelief. Emily's face lit up. She screamed back and rushed to usher Lucy outside, throwing her arms around her.

Malton looked past Emily and her friend, across the bar to the entrance where the man who he'd nearly fucked less than an hour earlier, had just entered the room: Lucy's husband, Greg.

60

Dean cycled as if his life depended on it. He wasn't sure that it didn't.

After crashing Malton's car his first call had been to Malton Security, hoping against hope that it wouldn't be Malton who picked up the phone.

Dean had never been happier to hear Alfie's voice. Initially Alfie had refused point-blank to lock up the office and drive to the town centre to deal with the aftermath of the crash. It was only when Dean told Alfie that it was Malton's car he'd crashed that Alfie thought he smelled blood and headed over, eager to turn Dean's misfortune to his advantage. Exactly as Dean hoped he would.

Once Alfie arrived on the scene, before he even had time to gloat, Dean tossed him the keys and fled. He knew exactly where he was going. To discover the final piece of the puzzle, the thing that would tie everything together.

Piccadilly station was on the other side of the city centre to the university but between the two lay a string of student halls. And where there are student halls there are bicycles.

Malton was right, the best way to break into a place was to find it open. The easiest way to steal a bicycle was to find one that someone hadn't even bothered to lock up. Among the cash-rich students who could afford the private city-centre accommodation such a bicycle was easy enough to find and even easier to steal.

Dean hammered the pedals as he sped through Moss Side and on through Fallowfield, heading south out of the city centre. He felt his clothes sticking to his body as the sweat poured off him. But he didn't for a minute slow down.

He'd lost Keisha. He'd wrecked Malton's car. There was only one way to rescue the situation. He needed to discover the key to it all. Who had Paul Bistacchi.

Leon Walker's daughter had told him that it was Keisha who had given her father the shotgun and, what's more, that she had given Cody the gun he'd used to kill Lorraine.

But firearms wouldn't be enough. Leon Walker was a helpless addict. Cody was an angry teenager. Neither of them would have the imagination or resources to discover where Malton lived or know that Lorraine's café was being used as a drop house for Danny Mitchum.

Keisha hadn't just armed them, she'd aimed them at their target: Craig Malton.

All this chaos caused by one woman. The same woman who'd turned up asking Malton to find her kidnapped husband. It didn't take a genius to make the final leap.

Right now, all Dean had was the word of Leon Walker's daughter. That wouldn't be enough. If he was going to convince Malton that his ex was out to destroy him he'd need something more solid. Or to be more precise: someone more solid.

A lifetime of cycling had given Dean a near-photographic recollection of the streets and suburbs of Manchester. It was easy enough to find Adam Cornforth's house. Didsbury was quiet this time of evening. Wrapped in dusk and the wet, leafy smell of suburbia.

As he ditched the bike on the overgrown driveway he saw that the downstairs lights were on. Rushing to the front door, he took a breath. He could feel the sweat running off him and wiped his face on his sleeve, running a hand back through his hair as he tried his best to look halfway presentable.

He needed Adam Cornforth. After the incident with Fury the dog, he knew that threats and violence were not his strong suit. He would need words to convince Adam Cornforth to give up what he needed.

Calmly Dean knocked on the door and waited.

The door opened on the chain and Adam Cornforth's face appeared in the gap. He recognised Dean straight away and went to close the door.

Dean was quicker and stuck his foot in the gap. 'Please, I don't want to come in.'

'I told you everything.'

'I know. But there's just one more thing I need to know. I just need a name and I'm gone. Just a name,' said Dean.

'I don't know anything,' said Adam Cornforth.

Dean felt breathless. He wasn't sure if it was the bike ride or the thrill of being so close to the truth. He tried not to sound too excited.

'The other day when we were here, there were two plates in the sink. Two cups. Someone had been round.'

'It was my wife,' said Adam too quickly, before glancing away for just a second. He looked back to Dean and they both knew he'd been caught in his lie.

'You said you hadn't seen your wife for months,' said Dean.

'I made a mistake. She came round. It was her,' blustered Adam.

Dean was running out of time. Delivering Malton everything was his only hope. At this point he had nothing to lose. Unfortunately for him, neither did Adam Cornforth.

'I've said everything I know. Please leave me alone.'

Adam sounded defiant. As if he'd realised the balance of power. Dean had a foot in the door but that was all he had. He was fishing.

With no other option Dean took a leap of faith.

'That second plate. It wasn't for your wife, was it? It was for Keisha Bistacchi.'

The look on Adam Cornforth's face told Dean all he needed to know.

61

Over the past hour Malton had learned that Lucy's husband Greg, the chubby white man from the Locker Room, was also a secondary school maths teacher and that he was a talker. A big talker.

When Greg had asked him all the usual polite questions one might ask a stranger, Malton had made a point of looking him straight in the eye as he explained what he did for a living, how many people Malton Security employed and the kind of routine violence that went hand in hand with working in security.

Far from this subduing Greg, a combination of nerves and alcohol seemed to be having the opposite effect. Greg was a lot more confident with his clothes on. He kept peppering Malton with questions: *Have you ever been to prison? How do you knock someone out? Have you ever been shot?* Malton couldn't believe it. Greg was playing with him.

Every joke was a test of Malton's newly regained self-control. Malton had once been kidnapped off a job and tortured. He'd had an iron pressed into his flesh to get him to reveal the name of the man who'd hired him. In all that time he'd said nothing.

It bothered him how much trouble he was now having keeping it together over a maths teacher.

Lucy and Emily competed to spot the most famous person at the bar. There were regional newsreaders alongside the soap stars and footballers. A couple of semi-famous local millionaires and a glamour model whom Greg unsuccessfully affected to not recognise.

While Malton and Emily were teetotal both Lucy and Greg drank freely – all the more so upon learning that drinks for the night were on Malton. Emily had broken the news to her friend about the IVF and after hugs and tears Malton ordered a bottle of champagne, hoping to move the conversation on with free booze.

Malton watched as Greg made his way through the bottle, polishing it off almost single-handedly while he launched into a meandering story about an Ofsted inspection.

But eventually the dam broke and Greg rose to go to the toilet.

No sooner was Greg out of the room than Malton made his excuses and followed along after him. He needed to prove to himself that his visit to the Locker Room had worked. That he'd turned a corner and was back in control.

He would go into the toilets and give Greg a warning. Nothing more. Remind himself that the threat always trumped the act.

Greg looked up from the urinal as Malton walked into the toilets. From the way he began nervously fumbling with his trousers he knew he was in trouble.

Malton deliberately took the urinal next to Greg's. Suddenly he felt the familiar pattern returning. His senses slowing down to a crawl. The gentle lighting and the mixture of expensive soap and inexpensive disinfectant. This was Malton's stage and he was ready to play his part.

As Malton undid his trousers, Greg spoke up.

'I'm sorry. Out there. I'm sorry. I'm just nervous. You were at the sauna. You were right. I shouldn't have been there. But I won't tell anyone, I promise.'

Malton let rip into the urinal, letting the sound of piss on porcelain punctuate the silence. He almost smiled. To think there'd been a tiny speck of doubt in his mind as to whether he would handle this well. If the dark ferocity that had erupted the day before would return. Whether it was Greg or Danny Mitchum himself, Malton knew now that he was firmly back in control.

He finished up but didn't put himself away. Rather he stood there, his flaccid penis hanging over the urinal. He turned to Greg who still had not managed to go.

'If you ever mention anything, a tape will arrive at your house,' said Malton.

Greg looked over, doing his best to look Malton in the eye and not be drawn down to the sight of his large, thick member hanging free.

'They can't film in a . . . in a place like that. Can they?' said Greg, the thought of it suddenly dawning on him.

Malton saw how nervously Greg held his gaze. He didn't want to look Malton in the eye but knew that if he looked down then he was lost.

'They can and they do. I helped them set up the cameras. All sorts of things go off in a place like that. Sex and guilt and drugs and men. That's a hell of a combination. You need security,' said Malton.

'They film it?'

'Everything. You'd be amazed who you get turning up at a place like that. People who shouldn't be there,' said Malton.

'I won't say anything,' said Greg. He finally flinched and for just a moment his gaze went down to Malton's exposed penis.

Malton shook himself dry and put himself away.

'Out there, you were making jokes? Telling stories. You're a funny guy,' said Malton.

'What?' said Greg, struggling to keep up.

'So we're going to go out there and you're going to be the life and soul of the party. Just like before. No one will know we've had our little conversation. Why should the girls' night be ruined because of us?'

'I can do that,' said Greg. He seemed relieved that this ordeal was coming to an end.

'I'll follow you out. Don't want to come out together. Looks a bit gay don't you think?'

Greg started a nervous laugh and then stopped abruptly as if unsure if that would make things worse.

Malton watched him scurry out of the toilets and then turned to the mirror over the sinks.

Looking back at him he saw a short, squat man in a suit with an open collar, brown skin and a thick, aged scar running down his face. He saw a man who could gain access to any room in the city. A millionaire several times over. A man who was rightly feared by some of the most violent people in Manchester. A man who had a beautiful partner, an expensive car, several properties, his own business and a family on the way. The most powerful man in Club Brass.

Just for a moment he saw a man who was terrified that despite all of that he still didn't belong. A man who if he stopped for even a second would be exposed as the interloper he was.

By the time Malton rejoined the table he'd pushed those thoughts to the back of his mind. Greg was doing his part, telling some story that had Lucy in fits. Emily seemed quieter but he put that down to seeing her evening being eaten up with Greg's ceaseless prattling.

Malton gazed out over Manchester. An endless blanket of darkness, punctuated by tiny pricks of light. He'd had his night off. It'd been fun but now he was getting restless. He started to count the seconds until he could leave all this behind and return to his world.

A world of violence and fear. A world where if he pushed hard enough he might still have a chance of coming out on top.

62

Malton drove them home in Emily's bright red Ford B-Max. Emily sat dozing in the passenger seat. Every so often he'd catch her out of the corner of his eye, staring at him with a look of deep contentment.

Greg had done his job. He was just as loud and obnoxious as he'd been before their conversation at the urinals. Despite everything even Malton had found himself enjoying the evening.

It had been just after midnight that the four of them had said their goodbyes, promised to do this again soon before vanishing into the night.

Malton sped through the dark empty streets in silence. There was no need to speak. He felt something warm inside him. Something he hadn't felt since James had died.

The feeling so threw him that he put it to the back of his mind, focusing instead on the work to come.

Malton was sure now he knew where Paul Bistacchi had ended up. He had been groping in the dark until the boy from the robbery at Lorraine's had given him a name. It was a name that initially made no sense but, as time went on, slowly everything had come into focus. The burned-out cars had simply confirmed it beyond any doubt.

It was unfortunate that Danny Mitchum had become involved but now Malton saw that that too was no coincidence. It all pointed to what he now knew – the identity of Paul Bistacchi's kidnapper.

He had an unwelcome suspicion that returning him wouldn't be the end of this mess. Nevertheless, first thing tomorrow morning he would liberate him, return him to Keisha and do his best to wash his hands of the whole affair.

After a flurry of missed calls from Dean that he didn't bother returning, Malton hadn't heard from him all night. Whatever the initial problem was it seemed like Dean had managed to get a grip on it. Just as well; this would all be much easier with Keisha safely tucked up at the Bistacchis'.

There were just the loose ends to deal with and this whole sorry affair would finally be behind him. The video of him leaving Susannah Harper's was unfortunate, Danny Mitchum getting involved even more so. But they could both be handled.

He was so caught up in his thoughts that if Emily hadn't screamed as he pulled into the driveway he would have run over Keisha, who was standing outside his house looking like she'd just had the worst night of her life – clothes torn, hair a mess and wrapped in a borrowed overcoat.

Malton pumped the brakes and cut the engine. 'Stay in the car,' he said, slipping easily into damage limitation.

'Who is she?' said Emily, pushing herself back into her seat, unable to take her eyes off Keisha.

'Nothing to do with you. Stay in the car.'

Malton heard his own voice and inwardly cursed. He spent so much time and energy keeping Emily from that man. The man who spoke to people like that. And now here that man was, on his driveway, telling Emily what to do. But there was no time for apologies.

He left Emily sat in the car and strode across to Keisha, put his arm around her, and steered her away from Emily's gaze while with the other hand he got out his keys.

'What the hell are you doing here?' he growled.

'I didn't know where else to come.' Keisha sounded like she'd been crying. Her hair was half combed out and her dress was ripped. She clung to the coat she'd wrapped around herself.

Malton didn't dare turn back to see the look on Emily's face as she watched him open the front door and lead Keisha inside.

Malton shut the door behind them and stopped in the hallway. He grabbed Keisha roughly.

'You don't ever come here,' seethed Malton.

Keisha looked up at Malton, her eyes filling with tears. He softened, just for a moment.

'You know you don't ever come here,' he repeated, more gently this time.

'Where else do you want me to go?' pleaded Keisha. 'He hit me. Beat me up. Johnny.'

'Johnny Bistacchi beat you up?' Malton felt his hands bunching into tight fists.

'He's lost it. Him and his mother. I tried to stop him. He wouldn't listen. Said me and you were plotting behind his back. That I knew where Paul was and was using you to take over the family. I thought he was going to kill me . . .'

Keisha broke off and began to sob. Malton watched her, his own emotions a raging torrent of violent anger.

'You're coming with me,' said Malton, hauling Keisha along.

'Where are we going?'

But Malton didn't answer, his jaw was too tightly clenched to even think about saying another word.

He opened the front door and led Keisha back outside.

'Wait here,' he said to her and, leaving Keisha where she was, he walked across the driveway to Emily's car. He went to open the driver's side and to his dismay found that Emily had locked it. He waited a moment as she looked nervously at him through the car door window before reaching over and disengaging the central locking.

Malton opened the car door.

'I know her,' said Emily.

His blood ran cold.

'How?'

Emily sounded terrified. 'She came into the shop. I recognise her. She ordered a cake. I made her a cake.'

'You don't know her,' asserted Malton.

Keisha stood on the driveway, bedraggled and torn but still exerting a dark gravity over Emily. 'Who is she? Why is she here?'

Malton could feel himself losing control again. He scrambled to hold it together.

'Go inside, lock the door and don't answer it to anyone but me. I'm dealing with it,' he said.

Emily missed the edge in Malton's voice. She finally found her courage.

'No. What the hell's happening? This is my house too. You have to tell me. Now!'

Malton gave up. 'Go inside.' For the second time that night he spoke to Emily in that voice.

He saw her looking up at him. Saw the fear in her eyes. He became aware of his hand on the car door, its size and the hundreds of tiny scars covering the fingers and knuckles. A lifetime of violence.

Without a word, Emily got out of the car, brushed past him and headed inside. As she passed Keisha coming the other way, for just a moment Malton saw the flicker of a smile threaten to break out over Keisha's face.

Finally it all made sense. The reason he couldn't put it all together. He wasn't doing the puzzle wrong. He didn't have all the pieces.

Until now.

63

After leaving Adam Cornforth, Dean checked in with Alfie that Malton's car had been taken care of and was about to call Malton when his phone beeped with a message. It was Malton. The message simply said, '*Get to the office now.*'

Dean didn't need telling twice. He had everything. Not just who but how and why. He'd figured it all out himself. Dean had no idea what Malton would do about him totalling his car, but he knew he couldn't hide from Malton and he definitely couldn't out-bluff him or out-muscle him.

All he had to protect him was the truth. He hoped it would be enough.

Waiting outside the locked offices of Malton Security at two in the morning was strangely peaceful. The roads were empty and Dean had made it in record time. It gave him a chance to rehearse it all in his head. His insights, his detective work. How he'd pieced it all together. As he was going over his grand reveal a red Ford B-Max pulled up.

Malton got out of the car alone. He looked furious and made a beeline for Dean.

'I know about the car. I don't care. Things have got worse. Much worse. Come with me.'

Malton turned and headed back to the car. Dean hesitated. Malton was always intense but right now it seemed like the very air around him was on fire. Suddenly all Dean's cleverness seemed a lot less clever.

Malton opened the back door to the car. There on the back seat, lying under a pile of coats, was Keisha Bistacchi.

She and Dean locked eyes, neither one of them expecting to see the other again so soon. If she was surprised Keisha didn't show it.

'Take me inside,' said Keisha, extending a hand to Malton, who almost lifted her out of the car and headed towards the office, one arm protectively around her shoulders.

Dean silently followed behind, more terrified and confused than ever.

As Malton led Keisha into his office, Dean saw his last chance slipping away.

'Wait!' cried Dean.

Malton stopped. He closed the door, leaving Keisha alone in his office, and turned to Dean. It was now or never.

'What?' For the first time since Dean had known Malton, he sounded tired.

Dean sucked up all his courage. 'I know who kidnapped Paul Bistacchi. And who shot up your front door. And who was behind the robbery at Lorraine's. I've worked it all out.'

Malton didn't move. He looked at Dean. Stripping him down, figuring him out. Dean knew he'd have to say the name. Risk the wrath of the silently dangerous man stood before him. He became unpleasantly aware of just how solid Malton was. Every inch of him unmoving and coiled.

'You know who it was, do you?' said Malton.

There was no room for doubt now. He'd made his pitch. It was time to call. 'Yes,' he said.

Malton held his gaze, daring him to say the name.

But before he could Malton spoke.

'So do I,' he said and went into the office, leaving Dean unsure whether he'd just aced the test or signed his own death warrant.

64

'What are you going to do? About Johnny? If he thinks we're in it together, he'll be coming for you too.'

Keisha paced Malton's office, giving vent to her thoughts. She hadn't expected the young lad. Not at this time of night. Craig had said something to him before he joined her in his office. Whatever it was, Keisha resolved to stick to the plan. He would eventually learn all the sordid details of what she'd been up to but as long as she could get her story straight over the next few minutes whatever that boy told Malton would be meaningless in the face of her version of events.

It had taken thirty years of patient planning to put her in this room. This was the plan and she was going to stick to it until the last.

Craig sat at his desk watching her. He was dressed in an expensive-looking suit. Keisha liked it. When they'd been together all those years ago he was never out of a tracksuit. A bit of money suited him.

Keisha tried not to look at the pristine white cake box sitting untouched on the desk.

'Tell me again, what he said. Exactly,' said Malton. Keisha recognised that face. Craig was slowly figuring it all out.

'After he finished beating me, he was ranting. He said that he knew you'd taken Paul.'

A pause and then Malton said, 'He thinks I have Paul?'

'I know. He's lost it. After Johnny escaped Danny Mitchum he ended up walking twenty miles back home to

Hattersley with a bag full of guns. Then his mum shoots his ear off.'

A look of confusion came over Malton's face. 'Wait. His mum shot his ear off?'

Keisha smiled and made eye contact. 'I know. Fucking Hattersley. She thought he was breaking in and shot him.'

'And then he beat you up?'

She had him now. All the build-up, all the planning. Keisha could feel Craig coming back to her.

'He was full of painkillers and booze. He started asking all these questions. How did Danny know where we were? How come they took him and not me? He convinced himself that I'd been talking to Danny Mitchum through you.'

'And what did you say to that?'

'I laughed. It's ridiculous. Why would you be telling Danny Mitchum anything?'

Keisha stopped and leaned over Craig's desk. She rested a hand on his.

'I'm scared he'll do something stupid. Something that'll get you hurt.' She paused then took the plunge. 'You know I still think about you?'

Craig took her hand in his own. Keisha did her best to hide the rush of joy the sensation gave her. She was so nearly there. So nearly back.

'I still think about you too,' said Craig.

Keisha couldn't help but smile. 'You do?'

'Yes.' He took a breath. 'I think about why you paid Leon Walker to shoot a shotgun at my front door. Or why you had your own husband kidnapped. But most of all I think about why you turned up on my driveway in the middle of the night with this bullshit.'

Keisha pulled her hand back and did her best not to let the bubbling rage inside her show.

'Why now? It's been over thirty years since I walked out,' said Malton.

Keisha wanted to tell him what really happened thirty years ago. To rub his face in the private grief that for three decades she had carried alone. But she knew better. That was her final play, the last card, and she would only reveal it to Malton on pain of death.

Instead she stuck to the plan. She crossed the room and sat down on the sofa, trying to look like she belonged here as much as the weights or the faded maps or Malton himself.

'I see you,' said Keisha. 'You can pretend all you want. With your posh cow and your expensive clothes. Go and live in Chorlton or Didsbury or wherever wankers are living these days. Tell the world you run security and you're straight and you're middle class. I know what you are.'

She felt Malton looking her over. His eyes examining the bruises around her neck, the split lip. 'Johnny didn't do that to you, did he?'

Keisha smiled. It hurt a little. 'It doesn't matter. By now he'll already be there.'

Uncertainty crossed Malton's face. She still had the upper hand. There was still a chance.

'Where?' he asked.

'I know you care about me, Craig. I know you do. And I know how much you love to save a damsel in distress. Well right now I'm in real trouble. You see, Maria got it into her head that the best thing to do with all those guns was to go on the offensive. Right now, she's sending Johnny off to break into Danny Mitchum's house in Hale.'

Keisha saw the surprise in Malton's face. She leaned forward, drinking it in.

'He wouldn't dare,' said Malton, leaning back in disbelief.

'*You* wouldn't dare. Because you're not a fucking idiot. Johnny doesn't have that problem,' said Keisha, laughing.

Malton rose to his feet, the urgency of what he'd just been told suddenly shaking him into action. Keisha watched him hungrily. There was still a chance the plan might work. She was still in the game.

'He'll get himself killed,' said Malton.

'Oh I hope so,' said Keisha, getting to her feet. 'And then Danny Mitchum comes looking for the rest of the Bistacchis. And where's Paul's wife? She's being kept nice and safe by Craig Malton. The same Craig Malton who's already warned him off the Bistacchis. After Johnny gate-crashes Danny's place you think he'll be quite so ready to believe it's just another job?'

'You have no idea what you've done,' said Malton, grabbing Keisha by the wrist.

Keisha let him manhandle her. It just brought her closer to him. She was up against his chest now, able to look him in the eye, smell his aftershave and feel the heat of his body. She was as close as she needed to be to strike the final blow.

'Oh I do. That's why I did it,' she said. 'That's why I got Paul kidnapped. And why I went to you for help. You can't resist being the white knight. Go with it. Ditch that boring bitch. Let's do it for real. Me and you. Right now you're at the top of Danny Mitchum's shit list. You can fight him alone and die or you can come with me and we'll show him just what we can do. Between the two of us he doesn't stand a chance. Fuck the Bistacchis. Fuck Danny Mitchum. Fuck 'em all.'

Keisha was inches from Malton's face. The two of them hung there for a moment. Apex predators sizing each other up. It would all come down to who blinked first.

Malton let go of Keisha's wrist and took a step back.

'We're not doing a thing. You're staying here and I'm sorting this mess,' he said and moved to the door.

This couldn't be happening. The plan had worked. She'd drawn Craig in, set him against insurmountable dangers and positioned herself as the only way out. She'd given him the chance to show the world who he is, and to do it with her by his side.

Keisha felt everything slipping away.

'Wait!' shouted Keisha. 'I heard how you spoke to that girl back at your house. I saw the look in her eyes. She's never heard you speak like that before has she? She has no idea how deep you go. She's weak. And that makes you weak.'

Malton's voice dropped an octave to a low growl. 'If you touch her . . .'

Keisha had one last throw of the dice. To do the thing she hated most in the world. The thing she had never done for Paul throughout their marriage. She let her guard down and spoke from the heart as Keisha McColl.

'I know you, Craig. I know everything about you. And I don't care.' Her shoulders dropped, the lithe, readiness with which she held herself gave way to the fatigue she felt.

'All of this? I did it for you. To wake you up. Remind you who you were. Who you could be. I thought maybe I'd gone too far, pushed you too hard. But you did it. You worked it all out. And now you're here. You with Malton Security, me with the Bistacchis. Together we'd run this town.'

Keisha felt all the emotions that she'd assumed were long dead inside her welling up. Thirty years of blood and guts and it was all she had left.

'So what do you say? They're weak and we're strong. Why waste your time protecting them when we could take it all from them?'

Malton didn't move a muscle. 'Did you give that kid a gun and tell him to shoot Lorraine for me too?' he said.

At that moment Keisha knew it was not enough. She had lost Craig. Imperceptibly she raised her guard and resumed being Keisha Bistacchi.

'I know. Very sad. But I had to get you in trouble with Danny Mitchum. Make him doubt you. If it's any consolation, I'm sorry.'

'You're done,' said Malton, opening the door to leave.

'You've got a present. On your desk,' said Keisha.

Keisha enjoyed watching Malton notice the box on his desk for the first time that evening. This was all that was left. To burn it all down.

'What is this?' said Malton.

'Open it,' said Keisha.

Malton tore the top off the box and there sat the beautiful cake bearing the inscription: *ONE LAST CHANCE*.

Keisha enjoyed seeing the look of horror on Craig's face.

'She's your weakness,' she said.

A deep, furious, primal sound that started way down in Malton's gut erupted from his mouth. A terrifying bellow as he scooped the cake up with one hand and hurled it at Keisha who ducked just in time as the cake sailed over her head and smashed into pieces on the wall behind her.

'You went to his funeral,' shouted Malton.

'The guy Johnny ran over? What does that matter?'

'That's *your* weakness.'

'That's my strength,' said Keisha. 'Look at you, trying to be like them, terrified they'll sniff you out. So eager to please them. I don't give a fuck. I go wherever I want. I can be whoever I want. I can walk into a room and listen to the heartfelt tributes to a man whose murder I covered up and cry along with the rest of them. I could have given you that.'

'She saw you there. His wife. She knew it was you. If you hadn't gone to that funeral, his wife would never have called me.'

Keisha looked taken aback.

'So you really are playing both sides?'

'And if she'd never called me I would never have made the connection. You burned out both cars didn't you?'

Keisha suddenly felt sick. All her planning. Every little detail she'd laid out end to end. And this was where it all came crashing down?

'I go where I want. I do what I want,' she said.

'And that's why I knew for sure it was you who kidnapped Paul. I knew that it was you behind Lorraine's and pulling the strings with Leon Walker. But I didn't want to believe you'd do something this insane. Kidnapping your own husband, goading Danny Mitchum like this. Part of me didn't want to look at what was right there in front of me. But then the burned-out cars? Then I knew.'

As everything came crashing down Keisha couldn't help but be impressed. Craig was every bit as brilliant as she thought he was.

'I care too much but you, you don't give a shit. And that makes *you* weak,' said Malton opening the door to his office and gesturing for Dean to come inside.

Sensing the mood in the room, Dean kept his mouth shut.

'I need to go and sort something,' Malton said to Dean. 'Something urgent. You stay here. Lock yourself in. Don't let her leave.'

Malton turned to go.

'You won't make it in time. Soon as Johnny gets inside that house it's over for you. You need me. I'm your only hope,' Keisha called after him.

Malton looked to Dean. 'Don't let her leave.'

'Craig! Wait!' said Keisha. 'You know you're dead, don't you?' she shouted after him.

Malton's silent scowl as he shut the door behind him let her know that he was all too aware of the possibility.

65

'It's happening now!' shouted Malton into his phone as he pushed the B-Max past fifty, tearing through empty North Manchester streets. Right now he needed to be in several places all at the same time. With that being an impossibility, he was racing towards the most urgent situation and hoping that what he couldn't fix he could delegate.

'What's happening?' said Benton, her voice still sounding half asleep. 'It's the middle of the night. This better be good.'

Malton accelerated through the upcoming lights as they turned red and thanked his lucky stars that the morning rush hour had yet to kick in.

'The Bistacchis are making a move on Danny Mitchum. They have guns and are planning to storm his house and murder him. Is that good enough?'

He could hear Benton thinking on the other end of the line. 'You know what this sounds like?'

Malton made it across an empty city centre at record speed and was now tearing down Princess Parkway. 'I don't give a fuck, Benton. Greater Manchester Police need to move or there's going to be a bloodbath.'

'Paul Bistacchi going AWOL has tanked a year of police work. No one has an appetite for chucking good overtime after bad,' said Benton down the line.

In a few hours it would start getting light. Right now the world was cold and grey. Waiting for the sun to emerge and start the day proper.

'Can you make this happen or not?' said Malton.

There was a long pause.

'I don't have that kind of juice. Not anymore. Not without hard evidence,' said Benton.

Malton was near his destination. He didn't have time for this.

'If you don't stop this then there's a very good chance that a full-scale gang war is going to erupt and then we're all fucked.'

'You mean you're fucked,' said Benton.

Malton took a breath.

'If you don't stop this they'll kill me, they'll kill Emily and they'll kill a whole lot of other people who don't deserve any of it. If you ever had any pull in the Greater Manchester Police, any favours, any contacts, anything. Now's the time to call them in.'

Malton pulled up and stopped the engine.

'I'll do what I can.' Benton hung up.

Right now Johnny Bistacchi and whoever was stupid enough to follow him were tooling up and getting ready to raid the heavily guarded home of the most dangerous man in Manchester. Malton had been inside Danny Mitchum's house. It was a fortress. You'd need a tank and heavy explosives to get in. And if you did get in there were never less than a dozen bodies inside, all of them being paid handsomely to fuck up whoever Danny told them to fuck up.

The Bistacchis were walking into a massacre and when it happened, thanks to Keisha, the trail of blood led all the way back to Malton.

Malton did his best to put it out of his mind. His night was far from over.

66

Claire would be the first to admit that her plan sounded crazy. For her and her daughter Jessica to run away, leave that very night and spend the rest of the time Claire had left seeing the world, just the two of them. But she was running out of ideas.

It would mean turning her back on proton beam therapy. Losing her best shot at beating the cancer in order to ensure that Jessica was as far away from this madness as possible.

Claire knew exactly how insane it all sounded but after what had happened to her at the police station she felt truly desperate.

She'd talked to an officer named Benton. At first Benton listened but as soon as Claire had mentioned the video that was all she wanted to talk about. More than that she had insisted Claire hand it over. If her manner hadn't been so odd then Claire probably would have done just that. But something about Benton spooked her. She'd listened as Claire outlined everything she knew about Craig Malton and hadn't blinked an eyelid. It was like she already knew and had decided that she didn't care. Just another criminal under the protection of the Greater Manchester Police force. It was only the mention of the video that got any sort of response.

When Claire stood her ground Benton changed tack. She'd started warning Claire about the man in the video. Telling her how dangerous he was. It seemed almost like she knew him.

Claire had made her excuses and left.

At the time it felt like a victory but now the video on her phone felt like a bomb waiting to go off. She knew Malton would somehow find out that she'd spoken to the police. Maybe it was even Benton who would do the telling. Whether or not her fears were rational, now that she had tried and failed to do the right thing it was the turn of irrationality to take a driving seat.

Hence the trip around the world.

She'd returned home armed with a takeaway and over a couple of hot, greasy pizzas Claire had tried to convince Jessica why it made perfect sense for them to pack their bags and jump on the next plane. Jessica had been unusually quiet but Claire pushed on. She omitted to mention the proton beam therapy or what Dr Rosenbaum had told her about her chances of survival if she chose to try it.

What was the point in surviving the cancer only to be killed by Craig Malton? If she died from cancer then the trail ended with her. The only way she could protect Jessica was to let the tumour in her head carry her away.

So she explained to Jessica how with the time she had left they should see the world. Tick off a whole bucket list of experiences and enjoy themselves.

After they finished eating, Claire jollied Jessica upstairs and between them they'd dragged two suitcases down from the attic, dusty and covered in cobwebs. One for each of them. The last time she'd used them had been when she and Marcus spent the weekend in Rome for their anniversary. That seemed so long ago. Like someone else's world.

Claire left Jessica to pack while she went to her own room and tried to condense down her entire life into one suitcase. As far as Claire was concerned this was a one-way trip. She wasn't coming back. She would make sure she put enough cash aside that when her time came she would be taken care of and Jessica returned to the UK. It was heart breaking but it was the only way.

Claire filled and refilled the suitcase. Trying her best to imagine how she saw the next six months. Try as she might all she could think about was Craig Malton. Shaking the image out of her mind, she went to check on Jessica.

When she put her head round Jessica's door she saw that her daughter had yet to pack a single thing. 'Come on. I've ordered a taxi to be here in an hour. We'll go to the airport, see what flight takes our fancy. And then we're off!'

'What about the proton beam therapy?' said Jessica.

Claire froze. *How had Jessica found out?*

'It's not a cure,' said Claire brusquely, as she started pulling clothes out of her daughter's cupboard.

'What did the doctor say?' said Jessica, her voice full of desperate hope.

Claire welled up. The absurdity of her plan began to become impossible to ignore. She was going to lie. She was going to throw away her chance at beating this cancer. Throw away old age and seeing Jessica into adulthood. All because of Craig Malton.

She felt like a coward as the words stuck in her throat.

'Because I read that it can be fifty-fifty,' said Jessica. 'Maybe more. With your kind of cancer. It's got to be worth a shot, right?'

Claire felt numb. She looked down at the mess of clothing stuffed into the suitcase in front of her. She could smell the fabric softener on the dress she clutched in her hand. It smelled like Jessica. Like Marcus. Like home.

She sat down on the bed and then she told Jessica everything. Tracking down the Bistacchis and witnessing Paul's kidnapping. The day Yaya brought the business card into her office and how she brought Craig Malton into her life. Even her suspicion that somehow Marcus might be connected to the Bistacchis.

When she'd finished, Jessica sat in silence for what seemed like several minutes. Claire let her daughter think. She knew how it all sounded. The insanity of it. Finally Jessica spoke.

'I'm not scared. I want you to stay and get the treatment. Whatever happens, I want you alive.'

'But I can't protect you,' pleaded Claire.

'Running away isn't protecting me,' said Jessica. 'What do I do if you get ill and we're halfway round the world? You belong here, fighting it. If you let yourself die from the cancer it's like he's killed you and you let him do it.'

The clarity of Jessica's words filled Claire with a dull sense of shame.

Jessica continued. 'I miss Dad and I'm scared about losing you. And I know that you miss him too and I know that you only did what you did because you were hurting. That doesn't make you a bad person. You still deserve your shot at getting through this.'

Claire felt the tears pouring down her face before she even realised she was crying.

Jessica threw her arms around her mum and held her tight.

Claire had said the words and the world hadn't ended. She'd seen the hope in Jessica's eyes and now she couldn't go back. Seeing her daughter's bravery made the fear Claire felt about Craig Malton and the darkness he brought with him seem like the cowardice it was.

Finally she knew what she would do. She was a mother and a fighter. She would face down cancer and face down Craig Malton. For Jessica.

67

Malton sat in his car next to Adam Cornforth. They had pulled over to the side of the road when the call had come in and now they sat listening on Malton's speakerphone.

From the other end of the line the sound of barked instructions were just about audible. Malton made out 'ARMED POLICE! GET ON THE GROUND!'

There followed the sound of glass being broken and more shouting. Adam Cornforth did his best not to look too scared at whatever it was he was hearing.

More shouting. 'STAY ON THE GROUND! STAY ON THE GROUND!' And then a single gunshot followed by the sound of a scuffle. Then silence.

'Benton?' said Malton. 'What's happening?'

Benton's voice came on the line. She sounded like she was smiling.

'What's happening is I've just provided the intelligence that led to the boys with guns doing a hard stop on a minibus full of East Manchester's finest.'

'I heard gunfire.'

'You heard what happens when someone who doesn't know what they're doing tries to turn a starting pistol into a viable firearm. It went off when they were arresting them.'

Malton couldn't quite believe it. Benton had done it.

'You got them all?' said Malton.

'Johnny Bistacchi and four others. Unless you know of an imminent pincer movement on Danny Mitchum's mansion then I'd say we got them all.'

Malton heard the sound of officers congratulating Benton and Benton soaking up the praise.

'I won't forget this, Craig,' said Benton.

'Me neither,' said Malton. 'I have to go. One or two loose ends left to tie up.'

He hung up and noticed Adam Cornforth had gone pale. Ever since Malton had turned up on Adam's doorstep and frog-marched him into the car he hadn't said a word.

Until now.

'I just need to explain,' started Adam Cornforth.

'You'll explain everything. Not here though,' said Malton and he pulled out and carried on driving.

They headed south, down the A34, through the tiny village of Alderley Edge lined with footballers' mansions, and onwards towards the Edge itself, the strip of land high up, overlooking all of Manchester.

As Malton turned off the main road and down a dirt track, close to the Edge, Adam spoke up again. A quiet, defeated voice. 'Make it quick. Please.'

Malton said nothing. He kept on going for another few hundred metres. By now the track was narrow with dense woodland on both sides. Winter had thinned out the canopy, leaving skeletal arms and revealing the views down from the Edge out over all of Manchester.

Malton parked up and got out of the car. He walked around to the passenger side and let Adam out.

'Follow me,' he said.

Wordlessly he led Adam deeper into the woodland. It was early morning but they saw no one. No joggers or dog walkers to spoil their splendid isolation.

They started moving uphill. Turning back, Malton saw Adam was struggling to keep up. Malton stopped and stood waiting until Adam reached him. Without giving the other man a moment to catch his breath Malton started moving again, marching uphill.

Malton suddenly stopped and shouldered his way through a bush to the side of the dirt track. Adam followed and found himself stood next to Malton on the edge of a steep cliff that towered over the lower hills of Alderley Edge. The woodland fell away beneath them and they could see clear across the whole of Manchester.

They saw the Beetham Tower surrounded by dull pretenders to its lofty crown – student accommodation and Chinese-financed flats. They could make out the AO arena and the dome of the Palace Hotel. Somewhere down there in a nice street in Didsbury was Adam's home.

Malton sat down, his legs dangling over the edge.

'Sit,' he said and Adam obeyed.

The morning view over the city seemed to have an effect on Adam Cornforth. Suddenly his own troubles seemed just a little smaller. Whatever was about to happen he couldn't stop it now. It was over and he knew it. 'I want you to know I didn't mean for any of this to happen,' he said.

'But it happened,' said Malton.

Adam nodded. 'And I know it's my fault. I did it all.'

Malton kept staring out across the vastness of Greater Manchester. From up here it looked almost peaceful.

'What did the police tell you about Lewis?' Malton said.

Adam shook his head angrily. 'Nothing. They said there wasn't enough evidence. A whole bar full of people saw it. How could there not be enough evidence?'

Malton felt the heat of the sun slowly beginning to make itself felt through the grey cloud. It would be a beautiful day. He waited for Adam to continue.

'I wouldn't let it lie. I was writing letters. I spoke to our MP. My wife, she just wanted to forget. But you can't forget, can you? It wasn't right. It shouldn't have happened like that.

And yet everyone I spoke to, no one could do a thing. They knew who that man was and no one did a thing.'

'Paul Bistacchi?'

'My wife moved out in the end. We were fighting all the time. She couldn't bear to think about Lewis or the man who killed him. She was right.'

Adam gazed out at the horizon. Malton knew he wasn't seeing any of it. Too blinded by his own grief and regret.

'And then you met Keisha Bistacchi?' said Malton.

'I told all this to your younger colleague,' said Adam.

'And now you can tell me,' said Malton, his gaze fixed on the blinking lights atop the cranes of Manchester's building boom.

'She was at Lewis's funeral. Of course, I didn't know her at the time. There were lots of well-wishers there. It'd been in the paper, Lewis getting attacked. People were very good to us. She told me straight out who she was. His wife. And what he did to her.'

Malton made a clipped little sound in his throat. Like a stifled laugh.

'She was kind. She listened. She was . . . Since Lewis died there'd been nothing. The fight was keeping me occupied but it wasn't living.'

'And then she asked you to kidnap Paul Bistacchi?' said Malton.

Adam looked at his feet hanging over the edge. It was a long way down. 'Of course I was angry. But kidnapping? Have you seen the size of Paul Bistacchi?'

Adam laughed to himself, tickled by the absurdity of it all.

'But she kept on. And eventually I thought, why not? Whatever you say, he killed my boy.'

Adam turned to Malton. For a moment he was steadfast. It all made sense to him. But only for a moment. He shrugged and looked away. 'What do I care anymore? Go on. Do it. You're going to throw me off? Make it look like a suicide?'

Malton looked genuinely surprised. 'Why would I do that?'

'Then why are we here?'

Malton gestured towards the horizon and the dawn. 'The view. I love the view. Don't you?'

They both took it in. From mills and slums to tower blocks and commerce. A city driven by the will of its people. The city he'd lived in his entire life. When you were down there it was hard to see it all. Impossible to realise how every piece of the city connected to every other piece, a giant puzzle that you could only fully appreciate by stepping far enough back to see the whole picture.

The morning light revealing everything.

'I'll turn myself in,' Adam said.

'Don't do that. Just tell me where Paul Bistacchi is and I'll sort the rest,' said Malton.

'You? But why?'

'Do you need to know?'

Adam looked like slowly, finally he was beginning to understand the rules of the game he'd found himself dragged into.

'What if he finds out who I am? He'll come after me. I'll never be safe,' he said.

'I'll have a word,' said Malton.

'What about Keisha?'

Malton screwed up his face. 'That's a bit trickier.'

68

Dean was glad Keisha had stopped talking to him. The moment Malton left the room she had been all over him. Begging, threatening, trying to make some kind of deal that would result in him letting her out of that office. Dean wasn't totally sure that if she rushed him he'd be able to stop her leaving. She was small, but there was something about her that left him in no doubt that he didn't want to fight her.

So now she was sitting on Malton's sofa – staring at him. Silently judging him. Dean was starting to miss the talking.

It got so bad that after ten minutes of uncomfortable silence he had excused himself, locking her in, only to return a few minutes later with cleaning supplies. He began to clean up the cake that Malton had hurled at the wall.

It was something to do and even though it meant that he had his back to Keisha he could look up at one of the several mirrors Malton had on the wall of his office to check that she was still sitting on the sofa.

As he scooped handfuls of ruined cake into a black bin liner he glanced up and saw Keisha was still staring at him. She caught him looking and smiled. Instinctively Dean smiled back. Keisha kept on smiling until Dean had to look away.

When he looked up again a few seconds later, he saw she had moved.

She was on her feet by the sofa.

'Sit down,' said Dean, hoping he sounded like he meant it.

'You asking or you telling?' said Keisha. Dean realised this was the first time he'd seen her without her sunglasses on. Her eyes were dark and angry, the strip lighting of the office casting her face into sharp relief. She suddenly looked older. Harder.

'The door's locked. We're not going anywhere. Sit down,' he said, trying his best to sound like Malton.

Keisha didn't move. 'You missed a bit,' she said, pointing to the cake all over the wall.

Realising that this was an unwinnable conversation, Dean turned his back on her and went back to cleaning. Out of the corner of his eye he could see her start to wander back and forth.

'I planned all this you know,' she said casually.

'I know. I spoke to Leon Walker's daughter.'

Keisha seemed surprised. But only for a moment.

'So you know I got Leon Walker to shoot up Craig's front door? Get his attention?'

'Yeah. I saw him scoping out Malton's house. I tracked him down, found out who he was.'

Keisha looked impressed. 'Aren't you a clever boy? I guess you saw him back there in town too? Before you totalled Craig's car.'

Keisha started giggling. Dean carried on cleaning.

'Didn't he do a good job of roughing me up? Terrified of laying a finger he was. I told him – if you don't slap me about then I'll slap you about. That got him on board.'

Dean could well believe that despite his size and vicious reputation Leon Walker would need convincing to lay a finger on Keisha.

She started to move towards the weights.

'Stay away from there,' said Dean forcefully.

Keisha smiled and made a show of backing away.

331

'Don't want me braining you with a 10-kilogram plate do we? So did you also know it was me who set up the robbery at Lorraine's?'

'Yeah. I figured that too. You needed to drag Danny Mitchum in but you needed Malton on the back foot before you did it.'

Keisha gave Dean a sarcastic round of applause.

'That's right. It was a two-for-one. I can see why Craig likes you so much.'

Dean didn't say anything but despite knowing full well Keisha was a murderous, psychotic liar he chose to take it at face value that Malton had been singing his praises to her.

'And you must have known it was me who had Paul kidnapped?' coaxed Keisha.

'It all fits together. You just need the right pieces,' said Dean. 'There's just one thing I don't get. What if Danny Mitchum had killed Malton or killed you?'

Keisha burst out laughing. She didn't stop. Whatever it was that Dean had said, had uncorked a reservoir of long-suppressed mirth. Finally she wiped her eyes and took a breath.

'That's why even Danny Mitchum knows to handle Craig with care. That's why I nearly got away with it. If you're worried that one day someone might catch you and hurt you or kill you, then you don't do any of this. You become a teacher or an accountant or whatever other sort of wanker gets to live out their quiet, safe little life without ever knowing how it feels to risk everything.'

Dean finally got it. Keisha wasn't locked in here with him. He was locked in here with her. He began to wonder when Malton would be back.

Despite his mounting fear Dean was resolute, nothing Keisha could say or do would make him open that door and so he carried on cleaning.

Keeping her in his peripheral vision, Dean saw Keisha walk to Malton's desk. There was nothing but a few unopened bits of mail on it. Nothing that could be used as a makeshift weapon.

Dean had nearly finished scraping cake off the wall. He turned to face Keisha.

'You did all this just to get back at Malton?' he said, incredulously.

Keisha sat down in Malton's chair and leaned back. Her face was smiling but her eyes were cold.

'No. I did all this to get him back.'

Dean looked puzzled. Sensing his confusion Keisha leaned in low over the desk, spreading herself across the surface like a coiled snake, looking up at him with those cold, dangerous eyes.

'I planned everything. Right down to the last detail. Like what would happen when I turned up on Craig's driveway with my sob story. He'd take me to his office, because he couldn't very well keep me inside his house, could he? Not with his posh little girlfriend there?'

'But he already knew what you were up to.'

'Oh I know. That was unfortunate. He's a clever one that Craig Malton. But I had a plan for that. I thought maybe I could still talk him round.'

'It didn't work, did it?' said Dean.

Keisha looked sad.

'No. It didn't,' she said reaching under the desk. 'But that's why the very first time I came into this office I made sure to leave a little something behind. Just in case.'

Keisha pulled her hand out from under the desk. She was holding something. Something small, and black and metallic.

Keisha stood up and pointed the miniature handgun at Dean.

'Go on. Tell me how fucking clever I am,' said Keisha with a flourish.

'What do you want?' said Dean, backing away.

'He's got handcuffs in his drawer. Take them out.'

'He'll find you. You can't run from him.'

'You still don't know who I am do you?' said Keshia pityingly.

Dean tried to not look as scared as he felt. 'You're Keisha Bistacchi.'

Keisha frowned indulgently. 'Nearly but not quite. I'm the woman who made Craig Malton.' The sing-song lilt left her voice, 'Now get me my fucking handcuffs.'

Dean recognised that tone of voice. He'd heard it dozens of times. It was the tone of voice that suggested a terrible, cold violence was about to erupt and only absolute obedience could stop it in its tracks. It was how Malton sounded.

Dean walked to the drawer and sure enough there were the handcuffs.

'Now unlock the door. Give me the keys and then go and chain yourself to his weights bench.'

She waited as Dean chained himself to the weights bench. He raised his hand to demonstrate his complete helplessness.

'Where are you going?' asked Dean.

Keisha smiled. 'Away,' she said before she raised the gun, aimed it squarely at Dean's face and pulled the trigger.

69

Paul Bistacchi lay on his back conserving what was left of his strength. A lightbulb hung directly above him, the stark downward glare constantly tugging him back from the brink of unconsciousness. Paul could no longer feel his legs. The pain had progressed to an aching numbness.

If he flexed he could feel the burned skin on his chest where the cattle prod had struck. His hair scorched to stubble and flesh lightly cooked. It may well have hurt, but at this point Paul Bistacchi was beyond pain.

Turning his head to the left, he could see light around the garage door where someone had roughly propped it back up, stuffing it into the broken frame. It had taken all his energy to break out and enjoy those few sweet seconds of freedom. Now he was right back where he started.

The concrete floor began to feel very cold indeed. He felt the darkness close behind him.

He lay on his back and concentrated on all the violent things he was going to do to all the people who he held responsible for him being there. It kept him just a few steps ahead of the dark.

That's where he was when Malton let himself in.

'You look like shit, Paul,' said Malton.

Paul was so shocked to hear his voice he almost sat up before the weight of his injuries hit him and sent him right back down to the floor.

'What happened to your legs?'

'Get me out of here,' barked Paul.

Malton did as he was told, heaving Paul to his feet. Despite everything he'd gone through Paul was still a big man. He easily had a couple of stone on Malton.

Upright, the blood began to circulate around Paul Bistacchi's body. The numbness in his legs slowly started to melt into excruciating pain.

He nearly fell but Malton's solid frame kept him upright.

'It's his fucking dad,' muttered Paul.

'What gave it away?' asked Malton, leading Paul out of the garage and onto the lawn. It was early morning and still chilly out.

'What the fuck you doing here?' said Paul as they staggered their way across the driveway to Malton's waiting car.

'Keisha hired me to find you,' said Malton.

'Clever girl. Playing both sides,' said Paul.

'What's that supposed to mean?' asked Malton, not giving anything away.

'You're not half as smart as you think you are. That's your problem.'

Paul was near enough to the car to shake Malton off and take faltering steps on his own. Every part of his body screamed in protest but there was no way he was going to accept any more help from Malton than was absolutely necessary.

He reached the car and stood waiting.

'Just got cramp,' he said unconvincingly. 'All that sitting about and that.'

Malton walked around to the other side of the car, taking his time. Paul leaned across the roof and grinned with malice.

'I'm betting Keisha paid you good money to find me. My fucking money. Now come on, take me home. So I can thank her personally.'

70

Malton had put down plastic bin liners to protect Emily's car from the blood. Paul Bistacchi sat in the passenger seat silently glaring out of the window. Malton couldn't help but sneak a satisfied glance at the scabbed wounds on his legs.

Malton drove up the entrance ramp to the inner ring road and began the short drive to the A57 and onwards to Hattersley. In the Sixties there were grand plans to throng Manchester city centre with elevated roads. This small stretch, dubbed the Mancunian Way, was as far as they got. But it afforded the driver a bird's eye view of the increasingly dense city centre. Half a dozen buildings were being thrown up on one side, and on the other brownfield land was being cleared for yet more growth. And dotted beneath the flyover – what were once some of the worst-situated council houses in the world. Houses that now found themselves in the beating heart of a resurgent city.

'You can't harm Adam Cornforth,' said Malton as they passed Piccadilly.

'The fuck I can't. Look what he did to my legs!' Paul shuffled his bloody thighs for emphasis. 'I'm going to take the bastard to bits.'

'You can't, cos I said you can't,' said Malton matter-of-factly.

'Or else what?' sneered Paul. 'You going to watch him 24/7?'

'No. I'm not going to do anything. I'm just going to ask you nicely. Please don't ever contact Adam Cornforth again.

Don't send people round. Don't post shit on Facebook. Let him live his life. You got some new holes in your legs; he lost his son. You're up on the deal.'

Malton's attention was on the road as he merged onto the motorway to Hattersley.

Having failed to get a reaction from Malton, Paul settled back in his seat and did his best to not let on how badly his legs were hurting.

'I suppose Keisha paid you for this bullshit too?' he grumbled.

'No,' said Malton with a wry smile. 'This is bonus bullshit.'

Malton wound his way through Hattersley towards the Bistacchi house. The sight of his territory seemed to be having an effect on Paul. He was sitting up, scanning the pavements for faces he recognised. Making sure that anyone he did recognise noticed him. Saw he was back. The kind of power Paul Bistacchi had required a constant application of pressure. He could never rely on loyalty or shared interest. It depended on fear and fear alone. Paul knew that even being absent for a few days could be enough for that fear to wane sufficiently for someone to fancy their chances.

Malton pulled over at the top of Burns Avenue.

'You not dropping me off?' asked Paul, warily eyeing the long walk to the bottom of Burns Avenue.

Malton turned to Paul. 'I'm going to ask you one last time. Do you agree to leave Adam Cornforth be?'

'Fuck off,' Paul retorted. 'And so you know, I wasn't kidnapped by some no one off the street. This was all a set-up. This was all Keisha. She played you.'

Malton tried to look surprised. 'You think your own wife had you kidnapped?'

'I know she did. I heard her talking to him, didn't I? Outside the garage. Didn't know that about your ex, did you? That she was a lying, little bitch?'

Malton kept quiet.

'So now I'm going to take a shower, eat a load of McDonald's and then I'm going to be asking her a few questions. I'm going to show her exactly what it feels like when someone takes a fucking power drill to your legs. And there's not a fucking thing you can do about it.'

'I can ask you nicely not to,' said Malton.

He waited for an answer. What Paul said next would decide whether Malton would drive Paul down his cul-de-sac and deliver him to his door or whether things would get more complicated.

'Fuck you,' said Paul. 'Now drive me to my fucking door.'

As Malton steered the B-Max down the narrow cul-de-sac he reflected. Keisha was right about one thing: people don't change. Paul Bistacchi was living proof of that.

Malton watched Paul struggle out the car and up to his front door. He saw Paul take in the boarded-up windows and the broken glass. Paul knocked. No one answered. He knocked again.

Malton almost felt bad for Paul.

'Mum! Open the fucking door!' barked Paul.

The door swung open and two sets of hands grabbed Paul Bistacchi, hauling him inside. A moment later Stevie Mitchum's piggy face peered out of the doorway, locking eyes with Malton.

Neither man moved a muscle until Stevie swung the front door shut and Malton did a neat, three-point turn and headed home.

It had been a very long night.

71

The first thing I need to say is that I love you. And I'll always love you. I was in the darkest place and you were my light. I'll never fully understand why, but you didn't see a silly little rich girl slumming it out of her depth. You saw someone who desperately needed rescuing and you came to my rescue. I will always love you for that. But I can't stay.

I know what you do. Or at least as much as I want to know. It's my fault I've turned a blind eye. Every time you came home with bloody knuckles. Every time I found rolls of money in your clothes. When we go out and the most dangerous-looking men treat you like some kind of celebrity, I'll admit I enjoyed it. I liked being on the arm of the man people were scared of. It made me feel safe.

But now I'm the one who's scared. I don't know who that woman on the driveway was or what she means to you but I do know what it felt like to hear you talk to me like that. To order me. Like there was no option but to obey. I remember exactly how that feels from my life before you.

I cannot and will not bring a child into that. This might be my last chance to be a mother but if I have to give it up to protect the child that will never be born then that's what I'll do.

This is the hardest thing I've ever done but I know I need to do it. And if you love me then please understand why I've done this. Please don't try to contact me. Please let me go.

Emily

72

Malton had found the note on the kitchen table. He'd come home assuming Emily would still be in bed after he left in the early hours of the morning. He'd stopped at a local deli to pick up free-range eggs, thick-cut bacon and a still-warm sourdough loaf. His plan was to make breakfast, and he was looking forward to the chance for him to shut his brain down for half an hour while he fried up bacon and brewed coffee. Then he'd carry it up to their bedroom and act like the previous evening had never happened.

If she asked he'd tell her that it was a work thing. He would rely on his absolute confidence to persuade her that to probe any further was unnecessary. It was one of those things. He wasn't worried so it would be foolish of her to worry. Then he'd move the conversation on to what was really important – the future. The IVF and finally starting their family. The happiness that it had taken him so long to accept.

He didn't get a chance to do any of that.

He read the note just the once. He understood what it said and as much as he might wish otherwise, reading it again wouldn't change its meaning. Stood alone in the kitchen, he felt a cold numbness begin to flood over his body. Maybe it was tiredness, maybe it was grief. He swallowed hard, flexing the stiffness out of his thick fists as he fought to stifle what couldn't possibly be tears.

If you love something, it will leave you.

The sound of his phone going off pulled his focus. It was Dean. Malton already knew what he would be calling about – Keisha had escaped. Malton had debated whether to go and check on Keisha before coming home. His instinct had told him that Keisha would make a move and that when she did, Dean wouldn't be ready for it. But something louder had told him he needed to be with Emily. That the events of the previous evening needed dealing with.

So many fires and so little time to put them out.

Malton answered his phone. Dean's voice sounded faint on the other end. 'She shot me. I'm dying.'

Malton snapped back to life. He'd lost Emily; he wouldn't lose Dean too. But first he needed to address the final threat. 'Where's Keisha?' he asked.

'I don't know. She got away. She shot me. In the face.' The words squeezed out between clenched teeth, Dean's breath shallow and tight.

'Did she say where she was going?' Malton knew he was pushing the boy but he couldn't afford to walk into another trap.

'She said "away".'

Malton took a moment to consider. Then another. Then another.

'I didn't want to call an ambulance. Get you in trouble.' Dean sounded in a bad way.

Malton felt the thrill of urgency filling up the empty space left by Emily's note. He seized on it. Told himself that underneath it all he had been right. His desire to have a family *had* made him weak.

He wouldn't make that mistake again. He would keep moving, never let himself be tied to anyone or anything. He would embrace the darkness. Make it work *for* him.

Malton could hear Dean's faint breathing on the end of the line.

'Stay in the office,' he said. 'I'm coming to get you.'

343

73

Malton never forgot the first time he was shot. It was like the first time he had sex. Looking back and thinking: *Is that what all the fuss was about?*

But just like having sex, the world divided into those who had and those who hadn't. Now Dean was one of those who had. Malton found him on the floor of the office, passed out from his wound. He scooped him up, laid him out on the sofa and was dabbing his face with iodine when Dean came to.

It took a moment for the pain to register but when it did Dean shot up with a scream. Malton had to hold him down, the combination of his strength and the implied threat that strength carried being enough to convince Dean to lie back and endure.

Malton explained the damage, and told him how lucky he was to not have lost an eye or his tongue. Malton prepped a syringe full of liquid ketamine. Dean was in a bad way and while morphine would solve his pain he couldn't run the risk of the boy's lungs giving out on him. Ketamine would take the edge off just enough until he could get him to a doctor. As he slid the needles in he smiled and told Dean at least he'd end up with a menacing scar. Just like his.

Dean had laughed. The drugs Malton was injecting into him and the sight of Malton running a thick finger down the scar on the side of his own face proved too potent to resist. And then he passed out.

By the time he came to, Malton was on the move again. He'd strapped Dean into the passenger seat of the Ford B-Max and was heading across Manchester.

'I think I need a hospital,' garbled Dean, his voice muffled by the wadding and clotted blood filling his mouth.

'You do,' said Malton. 'But there's one more thing to deal with first.'

Dean went to talk but Malton stopped him.

'Don't say a thing. Just lie back, enjoy the ketamine and think happy thoughts. Whatever you do, don't go to sleep.'

Dean shuffled up in his seat. It was clear to Malton that he was in a great deal of pain. Malton didn't show it but he was worried he was going to lose him. This whole night had been a collection of last-minute judgement calls. So far the dice had mostly rolled in Malton's favour. If he could tie up the last loose end before taking care of Dean then he could finally rest.

'Let me tell you a story,' he said. 'Listen to my voice and stay awake. Can you do that?'

Dean feebly raised a hand and gave a thumbs-up sign.

'It wasn't Danny Mitchum who kidnapped Johnny Bistacchi. It was me.'

Dean's eyes were wide with surprise. Malton allowed himself a pleased little smile.

'The Bistacchis were always planning to hit Danny; Keisha was just speeding up the process and putting me in the crosshairs. So I decided to give her what she wanted.'

Malton kept talking, all the while keeping one eye on Dean. Making sure he was still with him.

'I sent a couple of my guys out to intercept them on their way back from getting the guns. Keisha had told me where they were going. That part of the world, it's small, not many roads. With a bit of luck and surveillance it was easy enough to know where they'd be. I knew Maria wouldn't be able to back down if she thought Danny Mitchum had lifted both her boys. Suddenly Keisha got what she wanted. A war between the Bistacchis and Danny Mitchum. A war she knew they'd lose.'

Malton looked over to Dean. His eyes were alert, taking it all in. Malton continued.

'To make sure she got the message I got a couple of the guys from the office to go round to the Bistacchi house. Throw a few bricks. Keep them on their toes.'

Dean was smiling. The effort of it was clearly hurting him but he couldn't help it. Malton's plan had been the perfect combination of brutality and daring.

'I let Johnny think he'd escaped Danny Mitchum in the hope that he'd go back to the Bistacchis and convince them it was a war they couldn't win. And if he couldn't convince them, then I hoped Keisha would at least realise just how risky her plan was and call it off.'

Dean took a breath and very slowly started to speak. 'Why . . . let . . . him . . . keep . . . the . . . guns?'

Malton smiled. 'Good question. Say I let him go with nothing? That's them fighting for their lives, and there's no telling what a cornered animal might do. But give them just enough firepower to feel safe, then they hole up and wait it out. Enough time for me to unravel everything. At least that was the plan.'

Dean sat back in his seat, taking it all in. Malton drove on in silence. He had run out of things to say. It had been very satisfying to lay out his thinking over the past few days. He had never had someone like Dean before, someone he felt would not only understand and appreciate it but who would also learn from it.

Malton desperately hoped Dean would survive his gunshot wound. If he did then from here on in there would be nothing he wouldn't do for the boy. He'd been shot in the face and his first phone call was not to an ambulance but to Malton. He'd been tested and he'd passed with flying colours.

Malton pressed a button and the windows rolled down. The cool morning air rushed into the car. Next he turned the radio on and pushed the volume right up. Loud music filled the car.

It was early, still an hour or so before rush hour and they had Manchester to themselves. They wound through the city centre, hugging the inner ring road and on through Moss Side. The terraced streets were as scruffy as ever. The loose cables from makeshift aerials hanging down over the fronts of crudely subdivided homes. Alleys choked with litter and broken furniture. A half-mile square putting up the fight of its life against the forces of gentrification emanating from the city centre.

They passed through Fallowfield with its mixture of student housing and grand Victorian villas. Properties that cost near to a million pounds but sat cheek by jowl with crumbling flats stuffed with those students who couldn't afford the new luxury blocks in the centre.

They crossed the A34 and turned towards Stockport and the Heatons. There were more trees now, the city making a concerted effort to trick you into thinking that maybe you weren't living in an urban sprawl of four million souls.

Paul was most likely already dead at the hands of Stevie Mitchum. Johnny was in police custody thanks to Benton, and Keisha was in the wind. There was just one loose end left.

Malton pulled into Claire Minshall's driveway and, leaving Dean in the car with the radio on loud to keep him from passing out, went round to the car boot to check on his other passenger.

74

Claire had woken up feeling nauseous. Jessica was asleep next to her in the bed, where Marcus used to sleep. Claire tried to swallow down the urge to vomit. Was it fear or cancer or both? Lately every little niggle had her worrying. When she felt the cold, or was a little stiffer than usual in the morning, all she could think was whether or not this was the start of the end, the swift downward spiral into hospital and hospice and the grave.

But now she had hope in the form of the proton beam therapy and she had strength in the form of Jessica, the brave daughter sleeping beside her. Claire was now ready to choose life, for however long it lasted.

The sickness started to pass and Claire turned to spoon her sleeping daughter. Marcus was dead. Jessica was her world now. Johnny Bistacchi and Craig Malton meant nothing when you put them up against that. Claire wasn't prepared to let fear and grief have any more of her time.

Lying there she made a promise to herself. In half an hour the alarm would go off. She'd get up and help Jessica get ready for school, cook breakfast and send her on her way. Then she'd head off herself, go into work and start another school day, reset her life to before Marcus died and all this happened. She was going to go back to being normal.

Claire had spent her whole life taking charge. Running failing schools as well as a home, and raising a daughter. She'd never walked away from a challenge or stopped fighting for what she knew was right. Now she saw calling Craig Malton all those days ago for what it was – blind panic. She had felt helpless for just a moment and in that moment she'd made a terrible choice. But now she was back in control.

Five minutes before her alarm was due to go off, someone rang the doorbell.

Her heart sank as she looked out of the window. There on the driveway waiting for her to open the door was Craig Malton.

75

Keisha had never not had a plan B. Craig wasn't the only one who knew what it took to start again from the ground up. She relished the challenge. A clean slate with only one pre-condition: whatever she did from now on there was only one goal – to strip Craig Malton of everything he loved, to expose him to the world and finally, once he was broken beyond salvation to hear him beg to take her back. And if he didn't, she'd kill him.

The Bistacchis had half a dozen properties around Manchester. Keisha had offered to manage them and Paul had gladly let her take over the paperwork. In no time at all Keisha had remortgaged every property. Using inflated valuations, she leveraged the maximum amount of money from each property. She used that money to purchase a small, detached house on the outskirts of Bury in her name and what she had left over she converted into gold Krugerrand and luxury watches. Underworld currency.

Keisha was at that house in Bury now, getting ready to disappear. She had lost the element of surprise. Craig knew she would be coming for him. But at least he had no idea when or where the move would come from.

On the kitchen table was Keisha's go-bag – everything she'd need to go on the run indefinitely. Over fifty thousand in gold and watches, a couple of fake passports and a change of clothes. Keisha had survived on a lot less.

And she still had her secret: that hateful day thirty years ago, the memory of which had put all of this in motion.

She still had that tiny, burning seed inside her. As long as she had that she would never stop.

But before she left she had one last thing to do.

Keisha was packing a shoebox with bubble wrap. Into the small hollow centre she tossed a syringe, a dozen hypodermic needles, a rubber tourniquet and finally – a five-gram bag of uncut heroin. She took a Post-it note and neatly wrote on it 'One Last Chance' before sticking it in on top.

She made sure everything was packed snugly with more bubble wrap before putting the lid on the box and sealing it up with tape. Next, she wrapped the box neatly in brown packing paper and taped it shut.

Keisha was going to deliver this personally, to make sure it ended up where it was meant to go – into the hands of the person who would unwrap it and be unable to resist using what they found inside.

To make sure there was no doubt whatsoever, Keisha took a thick black marker and wrote a name on the top of the box.

Now she was ready. She just had to deliver this parcel and then she would be in the wind until such a time as she decided to strike.

She picked up her go-bag and the shoebox, which bore the name 'EMILY' in elegant, blocky capitals, and headed out.

76

'I know you're in there,' called Malton through the letter box.

He had seen the upstairs curtains twitch as he arrived. Claire's car was still in the driveway. He knew she was home. She was a loose end he had no intention of leaving unattended.

He glanced back to the car. Dean looked in a bad way. Malton needed to get this sorted and get it sorted now.

He went to ring the bell again but before he could, Claire opened the door defiantly. She had thrown on jeans and a blouse and tied back her hair. Doing everything she could to muster a little dignity and presence for this confrontation.

'If you don't leave now I'm calling the police,' she said.

'That's up to you,' said Malton. 'But I just came to give you some good news. You don't need to worry about the Bistacchis anymore.'

Claire's face darkened.

'You killed him, didn't you?'

'Not me. But by now Paul Bistacchi is most likely dead. His mum too I'd imagine. Johnny Bistacchi is in police custody about to be charged with firearms offences, and the woman who came to your funeral . . .' Malton paused searching for the right word. 'She's gone.'

Claire's mouth opened and closed, words eluding her as she took it all in. Finally, with a trembling but determined voice she said, 'I need to know, was this because of Marcus? Did he do something? Was he involved with the Bistacchis? You promised me that.'

Malton almost smiled. After everything that had happened, this was what had stuck with her the most.

'Your husband had never met the Bistacchis before. He did nothing wrong.'

Relief flooded Claire, but only for a moment. Then the horror of what Malton was saying hit her.

'You mean all of this, it was just . . .'

'Bad luck,' said Malton.

Claire stood taking this in. She seemed unsure whether to laugh or cry.

'And it's over?' she said.

'Yes. I've made sure of that. But now I need something from you.'

Claire knew exactly what he meant. She stood up a little straighter and put her chest out defiantly.

'I'm not giving you the video. If I give you that what's to stop you killing me?'

'Why would I do that?'

It was the most chilling question Claire had ever heard. She took a step back, her hand on the door.

'I've got an offer,' said Malton.

Claire watched as he walked to the boot of the car he came in, opened it up and helped a hooded figure to clamber out.

Malton guided the hooded figure onto his feet and walked him back to Claire. She was looking less and less composed. Exactly what Malton wanted.

'You said Johnny was in police custody,' said Claire, an edge of panic to her voice.

Malton reached up and pulled the hood off to reveal a scared, pale-looking Cody Harper.

Claire gasped and visibly shook for a moment before her years of teaching kicked in and she held it together. For Cody's sake.

Malton let her look at the pitiful youth for a little longer. Every step here was calculated. This was theatre and he was the director, manoeuvring Claire to exactly where he wanted her to be. The perfect outcome: a compromise. Letting everyone walk away feeling like they snatched victory from the jaws of defeat. Just.

'Where have you been? The police, they said you . . .' Claire looked down and saw the stump where Cody's hand had been.

Cody looked to Malton as if waiting for permission to speak. In that moment Claire knew it was all true. Her pupil had killed a woman and Malton had cut his hand off, stopping him.

Suddenly Claire Minshall the head teacher came roaring back to life. She turned on Malton.

'What have you done to him?'

'I saved his life,' said Malton.

'You cut his hand off,' said Claire. 'You can't get away with this.'

'He killed a woman,' said Malton gravely. He let it hang. The impossible web of immorality that surrounded everything he touched.

Claire turned back to Cody. She was struggling to hold it together. 'I told your mother you were dead.'

'He is,' said Malton. 'Unless I help him.'

'You brought him all this way to tell me you're going to kill him unless I give you the video?'

'No. Not me. A very dangerous man. The man who owned the café Cody here robbed. He can't be seen to be ripped off and not do anything about it. Soon as he knows Cody's alive he'll make his move.'

'Give him to me and I'll make sure he turns himself in,' pleaded Claire.

354

Malton shook his head. 'The man I'm talking about has a long reach. Prison is more dangerous than being on the outside. Cody here would be dead within a week.'

Claire reeled. Malton watched her trying to process it all in her head. She was finally getting it.

'But if you tell this man not to, you can save Cody's life?' she said with resignation.

Malton made a show of looking down, trying his best to summon an air of disappointment and apology.

'It's not that easy. Cody has crossed a very dangerous man. The only way I can convince that man to spare Cody is to offer him someone else in his place. An eye for an eye.'

'You want me to choose?'

Malton had finally reached his destination. Claire Minshall was a clever, successful woman but she had never done half the things Malton had done to succeed. Her imagination was hemmed in by things like decency and empathy. She was fighting with one hand tied behind her back.

'It's not a choice. There's only one man who'll fit the bill. Johnny Bistacchi.'

It would be a stretch but Malton was confident he could make the trade. The Bistacchis had waged war on Danny Mitchum. It was no different to Leon Walker shooting at Malton's front door. If the underworld saw a challenge go unanswered then the spell would be broken and it would be open season. That was worse than any drop house robbery. In return for the boy's life Malton would give Danny Mitchum Johnny Bistacchi and thus restore Danny's reputation as top dog.

'You said he was in police custody,' said Claire.

'He is. That's no guarantee of anything,' said Malton coldly.

'Who is it?' Jessica's voice came from upstairs. The sound of it seemed to bring some kind of clarity to Claire's thoughts.

She stepped forward and closed the door behind her.

'This is the deal,' she said. 'You give me Cody now. I will take him to his mother's house and stay there until the police arrive. I assume you've already threatened him to keep quiet about you. I know you want me to choose between the man who killed my husband and one of my pupils because it appeals to your twisted sense of justice. And I choose Cody. But not because I'm like you. Because I'm nothing like you. I'm making that choice and it's going to haunt me forever. But I know you won't think twice about any of this. And my final condition. I keep the video. You have my word I won't show it to another soul. But I'm keeping it. You can either trust me or not. That's the deal.'

Malton was genuinely impressed. It's true it gave him a morbid satisfaction to have put Claire in this position but he had expected a tearful capitulation. This was very different. This he could respect.

'That's my deal,' said Claire, holding out her hand.

77

'Thank you, Miss,' said Cody quietly from the passenger seat of Claire's car.

It was only a short drive from Claire's house in Didsbury to Susannah's in Hulme but thanks to the rush hour traffic she had been slowly crawling down Princess Parkway for the past twenty minutes.

She tried to focus on the road and ignore Cody's hand. Or rather the stump where his hand used to be. It rested in his lap obscene and lifeless. Malton had dressed the wound and kept the boy alive but it was clear he would need proper medical attention as a matter of urgency. And then there was the matter of the robbery.

Claire kept her eyes on the traffic as she spoke. 'You know you have to talk to the police. Tell them everything?' She was talking in her headmistress voice.

'Everything, Miss?' said Cody, sounding like the child he still was.

Claire knew exactly what he meant. She hated that she was being forced to go along with the lie, to cover for Malton and whatever it was he'd been doing to Cody for the past few days.

'Everything about your part in the robbery. You were alone?'

'Yeah,' said Cody. As young as he was, he knew what was happening here.

Claire remembered Cody when he was just starting school. He was a small boy. He hadn't yet had the growth spurt that so many of his peers were already enjoying. He was always talking, and it soon became clear that the constant chatter was a coping mechanism. A way to evade being called on in class. To avoid anyone finding out all the things he couldn't yet do. The things that his peers found so easy.

'Whatever that man said to you, you need to know, as long as I'm here, he won't touch you or your family.'

'I know, Miss. He promised,' said Cody.

The traffic was still crawling. Claire turned off and started to cut through the Alexandra Park Estate towards Hulme. Thirty years ago the estate was home to two notorious gangs of kids not much older than Cody. There were drugs and guns and deaths. Thirty years ago, and it was still happening now. Claire felt sick.

'Miss . . .' started Cody.

'Whatever he told you, I don't want to know,' said Claire.

'It's not that, Miss. I just want . . . I'm sorry, Miss. I was a little bastard, wasn't I?'

Cody smiled just a little. Claire couldn't help join in.

'Just a bit,' said Claire.

'I was dumb. A little kid. I know now, you weren't out to get me. You were one of the good guys, Miss. Thanks.'

Claire felt a lump in her throat as she pulled up outside Susannah's house. She spoke to Cody, not as a headmistress now, but as a mum.

'We go in and you've got half an hour with your mum and Yaya before I take you to a hospital and call the police. Is that a deal?'

'It's a deal, Miss.'

Cody looked very small and very young. Claire thought back to Malton. He said he went to school in Moss Side and had grown up just like Cody. Malton seemed like he'd never been young. Never been scared. Never been anything except

Malton. Claire hoped she'd never see him again as long as she lived.

'Let's go and make your mum's day.' Claire beamed.

The two of them got out of the car and the look on Susannah's face when she opened the door made Claire forget all about the horror of the past few weeks.

At least for a little while.

359

78

After Malton got back in the car Dean had expected they would take the short drive to Manchester Royal Infirmary, the city's largest hospital. Instead he found himself slipping in and out of consciousness as they headed south, out through Didsbury and on into the suburbs.

Dean remembered seeing glimpses of Chorlton high street with its organic delis and vegan takeaways and later a stretch of road he recognised as running alongside Sale Water Park. He was unsure where they finally ended up but his best guess was somewhere in the leafy anonymity of Urmston.

He didn't remember arriving at the house or indeed being taken in. His first memory was of waking up alone in a bedroom that looked a lot like someone's spare room. There was a rail of clothing by the window and boxes stacked on top of the cupboards as well as lining the walls. A musty, wet smell hung in the air.

The room looked like someone had been in a rush to make it habitable. The only functional piece of furniture apart from the bed was the clean, steel surgical trolley, which held fresh boxes of dressings as well as sealed packets of syringes and medicines.

Dean's next memory was of pain. He tried to raise his hand to his face but found he couldn't move. His head throbbed. It felt twice its usual size. Tentatively he'd tried moving his jaw and found his whole face bandaged tight.

Over the next few days Dean would meet the man who'd saved his life. He introduced himself as Dr Smith.

Going off the fact the doctor was clearly South Asian, Dean assumed it was a fake name and he didn't push it any further.

Dr Smith explained that he'd taken the bullet out of his jaw and reset the bone before stitching his face back up. He'd apologised that with what he had to hand he hadn't been able to do a neater job. Malton was right. Dean would have a scar.

As well as Dr Smith there was an older woman who came in and fed Dean. Every day she appeared in a different, brightly coloured sari bearing his food.

Dean was tormented by the smell of freshly prepared curries cooking somewhere in the house. But when the woman visited him all she brought was flavourless protein shakes, which she fed him through a straw.

Dean sucked them down and tried to pretend he was eating the delicious food that his wired jaw was incapable of consuming.

In all this time he'd not seen or heard from Malton. Dr Smith told Dean that Malton had spoken to his mum. As far as she knew her son been taken down to London on an urgent security job. Dean knew his mum wouldn't buy that for a second but he also knew that she trusted him enough to play along.

When he went home and she saw the scar that would be a different matter.

But he didn't care. Malton couldn't have taken him to hospital. He'd know Dean wouldn't talk but the bullet wound would have brought questions. Even if Dean had kept his mouth shut he'd be on the police radar from there on in. Malton clearly had other plans for Dean.

On the fourth or fifth day as Dr Smith was finishing up his daily check-up, he'd told Dean that he had a visitor waiting for him downstairs.

Dean was so excited he shot up in bed and instantly regretted it. The heavy pain medication dropped him like he'd been coshed. Dean didn't care. He had a visitor. It had to be Malton.

Dr Smith told him to take it easy and that he'd send the visitor up. After the doctor had left, Dean slowly and painfully hauled himself up into a sitting position. He wanted to show Malton how quickly he was shrugging off Keisha's attempt on his life.

Whether it was the pain medication or the surprise at who his visitor was, Dean was struck dumb at the sight of them.

Leon Walker's daughter Vikki gasped at the sight of Dean.

It took him a few moments to recognise her. She was wearing clean clothes and looked like she'd washed recently. Her hair, which had always been held back in a lank ponytail, was hanging down to her shoulders, shiny and freshly cut.

In her hand she had a bouquet of flowers, which she let hang awkwardly as if unsure whether they were the right thing to bring.

'They said you were shot in the face,' she said.

Dean went to speak but the best he could do was a kind of low murmur of agreement.

Vikki kept looking at him in horrified fascination.

'I called your card and the man at the other end told me everything. He said he was your boss?'

Dean managed a smile of encouragement and she continued.

'Anyway, I told him who I was and next thing I know he'd driven round personally and paid for someone to come and sort out the flat. I thought he must be after something, but I didn't really care. He got new furniture and everything. He could have taken what he wanted. But he didn't want anything.'

Dean started to laugh and instantly wished he hadn't. The sensation of laughter was agony, every movement of his jaw sending shooting pains up and down his body. The laugh turned into a muted grunt.

Vikki sat down on the bed with a look of concern on her face. Dean's eyes gave her a reassuring smile and she continued.

'He said he knew about my dad and wanted to help. Told me if I keep going to school he'd make sure I was safe and that there would be food in the flat. Why would he do that?'

With great effort Dean gave what he hoped was clear to be a shrug.

'He gave me these and told me where to find you.' She put the flowers on the bed. A guilty look flashed across her face. 'Thing is, when I called you, after what you did in the flat, you'd said if there was anything I needed . . .'

She hesitated, willing the words to come. Dean leaned forward, intrigued. This was something new. Something that clearly meant a lot to Vikki.

When she spoke, she sounded scared. 'My friend Olivia, she's gone missing. And I know she's not sleeping over somewhere or back in care. She's gone. She left her phone. She got all her pictures of her dead mum on that phone. She wouldn't ever leave it.'

Dean felt his heart start to race.

'I didn't want to tell your boss. He'd already done so much and it seemed silly. But I remembered what you said and I told you all that stuff about my dad. You owe me.'

Her words were tumbling out. Suddenly the scared, little girl was right back in the room.

'I know right now you're recovering, but when you're better . . . Can you help me find her?'

Dean's mouth felt dry. He could feel his jaw strain and the throbbing holes where shattered teeth had been extracted.

With great difficulty he swallowed and started to speak. Through the unbearable pain all he could manage was, 'Yes.'

Vikki was about to throw her arms around him, only at the last moment realising just how delicate Dean's condition was. She contented herself to smile down at him.

For the first time since he saw her Dean noticed her smile.

'There's something else I wanted to tell you,' she said. 'Something I didn't want to tell when we first met.'

Dean braced himself but Vikki looked less stern, more embarrassed.

'My name's not really Vikki. My dad, he likes this awful band called the Sex Pistols. Old-man music. Well anyway, he named me after one of them, even got the tattoo. Vikki? It's short for Vicious.'

79

It had been over a week and Malton hadn't heard from Emily. She hadn't been back to the house and she wasn't answering her phone. There'd been letters addressed to her from the hospital. He'd opened them and found out that she'd cancelled the IVF. The letters were warning her that at her age the effectiveness of the treatment would drop steeply with every passing year.

Out of curiosity he'd called in on the cake shop and found it shut with a small pile of mail collecting behind the front door.

Dean was on the mend. Malton had fixed him up with a doctor friend of his who'd stitched his face back together and was keeping him safe while he recovered – no questions asked. He'd also put Dean on a permanent contract, given him a huge pay rise and made a point of dropping in on his mum to lie to her about the big job Dean was doing down south. The kind of loyalty Dean had shown was rare and Malton was more than happy to reward it.

Dean's mum had instantly taken to Malton. He liked her. She was uncomplicated. She'd shown off the Ugg boots Dean bought her for her birthday and told him to watch out for her boy. He didn't tell her about the gunshot wound. One thing at a time.

Adam Cornforth had sold his house and moved on. Malton had driven past the place and seen builders halfway through gutting the old place, pulling out everything that had made it a home and getting ready to replace it with an expensive imitation. Another bit of old Didsbury gone forever.

He'd got the address of the scrapyard where Alfie had sent his written-off Volvo – it was currently in a garage in Oldham being returned to its former glory.

Keisha had gone to ground and Malton knew her better than to imagine he'd find her any time soon. When she wanted to appear she would, but in the meantime she'd be lying low somewhere, working out her next move. Malton was worried to find himself spending more time wondering what had become of Keisha than of Emily.

Claire had taken Cody to the hospital before calling the police. Thanks to Benton, Malton had made sure the boy was in protective custody until he had managed to reach out to Danny Mitchum.

For the past week he'd been trying to pin Danny down without success. Malton was on the verge of stepping things up a notch when he had received a call from Danny Mitchum's people. Danny wanted a word with Malton. An urgent word.

Malton knew that when it came to dealing with Danny there were no certainties. Danny had the power of life and death and he knew it. Ordinarily Malton would ensure when they met it would be somewhere neutral. A location that afforded escape routes and witnesses.

Danny wanted to meet at his mansion in Hale. Danny's home turf. It was a risk but Malton had no choice but to accept.

He dressed casually in heavy, Japanese denim and a thick gansey sweater, clothes that he knew could at least slow down the progress of a blade. It wasn't much but it was better than nothing. He threw his battered Barbour over the top and slipped his hatchet into the gamekeeper's pocket. If things did go badly Malton had no illusions that he'd make it out alive. But at least he could make it difficult and bloody.

Malton rang the buzzer outside Danny Mitchum's place. It was set into the thick, stone wall that ran all the way around the house. The wall was covered in off-white render, which did little to distract from how much like a fortress it made it look.

Malton marvelled at how on earth the Bistacchis imagined they'd storm this place and kill Danny Mitchum.

Staring into the video doorbell, Malton confirmed his name and the heavy, eight-foot-high, reinforced gate slid open to reveal a front garden that had been paved over into one enormous driveway and beyond it, Danny's vast house.

Malton was interested to note that apart from the two men who met him at the gate there were another half a dozen lurking around outside in the grounds. From the way they were dressed in thick coats and hats, Malton guessed they must have been outside for some time. They seemed too concerned with the bitter cold to take any notice of Malton as he was led into the house.

Something was wrong. Suddenly the weight of the hatchet in its leather lined gamekeeper's pocket felt very reassuring. Even more so when the two men who led him into the house made no effort to frisk him. They clearly had their minds elsewhere.

There were too many rooms in Danny Mitchum's house to realistically fill with furniture. And so for every lavishly decorated, double-height living room they passed by there was a virtually empty bedroom or an unused bathroom.

The house was carpeted throughout in pale ivory Berber. A filthy trail of footprints indicated which rooms were in use. A single family using the house would have struggled to keep the carpets clean. For Danny Mitchum, with dozens of associates constantly on hand, there was no chance. Being blind,

Danny Mitchum must have been oblivious to the effect and it was clear no one felt brave enough to tell him.

Malton was left to wait in a room lined with framed Manchester City football shirts. The only way out was the door through which he came. That or the window. He was on the first floor but Malton knew he could make the jump with a good chance of not breaking anything. Whether he could make it to the wall surrounding the house, or get over it, was another thing.

He walked around the room reading the names on the shirts and thinking about how the names told their own history of the city.

Malton's thoughts drifted back to Emily.

The whole time they were together Malton lived in constant fear that somehow the violence of his world would come catch up with her. Or that she'd finally see him for who he really was and run for her life. That had all come to pass and yet the world had not ended. Malton had found himself profoundly unmoved. He still felt as alone as he ever had. But this was different. Suddenly there was nothing left to fear. Nothing to feel but numb.

He'd been so worried about protecting Emily that he had failed to realise that the one thing she needed protecting from most was him.

'Malton, you cunt, I can smell you!'

Malton turned to see Danny Mitchum leering at him in the doorway. He was flanked by two large men in bulletproof vests, neither of whom Malton recognised. They didn't have the slightly feral air of most of Danny Mitchum's hangers-on. From how they held themselves Malton guessed ex-military.

Danny too was wearing a bulletproof vest over a bright purple tracksuit. He seemed oblivious to how cumbersome it made his movements. Like he was wearing a fat suit.

'It's Jean Paul Gaultier,' said Malton without any hint of annoyance in his voice.

Danny didn't seem to hear and carried on into the room. The two large men split up. One stayed by the door, one went to the window. Both kept scanning their surroundings, constantly alert.

'You still owe me the kid who shot Lorraine.'

'I wanted to talk to you about that,' said Malton.

'I bet you fucking did. Took him back to his mum? Got him arrested? You think I can't get to him? Fuck it, lot easier in prison. Number of dickheads I know who are never getting out. Don't matter what they do, does it?'

Malton knew Danny was bluffing. If he could have reached Cody by now he would have done. Benton had done her job and kept the boy safe.

'I want to offer you a trade,' said Malton.

Danny Mitchum spun round. From what was left of his face Malton guessed he was trying to look sarcastically intrigued.

'Oooh, a fucking trade. Lucky me. What you got for me this time?'

'How does Johnny Bistacchi sound?'

'Fuck I want him for?'

'Well I hear the Bistacchi family are something of an endangered species. I thought you might want the set. I see you're a natural collector,' said Malton, his voice full of flattery.

He gestured to the shirts on the wall, knowing full well Danny couldn't see him do it. Danny smiled.

'You like my shirts? Three hundred grand's worth in this room.' He shrugged. 'Fuck it – only money right?'

Malton did his best to sound humble. 'The boy's gone to prison for murder. The robbery is on me. Johnny Bistacchi is my way of saying sorry,' he said.

Danny blew out a breath and started fiddling with his bulletproof vest.

'Interesting new look,' said Malton.

'You don't know the fucking half of it,' said Danny. He momentarily sounded annoyed before slipping back into his usual blend of perky, foul-mouthed antagonism. 'Fuck it. Fuck it. Done. Bistacchi's in isolation. Someone clearly thinks that I might want to hurt him. Can you sort that?'

Seeing as it was Malton who had advised Benton to put Johnny there in the first place he was confident he could.

'If I couldn't, I wouldn't have made the offer,' said Malton.

'Fuck it. Done. Fucking done.'

Danny strode right up to Malton and stuck his hand out. Malton looked into the landslide of flesh that was Danny Mitchum's face.

'Done,' he said shaking Danny's hand. But Danny didn't let go.

He pulled Malton close. Malton could smell Danny's breath. He could see every ruined pore, the weeping red flesh. Danny Mitchum looked on the outside exactly as he did on the inside. A complete nightmare.

'Is that a hatchet in your pocket or are you pleased to see me?' asked Danny, stepping back.

Malton was surprised he'd got this far without anyone realising he was armed. The two military men started towards him. Danny threw up a hand.

'Let him keep it. Evens the score a bit.'

He laughed and threw up his fists in a boxing stance. Malton had often wondered what would happen if he ended up fighting with Danny. How much damage had he taken that wasn't obvious? How on earth could he put up any kind of a fight without eyes? At the back of his head Malton knew one day he'd find out the answer to all those questions. But not, he suspected, today.

'That's not why I wanted to speak to you though,' Danny said.

Malton had been waiting for this. The men outside, the new recruits, the bulletproof vest. Something was very obviously wrong in the world of Danny Mitchum.

'Oh?' said Malton, sounding as innocent as he could.

'Don't you fucking "oh" me,' said Danny. 'I know you're a clever fucker. You seen the boys outside, and these two.'

He pointed with unnerving accuracy to the two large men in stab vests.

'What would you say is going on?' Danny asked.

Malton took a moment for dramatic effect.

'I'd say you've pissed someone off. If Danny Mitchum's scared then whoever it is must be someone pretty heavy.'

Danny Mitchum threw up his arms and smiled.

'What the fuck did I tell you? Craig fucking Malton knows what's what! These two units, they're special forces. Well not anymore. Now they protect fuck-ups like me. I told them, I said, "You two aren't shit compared to Craig Malton. He's a wily fucker: Craig Malton. He's Wile E fucking Coyote."'

Malton was beginning to get bored. Danny Mitchum's unlimited wealth and power meant that most of the time he was talking his stream of nonsense it was to eager sycophants who lapped up every word. It had given Danny an unusually grating way of expressing himself. Malton still hadn't forgotten the threat towards Emily. He definitely hadn't forgiven it.

'You know what an Osman warning is, don't you?' said Danny.

Malton did but he played dumb. It was clear Danny wanted to tell him.

'When the filth know someone wants to dead you, they got to tip you off. Else they get in all sorts of trouble. You get an Osman warning. Fuck knows why it's called that.'

Malton knew that it was named after a poor bastard who didn't get one, but he kept quiet.

'They totally forgot to warn me about the piece of shit who did this to my face. Cost them two million quid. Cost the piece of shit who did it a lot more.'

Danny smiled widely. His reconstructed lips struggled to stay anywhere near his teeth as his tongue slipped out of his mouth and wetted his dry gums.

'So now whenever they hear someone has it in for me they give me a bell. Like when your mate Benton called the other day and told me the Bistacchis were coming over.'

'So where do I come in?' said Malton.

'Usually when my good friends the Greater fucking Manchester Police tell me my life's in danger, I take care of things. Threats get a lot fucking more than fucking threatened. Yeah?'

Malton was getting bored now. It was time to cut to the chase. 'Who have you pissed off and what do you want me to do about it?' said Malton.

Danny paused for effect, a dopey grin spreading across his face.

'The Scouse Mafia,' he said. He sounded almost apologetic. But only for a moment.

'So you mean a South American drug cartel,' said Malton.

'I don't know who those Scouse fucks hang out with do I?'

Malton knew Danny Mitchum would be fully aware of the close ties between the gangs on Merseyside and some of the most dangerous criminals in the world. People who did much worse than threaten to kill you.

'Where do I come in?' asked Malton.

Danny Mitchum slapped his hands together with glee. His habitual mania was back in full effect as he turned theatrically to one of the military men.

'I thought he'd never ask,' said Danny before turning back to Malton. 'Those prickly Scouse fucks think I've been thieving from them. Thing is, I have been.'

Danny cackled to himself.

'And you want me to find out who it was told them?' said Malton.

Danny clapped his hands together with delight.

'Got it in one. Clever fucker this one. Clever. Fucker. But not just that. See I want to be alive when you find the pricks. So until you do . . .'

Danny Mitchum spread his arms wide.

'Malton, you are going to be my fucking bodyguard!'

Epilogue

It was the middle of the day but the rain was falling so hard on Southern Cemetery that it may as well have been the middle of the night. The enormous cemetery was deserted, the rain driving all but the most determined mourners indoors. Huge fat droplets smashed down on silk flowers and teddy bears, turning cards and messages to illegible pulp.

Picking his way between gravestones, Leon Walker focused on the bag of heroin waiting for him back in the car. His clothes were soaked slick to his skin and in his hands he clutched the spade he'd been given.

Ever since he met Keisha all those months ago his life had become dangerously simple. She gave him drugs and he did whatever she asked. He didn't question or hesitate. He enjoyed no longer having to worry about anything other than doing as he was told.

A few paces behind him, her Burberry trench coat and umbrella keeping off the worst of the rain, followed Keisha. Her wellington boots plodded through the wet grass, scattering graveside tributes as she went. Her sunglasses hiding whatever it was that was going through her mind.

As they headed deeper into the cemetery, the graves began to change. The decades-old, weathered headstones gave way to smaller, more modern black granite, embossed with photos of loved ones. And eventually these graves began to give way to smaller plots with stones shaped like hearts and engraved with pictures of footballs and toys. Children's graves.

Passing between the graves Leon briefly wondered what ever happened to Vicious, his little Vikki? The last time he'd seen her had been a couple of months ago, right after he'd shot at Malton's front door. He'd dropped in to hide the shotgun. He hadn't even stayed long enough to speak to her.

He loved her as much as he could love anyone but he also knew he could never be a father to her. She deserved better. He hoped someone better than him could look after her.

As they pushed deeper in the graves became newer – crowded with flowers and soft toys. Silent screams of the intense sadness of a parent burying their child.

'Stop!' shouted Keisha as Leon nearly fell over a gravestone in the shape of an angel.

He turned back and saw Keisha standing still, looking down at a gravestone. There were no flowers on this grave. No toys. It was older than most of the graves around it. Moss had begun to grow up the sides.

Leon staggered back to stand alongside Keisha. Peering, he tried to make out the inscription.

Anthony Malton 01.07.1992 – 01.07.1992

Leon could have sworn he saw Keisha's bottom lip quiver just a little. He felt the weight of expectation, the need to fill the tiny gaps of silence left by the hammering rain.

'I'm . . .' But he didn't know what to say. He was an addict. He'd stolen from his loved ones. He'd seen his friends die. He'd abandoned his own daughter. He'd done too much and been the cause of too many tragedies for his words to have anything like the weight needed. For once in his pathetic life, Leon Walker did the right thing – he shut up.

Keisha didn't take her eyes off the grave as she spoke. 'This is my secret. I am the only person alive who knows about this. Do you understand?'

Leon Walker understood completely. He wouldn't tell a soul. Besides, after everything he'd put himself through, he was already dead. His body just hadn't quite got the message yet.

But Keisha wasn't finished. 'I've been beaten black and blue. I've watched grown men in so much pain they begged to be put out of their misery. I've put them out of their misery. I was never scared. Not once. You can't be. Not in this life. You got to be made of stone.'

Keisha stopped. Her voice breaking, her jaw clenched against the emotion.

'Or else something really bad happens,' she said, her hand reaching to cover her mouth.

They stood together in the rain, looking down at the small, sparse grave. Leon became more and more aware of the spade in his hand.

Finally Keisha turned to him. She said one word: 'Dig'.

Leon was all elbows and knees. But he dug with the furious energy of a junkie who knew his next fix was waiting for him. The spade cut through the soft earth and Leon haphazardly threw out piles of wet mud over the adjacent graves. Keisha didn't seem to care.

'There's something there,' said Leon, standing back and looking to Keisha for guidance. 'I think I hit something.'

'Dig it up,' said Keisha.

Leon didn't need telling twice. Dropping the shovel, he fell to his hands and knees and began to claw at the grave with his hands. The sandy earth drove deep under his nails – the loamy smell filling his nostrils.

His hand hit something. Not the hard coffin lid he was dreading. Something soft. Fabric.

Leon scooped out more earth and found it was a handle. A handle for a holdall. He wrapped his muddy hand around it and struggled to his feet, pulling the large bag from the sodden earth. It was heavier than it looked. Leon put his whole weight behind the bag, finally freeing it from the mud with a sloppy gurgle. He fell backwards, scattering the flowers on the grave behind him.

Keisha stepped over him and bent down over the bag. Discarding her umbrella, she fumbled for the zip and opened it up.

From where he sat on the wet ground, Leon looked past Keisha's legs and peered in the bag. It was packed full of guns.

'Fuck me,' said Leon. 'You've got enough there to start a war.'

Keisha zipped the bag closed and stood back up. She looked down at Leon and smiled.

'Enough to win a war.'

Acknowledgements

Dr Hughes for all her work in making every part better. My agents Gordon Wise and Michael McCoy for getting this across the line. My editor Bethany Wickington and copy-editor Helena Newton for raising the bar. Mayer Nissim, Chris Mettam and Thomas Mckennan for taking the time to read early drafts. J. J. Connolly and M.J. Arlidge for their encouragement. Ken Blythin for making it all much clearer. And my parents Anne and Dave. You know what you did.

Read on for a sneak peek of the second book in Sam Tobin's gritty Manchester Underworld series.

Out January 2023.

Prologue

Standing on the pavement, it was impossible to know the strong room was even inside.

The house itself was one of a row of large, Victorian semi-detached homes on the outskirts of Bolton town centre. To their rear was the densely packed terraces of Daubhill, home to Bolton's South Asian community. Ahead of them lay a patchwork of fields and housing slowly falling away as the land climbed up towards Winter Hill, the peak that towered over all of Bolton.

The strong room lay deep within the footprint of the house. It had no windows facing the outside world, nothing to reveal its presence to the casual observer.

The walls, floor and ceiling of the safe room had been specially constructed with steel-reinforced concrete. The kind used for bank vaults. It had cost tens of thousands of pounds but when set against the value of what was inside the room it was a drop in the ocean.

There was a single way in and out: a heavy, metal door set into an equally sturdy metal frame. The door had no handle inside or out and on either side of it Set in was a keypad. Without the eight-digit combination there was no way to get in or out of the room short of industrial strength explosives.

The formidable door lay wide open. Someone was inside.

Slow, deliberate footsteps pressed down into the thick, burgundy pile of the carpet as a young woman crept past the exquisitely crafted, bespoke cabinets that lined the room.

Made from imported Brazilian hardwoods and finished with a genuine gold trim, each cabinet was glass-fronted to better display its contents.

Racks of solid gold jewelry. Necklaces, earrings and bangles. Hundreds of thousands of pounds' worth. Rows of Rolex watches, each larger and more ostentatious than the last, sat proudly beside their boxes and certificates of authenticity. Treasures that glistened softly beneath spotlights set into the ceiling.

The young woman passed the glittering haul without so much as a second glance. She had something far more valuable in mind.

She wore skinny, blue jeans, white trainers and a crop top beneath a knee-length black, padded jacket. The standard uniform of a million northern, teenage girls.

Her hair had been scraped atop her head into a tottering bun, which gave a clear view of her face. She had the determined, thickly applied makeup of someone well used to passing for much older than her young years. But beneath the foundation, contouring and darkly painted eyebrows there was no mistaking that she was barely older than a child.

This was her first time in the strong room but she knew exactly what she was doing. It was just as it had been described to her. The only surprise was the smell. The strong, solvent-clean stink of the brand new. Trapped within the confines of the sealed room it was almost overpowering.

As she passed through the room something caught her eye. She stopped dead in her tracks, all thoughts of urgency deserting her.

There on the wall hung a painting. The girl didn't have to look at the signature to know who painted it. Back before she was permanently excluded, art was the only subject to ever catch her desperately divided attention. It was an L.S. Lowry. A *genuine* L.S. Lowry.

She held her breath, in awe to be so close to true genius.

Absent were the painter's iconic scratchy figures and crowded terraces. This painting depicted a hillside view across Bolton. A dark church nestled between smoking mills with the city stretching away into a grey horizon broken only by chimney stacks. Bolton had changed immeasurably from when Lowry had sat atop a hill to paint it. The mills and chimneys were long gone. The churches deserted or converted into Mosques. But the girl instantly recognized the endless, grey horizon. Some things never change.

Overwhelmed by the beauty of it she reached out, brushing her fingers against the frame, eager to somehow be closer to what she saw.

A noise came from outside. The distinctive sound of Urdu being spoken with a thick Bolton accent. Someone was home. The girl broke away from the painting and turned her attention to what she'd come for.

The safe sat alone on the floor, no taller than waist height. Unlike the wooden cabinets it was a new addition to the room. It stood out like an ugly afterthought by someone unconvinced of the ample security already on offer.

The girl knelt down, her knees sinking into the soft carpet. The voices were getting louder. She didn't have much time.

She looked to the back of her hand. Two sets of numbers had been scrawled there in biro. The first set were the numbers that had got her into the room. The second set she began to quickly type into the safe.

A small, red light came on. The safe gave a short, sharp buzz and remained closed.

The girl looked down at her hand. She was sweating. The numbers had begun to smudge. She took a breath and moving slower this time put the numbers in again. One digit at a time. Check the hand, type the number. Check the hand. Type the number. She willed herself to ignore the voices outside, to forget who it was she was stealing from and what he'd do if he caught her.

She pressed the final number and a small, green light flashed on to the accompaniment of a satisfyingly solid, clicking sound. The safe door swung open.

She was greeted with the sight of stacks and stacks of notes and half a dozen velvet bags. Despite the voices outside the room, her curiosity got the better of her and she risked a glimpse inside one of the bags. Dozens of uncut diamonds spilled out. Scattering through her fingers and into the deep pile of the carpet. There was no time to pick them up. She stuffed the bag back in the safe and ignoring the cash and diamonds, reached in to take what she had come for. The thing which was more valuable than everything in that entire room combined.

She slipped her prize into the pocket of her padded jacket and before shutting the safe pulled out a handkerchief with which she wiped down the keypad and door for prints.

Moving as fast as she dared, she crept out of the room, pulling the door closed behind her, again wiping over every surface she touched.

By the time the heavy, metal door had closed she was already halfway out of the window of a downstairs bathroom.

By the time anyone realized what was missing she had disappeared over that grey, endless horizon and vanished off the face of the earth.

1

The man in the blue shorts swung a leg up and brought it smashing down on the back of the man in red shorts' head. Red's face registered the shock and pain and for a moment he staggered, threatening to fall.

Smelling blood, Blue pressed his advantage, launching a savage cross into Red's faltering guard.

But Red wasn't out yet. He leaned back and as Blue's looping punch missed him he reached up and grabbed Red's extended arm, before pulling him tight to his body and taking them both down to the mat with a well-timed trip.

The fighters' bodies hit the canvas with a sickening thud. Blood and sweat splattering across the canvas of the ring.

When it had looked like a swift, violent knock-out the crowd had been on their feet, screaming for satisfaction. Now that the fight had progressed to the slow attrition of grappling, the crowd's interest waned and they retook their seats as the monolithic roar died down into the hubbub of drunken conversations.

At the back of the room one man remained fixated on the fight, never once taking his eyes off what was happening in the ring. He sat alone at his table, a glass of water untouched in front of him. He stood out like a sore thumb, his mixed-race complexion alone in a room full of white faces. A shaved head and deep scar running down the side of his face. Beneath his waxed jacket he was nearly twice the size of the men fighting in the ring. Craig Malton was here on business.

Malton had travelled all the way out to Hindley, an unremarkable former mining town on the periphery of Greater Manchester, to witness this fight. West out of his hometown of Manchester and out towards Wigan. Having grown up in Moss Side, anywhere this far out felt like countryside to Malton. Out here he was on his own.

But working alone was how he liked it, it meant that the only people who got hurt were the people who he decided should get hurt.

Malton glanced around the town hall where the fight was taking place. Parquet floors and ornate details spoke of an era when, thanks to the Industrial Revolution, Hindley had been prospering. A time long since passed. Nowadays the hall was the kind of place that at the weekend would be hosting a local wedding; folding tables of buffet food, a travelling DJ and everyone having the time of their lives. But on this wet Thursday evening it was violence that had brought people out. An evening of mixed martial arts fighting.

Malton noted the hall had several exits: the double doors that led from the entrance, a couple of doors leading to toilets and another couple leading to backstage. Too many escape routes for Malton's liking. He'd have to be quick.

He turned back to the man he was here to see. The man who was kneeling over his opponent, raining down blows. The man in the red shorts - Bradley Wyke.

Officially Malton ran Malton Security, a firm that ran doors, protected building sites and installed security systems. Unofficially, and if you could afford if, Malton was the man you came to when you needed something looking into. Something that you'd rather the police didn't know about.

Malton solved crime for criminals. With a mixture of cunning, brute force and a lifetime getting to know Manchester's sordid underbelly there was nowhere he couldn't go. Nothing so well hidden he couldn't drag it kicking and screaming into the light.

Malton wanted a word with Bradley Wyke and Bradley knew it. He'd not been at his flat this past week and hadn't turned up to the gym he ran either. But this fight had been booked in for months in advance and Malton was sure that however scared Bradley was, there was no way he'd waste the months of training and the chance to beat another man to a pulp in front of an adoring crowd. Not to mention the thousand-pound purse on offer to the victor.

Malton felt a buzzing in his pocket. He knew straight away who it would be. The man who was paying him to come all the way out to Hindley on a wet Wednesday night. The most feared man in all of Manchester - Danny Mitchum.

Danny Mitchum sat at the top of a vast pyramid of criminal ingenuity. He didn't just oversee the wholesale importation of drugs from both South America and Central Europe, he commanded a sprawling network of middlemen and street dealers. Despite his operation generating millions of pounds a year and being the responsible for the majority of drugs sold in Greater Manchester Danny was also more than happy to get his hands dirty.

Through a combination of fear, respect and extreme violence Danny Mitchum had become king of the Manchester underworld.

But he'd got greedy. Word had leaked out that he'd been ripping off his suppliers. The sort of people who sold drugs to Danny Mitchum were not the sort of people who took kindly to being ripped off.

While Danny went into hiding he'd tasked Malton with ferreting out the leak in his organization.

For the past three months Malton had been wading through Danny's crew. Men like Bradley. Danny Mitchum worked with the absolute dregs. Serial offenders, domestic abusers, sociopaths, bottom feeders and violent alcoholics. Any one of them could have been the leak. It was Malton's thankless job to find out which one.

Malton hadn't wanted to take the assignment but he knew well enough that you don't say no to a man like Danny Mitchum. Ever since taking the case he'd been bombarded day and night by Danny's calls. Most of which he chose to ignore. Danny didn't text. He couldn't, he was blind. And so instead he left long, foul mouthed voice notes which Malton was forced to trawl through at his leisure.

Malton let the phone in his pocket ring out.

Bradley was on his opponent's back, his arms and legs hooked around the man's torso, pinning him to the mat. Blue tried to stagger to his feet as he attempted to muscle Bradley off.

Both men were at the peak of physical fitness. Lithe, gym-honed bodies, each covered with a mess of tattoos. Blue's thick legs flexed as he attempted the impossible, raising his own weight and that of the man on his back. For a thrilling moment it looked like he would make it. The crowd rose in volume only to crash into disappointed heckling when the weight proved too much and Blue crashed back down to the mat. Bradley kept his grip but for just a moment looked up from the fight and out into the crowd, directly into Malton's eyes.

Malton saw straight away that Bradley knew who he was and what he was there to get from him. For just a moment Bradley froze in the ring. Torn between finishing off his opponent or turning to run. Fight or flight?

The phone in Malton's pocket started buzzing again. He kept his eyes on the fighting and let it ring out.

Bradley made his choice. He loosened his grip on Red. For just a moment the man's tired arms slipped down to his sides. It was the opportunity Bradley was hoping for. Without hesitation he started hammering blows into his opponent's exposed face. The first punch hit so hard that before he knew what was happening Bradley had already unloaded half a dozen more hits.

Scenting blood, the crowd rose to its feet and Malton was forced to stand to keep eyes on Bradley. He saw him smashing his fists into the face of his opponent. The referee hovered, unwilling to intervene too soon but it was clear the fight was over. The man in the Blue made no attempt to protect himself. His head swung left and right, his neck loosened by each crushing blow.

Finally the official stepped in and pulled a frenzied Bradley Wyke off what was left of his opponent. He hauled Bradley to his feet, holding his arm aloft in victory.

Malton was already moving towards the ring, pushing past the groups of men intoxicated as much with violence as with alcohol. He felt a hand grab at his shoulder as he barged through the throng. Without dropping a step Malton's own hand reached back, clenched the offending hand at the wrist and sharply twisted. The hand shot back and Malton kept going. Making a beeline for the ring.

Bradley was lost in the moment. Soaking up his victory. The crowd bellowed their approval and he bellowed back. The sight of Malton at the apron shook him to his senses.

Malton frowned as Bradley raised his arms and beckoned to the mob.

'Come on!' he shouted, urging them into the ring. The effect was instantaneous. As one the crowd surged forward, screaming obscenities and hurling pints high in the air. Malton was powerless to do a thing as hundreds of bodies flooded the ring.

The last Malton saw of Bradley Wyke was his bloody, sweat-stained torso shaking off well-wishers and then slipping out through one of the doors that led backstage.

Malton was outside in the car park just in time to see Bradley's beat-up Mazda tearing away into the murky Wigan night.

Already he could feel the sweat chilling on his bald head in the freezing night air. Now he was no longer in the hall he became aware of the stench of the crowd – beer and BO.

The phone in his pocket was ringing again.

Ignoring the phone Malton got into his racing green Volvo estate and set off back to Manchester. As he drove through the night his resolve began to harden. In his mind he replayed the grind of the past few months, culminating in tonight's almighty fuck-up.

By the time he was on the outskirts of the city his mind was made up. He was going to tell the most feared criminal in all of Manchester he quit.

As he drove he imagined how Danny would react to the news. The thought made him smile.